The Dragon and the Gnarly King

The
Dragon *and the*
Gnarly King

Gordon R. Dickson

TOR®

A Tom Doherty Associates Book

New York

THE DRAGON AND THE GNARLY KING

Copyright © 1997 by Gordon R. Dickson

Tor® is a registered trademark of
Tom Doherty Associates, Inc.

ISBN 0-312-86157-5

First Edition: August 1997

Printed in the United States of America

This book is dedicated to
Ben and Barbara Bova.

The Dragon and the Gnarly King

Chapter 1

Heads down!" shouted Jim. "The next man who looks up at the arrows gets taken off the wall! Pass that along."

He could see heads turning along the catwalk below the embrasures in the curtain wall as the word was passed. Threatening to take them off the wall was probably the best way of making the men obey.

He saw a few heads tilt down quickly on this front part of the wall where he himself crouched; and a second later the wide-bladed war arrows rained down upon them, harmlessly for the most part on the stone of the embrasures, the catwalk itself, or the open courtyard of the Castle behind them.

Only one man, sitting crouched on his heels, fell over backward at the impact of an arrow falling from a considerable height and driving into, if not through, his shoulder.

"You there!" called Jim. "Get down to the Bake-House and have them take that arrow out. Don't try to do it yourself. Someone—Little Ned, there, I mean Ned Bake-House, help him down the steps! Give his helmet and spear to someone else and send them back up to the wall."

"Yes, m'Lord!" floated back the voice of Ned Bake-House, the somewhat roly-poly elder brother of Little Ned, both Castle servants. He ran along the catwalk, crouching, hurrying to obey—which was only proper, since the Baron, Sir James Eckert, the Lord not only of Malencontri Castle but of its fairly extensive lands (ninety-eight percent Somerset wilderness though they were) had given him a command.

It was one of the tenants, rather than one of Jim's handful of men-at-arms or even one of the Castle servants, who had been hit, thankfully; though to be sure it was really not because he was looking up. It had just been blind bad luck. But everybody else on the catwalk around the walls would think he had, which would help the others to keep their heads down as Jim and the veteran men-at-arms had warned them to do.

But the urge to look was strong. Jim was not without sympathy for those who did lift their heads. The sight was almost hypnotic. He had needed to fight hard against looking, himself.

On long shots the arrows looked like a cloud of small black matchsticks, rising and rising, until they abruptly nosed down and began coming back to earth with unbelievable swiftness. Look up at them as they rose, and you risked an arrow in the face or throat when they fell. Keep your eyes down, and the three-foot shaft with its two-inch-wide triangular warhead might knock you down; but it would have to glance off your helmet or lodge in a shoulder. In the second case, at least, you had a chance of surviving.

The problem was more than getting the servants and tenants to keep their eyes down. The force threatening Malencontri right now would be a real danger only if allowed to develop into one—if, for instance, they noticed that the spears and helmets showing above the battlements were on tenant farmers rather than experienced fighting men.

Unlike the raiding party, led by Sir Peter Carley that had attacked the Castle last winter, these attackers could not be ignorant of the fact that this was the residence of a magician. Among the lower classes all was known, when peasants came together—and these hundred and fifty or two hundred men outside his walls were peasants, probably a remnant of a large peasant march.

Jim remembered, from the history he had known before he came here from the twentieth century, that there had been a number of such revolts during this fourteenth century; of which the best-known was that led by Wat Tyler. Tyler's group had broken up after he was pulled from his horse, during a confrontation near London, by the Lord Mayor, Sir William Walworth, and eventually killed.

After every such revolt, many of the peasants who hadn't been killed found themselves unable to go home. Some held together and began to move about, living off the land.

They were the ones who had nothing to go back to—either they had been put off their tenant land to begin with, or they were runaway serfs, or they knew they would not be accepted back by their particular lord, master, or superior. Some had been robbers or outlaws even before. Now homeless, hunted, and desperate, they no longer put much value on their lives anyway; that might explain why they were willing to attack the castle of a known magician—and the countryside generally believed that magicians, like dragons, had hoards—wealth beyond imagining.

For the outlaws and other human flotsam attracted to the group, taking Malencontri would be a long hope at best. That part of the group would only become a serious threat if a weakness were seen in the Castle's defenses. Unless the bitter, wild hatred of the homeless men reached the point where they stormed the walls simply because it was a castle with people in it like those who had starved, dispossessed, or even killed them and theirs. For some, death was unimportant if they could take some fat lordling to Hell with them.

They had no siege engines, but a number were certain to be unemployed men-at-arms, with some training, and able to build scaling ladders; with them they could put more men over the curtain wall at one time than Jim, with his dozen armsmen plus perhaps forty untrained servants, could throw back.

This was another reason to keep their heads down, so that only spearpoints and steel helmets should show above the stone. But the issue of a helmet and spear to the servants and tenants had aroused a misplaced enthusiasm for a fight in many who had seldom been close to a battle.

"M'Lord?"

Jim stood up, backed from the battlements, and turned.

"Oh, it's you, John," he said, getting an unpleasant jolt at seeing the tall, stocky, middle-aged man who was his Steward, the head of all his servants. John's duty was not on the battlements. It was anywhere in the Castle, overseeing matters there. Alarm stirred. "Why are you here?"

"M'Lord!" said John, in a deep, portentous voice. "Boomps!"

"Oh, those!" said Jim. They had been having mysterious noises in the Castle starting about the time the first of the peasants at the gate began to drift into this part of Somerset. He himself had been the one to name the noise, vastly underestimating the superstition of those who worked for him and regretting it later. The name came from an old Scottish prayer he had found while writing a research paper for graduate school, hundreds of years in the future:

"From Ghoulies and Ghosties and lang-leggetty Beasties,
and Things that go boomp in the Night,
Good Lord deliver us!"

The word had fitted too exactly the sound of the noise, and the Castle's people had seized upon it immediately. Naturally, a Lord and knight who was also a magickian would know the safe name for such a thing—"Naming calls," went the popular lore. The people were happy to have a name to call the noises by that would not somehow conjure up the things causing them.

A faint paleness showed on John's large, clean-shaven face. As he saw it, he had come with terrible news. News that deserved some alarm in the hearer.

Unlike Jim and Angie (the Lady Angela), he and the other servants were terrified by the boomps in the walls. The Castle people outdid each other in trying to imagine the horribleness of whatever was causing the noise, and most were certain that something was coming to eat them alive, one by one. Now John had come, bringing desperate news that, as he saw it, deserved a reaction, even under siege conditions. But, it was plain that after Jim's response he felt both helpless and hopeless.

—And Jim could not afford to have his chief servant losing all heart. The whole servant cadre would see that he had, and disintegrate.

"John, there's no need to worry, now. We'll take care of the boomps, and they won't hurt anyone in the meantime."

He had reassured all the servants repeatedly; but reassurances did not help. He was supposed to act, not talk. That was what lords, knights, magicians, and other strong people were for. Only those who could not act, talked.

"Who heard it this time?" he asked.

"Meg and Beth both heard it," said John, faintly, "just now. They were in the Still-Room, and they heard it in the wall right beside them; and others just outside the Still-Room heard. They two screamed, and then fainted— dead away. They were carried to the Serving Room, where they are being fanned and given sommat to drink."

Jim reflected for a moment.

The walls of Malencontri, like those of most large stone castles, were every- where from three to twenty feet through, thickening as they went down to- ward the base, to carry the weight above them—and the Still-Room where the beer was brewed was on the ground floor. Plenty of thickness there for Something to be tunneling through; provided, of course, It could tunnel noise- lessly, except for an occasional boomp.

"Never mind, now," Jim said, suddenly weary. "The boomps have been only in the walls so far. They won't be coming out; and I'll take care of them as soon as I have time. I give you my word as a magician on it."

A faint smile, an equally faint gleam of hope lit up John's face. A knight's word could be counted on—a magickian's must be twice as unbreakable.

"Yes, m'Lord." John started to turn toward the nearest steps down to the courtyard.

"Oh, and you can tell Beth and Meg I'm sorry they had to be right next to the boomp, but we can be pretty sure now no one'll hear it in the Still-Room, since it's never sounded twice in the same place."

"Yes, my Lord." It was the ultimate submission. When no stranger of rank was present it was the habit, and privilege, of the Malencontri people to slur the two words of Jim's formal address together in familiar fashion. Only when visiting gentry were present—or in moments of great stress—did they answer as John had just done. But Jim looked at the Steward sharply. The pale cast was gone from John's face, and there was a touch in his voice of an almost consoling tone.

But John turned and went; and Jim put him out of mind, having other things to concern him. The fuss about the latest boomp had given him an idea for dealing with the besiegers.

If there were left in them any of the superstition the servants were now showing, a magickian could still seem to be a fearsome opponent. Many among them might no longer care what happened to them; but the fear of something other than human, instilled in them from birth, might override even their desperation and hatred. If, for instance, something equal to the boomps sounded from the woods around them. . . .

"Theoluf!" he shouted.

"Yes, m'Lord?" came the prompt answer of his squire from behind him—everybody was coming up behind him today, for some reason.

"Take over—I'm going out. Keep a runner beside you at all times to send with any necessary message to the Lady Angela."

"Yes, m'Lord."

"I'm going to *fly* out of the Castle." Jim's emphasis on the word "fly" meant that he would be changing shape. "Watch and tell me what those outside do. If any run off into the woods"—Malencontri, like all castles, was surrounded by an area cleared of trees and shrubs, so attackers would have to come out into the open—"looking as if they're deserting, be ready to tell me how many and where. Stand away from me."

Theoluf and the nearest men backed off to give him room for a much larger body; and Jim changed into his alternate shape as a very large, very fierce-looking dragon. He dived over the battlements and down upon the men below.

The desperation and hatred of those men might have made them immune to the paralyzing fear of the supernatural and magical that had been fed them as children; but it had done nothing to dull their survival instincts. They scattered out of the line of Jim's apparent attack like chickens under the dive of a hawk on their yard.

Jim, of course, had no intention of attacking even one of them—lingering to fight here, once they had recovered their wits, would be sure death even for the strongest of dragons. So he pulled out of his dive at the last minute—making a fine noise as his wings caught the air like a parachute—and he began to explode skyward on their full climbing power.

That power was considerable. He went almost straight up, like a fighter plane of his own later century; but it was necessarily limited by the energy stored in him. He was like an opera singer who could hold a high note for an amazing length of time; but when his physical limit was reached, no more was possible.

Still, that much took him up until he was a small airborne shape in the sky over their heads. Breathless, he extended his massive wings, tilted them to the flow of the air current he had just passed through, and, like a latter-period sailplane, began his effortless soaring.

He had ended up soaring westward, toward Castle Smythe, home of his closest friend—and literal life-saver on occasion in this bloodstained fourteenth century—Sir Brian Neville-Smythe. He had been worried about Brian lately: Brian had been preoccupied with the recent growth in Royal taxes. He was hardly alone in his feelings. But while such as the Earl of Oxford were powerful enough to talk so about them in public, and get away with it, Brian and those he spoke to were not.

Jim put it out of his mind. One worry at a time.

He glanced down and saw that, although the attackers had not been scared off, they had withdrawn from the walls and clustered in a tight group that seemed to be arguing among themselves, faces occasionally flashing upward, like table plates being dried in bright sunlight.

Good. They could watch him apparently heading off to the west and wonder. Where was he going and why? What might he bring back?

Actually, his line of travel was not straight west, but the beginning of a circle that would swing him around Malencontri at a distance of a mile or so. Dragons, like most large birds of prey, had near-telescopic distance vision. He could keep the Castle and its attackers in sight without being suspected, while he tried to figure out some way to handle the situation.

It was too bad he couldn't think of a way for boomps to sound in the earth around where the peasants stood. At the very least that should scare off half of them—

"M'Lord!" roared a distant voice, completely ruining his train of thought. "M'Lord! Oh, m'Lord!"

Jim gritted his teeth, refusing to look toward the voice. It was far too low-pitched—about that of a good operatic basso hitting a baritone note—and far too high off the ground, to be any but the one possible source of interruption he had completely forgotten could reach him here in mid-air.

"M'Lord, m'Lord!" This time, the voice rose half an octave, to an anxious pitch.

Jim sighed, and looked back over his shoulder. Sure enough, there, less than two hundred yards distant and soaring along on a river of air coming to meet his, was another dragon. A young, half-grown dragon. Past any doubt, one of the younger generation of the Cliffside Dragons, his imagination pumped full of lurid renditions of Jim's adventures. The pumper being Secoh, the feisty little mere-dragon who had been with Jim, Brian, Dafydd ap Hywel, Aargh, and Smrgol—granduncle of Gorbash, whose dragon body Jim had been in—when they had all won their famous battle with the Dark Powers at the Loathly Tower.

Possibly, this young Cliffsider had a message for him. If he did not, he was an unusually brave immature dragon to approach Jim now, on his own initiative.

He was about two-thirds the size he would become as an adult, certainly no more than sixty or seventy years old; and his voice had not yet broken—otherwise Jim would have heard it booming at him from twice the distance.

"It's me—Garnacka, m'Lord!" said the young dragon. He had already transferred to Jim's air current and been sidling closer, with little pumps of his wings, until he was no more than fifty feet away. He sailed along side-by-side with Jim for a few minutes of silence, evidently feeling his name ought to explain everything about his being here.

When Jim said nothing, Garnacka lowered the volume of his voice self-deprecatingly. "Actually, I'm Garnacka, because I was named after my grandfather. But everybody calls me Acka."

"What do you want, Acka?" asked Jim.

"Well, m'Lord," said Acka, and paused again. He was looking as winning as possible, like a young dragon about to ask one of his parents for something which he was almost sure would be answered by a thunderous roar of *"Certainly not!"* Dragons did not use the same facial expressions as human beings. Acka's four protruding young fangs were pressed tight back against the otherwise-closed crocodile-like lips, his eyes were very bright, and his ears were erect, wiggling slightly at the tips, ingratiatingly. "Pray forgive me for intruding upon you, m'Lord."

Language like that was absolutely unnatural for a dragon. Acka had to have learned it from Secoh, who in his turn had learned it from the servants, when he came visiting Jim at Malencontri.

"That's all right," said Jim, as pleasantly as he could, but very distinctly. "What . . . do . . . you . . . want?"

"I just wanted to tell your Lordship," said Acka, "that you can call on me at any time. You don't need to wait to have Secoh go and find me or any of the other dragons. If you just call or send a message directly to me, I'll be there right away, before anyone else!"

"Good. I will," said Jim. "Thank you, Acka. Good-bye."

"Under any circumstances," said Acka, earnestly. "No matter how dangerous it is, you can count on me. If you can just get me by magick—why don't you do that? It would save time all around."

"I'll think about it," said Jim. "Now, farewell, Acka!"

"Farewell, my Lord," said Acka, sideslipping away regretfully. "Honored to have talked to you. . . ."

Jim watched him go. Acka had dropped to a lower air current but one still running westward. The Cliffside Eyrie which was Acka's home was in the opposite direction. He was adventuring even farther than Malencontri—in the middle of the day when most mature dragons would be heading for the coolness of their tunnels and caves.

Probably, he was showing off how fearless he was. Oh, well, Jim's own route was curving away from the youngster's, now; and he had no actual authority over Acka anyway. The other would soon get tired of whatever game he was playing, once Jim was out of sight, and go home.

Now, back to the besieging peasants—a thought occurred that possibly he could use Acka somehow to give the idea he had gone to get other dragons as reinforcements. No—he had forgotten the archers. They had been too startled to get off any shots during his brief appearance in the clearing, but that would not be so again.

A dead Acka looking like a pin cushion, with shafts sticking out all over him, was not something Jim wanted to explain to the young dragon's family at Cliffside—

He noticed suddenly that the dot that was Acka was now once more growing larger. For some reason, he was headed back toward Jim. Ten to one he had thought of some reason or excuse for prolonging the conversation and was coming back to have a further try at it. That should be stopped before it had a chance to get started.

Jim filled his capacious dragon lungs. Acka was still too far away for his youthful voice to reach Jim; but with Jim's mature dragon's voice and the younger dragon's acute hearing, Acka should be able to hear him—putting Jim in the happy situation of being able to send the youngster home without having to listen to his excuses not to.

"Acka!" he bellowed. "Go home!"

The dot that had just enlarged into a head-on dragon-shape hesitated, bobbled uncertainly in mid-air, and shouted something back—that, just as Jim had expected, was unintelligible.

"Go home!" repeated Jim.

But Acka kept on coming.

"M'Lord! M'Lord . . ." he was shouting.

"What is it?" said Jim, angrily.

"There are a lot of georges coming down the trail from Castle Smythe toward Malencontri!" Acka's relatively high-pitched voice called back. "A *lot* of georges, m'Lord!"

The information made no sense at all. Georges were what dragons called humans, of course; but in his somewhat run-down home Sir Brian Neville-Smythe never entertained, and there was no one . . . he thought of Brian's recent interests in politics, and a coldness began to form inside him.

"—And they're all on horses!" Acka's voice reached him again.

"On horses?" This made the coldness increase. Only gentry, knights, or men of higher rank rode, except for the occasional courier or special servant.

"I'll take care of it!" Jim shouted at Acka. "Now you go home. GO HOME!"

Acka stopped shouting, bobbled for another second or two, and then began to dwindle again—this time in an easterly direction, toward the Cliffside caves. Jim angled himself to the wind, to head northwest by west, which was roughly how he had to go to overfly the forest trail that was occasionally dignified by—but didn't deserve—the name of "road" between Malencontri and Castle Smythe.

He soared along, looking down at the treetops, and waiting for the break in them that would show him at least a portion of the trail. However, some little time went by, and he did not find it. Puzzled, he turned at last and headed back in the opposite direction. It seemed impossible that he could have missed it—or perhaps it wasn't all that impossible, after all.

It was full summer now. The trail was very narrow, and the leafed-out treetops hid most of it from the air unless you were looking down at the right angle to the ground. Acka must have been doing just that to spot what he did.

Jim's feeling of alarm began to subside. Probably, he thought, a couple of pack-pedlars with their donkeys had caught Acka's eaglelike vision. He had just exaggerated.

In any case, whatever the young dragon had seen couldn't have been this far away.

Jim worked back along the line of where the trail should be visible, now headed toward Malencontri. He knew the trail well, from traveling it on foot—or, more accurately, on horseback. Except for little twists and turns, to go around an unusually large tree or awkward clump of bushes, it made a fairly straight line toward the Castle, this close to Malencontri.

He located it at last—just a glimpse of a narrow, greenish-brown thread between the trees, unused enough that grass was partially covering it. But no one was in it—he must now be beyond whoever was approaching Malencontri. He turned once more and began to soar outward again on a breeze that carried him only about a hundred feet above the treetops. This close to the ground, he could see the trail clearly; and eventually he did catch sight of some movement up ahead.

He checked his momentum and angled his wings to put himself into a tight circle above the treetops, so that he could watch and wait for whoever was approaching. They should be putting in an appearance within minutes—within seconds, if they were on horseback.

Even as he told himself this, there they were. A long line—clearly a knight, leading a very long double line of men on horseback, all wearing identical red surcoats with a badge on them, over their armor . . . Jim adjusted his dragon sight for distance, now seeing like a falcon . . . this shade of red was the royal color, and the badge on the breast of the surcoat was the head of a lion—leopard, it was termed.

These were the English King's men-at-arms, and their line stretched back out of sight among the trees. Acka had not exaggerated after all.

These were indeed a remarkable sight to be seen coming along the track from Castle Smythe. There must be thirty or more of them—an unreasonable number, ordinarily, for quiet, peaceful Somerset on a bright summer day; and the King's costly men-at-arms would not be out here just to pursue renegade peasants. . . . The man who rode at their head would be their commander, a knight wearing his own coat of arms on his shield.

The thought occurred that this might be Sir John Chandos, who had visited before—though not with such an escort. Jim's angled view did not let him make out the coat of arms the knight was wearing. He made a turn in the air and angled toward the front of the column to get a better view.

Abruptly, he had it.

The knight's coat of arms showed two heraldic hounds attacking a boar.

It was not Chandos, but some other King's officer—in force; and if he and his men were coming from Castle Smythe—from which Jim had received no message on any such matter—then anything could be in the wind, and that wind might bode ill for his and Angie's closest friend in this world, Sir Brian Neville-Smythe.

Jim spiraled upward from the trees—not pumping his wings but riding an updraft, because he did not want to be heard below, but gaining as much altitude as he could before heading directly for Malencontri again, as fast as he could fly.

Chapter 2

The Lady Angela Eckert, erstwhile twentieth-century graduate student and wife of Jim, Baron of Malencontri, and in her own right Chatelaine of its Castle, had been moving around that Castle and its grounds most of the morning, taking care of things automatically as she came upon them—as good Chatelaines will. She had been correcting a mistake being made here, chiding a daydreaming servant who should have been working there, and settling a dispute between two workers someplace else.

She had dreamed once of herself as working away, turning a large crank whose shaft entered one of the Castle walls. All around her had been people belonging to the Castle; and as long as she kept cranking, they went busily about their proper duties. But when she stopped to catch her breath for a moment, they all instantly stopped, too, and stood like clothing dummies until she began to turn the crank again—at which moment they all began to move once more.

The image of everything and everyone brought to a halt had come back to her mind just minutes before, as she had passed the Serving Room just off the Great Hall and heard voices raised in argument there. She had made a mental note to check up on it, but not right at this moment.

The Castle's work could not be let to be interrupted by a little thing like an attack by a band of marauding outlaws. The thunder of Jim's wings as he dived at the peasants had drawn her to one of the windows. She had recognized him in his dragon-shape, and watched with relief as he sensibly flew off before the attackers could recover.

Still watching, she had seen, a few minutes later, another dragon flying overhead. The attackers, already turned somewhat irresolute, had spotted it. Then it had returned, coming back in the other direction. It was clearly a younger, smaller dragon than the first that had attacked them; but the idea of more than one such beast above them had clearly been upsetting for the former peasants.

Then a few of their party came running out of the mouth of the road to Castle Smythe, pointing back the way they had come. At this the archers and some of what were probably the more experienced hands in the group disgustedly shouldered their bows and trudged off toward the south. The rest hurried to follow; and it was all over. There were not even any bodies to clear away

The attackers were probably no longer a danger, but she ought to send a warning to their friends, anyway.

She had been planning to get together with Geronde, in any case. The Lady Geronde Isabel de Chaney—Chatelaine, and in all but name, ruler of Malvern Castle—who was Brian's bride-to-be, was someone much more experienced with fees, bribes, and other practicalities, than Angie herself. Climbing the tower stairs toward the pigeon-loft and dispatching one of the homing pigeons to tell her of the attacking party on the loose, and invite her to Malencontri, was the first step. The Serving Room problem could be looked into on Angie's way back downstairs.

A present to the Bishop of Bath and Wells, who had been so helpful in badgering the King into giving the wardship of little Robert Falon to her and Jim, was overdue. What Angie had in mind was some real Chinese silk, something Carolinus ought to be able to get for her through his connections with other magicians in the Far East. But paying for such a present would be a large extra expense—particularly right now, when the King was driving everybody up the wall by increasing taxes on everything conceivable.

She had never realized that back here in the fourteenth century, one of the things she would have to worry about would be income tax. It was not called by that name here and now, but that was what it was. She and Jim had to pay his Royal Majesty, Edward the Third, ten to fifteen percent of everything they gained during the year; from rents, anything sold, earned, or derived from any other means of income.

They had already bribed the King—more or less directly—with over thirty pounds for the wardship itself; and there would be further necessary payments to the Court functionaries who would be handling the legal paperwork—not merely the Court of Chancery, but the Chief Clerks there, and even some of the subsidiary Clerks.

Finding money—or some equivalent—to pay for a bolt of white Chinese silk—even though a bolt of cloth in this time was nowhere near as wide as the ones she had been used to in the twentieth century—was going to be a problem, the way money had drained out lately.

As she finished thinking this, she had finally reached the floor where the pigeon-loft was, two stories down from the tower-top—in fact, right below the Solar, that was her bedroom and Jim's, and where there was a smaller room that had been partitioned off for Robert.

The pigeon-loft was a long narrow room, curved because it was fitted to the curve of the tower itself; with a companionably curving shelf running at waist height its full length. On the shelf were cages, most with a homing pigeon in them.

A quiet cooing became somewhat more clamorous as she appeared, just in case it might be feeding time—even though the pigeons knew very well it wasn't. She looked at them with approval. Yes, there were plenty of Malvern pigeons, ready to take off for their home loft the minute they were set free with a message, their destination firmly fixed in their small pigeon heads.

Angie frowned. The Pigeon-Keeper, who was new on the job, was nowhere in sight, nor had she encountered him anywhere on her way here.

Still frowning, she followed the curve of the room around toward its far end, and there discovered him on the floor, huddled in a corner and not moving.

Her first thought was that something had happened to him; but her frown came back like a thundercloud as she stood over him and smelled the strong reek of beer. A closer examination confirmed the fact: the fourteen-year-old Keeper was dead drunk, passed out.

Angie repressed a strong desire to kick him in the ribs. She did not; for one thing, she was still not that much of a medieval person, even after living in this world for almost three years now. Also, she remembered, she was wearing the shoes of the period, which were more like heelless slippers than anything else—kicking would have hurt her toes and probably not even awakened him.

Following up these thoughts was the sudden worry that the boy might be a confirmed drinker, rather than someone who had just happened to fall off the wagon on this particular occasion. It was not impossible, given the fact that everybody—regardless of age—drank at least the local home-brewed beer or ale. It could be that the lad was already addicted to alcohol.

If that was the case, he could not be kept on at the Castle. Dismissing him would be hard on his family, and doubly hard on him when his family learned about it. They had undoubtedly celebrated his being given the chance to take care of the pigeons here, telling each other that once on the Castle staff, his ambition need know no limit. The boy could end up as anything—Master of Hounds, possibly. Maybe even . . . wild dream that it was . . . he might some-day even become the Castle Steward.

There was little doubt that his nearest and dearest would handle him very roughly if they discovered he had lost his chance at rank and riches simply because he did not have the wit to know when it was safe to get drunk.

But she could not risk having an undependable servant. Nor did she have time to try and wean a young alcoholic from his addiction, even if the servants around the Castle would back her up in her efforts—which she doubted. In fact, they would probably sneak drinks to him—if not out of mere sympathy, then out of a coarse sense of fun at getting him in trouble.

This was the kind of thing Angie hated. Neither she nor Jim had been able to bring themselves to order the beatings, floggings, and such that medieval people in authority used to control those under them . . . of course, she could have the boy thrown into the Castle dungeon, which like the dungeons in most castles was simply a dirt pit on the basement level.

She had had the dungeon at Malencontri cleaned of filth—there were no facilities available for those thrown into such places in this era—in fact, prisoners were lucky if food were also thrown at them occasionally—but it was still lightless, unfurnished, and within the foundation walls, the thickest stone walls of the Castle. These walls never really warmed up, even at the end of summer. As a result, dungeons were always miserably cold.

A night in one might bring the boy to his senses as far as his duty was concerned. The usual lot of those imprisoned in this fashion was never to come out alive, or else to be taken out only to receive such severe punishment that they died. Such a prospect might scare the boy into sobriety. Or maybe it would scare him only until he was released, after which he might well slip back into his old ways.

Angie's mind was still wrestling with the problem when she heard the tinkle of a bell that announced the arrival of one of their own pigeons at the cote. She turned to it immediately, but it had no message banded to a leg. It was certainly a Malencontri pigeon, lent to Brian or Geronde to send her or Jim a message; perhaps it had managed to escape its keeper and come home on its own.

To Angie's surprise, however, it was almost immediately joined by another pigeon that Angie had not noticed loose among the cages until now; and which was wandering about, helping itself to grain spilled or kicked out of the other cages. This bird did have a message band—bulging with a message that should have been delivered to her or Jim by the boy now unconscious in the corner.

From its calm and peaceful air this second bird had not arrived within the last few minutes. It might have come before the boy got drunk enough to pass out. Another black mark against him.

Angie went to the bird, picked it up, and removed the message, before putting both loose pigeons into an empty cage. The newcomer protested, but she tossed them some extra corn, to sweeten the situation, and they immediately gave this all their attention.

Angie unrolled the message.

It was a strip of the thinnest paper then to be found; and the message itself read simply "*B ANT G CUM,*" printed in Geronde's personal version of fourteenth-century spelling. Since it was also in English, rather than the Latin written by Malvern Castle's resident priest, it was meant to be a personal note, signaling a personal visit.

Brian and Geronde, then, were coming to pay a visit. But when had the message been sent? From the state of the pigeon-boy, it could have been yesterday.

But even more disturbing was the personal element hinted at in the note. Ten to one they had some kind of problem and would be looking for help or advice. That would almost certainly mean a serious matter.

In the Middle Ages, there were no two meanings to the word "friendship." If a friend called on you for help, it was not a time to explain that you were busy right at the moment, or had a previous engagement. Your duty was to drop everything else and pay attention. To lend a hand or possessions, wield a weapon or even risk your life, to aid him or her. Else you were no true friend.

But just when had this message been sent?

How long had the messenger pigeon been here, and when might Brian and Geronde arrive? Beyond any advice the two might want, there would be a need for a certain amount of creature comforts. That meant that not only had the Kitchen to be set to preparing some special eatables, but two rooms had to be cleaned, aired, and readied. Angie left the loft on the run, dismissing the matter of the drunken bird-keeper from her mind, and headed swiftly down the spiral stairs on the inside wall of the tower, toward the Serving Room.

Now, as she approached it, she began to hear the same raised voices she had heard earlier. A passionate fight was going on between a woman and a girl; and since Angie knew the voices of the individual servants—who better?—she identified them immediately. The woman was Gwynneth Plyseth, Mistress of the Serving Room, where dishes from the outside Kitchen were kept hot or ready for serving to people eating in the Great Hall—and particularly the High Table, at which Jim, Angie, and any guests of high rank or importance would be seated. The girl was Gwynneth's new apprentice.

Angie, already irritated by the siege, drunken pigeon-boys, and impending visitors, stalked into the Serving Room; and there they were, standing nose to nose.

The apprentice was May Heather, a handful by anyone's standard, though only thirteen years old. She had recently been transferred from the Kitchen staff to be a direct understudy of Gwynneth. The image of them both, face-to-face, was striking—they could have posed for a picture titled AGE VERSUS YOUTH—AT SWORDS'-POINTS.

May Heather, short as she was, still stood only some three or so inches shorter than Gwynneth Plyseth. But the Mistress of the Serving Room had a good hundred pounds in weight over her opponent. Nonetheless, May was clearly ready to do battle with any weapons the other chose; and Mistress Plyseth was equally willing on her side.

Angie's appearance struck them both dumb, however. They stared at her.

"Mistress!" snapped Angie at Gwynneth Plyseth. "What's the meaning of this?"

She was shocked at the sound of her own voice. Once more she felt as she had in the moment when she had come very close to kicking the Pigeon-Keeper. It reminded her she had lately become aware the servants were saying that she was very fierce and dangerous to deal with, since she and Jim had acquired the wardship of young Robert Falon.

Too often lately, instead of having to pretend a Chatelaine-like outrage, she had found herself actually feeling it. She was feeling it now.

The two stared at her.

It was not that anything she said or did was unusual, coming from a superior to an inferior, in this age. But from the beginning, neither she nor Jim had acted like this with the Castle servants, the men-at-arms, the tenants, and the

serfs; and as their neighbors—Geronde among them—said, the Malencontri
servants were spoiled. But at the moment she was just as angry as the two she
was looking at; and they knew it.

"Nay—pray pardon, m'Lady," gasped Gwynneth, "forgive me, m'Lady, but
I must have a man-at-arms to beat this girl properly. She's too strong for me,
m'Lady. I get all worn out."

On its face, it was not an unreasonable request from a fourteenth-century
standpoint. But it was also not a usual service to be performed by a man-at-
arms, who would feel it beneath his dignity.

"She—" May Heather burst out passionately. But a look from Angie silenced
her. Angie turned back to Gwynneth.

"Why beat her? You know my orders about things like that! Well?"

"But I was teaching her, m'Lady!" said Gwynneth. "I have to teach her what
we do, here in the Serving Room. Only, she won't let me teach her proper."

"What's teaching got to do with beating her?" demanded Angie.

"Why, m'Lady," said Gwynneth, "how else can she learn? To teach a lass
like her, you must first show her what is to be done, and then beat her so
that she remembers it. This one is quick to learn—I'll say that for her—but
she's got a lot to learn yet; and I'm fair wore out, trying to beat her after each
time I show her something. She won't take her beatings. She fights me!"

Angie could believe the last. May Heather had once been willing to confront a dragon—who was actually Jim in dragon form, but May had not known
it then—with an ancient battle-axe she had managed to get off the wall and
could barely lift. Once again, now, she tried to talk and give Angie her side
of the situation.

"I remembers," she said earnestly. "Better than anybody. Listen, m'Lady"—
she began to chant—" *'hippocras: for parties large—in Kitchen made—for small, our
Lord and Lady guests—Serving Room is best—ginger—cinnamon—cardamom, few
grains—sugar, pepper (not for m'Lady)—blue blossoms heliotrope; add one quart red wine;
and for measure, ginger, six slivers, small, the cinnamon sticks'—*"

"Stop that!" said Angie. "Let your Mistress speak!"

May Heather stopped chanting, but added with the last of her final breath
"—anyway, she don't *need* to keep beating on me!"

"May!" snapped Angie. May Heather was mute. Angie turned back to the
older woman. "Now, Gwynneth. *You* explain what beating your apprentice
has to do with her remembering?"

"Why, otherwise, how will she ever remember it?" said Gwynneth. "There
are many, many important things to do in this Serving Room, m'Lady. Hundreds. Her young brain will be fair mazed by them, unless she has some reason

to remember each one separately. That's why I have to beat her after each showing."

Angie felt a new spasm of exasperation. Custom ruled among the servants, the tenants, the serfs, or anyone else on Malencontri land. If things had been done a certain way since time immemorial, they must be done that way forever. It was an attitude she was surrounded by, and which sometimes made her think that what everyone in this world needed was to have their heads opened up and a little common sense stuffed into them before being sewn up again.

"Mistress," she said grimly, "from now on you will show May Heather what's to be done, you will watch while she practices doing it, and when she has done it properly several times, then you can go on and teach her something more. There should be no reason to beat her unless she refuses to learn."

"Not beat her!" said Gwynneth, staring at her Lady. Her hands clutched at the fabric of her skirts. "But m'Lady, how can it be done without? Their little heads are too small to hold lessons unless those are thoroughly beaten into them. Everyone knows that. Why, if there is a new boundary post to be put up in the village, what do the men there do? They catch one of the village boys, take him to the post, and beat him. So as long as he lives ever after he can show people where the post is. Otherwise, how could they be sure he'd remember?"

The argument was sound, if you accepted Gwynneth's view of the world, and particularly of non-adults and the necessity to remember everything, because writing it down was unknown. It was like having witnesses at a wedding—they were there primarily so they could testify afterward that the wedding took place at a certain date and time. It was the one thing that could work in an illiterate society.

The only answer here was to stand on her rank.

"Well, we aren't going to do that here," Angie said, falling back on her own unanswerable authority over all things. "I'll tell you this once, Mistress, and I expect not to need to tell you again: you will teach May Heather the way I say, and that's an end to that. Now, May!"

She turned on the girl.

"This doesn't mean that you can get away with anything you shouldn't, May Heather," she said. "Mistress Plyseth will not beat you after every lesson; but she has a perfect right to beat you if you don't obey her orders; and you are to accept that like a good girl. If you don't, we'll have other ways of dealing with you. We'll trice you up like we would one of the men-at-arms in the courtyard and flog you. How would you like that?"

May Heather stuck out her chin and lowered her lip belligerently. For a heartbeat Angie was afraid her bluff was about to be called—because she could never actually carry through on such a threat to a half-grown girl. May could not possibly be dealt with as the Castle's fighting men were—and that was brutal enough even for grown men, in all conscience. But if a knight's banner should read *"Death before Dishonor,"* then May Heather's would certainly read *"Death before One Step Backward."*

"I knows what's right, m'Lady!" she said.

"No, you don't!" said Angie. "I do. And I tell you what to do. Do you understand?"

May's eyes dropped to stare at the Serving Room floor.

"Yes, m'Lady," she said.

Angie rounded on Gwynneth.

"And you, Mistress Plyseth?" she said. "Do you understand?"

"Oh, yes, m'Lady!" cried Gwynneth. But she was wringing her hands. "Though—well, I don't know m'Lady, I don't indeed. I'm sure, I don't know. It was the way I was taught when I was an apprentice in the Serving Room, and very grateful I am for the lessons, I'm sure; but if my Lady says I should teach her another way, I will do so. But—"

"No buts," said Angie. "You just do it."

"Of course, m'Lady," said Gwynneth, suddenly much calmer, now that it had become undeniable, an unyielding order—like rain, hail, and sleet, there was nothing more a Christian soul could do about it. "But I'm only not to beat her on the lessons, m'Lady? If she is pert or does things ill, or in a temper, it will be all right then?"

"That's what I just told her," said Angie resignedly—and suddenly remembered what had brought her downstairs. "But never mind any more of that. Right now I need food fixed for guests. Lady Geronde and Sir Brian are going to be here any time now."

"Yes, m'Lady," said Gwynneth, suddenly brisk and certain. She turned to May Heather.

"May," she said, "you will find my Lord in the front Hall or just outside. Take m'Lady's message—"

"Never mind!" said Angie, impatiently. There was no time to be lost, and she did not want Jim thinking that he could finish whatever he was doing before he came looking for her. "I'll go myself. You two go on about your business here."

She swept out of the Serving Room into the Great Hall, and saw that its long, high-ceilinged space was empty of any human form. There was no one at the High Table on the dais, which looked crosswise down the long length of the Hall at two long, lower tables, at which the less-than-honored guests would sit; and none at those tables either.

But at the end of the Hall, the door was ajar and a rectangle of bright sunlight gave her a glimpse of the courtyard. She could see no one there, but at that moment there was a heavy thump from somewhere just beyond the door and a confused shouting.

She ran down the Hall toward the doorway.

"Jim!" she called. "Geronde and Brian are coming!"

"I know," answered the deep-voiced bellow of a mature male dragon. "They're already here. They just rode in."

Angie was too familiar with that particular dragon voice not to recognize it immediately as Jim's. She opened her mouth to call back, but found that running was not leaving her with the breath she needed to shout. She would have something to say to Jim, however, once she reached him. What was he doing still in his dragon body, anyway? With unexpected guests coming into Malencontri's courtyard, it was no time to be fooling around.

Chapter 3

B ut the words she had in mind were never uttered, when at last she ran through the door into the bright sunlight and almost into Jim in his dragon body, who was sitting on the earth of the courtyard just outside. What stopped her was the fact that something unusual obviously was going on.

Theoluf was just finishing explaining to Jim about their besiegers having left, but there was still tension in the air.

Not only was Jim still being a dragon. Yves Mortain, the Chief of the men-at-arms, was running up the stairs to the catwalk; and John Steward was clumsily striding toward Jim across the courtyard, even as Geronde and Brian were riding their horses right up to the Great Hall door, while their escort peeled off to the stables. The Steward reached Jim before Brian and Geronde did, but Jim snapped at his squire first.

"Theoluf, all our archers to arrow-slits looking on the courtyard. Keep them out of sight, but ready to shoot down on any force that's come through our gate. The five new Welsh archers are still in the Castle, aren't they?"

"Yes, m'Lord," said Theoluf. "Trouble, m'Lord?"

"I hope not," said Jim, "but I want to be ready. We might be facing thirty men-at-arms or more. But be sure no one shoots unless ordered. John Steward—"

"Yes, m'Lord," puffed the very much middle-aged Steward, trying to regain his breath.

"As I just told Theoluf," Jim said, "we're going to have visitors—a knight and a good number of men-at-arms, bearing the Royal badge. You will meet them and tell them that I'm not here. The last you saw of me, I was a dragon, flying up into the air; and that usually means that I will be away from Malencontri. If the knight insists, you may let him see my Lady."

"What's all this, Jim?" asked Angie.

"I'll give you the details later," said Jim, in a quick aside to her. "Right now—"

"What arms, on the knight?" Brian's voice interrupted. He had already flung himself down from his saddle and was standing only a few feet away. Jim turned to him, and struggled to put his memory of what he had seen—the white hounds attacking a black boar on a gold background—into proper heraldic language. He could do it nowadays, where once it had been impossible for him, but it took a little thinking. "His arms were . . . *or*," he said after a moment. *"Two hounds blanc, dexter, and a boar sable, sinister; rampant, combatant."*

Brian frowned.

"I do not know those arms," he said. "He will be from the Court, no doubt, particularly if he has King's troops with him. You are wise, James, to avoid seeing him yourself at once, until you know what his intentions are. Thirty men-at-arms is too many to welcome happily inside your curtain wall—but you cannot close the gate on King's troops without reason."

"No," said Jim. He turned back. "Angie, why don't you take Geronde up to the Solar? You can take Brian too, as far as the chamber below the Solar, that looks out on the courtyard—the one we usually give Carolinus when he's here. Brian, I'm going to fly to the top of the tower, and then I'll come down in my regular body to join you in Carolinus' chamber."

"Good," said Brian briefly. He had already turned away to assist Geronde out of her saddle—in actuality, he simply lifted her out of it.

Geronde was perfectly capable of descending from horseback by herself; although it was something of a social art, in this period before the sidesaddle had been invented, to do so with proper ladylike grace. But it was a social requirement on the part of a gentleman to help a lady off a horse, and so Brian did.

He swung her down as if she had no weight at all, accordingly. It was still a little surprising to someone like Jim, who knew that Geronde, in spite of her small size, was all bone and muscle. But then, so was Brian. He was several inches shorter and lighter than Jim, but could undoubtedly match or excel him for strength in most bodily areas, except the legs—where Jim had been unusual even before coming to this century.

Brian took a couple of steps, half-raising his arms toward Jim, and then checked.

"Damme, James!" he said. "Much as I love and honor you, I cannot bring myself to kiss a dragon in greeting! In fact, I am not sure but what Holy Church forbids such things."

"That's all right," said Jim. "I understand."

He did. On the other hand, there was something now about Brian he did not understand. There was an excitement and tension showing in little ways that Jim could hardly have pointed out consciously, but which clearly registered as he watched his old friend.

It could be just this matter of a King's officer with men-at-arms about to descend on them that had triggered off some reaction in his friend. But Brian did not usually react so strongly for so small a reason. This armed visit could just as well be a thoroughly friendly one, in spite of Brian's talk lately—in fact, it was more likely to be friendly than otherwise—unless there was something new Jim did not know. His gaze sharpened on Brian, as he tried to put his finger on what exactly he was seeing that gave him the impression that Brian was almost keyed up enough to be ready for battle.

The bright sunlight told him nothing. It merely lit up Brian's bony face as he stepped back, a face that might have been called handsome if it had not been for a somewhat oversized, strongly arched nose. A Norman nose, as it was commonly called. On either side of that nose, Brian's blue eyes were bright with anticipation, but in no way concerned or upset. The result was a gaze something like that of a fierce, but friendly, falcon, a look Jim had seen in Brian before this, in moments when the two of them were about to find themselves fighting for their lives. Brian, unlike Jim, enjoyed fighting; and the anticipation of it always showed.

"But you'd better all start moving," Jim said, even as he studied Brian. "Angie, you can get everybody inside, can't you?"

"Certainly," said Angie. "Come on, Geronde. Brian—"

She turned and led the way into the Great Hall, Geronde and Brian following. Jim turned to find Theoluf gone, which he should have been by this time, but John Steward still there.

"John," said Jim. "I'm going to fly up to the top of the tower now, and you're to wait here to meet the knight and whoever he brings in through the gates with him. Don't let any of our people challenge or question him if he leads his men in. Just remember—the last time I was seen alive, I was a dragon."

"Oh, my Lord!" said John, wringing his hands.

"Don't be an idiot!" said Jim, more harshly than he ordinarily would have. "Nothing's going to happen to me. I only wanted you to be truthful when you say you saw me last as a dragon. Also, I want you to be able to take a church-oath on that, if necessary. Now, stand aside."

John hastily backed up. Jim sprang into the air with a thunder-clap of wings, flew with the usual effort up to the top of his own tower—and thumped down on it. The armsman on duty there saluted with his spear, and greeted him with the ritual cry that the servants had decided suited his two-body ability—a scream in the case of the women, a shout in the case of the men—whenever their Lord appeared before them in his dragon form. The man was just in time with his reaction; for Jim turned immediately back into his human self, clothes and all.

"We'll have visitors in a short time now," Jim told him. "There'll be no need to sound an alarm. John Steward will talk to them—nobody else should. They're King's troops, and Theoluf already knows they're coming."

"Yes, m'Lord. I understand."

Jim went down the stairs to the next floor, where he found Angie and Geronde on their way to the Solar. Geronde went on into the room, but Angie paused outside the door, and Jim filled her in on what he had seen from the air.

"So these men are coming from the direction of Castle Smythe?" she said. Jim nodded. "But Brian and Geronde came in from Malvern, in the other direction," she went on. "So they're not likely to know anything about this."

"That's what I think, too," Jim said.

"But you're very concerned about this, aren't you?" she said, looking at him. "What is it?"

"I don't really know," he said. "There's something going on, but I don't know what. Brian isn't acting his usual self, I think—or maybe I'm wrong about that. But it's just barely possible that word of his anti-tax sentiments has gotten back to the Royal Court . . . and that could be bad."

"Yes," she said thoughtfully, "I can see why you're not here just now." She looked up decisively. "I'll handle it, if John Steward sends for me." She stepped forward to give him a quick hug, then turned to the Solar door. "Go on down to Brian, now. He's already in Carolinus's room."

"Look," said Jim, on a sudden impulse. "There's something I want to talk to you about. It's about the servants."

"Fine," said Angie. "As soon as we get time."

"As soon as we get time," said Jim. He went.

Going down the stairs, he remembered that hug. Sometimes he wondered in all seriousness if Angie could be psychic. The possibility that Brian might be in danger from what he had been saying publicly about the new Royal taxes had reawakened a fear that had been growing in Jim lately—a fear for his and Angie's very survival: the suspicion that, in spite of the several years he had spent in this medieval century, people were beginning to see through him.

He was able to change bodies and be a dragon because of the accident that had brought him and Angie here. That same accident had stuck him with magical energy and with being a magician, like it or not. He was a knight— and therefore able to be a Baron—only because he had lied protectively about himself to Brian, the first time they had met.

He was no real magician—he only used knowledge from hundreds of years later to make himself look like one. He was no hand with a lance, and able only to hack and hew amateurishly with the sword, only because of Brian's earnest teaching. The manners of the time he had picked up by imitating those around him.

Face it, he was a fake.

He and Angie had been able to survive only because they had had the unbelievable luck to pick up great friends. Brian was a champion at tournaments—and there was no one as loyal as Brian. Dafydd ap Hywel was, probably quite actually, the Master of all Masters as an Archer, bowyer, and fletcher. And Carolinus, Jim's Master-in-Magic—who must have seen through him long ago—was one of only three AAA+ magicians among all the magicians in this world.

If he had learned one thing in the last few medieval years, it was that—in this time—you had to have friends to survive. All of those he had just enumerated would not give him away. But what of all the other people in England—to say nothing of the rest of the Earth.

Like his servants and men-at-arms here in the Castle. He was supposed to be a magickian as well as their Lord. It was his responsibility to get rid of the boomps, which they were all sure would come and eat them some night.

But he had not. The depth of their disappointment could be the beginning of a disillusionment about him, generally. He had noticed them recently indulging in familiarities, seemingly aimed at comfort and care and highly unusual for servants dealing with a Lord of their own time.

It was his own fault. He had been unable to bring himself to order the harsh penalties, like floggings, for their sins of failed duty, the way the usual

Lord of the desmesne would have done. He had talked to them too much, been too familiar in his own actions. They normally expected to fear their ruler and protector—otherwise how could he be someone who could defend them against their enemies? Friendliness came only after that.

Therefore, they had not really allowed him to make himself their friend because he had yet to prove himself. It was their duty to die for him, if necessary. It was his to prove himself by the usual actions, worth dying for. Their apparent care lately could be only pretended; and if so, why?

The trouble was, he was afraid he knew the answer to that—

He realized suddenly he was face-to-face with the door to the room ordinarily given to Carolinus when visiting at Malencontri. Walking in, he found Brian already peering out of one of the two arrow-slits at the courtyard below.

"Active fellow," Brian said, turning from the arrow-slit as Jim closed the door behind him, "and I have indeed never seen those arms before—although I may have heard them mentioned to me. There's something tickling in the back of my head about them; I may have heard the man's name. Broadbent? No, that's not it. Well, it'll come to me—"

He was interrupted as the door opened again; Jim turned to see Mistress Plyseth sailing in with a jug of wine, one of water, and four glasses. She was followed by May Heather, balancing a plate with small cakes on it. Both were beaming powerfully at the two knights. They brought their burdens forward to the table and set them down, curtsied, and then backed out as if leaving the presence of royalty, their determined smiles persisting to the point where Jim could not avoid wondering if the smiles would remain after the door closed.

As it shut, the answer came to Jim: May Heather was being given a lesson in one of the ways of the Serving Room. This must have been a demonstration of how to deliver food and drink to their Lord and his guest.

The curious thing was that this was not the way he was ordinarily served. Gwynneth had never before beamed upon him while serving him, that Jim could remember. In fact, if she ever delivered any food to his table or to him with her own hands, it was usually set down on the table with a very definite gesture, as if to say that he had better eat it and enjoy it. It was good for him.

None of this, however, seemed to have registered on Brian. He was already munching on one of the small cakes and pouring wine for both of them.

"Ah, well," he said, sitting down on the edge of the bed and leaving the room's one comfortable chair to Jim, "it doesn't matter. We'll find his name quickly enough, once your Steward comes up to tell you of his visit."

Since Brian had so pointedly left the chair open, Jim took it—although he had intended to perch on the bed and let Brian, as the guest, have the more comfortable seat.

"You're right, of course," he said.

"These matters unravel themselves in any case," said Brian, cheerfully raising his wine-glass. He checked himself abruptly and turned to the jug of water. As Jim watched, his old friend splashed some of the water into his wine.

Jim stared at him. Brian never watered his wine, except on formal occasions. Jim opened his mouth to ask about it; then closed it again. Brian—very deliberately, it seemed—did not notice. He drank off half of his watered wine almost at a gulp, and with an air of relief. "Ah, James, it is good to be with you again!"

"And it is good for me to be with you again, Brian," said Jim with great sincerity. Brian, he told himself, would get around to explaining the watered wine when he was ready.

Meanwhile, he also drank, and the two of them set their glasses back down on the table at almost the same instant.

"What's the latest news?" Jim asked. It was a socially acceptable way of inviting Brian to tell him anything he had come to Malencontri to say, without seeming to pry.

"Why, things are well enough, James," said Brian. "Not that I could not wish for happier days at Castle Malvern. You know how high my expectations were, when we brought Geronde's father home at last from the Holy Land."

"Indeed I do," said Jim.

The reunion of Geronde with her long-absent father, Sir Geoffrey de Chaney, had revealed a rift between daughter and father. Geronde had long been silently bitter about her father's wandering ways and his dreams of coming home laden with riches.

But the reunion had taken place months ago, and they were all safely back at Malvern Castle. Jim had assumed that father and daughter had been reconciled—nothing he had heard since had suggested otherwise. Brian was splashing more water into the wine that was left in his cup.

"Geronde," grumbled the knight, "has been driving me mad, wishing me to put water in with every damn glass of wine I take, just as if I was at a damned banquet."

He filled his glass with wine on top of the water-wine mixture already there.

"Makes some sense at banquets, where you sit together from noon until dark and want to stay half-way sober," he went on. "But by all that's holy, it spoils the taste of the wine! I told her I'd rather have nine glasses of water and one of untouched wine, than twenty glasses of watered wine. But she says practice will make it comfortable. Hah!"

Jim stared at him, surprised. This was the first time he had ever heard Brian grumble in any way about Geronde, and one of the rare times in which he had seen a sudden black scowl on his friend's face.

"—You know me, James," Brian was going on, "I am no wine-worm. Nor a malt-worm, even, like some I could mention, who think ale a harmless drink. If there is wine before me I partake. If there is none, I do not miss it—even as we are accustomed to rich times and lean ones as far as food is concerned, summer and winter. But by Saint Brian, my name-Saint, unwatered wine is a comfort to me!"

Jim looked at him closely.

"Is something wrong, Brian?" Jim asked.

"Outside of the wine—" Brian began, looking at Jim, hesitated, and then burst out, "—Yes, damme, yes! There is something much amiss! I have something great in prospect but cannot be happy about it because of what should not be!"

"Brian," said Jim, "empty out that watered wine in your glass."

Brian tossed the remnants of his refilled and adulterated glass—onto the floor, of course.

Once, Jim would have winced at seeing him do that. But the time he had spent here had accustomed him to behaviors like it—and it was quite true, of course, that the servants would clean it all up afterward. But Brian was already reaching for the pitcher again.

"No, no!" said Jim, holding up a warning finger; and when Brian hesitated, staring at him, Jim reached out, took the pitcher, filled Brian's glass three-quarters full of wine only, and pushed it toward him.

"You did not give *yourself* this cup of wine," he said to Brian. "I gave it to you. And it would be most un-guestly of you to refuse it."

"Oh? Ah—" said Brian, his eyebrows going up, and then down again as understanding took place. His hand closed around the wine-cup. "Yes, yes indeed, James. Most un-guestly!"

He took a large swallow from the cup, and his face beamed with sudden happiness.

"Aaahh," he said on a long, satisfied exhalation of breath.

"But you were saying something had gone amiss," Jim reminded him.

"So I was," said Brian, at least part of the scowl coming back temporarily, but then clearing again. "However, I should not bring my troubles to you, James—"

"I give you full leave, Brian," Jim said before Brian could finish speaking.

"And by my soul, that is like you, James," said Brian. "I'll not deny I rode over here with some notion of speaking of it to you. But speaking does not come easy. The man is one I will call 'Father' in a few months' time if all things go well. But I swear to you, I will not live under the same roof with him."

Jim looked appropriately shocked, but it was not necessary. Words were already tumbling out of Brian.

"—My Lord of Malvern is worse than the Devil's Ass, who could scarcely imagine a manger heaped full of fodder without immediately imagining two mangers, equally full—and thinking so would remind him instantly of four full mangers. I had expected to have the banns for our marriage published long ago, and to be married the month before this.

"Years now, Geronde and I have waited—and her life has been in danger more than once because I was not by her side. Because I was not there, she bears that scar put upon her face by that Hell-hound who owned Malencontri before you—you remember, when he would force her to marry him—and that mark she will carry for life! I tell you, it is close to more than a man can bear, and still pretend politeness!"

Jim felt a deep surge of sympathy. The Hell-hound at point of discussion— Sir Hugh de Bois de Malencontri—had lied his way into rich Malvern Castle, with sufficient men to take it over.

Trying to force Geronde into marriage was illegal, of course, since only Geronde's father—or the King, if her father was adjudged dead—could give consent to a marriage. But Sir Hugh was a great believer in doing things first and getting people to accept them afterward.

And there would have been a real chance of his succeeding. The King did not really want to be bothered with the troubles of his Kingdom, in spite of the best efforts of his Counselors. He much preferred to be left alone, and to leave the affairs of England to handle themselves. And a goodly bribe by Sir Hugh would have strengthened the Royal inclinations.

Jim made a mental note to check with Carolinus—the Master Magician whose apprentice in the Magickal Art Jim had become—and see whether magic could not somehow be used to take that scar from Geronde's cheek, after all.

He had grown so used to the brave way in which Geronde faced the world with it—and indeed, she had a remarkable, small, fine-boned beauty of feature, except for that one grim scar—that he had almost forgotten it was there. But Geronde must always be conscious of it, particularly whenever she met someone who had never seen her before.

"I'd guess Sir Hugh'd be dead, now," said Jim. "Certainly he wasn't moving, just lying on the ground, outside the protection of Carolinus' magic staff, the last time we saw him."

"But he was not there afterward—" Brian said, leaning forward, "after the rogue-Mage Malvinne had been drawn up like a hanged man, all limp and lifeless, to the King and Queen of Death. We cannot know for sure. But if de Bois lives, and if he crosses my path again . . ."

Brian's eyes had become unmoving, focused on something in his mind, and the falcon look was back on his face, but it was not the happy warrior look. It was his dangerous face, one Jim had seen only seldom.

"In any case," said Jim, to get off the subject of Sir Hugh, "you were saying that Sir Geoffrey had turned against you and Geronde for some reason?"

"You mean kindly by including Geronde," said Brian, his face more human, "but it is me Sir Geoffrey aims to trouble. James, he has set a bride-price on Geronde—a bride-price of eighty pounds! Can you believe such a sum? As if she was some fabled princess, loaded with jewels! Why, eighty pounds is nearly enough to keep Castle Smythe, and all of us within it, alive for two years."

"Hmm," said Jim.

"Oh, he says it is for Geronde's good, not his. He says he will immediately turn the sum over to her, that she have wealth therewith to protect herself in case something should happen to me. Damned nonsense! He first said two hundred, but Geronde beat him down, finally, to the eighty. There he stuck, but he's to hand it to her the moment I give it to him. Still, did you ever hear the like?"

"No," said Jim, seriously. He knew that the minimum necessary income of a landed knight, to keep up appearances, with something in the way of a decent stronghold and enough staff to run it, was at least fifty pounds a year. Brian's income was barely that in good years; and it came more from his winnings at tournaments than from the cultivation and rents of his meager lands.

A capful of gold pieces had been awarded after the tournament at the Earl of Somerset's Christmas party, last winter; but such a prize was highly unusual. A crooked gambler on Cyprus had taken much of that from Brian; in any case, the more normal award was something showy but of no great value. But because the horses and armor of the men Brian overthrew became his property, he could sell them.

Nevertheless, winning at tournament was an erratic and undependable form of support—particularly as it was quite possible to lose. Accidents or luck could favor a competitor who was almost as good as he was. To Brian's credit, that did not happen often.

"Well," Jim said, "if he's simply going to turn around and hand it to Ger-

onde, then Geronde can hand it back to you, if necessary, to keep Castle
Smythe going. It'll be her home as much as yours, after the wedding."

"Oh, and in need she will," said Brian. "She was quick to tell me so, as soon
as Sir Geoffrey was out of earshot. But I must have the wealth first, to hand
to him—and where am I going to find eighty pounds, James?"

He looked at Jim.

"I tell you," he went on, "that question has been driving me mad. I am like
a true madman, stamping up and down my Great Hall thinking of a hundred
different ways, but always coming back to where I started. All that I could
win in a year will simply not add up to that sum. Besides, Geronde and I have
waited a number of years already!"

"I know," said Jim. He would gladly have lent Brian the money if he had
it; and that was so well understood that it had not needed to be mentioned
between them. With Malencontri, he was a good deal better off than Brian.
His lands and other income brought in close to a hundred and twenty pounds
in a year. But that did not mean that at any time he had a spare eighty pounds
of cash in his hands.

"But what made Sir Geoffrey ask a bride-price, anyhow?" he went on.
"Something must have set him off, to think up a condition like that."

"The Devil if I know!" said Brian, refilling his own cup, hesitating, and then
putting a very small splash of water in it. "Geronde might guess, but I am
baffled!"

As it happened, Geronde could, and was busy telling Angie about it up in
the Solar.

Chapter 4

—Of course, he is dreaming of empires to be won and treasure-trove to be found, given only the money to begin to search with. He is as I always knew him, unchanged by the slavery Brian and James rescued him from. I tell you, Angela, that father of mine will drive me mad!"

Geronde had finally gotten around to the subject that had brought her here for this private talk with Angie.

Angie had listened with patience through the necessary preamble. Brian, when talking to Jim, could never bring himself to go directly to the matter in his heart; and so it was with Geronde. But once the preliminaries were out of the way, Brian went immediately to his main concern. Geronde, however, was like a hummingbird, hovering ever closer to her main topic—only to dart away unexpectedly on another subject before coming back to hover again.

Part of this, of course, was the manners of the period, but part also Geronde's reluctance—and to a certain extent embarrassment—to unload her troubles on a friend.

So Geronde had cooed over young Robert, who happened to be awake and looking at the world with his usual pleasure, waving arms and legs freely in the device called a "crib" that Angie had insisted on, in defiance of the medieval practice of swaddling—wrapping a baby into immobility with cloths that fastened him to an easily portable board. Everybody, including Geronde, had been privately sure that Angie's way would ruin the boy.

Having cooed, Geronde accepted some watered wine and spoke about the recent weather, the fact that the crops were doing well, that there had been born in the Malvern Castle stables a foal which looked promising to be her personal horse . . . to wind it all up, she checked with Angie on how things were at Malencontri.

Angie had listened patiently and answered appropriately, knowing that Geronde would get to the important matter in time; and so it proved.

Now, at last, she had begun to talk of what her real concern was—her father, home at last from a hapless attempt to find a fortune in the distant East.

". . . He is no different than I remember," she said to Angie. "I did not expect him to be greatly so; but I vow I had forgotten how wild his thoughts could be in certain matters. Now, having him back in the Castle, it returns to me how near to madness he has always been in his imaginings, his hopes and dreams of what only a Mage or a King could achieve. I remember seeing all these things clearly before he left me alone, with all of Malvern on my hands."

Curiosity got the best of Angie, in spite of her determination to be patient until her friend got to the topic she really wanted to discuss.

"Tell me, Geronde," she said, "were you really only eleven years old when your father left you alone at Malvern?"

"Yes, in effect, I was that age," said Geronde. "And I vow, there have been no lack of others like me—girls and women left as young, or as unprepared, to take care of equal ownings. Oh, it was not a thing I accomplished immediately. After he left me for the first time, he was home again several times afterward, but only for a matter of weeks each time; and then off again—until the time came when he said he was heading for the Crusade that was building in Italy and would come back with a fortune. By then I was full fourteen. But it all began when I was only eleven."

"I can't imagine it," said Angie. "What did he do? Just come to you and say 'You're Chatelaine'?"

"No, no, of course not," said Geronde. "There was a fool of a Steward, of course; I knew he was a fool before my father left him to handle all. But I still did not believe then that my father would not be back, or that I might have to take the full charge of Castle and lands into my own keeping.

"My father—the day he left first that year was a wet and cold March day. He rode off swearing he would be home by St. Mark's Day, when it would be April and dry enough for sowing. But he was not back by St. Mark's Day. Nor was he there on St. James' Day, on May first, or by the Visitation on May thirty-first; and by St. Barnabas' Day I had decided that there was no point in my sitting idle any longer."

Geronde's features hardened into grimness. "The Steward preferred to do nothing, rather than anything that might get him into trouble. He ended up sitting and drinking the day away. So I went to the men-at-arms in their quarters and had the Chief Man-at-arms—his name was Walter—call them together. When they were assembled, I spoke them all fairly. I looked at them, they looked at me, and I said 'I am the Lady of this Castle. Do any of you here deny it?'"

Geronde paused.

"And what did they say?" asked Angie.

"What could they say?" Geronde answered. "They looked at me, very uneasy; and after a moment, Walter himself said in a low voice, 'None here denies it, m'Lady.' It was the first time he had ever called me 'my Lady.'"

Angie nodded.

"'Then,' I said to them, 'our Castle and lands need a Chatelaine; and since I am its Lady, the Chatelaine can be none but me. It is to me you owe obedience, as you would owe it to your Lord. Is *that* understood?'"

Angie shook her head and gave a murmur of admiration.

"They hesitated," Geronde said, "but then all had to admit that my last words had also been true."

"'Very well,'" I told them, "'from now on you take orders from me and none from our Steward.' For there was much to be done. The fields had been neglected and the Castle was in disorder."

She paused, her eyes distant in remembering. "I set them, armed, to accompany me always, as I went about to give the orders that would set matters moving once more. I wanted it clear to all that I would brook no disagreement, and so it was. I moved into the room that had been my father's, and Walter set two men on guard there always.

"'When my father does return,' I told them, 'you will, of course, treat him as your Lord. But remember that the order of the Castle and lands is in my hands until he tells you otherwise; and from this day forward, I wear the Chatelaine's belt of keys. I will wear it before him, unless he orders me to take it off.'"

Geronde paused and breathed deeply for a minute. A little of the fierceness that had come into her voice as she spoke went out of her.

"My father did not return until St. Bartholomew's Day, when our apples were coming ripe for picking. He was with us then perhaps the better part of a month. He saw the Chatelaine's belt around my waist, he saw the way the men-at-arms and the servants answered my orders; and he said nothing."

Her look became fierce again. "It was all one to him, as long as he did not have to concern himself." Her look turned bleak.

"Then he was gone once more," she said, "for a matter of months; then back for a short while, gone again a number of times, and finally off to his Crusade. For a year or so I kept the Steward around, lest the neighbors should get notions that the Castle could easily be taken. For few would credit that it was really I holding the keys; but then I got rid of him. Since then, Malvern has prospered as you know it now."

Nothing was said for a little while; Geronde seemed lost in remembering and Angie waited.

"But that history is not what I came to tell you, Angela," Geronde said. "My father is back and Malvern is his—though I'm damned if I let it go to ruin simply because I'm not there. I'll keep my eye on it and see that things continue to run well; even though I will make my home in Castle Smythe—and that alone will be a large enough task, to bring order and something like an ordinary living to that nest of bachelors."

Her mood flashed to anger again. "My father," she went on, "has now determined to require a bride-price from Brian. He will accept no less than eighty pounds."

Angie looked shocked. Geronde pressed on. "My father has sworn that the money is for me; but I fear we cannot trust him in that, and he may wish to use it to finance some mad adventure once more. But there is no point in talking about that—I have done what I can to get the price down; and no one can do more than I in that endeavor. But it is of Brian I want to talk to you."

"Brian?" said Angie, a little startled.

"Yes," said Geronde. "This demand lies hard upon him—"

She broke off suddenly, almost ludicrously, dodging away from her subject again. "By the by, Angela, pray favor me in something."

"Certainly," said Angie.

"It is that, if you are at table with Brian, whether I am there or not—though it is not likely to come up if I am with you—if you see him taking a glass of wine into which he has *not* put some water, would you look at him curiously?"

"Look at him curiously?" said Angie, still patiently. "All right."

"You understand me," said Geronde. "I would like him looked at, not with censure, but with perhaps a little surprise that he should act so. That is all."

"I can certainly do that," said Angie. "Should I know the reason for doing it, though?"

"Of course you should," said Geronde. "I wish him to water his wine at all times. He is very loath to do so; and I cannot find it in my heart to blame him strongly. He is not an overdrinker—you will know that. While he may start by swallowing a cup at a draught, as others with him, those same companions do not notice later as he slows down, and gradually reaches a point where he drinks almost nothing. So he is never—almost never—what one might call drunken."

"True," said Angie. Now that Geronde mentioned it, she remembered Jim had mentioned, once, how he had noticed that Brian slowed his drinking as an occasion wore on, even when the people he was with were drinking more and more heavily.

"Indeed," said Geronde. "But it can happen in dinings such as last Christmas at my Lord Earl of Somerset's, that a servant fills the wine cups, and puts the water in at the wave of a hand. Not wishing to be different, Brian will, of course, wave it be done so with his, as well. This would not be bad, except that the amounts of water added are different, from time to time."

"I know what you mean," said Angie, who had been given a cup of almost unwatered wine at the Christmas gathering, after several cups of mostly water. In the overheated, overpopulated Great Hall, she had gulped thirstily at her cup—and almost choked.

"Often the servers themselves are not sober," said Geronde. "Under such conditions, Brian's skill at knowing when to make his drinking less and less is sent awry. He can no longer judge as well as if he was drinking the plain wine; and he either sits there dry, and gets into a foul mood, which with drunken companions may well end in sword-play—now or later—or he misguesses how even a little water added takes the curse of drunkenness off wine, and drinks more deeply than he ordinarily would."

When Jim and Angie had first come to this medieval world, Angie would at this point have tried to make Geronde understand that merely diluting wine did not reduce the alcohol in the total amount of wine, only spread it out. But she and Jim had learned better than to try to educate fourteenth-century minds with twentieth-century information. It never worked.

"So," she said, "you want him to get in a habit of watering his wine, so he'll be able to judge better how to pace himself? I know Jim said once he thought Brian kept a watch on his wine so he might be ready to use his weapons well in any emergency—in case somebody tried to put a quarrel on him, thinking he would be slowed down by drink."

"That, too, is true," said Geronde. "You do not mind helping us?"

"No, of course not," said Angie. "I'll be glad to. But what's this got to do

with your worry about the bride-price, and what needing to find it may do
to Brian?"

"What it already has done, you may well say!" said Geronde, angrily.

Angie stared at her.

There came a knock on the door.

". . . What it has done to me, this bride-price," Brian said to Jim, getting up
to take another look through the arrow-slit, "is set me searching for means of
raising money. Finally, unable to bear it longer, I swore a Great Oath—not
an ordinary oath, you understand, James, but an Oath before the altar of my—
well, of what's left of the chapel in my Castle. I swore I would find that bride-
price if I had to borrow it from the Devil, himself."

He turned away from the arrow-slit to sit down again. "And so, it happened,
James," he said, easing forward to tap Jim on the arm with one hard finger,
"that within the week a way came to me, unsought."

He sat back in his chair. Jim was clearly expected to look astonished, so
he did his best.

"Did you!" he said.

"I did indeed." He paused as if to marshal his words.

"You are aware that about the King there are other advisors than Sir John
Chandos? Some are earls and dukes, others large landowners or the wealthy.
A group of them have lately counseled him to lay on a number of new taxes,
such as the recent Aid, which is one-tenth of a man's income; and the Poll-
tax, that begins with a penny a year for the poorest and goes up to as much
as a pound for those of high rank; and new taxes on transfers of land."

Brian shook his head. "All this, on top of our yearly tithe to Holy
Church"—he crossed himself—"and others such as that, which of course we
do not mislike, but which, with these new collections added, eat away so
greatly at our available monies, that they have caused a mighty wrath among
such as the Earl of Oxford, and others. It has reached the point where they
are determined to act—not against the King, of course, but against those who
surround the Throne."

Jim was becoming uncomfortable. Mention of the Earl of Oxford made it
clear that Brian was talking about the very highest levels of the Kingdom's
politics, for that Lord had long been in bitter dispute with the Earl of Cumberland—a battle, in truth, for the King's ear, and a battle in which Cumberland had the great advantage of being the King's half-brother. This was
not, thought Jim uneasily, an environment for Brian to inhabit.

Ordinarily, he reflected, Brian would have known better; but perhaps his
frustration with Geronde's father had eroded his judgment.

As if following Jim's thoughts in the silence, Brian went on: "It is my Lord of Cumberland who leads his Royal Majesty—by the by, did I tell you Agatha Falon is back at Court and not only very well with the King, again, but close with Cumberland as well?"

"I didn't know that," said Jim, frowning. Agatha, young Robert's aunt, had once tried to kill the baby—and Angie as well. But Jim had thought she no longer had any power.

"As I was saying," Brian continued, "it is Cumberland and his group who take power in their own hands by advising our Royal Liege they will relieve him of burdens."

"Hmm," said Jim thoughtfully.

"I did not even have to search. An emissary came to me when I was not even thinking on the matter. James—"

He leaned forward to slap Jim's knee, emphatically.

"—they have offered me to join a force which they will raise. What do you think of that? One of them, or another, will find a dispute with the Earl of Cumberland or other such counselor, and as a result this force will harry some of Cumberland's lands. Having done so, it will withdraw and apparently be disbanded. Then another dispute will arise, and once more the force will be brought together, and harry another property, or such."

"But—" began Jim. Brian held up a hand to check him.

"You are about to ask, quite rightly," Brian said, "whether it is right and legal for me to be involved in such action. I will tell you that I went at once to my Liege Lord, the Earl of Somerset, from whom my lands are held. I asked his permission to fight in this cause."

"You did!" Jim stared at him. "Now everybody'll know you're involved."

"What does that matter?" said Brian. "He gave me permission, being in sympathy though not inclined to engage in the effort himself. The aim is merely to cause these greedy Counselors expense, while keeping the matter strictly between them and those who think otherwise—and away from the Throne. The result must surely be to draw the Counselors back to the care of their own lands and castles. Is it not a clever scheme?"

"Well . . ." Jim began slowly.

"I thought you would see the charm of it," went on Brian cheerfully. "It cannot fail."

"Yes, but—" Jim was beginning when Brian cut him short again.

"Hold, James," said Brian, raising his hand. "Let me tell you all. *They are willing to pay me the eighty pounds I need.* Forty pounds down and another forty once the force has acted!"

Jim opened his mouth to express his opinion of Brian's chances of ever getting the second half of his payment—then stopped. That argument was doomed from the start.

Brian was not basically a good businessman. He tended to believe in the honor of other gentlemen, deserved or not. On the other hand—eighty pounds, cash, paid immediately, was almost too much to expect for just about any martial service. Jim decided to try another tack, which might, indeed, be more important in any case.

"Brian," he said, as calmly as he could, "isn't there some danger that, though you're not actually acting against the King, the Counselors you're attacking might convince him that you're in revolt, or an outlaw who ought to be brought to justice? You could find yourself in a pretty fix."

"Pish, tush!" said Brian, smiling. "We would only come, there would be a pretty little flurry of arms around the castle of one of these Lords hungry to dip into a fatter Royal purse; and then we would be away again. No one would even know who had come. Meanwhile, those who are giving me my orders would be urging on the King that this must be a signal from a Kingdom dangerously upset about his new taxes. I cannot see any real harm or danger in it, beyond the usual possible hurt that may come when men in armor clash in earnest. The King will know nothing of it as a plan, of course."

"How can you be sure of that, Brian?" asked Jim. "He may have caught wind of this scheme already, or those close to him may. You know, when I first saw this knight and his party, they were coming down the road from your Castle."

"From Castle Smythe?" said Brian, sitting up very straight. "Why would he be coming from my Castle?"

"That was what I asked myself," said Jim. "But from what you've told me, it just might mean trouble. He's a King's Officer; and he's got a force large enough to take a small—a castle the size of yours, particularly with the advantage of surprise. Isn't it possible that the plan of these unnamed Lords may well have leaked—either to the King, or to those behind the new taxes?"

"I cannot believe so, James," said Brian, slowly. "There has hardly been time. Less than two weeks have passed since I spoke to the emissary who wished to hire me."

"Still . . ." began Jim.

Brian stared at and through him for a long moment. Then he relaxed and smiled.

"No, no," he said. "It could not be possible." He smiled reassuringly. "In any case, I have already agreed with them. No, I see what this is—and a very clever scheme it is, too. This business of a King's Officer looking for me is merely a plan of my employers, to get the word out about the country, that there are those already moved to rebel against being over-taxed. That is all it is. That is all it can be."

He sat back in his chair, completely relaxed, and took a deep drink.

Jim looked at his friend with a calm face, but with despair in his heart. At a loss for words, he got up and walked to the arrow-slit nearest him to look out and gain a moment of silence in which to sort out his thoughts.

For all Brian's dismissal of the idea, Jim thought, he was running the risk of being charged with treason. There was no treason in his heart, of course, but that would not matter if someone convinced the King otherwise.

Like a bolt from the blue, it suddenly came to Jim that if Brian were to be suspected of treason, so would be his close associates—Jim and Angie, for instance. That was the way minds worked at the Royal Court. And if that happened, arrest would come like lightning out of—well, that same clear sky.

Could that have something to do with why this knight had gone to Castle Smythe, and then come here? Jim looked more closely down into the court-yard.

"What do you know?" he said. "The man's leaving, and his men-at-arms with him."

"You say so?" He heard Brian's heels hit the floor behind him as the other jumped to his feet and took a few swift steps to the other arrow-slit. "By God, you're right!"

Gazing down on the courtyard, they could see the last of the Royal men-at-arms riding out through the open gate, over the drawbridge.

"Well, that's that!" went on Brian, turning from the arrow-slit and going back to the bed. Jim heard him pouring either wine or water—probably wine—into his cup. Jim turned back himself.

"It's a lot quicker than I expected," said Jim. "I wonder—"

He never got around to expressing that wonder out loud, however, because just at that moment the door opened and Geronde came in, closely followed by Angie. Jim rose from his chair, vacating it for whichever woman would take it over. Angie held back, and Geronde—as guest—hesitated only a moment before sitting down in it.

"How did you get rid of the man so quickly?" Brian asked.

"He had already asked if Jim were here," Angie answered, looking at Jim. "John Steward had already told him that you'd last been seen leaving the Castle in your dragon body. The knight asked me if you were engaged in one of your famous adventures with Brian, going on to say that he had just come from Castle Smythe, and Brian had been gone, too; so it had occurred to him that maybe the two of you were off together."

"What did you say?" asked Jim.

"I said I didn't know, of course," said Angie. "I told him you never told me about those sorts of things until they were all over—"

"And I," interposed Geronde, "said that Brian was just the same way. He never told me anything about his great adventures or feats of arms until they were all over. Then I went on to tell him that I was to marry Brian shortly, and he wished me a long and happy marriage."

"So," said Jim, "he seemed convinced by that?"

"As far as I could tell, yes," said Angie. She turned to her friend. "What do you think, Geronde?"

"Oh, he believed every word of it!" said Geronde. "After all, the husbands are damned few that tell their wives why they're going to be gone—any more than fathers tell their daughters."

"In any case, he gave up with that," said Angie. "He said that he had come by only to give you an order from Sir John Chandos in the King's name—"

She produced a piece of parchment that had been sealed with a large black seal, now broken. She passed it to Jim, who unfolded it and looked inside.

He could read twentieth-century printed Latin and, to a fair extent, speak Church Latin. But the stylistic flourishes of the fourteenth century—particularly the club ascenders, those tall verticals on such letters as "k" and "i" and "h"—stuck up before his eyes like the spears of a miniature army; and to him the whole page looked like a scribble of lines painstakingly drawn by somebody of kindergarten age. He passed it back to Angie.

"Can you read it?" he said.

"I already have," said Angie. "It's from Sir John Chandos. He asks you to hold yourself in readiness. By order of the King. You're to join a force he's taking into the North Country, to face some enemies of England. It doesn't say just who the enemies are; but Sir John'll be here, according to this letter, in the next day or two."

Chapter 5

... A day or two ..." echoed Jim dazedly. This was short notice indeed, particularly from a medieval point of view. On the other hand, superiors did not generally feel a need to consider that inferiors might need advance warning; and he was definitely the King's inferior—certainly in the sense of this letter—and, for the moment at least, Sir John Chandos' as well.

He turned to Brian.

"The North of England wouldn't be one of those places—" he broke off. "It wouldn't have anything to do with what you were talking to me about?"

"No," answered Brian, "nothing has been said to me so far about the North of England."

There was a noticeable silence in the room for several seconds.

"Well," said Geronde, briskly, "we now know why the King's men came riding—it was to deliver this message to you, James." She stood up. "Now, Brian, you and I had best be starting back if we want to reach Malvern while there is light in the sky."

"You aren't even staying overnight?" said Angie.

"Oh, no," said Geronde. "It was never our intent. Brian is guesting at Malvern for a few weeks, just to reacquaint himself with matters there. He and I went for a ride because it is such a bright day. Once out, the day proved so fine that we simply thought we'd keep riding until we got to Malencontri and look in briefly for a chat. But we must both be back by suppertime. You still have wine, do you, Brian?"

For a spur-of-the-moment visit, their coming had been singularly well prepared—with a pigeon-message sent beforehand. But no one mentioned this, though there were some unfortunate seconds of awkward silence before Brian answered.

"As a matter of fact, I do," he said, looking interestedly down into his cup.

"Well, Angela and I can give the order for the horses to be saddled and brought around, and you finish your wine and whatever words you still have with James. Then come down yourself. Angela and I will be either in the Great Hall or out in the courtyard. Come, Angela."

She and Angie swept out the door, their skirts rustling on the rushes as they went. Brian looked into his wine cup regretfully, and then drank off what was left of it at a gulp. He put the cup down on the table.

"You don't have to leave quite that quickly, do you, Brian?" asked Jim, pointedly seating himself in the chair Geronde had vacated.

"I must. I must," said Brian. "Geronde is quite right. If we want to be well back at Malvern by the time the supper table is set, we should leave now. Sit as you are, James. There is no need to see me out."

He turned toward the door.

"But what I was hoping for," said Jim, "was that you and I could talk about what we might do, if by chance we found ourselves on opposite sides in some situation."

"We would avoid each other, of course," said Brian. "Even if such a strange hap should come about, you and I can always find others wherewith to fight, besides our friends."

"I'd hope so," said Jim, but his heart sank. Brian was clearly determined to see no view of the situation but the prospect of earning the eighty pounds he needed.

"Besides," Brian went on, "I own I had come here with some hopes you might wish to join me, James. Would it not have been great pleasure for the two of us to fight together in such a sport of arms? But I understand how your orders from the King leave you no choice."

In spite of himself, Brian's face had saddened as he spoke.

"To be truthful," said Jim, "I'm not as interested in being mixed up in this as you are, Brian—for good reason, of course, on your part. But, even with this letter, I can't help but feel I've let you down."

Brian shook his head. He turned so as to pass around behind Jim's chair on his way out. Jim heard him move behind him. Unexpectedly, Brian's hand clapped down on Jim's shoulder and squeezed it with painful force. He spoke again, in a voice suddenly rough with feeling.

"Never think it, lad!" he said, deep in his throat. "Never think that!"

He released Jim's shoulder and went past him, out the door, closing it behind him.

It was early bedtime before Jim got a chance to talk to Angie alone, privately, and at length. But he could hardly have picked a worse time.

"What a day!" Angie was saying, as she fell into the large, soft bed in the Solar. "A nice quiet summer with you here at home for a change—and bang! In one day, an attack, the King's men looking for you, Geronde's father wants eighty pounds, and Brian's off to a small, but probably illegal, war to earn the money—with a King's man possibly already out to arrest him. Oh Lord, what next?"

"Well," said Jim, sitting up in the bed, "now that you mention it—"

"No, no, no!" said Angie, burying her head under a pillow. "Not now. Tomorrow, Jim!"

"No," said Jim, "now. Tomorrow, Chandos may come. Tomorrow anything could happen. You might as well listen."

He told her about his suspicions concerning the servants.

"Nonsense!" she said. She had taken the pillow off her head when he started talking. Now she sat up in bed. "It's just your imagination."

"I tell you," said Jim, stubbornly, "they're the first to see through me, here; and they don't like what they see. They don't like me—I'm almost certain of it. This concern of theirs is cover-up."

"If you think so, ask them."

"They'd lie to me—out of fear. Or politeness."

"Ask May Heather. If she doesn't like you, she'll tell you so, and anything else you ask."

"A thirteen-year-old girl? And new to inside the Castle? I couldn't do that."

"Well," said Angie, "it's the best suggestion I can make, right now, tonight. Let's both sleep on it."

Meanwhile, some miles away as his people trotted, pausing to investigate this and go a little out of his way to look at that, Aargh, the English wolf—another friend of Jim and Angie—paused to sniff at a faint whiff of a strange scent that had come to him on the evening air, before going on about a wolf's business.

*   *   *

True to the promise in his letter, it was no later than the next afternoon that Sir John Chandos, with twenty lances, rode in. So numerous was his retinue, that Sir John did not object—and Angie was not slow to suggest—that perhaps they should bivouac outside the walls. No one in his right mind let a large armed force into his or her castle, unless they had to.

Chandos understood, and accepted this with good grace, as did his men. The three younger knights with him were welcomed inside, even to being seated at the High Table with Sir John and their hosts. But experienced common soldiers like Sir John's men-at-arms expected to sleep out more often than in, and carried the makings of some kind of shelter that would keep them from the chill of the night and the morning dew.

Philosophically, they lit fires in the cleared space and looked forward to the food and drink that would be sent out to them from the Castle. Meanwhile, Sir John, his knights, Angie, and Jim settled down to a lavish, if early, supper.

"Being close," Sir John told them, once the preliminary courtesies and introductions had been made, "methought I would break my journey with you, since I have not seen you since last Christmas, and here is always a welcome meeting."

This, of course, was no more than polite formality, for the ears of any servants who might be listening. Jim and Angie smiled and accepted it as such.

Chandos sipped appreciatively from his mazer, a large, square-built wine cup that had no virtues, as far as Jim and Angie were concerned, except that it was large enough not to require frequent refilling. But it was what was called for for entertainment of honored guests. Having sipped, Sir John put it down again on Malencontri's best tablecloth.

"I am once again on my duties about the Kingdom on behalf of his Royal Majesty," he said.

"The Welsh border again?" said Angie, urging the process of pretense along. The last time Sir John had shown up with armed men, he had been heading in that direction.

"Not this time, happily," Chandos said. "This is another matter. Alack, there seems no shortage of them."

A servant came in and moved around the walls of the Great Hall lighting the cressets—open-weave iron baskets—already filled with dry firewood—to which he added a grease-soaked branch, already flaming at one end. The thin, dry willow stems set fire almost at once to the heavier pieces of wood in the cresset, adding light, as well as a certain amount of welcome warmth, to that of the three massive fireplaces, which had been kindled earlier. The illumination from the nearest cresset momentarily lit up the peaceful, handsome countenance of Sir John as the knight smiled engagingly at both Jim and Angie.

"Matters certainly keep you busy," said Angie, after the servant had gone.

"I'm afraid they do, Lady Angela," said the war-captain, spy-master, and Counselor to the King. "But such is life. And, to be truthful, I would rather be active than idle. Do you not find it so, yourself?"

"I don't seem to have much choice in the matter," said Angie. "But, yes, I'd rather be doing something than nothing."

"I would, too," said Jim. "But I don't seem to have much choice, either. In fact, as I look around me, nobody seems to have much choice, from the meanest servant to the highest Lord. We're all running full speed all the time."

"It is life. What would you?" said Chandos. "I—aah, those small cakes of yours that I like so well!"

May Heather had just come in, her lower lip caught between her teeth and all her attention on balancing a large serving tray holding the cakes to which Chandos referred. They were jelly-rolls, which Angie had introduced, along with some other twentieth-century eatables that were easy to make under fourteenth-century conditions. Chandos began to pick them up one after another in his fingers, eating them like miniature candies. May curtsied, with great care not to fall over, and departed.

"Well," said Jim, trying for a subtle way to get the conversation into some explanation of the order from the King, "what's the news at the Royal Court?"

"Ah, the news," said Chandos, stopping to wash a bit of jelly-roll down with a swallow of wine. "Well, first I should say that the Prince, young Edward, remembers you both most fondly. You and your various friends as well—I don't suppose you've been seeing any of those close Companions lately, particularly that wizard of a bowman. What was his name?"

"Dafydd ap Hywel," said Angie.

"That's right, I knew it was some such name. And, of course, the good Sir Brian and Sir Giles de Mer, and—oh, yes—the wolf."

"Aargh," said Angie.

"Also, come to think of it," said Chandos, "there was a time when we were besieged by Sea Serpents here, and you had in your courtyard a considerable giant. Would he be one of your close friends also?"

"A friend," said Jim. "Rrrnlf, a Sea Devil, a Natural. Not as close as the others you were just speaking about."

Actually, Rrrnlf had visited Malencontri only a few weeks past. He came to explain why he had not been able to answer a call from Jim, who during

the spring had sought his help. Rrrnlf had always promised to appear immediately if he was called—from anywhere in the oceans of the world.

He had a good excuse—he had come across a bottle at the bottom of the
Red Sea and, handling it clumsily, had accidentally released a powerful
Djinni—who then imprisoned Rrrnlf himself under an undersea mountain.

This had been annoying, but no great problem to the Sea Devil; he was
huge, powerful, and able to simply dig his way out from underneath the
mountain. However, it took him a little while; and so he had shown up here
somewhat late.

Curiously, while tunneling out he had come across another burrowing individual—man, or Natural, it was difficult to say which. The creature had
looked more or less human, but was less than four feet tall. It came along
with Rrrnlf on his visit, and said not a word the entire time—only stared at
Jim.

Rrrnlf had produced the little fellow from under his shirt—a rather ugly
manling, wearing a kilt apparently made of leather, and somebody else's oversized shirt of the same material. The sleeves were not only voluminous, but
so long they covered his hands, which seemed to be clutching the ends of
the sleeves from inside.

Rrrnlf had explained that he had found the small being tunneling, also, but
making relatively slow progress because of his smaller size. Rrrnlf, a kindly
type, had taken him along at the Sea Devil's own powerful rate—Sea Devils
could scoop solid rock out of their way as easily as a human being could
move piled-up dust. Since then they had been together.

The little man did not respond when Jim spoke to him, but only gazed
back with an open mouth, as if he could not believe what he saw. At least,
that was what Jim thought the expression on his face meant.

"Never says much," Rrrnlf had explained, gazing down at the small figure
with something like the fond pride of a pet-owner . . . Jim pulled his thoughts
back to what Chandos was saying.

"—Yes, yes," Chandos was continuing. "Now, your archer friend, for example, I could use him at this moment if he should not be at too great a
distance away. Do you suppose he would be interested in joining me, and
those men outside, in a small matter of dealing with a threat to disturb the
King's realm? He would be well paid."

"I don't think Dafydd would," said Jim, shaking his head. "He's never shown
any particular interest in fighting, except in his own defense; and, I don't
know if you ever heard him express himself on the matter, but my guess is
that, in any case, he wouldn't be particularly inclined to help Englishmen."

"Hmm," said Chandos. "Not an odd attitude for a Welshman, I suppose."

They proceeded from the small jelly-rolls to an omelet with beef marrow and chopped pork in it, which was considered an ideal sort of "summer dish." This was followed by a much heartier beef pie, and so the meal wore on.

Jim was thoughtful, mulling over the fact that Chandos had made only a single fleeting reference to a man he knew to be Jim's best friend—Brian. The omission was very noticeable. Chandos must realize that. But plainly no explanations would come until they were more private than they could be, here in the Great Hall.

Meanwhile, Sir John had now fallen into conversation with Angie, seated on his other side. Jim felt a slight twinge. He did not think of himself as being the jealous type; but the manners of this particular time seemed ideally adapted for the seduction of any lady that a gentleman might meet. In fact, it seemed to be something of a slight not to try to seduce any lady of equal rank you met; and it could not be denied that Sir John was a master of the manners of his day.

On this occasion, however, Jim had Brian too heavily on his mind to worry much about that—and anyway, he trusted Angie.

Angie, meanwhile, taking notice of Jim's silence—which was becoming almost as noticeable as the respectful silence of the three younger knights who had come with Sir John—began to wonder if possibly something about her conversation with Sir John was bothering Jim.

She was rather amused that this husband of hers showed a touch of jealousy where the older knight was concerned. Sir John was certainly in his forties, and might easily be into his early fifties, although he neither looked nor acted like it; and he undeniably was attractive. But if Jim were really getting concerned, she should probably back off a bit. After watching him for a moment, however, she decided that it was nothing to worry about and let herself enjoy Sir John's company.

Finally they were served a Faun Tempere—Gilly-Flower Pudding—the best Malencontri could do by way of dessert, most fruits not being ripe yet. It was a dish of beef broth, white flour, finely powdered cubeb berries, and ground almonds, atop which were sprinkled the petals of dandelions—basically for ornament. At this point, John Steward made his appearance, looking as formal as possible and carrying his staff of office, which under ordinary conditions he usually did not bother to lug around.

"Your pardon, my Lord, my Lady, Sir Knights—" he intoned. "Both the guest room for Sir John and the chamber for the other three gentlemen are now prepared."

He bowed and backed out of the Great Hall.

There was a clearing of throats at the far end of the table and Sir Charles Lederer, the oldest of the younger knights, spoke up.

"Pray pardon me, my Lord, my Lady, Sir John," he said. "But I find myself feeling faint. I have been somewhat unwell all day, and it may be something I, Sir William, and Sir Alan, here with me, together ate at breakfast this morning before our day's ride. I would greatly desire to retire now and sleep, with your kind grace and permission."

Chandos looked at Jim, who picked up the cue.

"Certainly, Sir Charles," he said. "Sleep is a sovereign cure for most ills. My Lady and I most certainly excuse you if you wish to go, though of course it will be a matter for Sir John to rule on."

"You have my permission, Charles," said Sir John. "And if either of you others are at all faint, or uneasy in the guts, you could do no better than to follow Sir Charles' example."

"Thank you, Sir John, my Lord, my Lady," chorused the other two politely, standing up immediately and bowing. "A good night and God's blessing on you all."

Jim and the rest wished them a good night in return; and, as the three left the dais, John Steward appeared instantly in the entrance to the Serving Room, to lead them to their accommodation.

"They are good lads," said Chandos, looking after them. "Mannerly and obedient. But they know nothing yet about real battle, or anything in the way of serious fighting. Yet, they all seem stout-hearted enough."

He turned back to Jim.

"We must talk, Sir James," he said. "We can do so here, if you think there will not be too many servants' ears close upon us. Or have you a more privy place for important conversation?"

"Our Solar, of course," answered Jim. The question had been a matter of form. Chandos was already familiar with their Solar.

So that was where the three of them went. Wine had been sent up, as well as more little cakes to nibble as they drank; but these went untouched. All three had already eaten more than they wanted—Chandos, out of polite compliment for the food; Jim and Angie to set a good example to their guests.

"A pleasant chamber," said Sir John, sipping his wine and looking out of the nearest of the windows that had resulted from Jim having the arrow-slits enlarged. These were now not only glazed, but framed in and hinged, so that they could be swung inward to open the Solar to the outside air.

That window was open now, and the twilight breeze moving through the room was probably welcome to Sir John, who, like most people of this time, was usually overdressed rather than otherwise. Clothes were considered to be for the purpose of keeping one warm; if it turned out that wearing them made you hot—well, of course, you could always sweat. Better to sweat for a few months than go cold the rest of the year.

"We like it very much," said Angie.

"I do not wonder at it," said Sir John. He looked at Jim. "It touches me with guilt, Sir James, to take you away from such pleasantness; but duty to our King calls us both, you and I. No doubt you have been wondering why his order reached you, putting you at my disposal."

"I assumed something was in the wind," said Jim, "but I didn't have any idea what—still don't, for that matter."

"We are both caught up in the cares and problems of our times," said Sir John, sipping at his wine. "For both of us it comes of having gained somewhat of a name, so that we are thought of when matters are at hand that can only be dealt with in certain ways. I will explain; but I would that the explanation be kept strictly amongst ourselves, the three of us here."

"Of course," said Jim and Angie almost simultaneously.

Jim turned in his chair and looked directly at the Solar fireplace, where a freshly laid, small summer fire crackled pleasantly.

"Hob!" he called.

"Yes, m'Lord?" answered the fireplace.

"Go someplace else, where you can't hear what we're talking about."

"Yes, m'Lord."

Jim turned back to Angie and their guest, and met Chandos' inquiring gaze.

"Just our Castle Hobgoblin," he said. "A staunch friend and ally. But he's likely to be in any chimney or fireplace we have. Still, I'd back him against any other Hob in England."

A small, happy sound escaped from the fireplace.

"Hob!" said Jim, over his shoulder.

"Yes, m'Lord. I'm going . . ." The voice faded away out of hearing.

"I give you thanks," said Sir John. "Well, it is a small matter of bickering between some of the nobles of the land; important only because on one side we have a gentleman who is sometimes overactive in his advice to his Majesty. On the other we have gentlemen who feel that the first has been giving ill advice to our ruler in the laying on of taxes in the last few years—you may even have heard some murmuring about the one or the others."

"Now I think of it," said Jim, "it seems to me I did hear about something like that, quite recently."

"Alas," said Chandos, "the complaints are all too common. I would you understood what is at stake here. Our Sovereign is determined to recover full control of Aquitaine, that portion of France which is his by rightful inheritance. And equally the Kingship of all of France, to which he also has claim, his grandfather having been King Philip the Fourth."

"That's right," said Jim, remembering his studies, "Philip of Valois was the one actually chosen by the French for their King, being a grandson of King Philip the Third."

"Yes," said Chandos. "In truth, our Edward had as good a claim as Philip. But it is not heritance alone that concerns those of us who are close to the King. We are concerned with the health of the Kingdom. The land of Aquitaine, of course, contains the wineries whence we get our wine of Bordeaux; and indeed, where all the world gets its wine of Bordeaux."

He paused to take another sip from his mazer.

"If we were to recover these lands and these wineries, the tax on the wine alone would make unnecessary a great many of these other small taxes of which our English people complain. So, in essence, by stopping individual quarrels between those about the King, and those who feel ill-counsel has been given, we not only keep the land peaceful, but in a way we answer the general unhappiness with some of these necessary measures."

He stopped speaking and looked at Jim.

"I see," said Jim. He could not bring himself to voice a heartier agreement. This was an Englishman speaking about his King's claim to the French throne, of course, Jim told himself. But the facts and reasoning were correct.

"I see," he said. "But what's all this to do with me; and what do you want from me at the moment?"

Chandos did not reply immediately, but got to his feet like someone who needs to stretch his legs, and sauntered over to the nearest open window, looking down on the interior courtyard of the Castle. With his back to Jim and Angie, he went on talking.

"In a word," he said, "your company most of all; but also your assistance. Word has reached us that your friend, Sir Brian Neville-Smythe, may be among those who plan to disturb the peace of my Lord the Earl of Cumberland—for you must know sooner or later whom we wish to protect."

Jim's heart sank.

"I understand," Chandos went on, "that Sir Brian has gotten permission from his liege lord, my Lord the Earl of Somerset, to engage himself with those who are currently at feud—shall we say—with my Lord of Cumberland." He seemed to shake his head.

"Meanwhile, all concerned wish to keep the matter as quiet as possible—though indeed it will not, in the long run, be possible to keep it unknown and undiscussed throughout the Kingdom. Sir Brian, from his name as a great lance and a winner of tournaments, will draw good men to the side of those who would now threaten Cumberland. I would make known the fact you are not with him, and as well add an equally weighty name to the other side.

"In any case I have the King's order for you; and I regret the promptness of such a going, but you and I must be leaving tomorrow, early. It is a necessity for us—"

He broke off suddenly.

"By Saint George," he said. "Your Castle is on fire! But a great many of your servants seem more interested in a fight that is going on down in your courtyard."

Chapter 6

Jim reached the window in two strides and looked.

"Oh, Hell, Angie!" he said. "It's May Heather and Tom, the Kitchen-boy. They're at it again!"

"And it's the Kitchen on fire!" said Angie, who had just reached one of the other windows.

They all three hurried downstairs.

When Jim, Angie, and Sir John came out into the courtyard, the smoke was beginning to thin, but the crowd was no smaller, and the fight was still going on; although the tall adult bodies of the servants hid the combatants, who were wrestling on the ground.

"Pull those two apart!" shouted Angie, as she, Jim, and Sir John strode rapidly up to the mass of watchers. "The rest of you stay here! You hear me? Stay! I don't want any of you leaving!"

The crowd, which had showed signs of scattering, reluctantly stayed, parting to let its superiors through to the center. Separation of the fighters was being managed, at the cost of some damage to those doing the separating; and it became undeniable that the combatants, as on several other occasions recently, were indeed May Heather and her opposite number on the Kitchen staff, a boy named Tom.

The two were the best of friends, but often at odds; and lately they had gotten into several of these battles-royal—which for some reason attracted every servant able to slip away from their duties. But not one servant could be made to explain why the fight was such an attraction.

"Beat thee again!" said May, triumphantly, as they were pulled out of each other's reach. Tom growled something unintelligible.

"Well?" snapped Angie. "What's it about this time?"

" 'Ee lied!" cried May Heather, forgetting in her passion her careful Castle pronunciation and dropping into the broad local speech.

"Didn't!" shouted Tom.

Both made a serious effort to break loose and re-engage. They were cuffed by those who held them prisoner.

"All right, leave them alone," said Angie. "I want answers, not a couple of deaf children. I've told all of you about hitting the young ones on the side of the head. Now, Tom! You tell me. What does May Heather say you were lying about?"

"There was a hole!" cried Tom, still at the top of his voice. " 'Twas by the big oven!"

"There's not! There's not!" shouted May Heather. "M'Lady, look for yourself. There's no hole there. It was his doing, the chimney getting stopped up!"

Getting the whole story in cases like this, Jim knew, was sometimes a slow affair, since those telling it tended to react to the last words said by those in opposition to them. Accordingly, he left Angie with the crowd and the two furious youngsters and went on into the Kitchen himself, accompanied by Sir John.

The air there was surprisingly clear. A few of the Kitchen staff, who had ducked back in there at Angie's first words, were now standing back in corners and looking guilty. Jim's eyes fastened on the Mistress of the Kitchen, who was standing with her lieutenant, the Bakery-Mistress, beside the oven.

This was a large kiln-like structure with walls of hard-packed earth. Low down at its center was a massive fire-box, with space above it where dishes could be put to cook, or merely be kept warm until needed. Behind, a chimney ascended from the fire-box, a chimney as massive in its own right as the oven.

The doors of the fire-box were open, and the fire appeared to be out, although a palpable warmth could be felt. As Jim and Sir John joined the two women, one of the under-servants of the Kitchen crawled out of the fire-box, his face and clothes now so thick with soot and grime that he was hardly recognizable.

" 'Tis blocked," he said, speaking to the Kitchen-Mistress, "with dirt. Hard blocked. We'll need rods to poke at it until it falls apart, and then we can shovel it out below here. By your leave, my Lord," he added, noticing the two knights.

"Clear blocked?" said the Kitchen-Mistress. "Our Tom couldn't ha' done that. Nor even that girl, though I wouldn't put it past her otherwise. It's too heavy a work for a lad and girl their sizes. Well, get the rods, and to work!"

" 'Twas the Fairies done it!" said the Baking-Mistress, lower-voiced, looking away from Jim. "Things like that happens when people coddle hobgoblins in their fireplaces. There's no hobgoblins in *my* oven, I can tell you! I've seen to that!"

The statement was ostensibly directed at one of the other servants against the farther wall of the Kitchen, who was now trying to look as if he had not heard a word. The very fact that such a statement was made aloud in Jim's hearing at all, however, was evidence of what Geronde called "the terrible looseness" with which servants were governed in Malencontri.

"Hobgoblins?" asked Sir John, looking at Jim, questioningly.

"The one you heard me speak to," said Jim, more sharply than he had intended. "It's here by my leave and will stay here—or anyplace else in my Castle!" For once he was honestly angry; and the tone of his voice plainly carried conviction to all his vassals within earshot.

They could not, without permission, step back from him. But they all leaned back a little as if in a strong breeze. The Baking-Mistress tried to edge behind the Kitchen-Mistress. A rather unsuccessful attempt, since both women were equally stout.

"Excuse me a moment, Sir John," Jim said, remembering Chandos was a witness.

He turned to the Kitchen-Mistress.

"How did the chimney get filled with earth?" he demanded. "And what's all this business about a hole?"

"I know not, my Lord," the woman answered, formally emphasizing the "my Lord" as two separate words, since a guest was watching. "Our Tom, who came into the Kitchen at a time when—well, there was none else watching, just before the chimney stopped up—says there was a hole in the floor."

She stamped on it.

Jim looked down. He saw earth, pounded hard by many feet over many years. She pointed to her right. "The hole was just over here, he said, my Lord, and you can see the earth has been at least loosened."

Jim and Sir John followed her to a rough circle on the floor, where the earth did indeed seem not to be so tightly packed. In fact, its top layer could almost have been swept away with a broom.

"This challenges belief," said Sir John. "If indeed there was a hole, and if indeed something like a fairy came up it, then went into the oven—was there a fire in it at the time, Mistress?"

"No, my Lord," said the Kitchen-Mistress. "The morning cooking was over, and the fire-box had just been cleaned out. Indeed, most of our people were having their own small bite of food before the evening's cooking should begin."

"Then not a fire-demon," said Sir John, turning to Jim, "but by all the Saints, it seems no Christian thing. Mayhap the talk of a fairy was not amiss?"

"I'll have to consult with Carolinus on that," said Jim, short-temperedly dodging the question.

"Fairy" was a term everyone of high or low rank seemed to use indiscriminately. As far as Jim's knowledge went, in this world there were no beings specifically called "Fairies." Rather, the term was applied to just about anything outside the usual range of living being—Naturals, Supernaturals, Goblins, Devils, Djinni, Demons—as well as Lords and Kings of Underworlds, Heavens, and Hells. . . .

Jim had never really figured out why it was that at some times these people seemed in mortal fear of even a mention of such creatures, but at other times gossiped eagerly about them—perhaps there was some nuance he did not totally understand, to the folk saying about *Naming Calls*, which as far as he knew meant that if you spoke such a creature's name aloud, it might come. To get you.

For a moment, Jim worried that Sir John, who was more intelligent than almost anyone else he had met in this fourteenth-century world, might be offended at the stiffness of the answer Jim had just given. But a glance at the knight seemed to find him completely satisfied. They went back outside to rejoin Angie.

She, it appeared, had sent May Heather back to the Serving Room, Tom to the Kitchen, and all the others—after a brief but sharp lecture on their own duties and not neglecting them to gawk at a couple of fighting children—back to work. The courtyard was emptying fast.

The three started toward the Great Hall, and as they went Jim explained to Angie about the hole in the Kitchen floor, and the fact that the chimney was mysteriously stopped up with earth.

"I wonder if there was a servant left anywhere else in the Castle?" he said. He meant it humorously, but Angie blanched.

"If there's something around the Castle that shouldn't be here—" she began, her face stricken—"if she's left that baby alone, I'll kill her!"

She left them, running ahead for the door, and disappeared through it.

"Why, is there danger about?" asked Sir John, his voice alive and interested. The note in it was very much like that Jim always heard in Brian's voice when it looked like there might be some entertaining combat in prospect; and abruptly, Angie's alarm registered on Jim.

"Excuse me, Sir John," he said, and broke into a run himself.

But Sir John ran with him. In spite of his extra years, the older knight seemed in as good condition as Jim. They went swiftly in through the Great Hall and through the Serving Room, past its Mistress, sternly confronting May Heather, whose face was now washed and her clothes at least straightened.

"—and are you to blame for that, too?" demanded Gwynneth Plyseth, looking back from the astonishing sight of, not one, but two knights running—*running*—through her Serving Room.

"Oh, no, Mistress," said May Heather, her freshly-washed face radiant with the conviction of complete innocence. "It was only a little dispute with Tom, I had."

Meanwhile, Jim had slowed somewhat on the stairs. Provokingly, Sir John also slowed, just behind him—but from the sound of his breathing, the older man did so more to accommodate Jim and stay with him than because he himself was running out of breath.

It was understandable—people like Sir John and Brian, to say nothing of the servants, had been engaged all their lives in daily physical activity to the limit of their strengths. Still, it was irritating to someone who had been rated AA-class in college volleyball, to find a middle-aged knight slowing down out of consideration for him.

They did, however, catch up with Angie, just in time to see her pounding on the door to the room that held Robert Falon and his nurse and shouting through the panel.

"Open up!" she was calling. "It's me, Lady Angela. Open up, I say!"

A squeaky answer came from within, not resolved into intelligible words. But a moment later there were sounds of heavy objects being dragged away from the door, and then of the bolt being shot back. The door opened, and in it appeared the absolutely terrified face of the nineteen-year-old nurse. Angie pushed past her and rushed to the cradle. She stopped, and heaved a great sigh of released tension.

"He's all right," she said. She breathed deeply for a moment, then whirled around to face the nurse—who backed away into Jim, who with Sir John was now also in the room.

"P-p-pardon, m'Lord," she quavered, then turned back and literally fell on her knees before Angie. "Oh, pardon, m'Lady! But I was so afeared!"

"Frightened? Why? Answer me!"

"Something tried to get in the door!" quavered the nurse. "I had it locked just like you said I should always do, m'Lady. When it couldn't get in, it hammered at the door. I called out 'who is it?' But there was no answer. Just this hammering and it trying to get in. So I shoved everything in the room, except his little cradle, against the door! Then I leaned against it myself. When you started knocking and calling, m'Lady, I thought it had come back!"

Jim and Sir John were already examining the outside of the door. It was no flimsy bit of carpentry, but a solid slab of wood a good two inches thick. Surprisingly, it did show dents . . . not around where the latch was, but level with it and more or less in the middle of the door.

"If you'll step out into the corridor with me, by your favor, Sir John," said Jim, grimly, "I'm going to set up a ward on this room."

Sir John followed him outside.

"A ward?" he echoed Jim.

"A magic protection, Sir John," said Jim. At the word "magic," Sir John backed across the corridor until his back was to the wall. Jim pointed his finger at the doorway.

Not long ago, he would have needed to work up a rhyming spell to set a ward on Robert's room. Now, however, he had learned how to concept—to build in his mind an image of the magic he wanted to create. In the back of his head he seemed to see it now, like invisible silver threads penetrating stone, wood, and empty air. He wove his finger back and forth before him for a moment, and it was done.

"Let no one who is not of this Castle enter this door or window," he told the threads, "unless taken in by Lady Angela or myself."

He turned back to Sir John, and saw no evidence of fear in the other man— but there was something else: John Chandos had a face that could go completely expressionless when he was most dangerous, and it was expressionless now.

"That takes care of it, Sir John," said Jim, speaking as lightly as he could. He spoke through the open door.

"It's all right, Angie," he said. "I've warded the room. Nothing can come through the door or the window—Matilda, you can feel safe now, but still keep the door locked—Angie, there's no more need to worry. Why don't you come back downstairs with Sir John and myself?"

"I pray your forgiveness, Sir James," said Chandos, "but what with dinner eaten and the fact that you and I should be ahorse at dawn, I believe I would rather go directly to my room, if a servant can be summoned to show me the way. You may have things to make ready also, and no doubt you yourself would prefer to go early to rest."

"Oh, of course, Sir John," said Jim, with a sinking feeling. In spite of the fact that Chandos had said he was expecting Jim to leave with him tomorrow, he had not connected that with leaving so early.

"You're on the floor below," he went on. "I'll take you there myself."

Having escorted their chief guest to the best visitors' room, Jim found Angie already laying out travel clothes for him in the Solar. Quietly, he joined her in the work. Sir John could hardly deny him the use of a sumpter-horse to carry extra baggage for his own use. He had learned the hard way to carry as much as he conveniently could, after experiencing a number of trips on his own and with Brian and Dafydd.

His mind began to make plans. Nor could Sir John object to his taking his squire as a personal servant—no, come to think of it, that wouldn't be wise. His squire, Theoluf, was the only real experienced fighting man in Malencontri; and the men-at-arms would need a leader in case of real trouble. To leave Angie and everybody else here lacking both their chief commanders at a time when outlaws were marauding, King's men were dropping by, and something unknown was invading the Castle—perhaps—would not be wise.

He could, of course, take one of the other men-at-arms, or one of the Castle's servants. But none of them had any real experience in this sort of traveling duty.

No. He would travel alone. One of Chandos's men-at-arms could lead his warhorse, Gorp, and the sumpter-horse.

Working together, he and Angie did not take long to get everything packed and ready to be taken down and loaded on the horse. Jim called the servant on duty outside the Solar and sent her down to summon John Steward. When John arrived, Jim pointed at his travel necessities.

"John," he said, "this is to be loaded tomorrow morn on a sumpter-horse; and a riding-horse, plus my war-horse Gorp on a lead rope, must be ready for me so I can travel with Sir John Chandos at dawn. If Gorp is fractious from being stalled so long, lately, someone should exercise him before sun-up."

"Yes, m'Lord."

"You will take care, of course, of providing breakfast, not only for myself but for Sir John and the knights with him; also for his men outside the walls, along with three more days of provision for them to carry—all of this should be in the Great Hall before we have to leave."

"It shall be done, m'Lord," said the Steward, without turning a hair. "All shall be as you desire. M'Lord would like to be woken an hour before sunrise?"

"A little earlier than that, I think," said Jim.

"Very good, m'Lord."

The Steward went out. Jim and Angie got ready for bed.

As they crawled into it—it was their latest version, very large and comfortable, with a complete canopy and side-curtains, to keep drafts out, as well as a sort of bubble of warmth enclosed—Angie said what had been in Jim's mind all the way along.

"I didn't think he'd take you so soon," she said, once they were settled in bed.

"Neither did I," said Jim. "But it's probably just as well. The sooner I leave, the sooner I'll be back."

The words were nothing more or less than Angie had expected from him; but she felt a sudden strong twinge of unhappiness at the thought of his leaving. Since young Robert Falon had come into their lives, she was not only full of intense protective feeling toward the child, but she also found herself wanting Jim around more—preferably where she could see him.

It was not that she was afraid of being left alone in the Castle. She had thoroughly adjusted to this rough period they now lived in; and Geronde had given her many lessons, information about many things useful to a Chatelaine managing a castle without her Lord. So it was nothing like that. It was just that she wanted him—Jim—to be there; and now that he had to leave, she wanted him back safely, and as soon as possible.

"You'll use your magic, now, won't you—if you really need it?" she said. "Won't you?"

"Oh, of course," said Jim.

But Angie knew that lately he had come to regard the magic energy he possessed as too precious to be used, except in the case of an absolute need such as the ward in Robert's room.

She closed her arms around her husband and snuggled up against him; but a small cold feeling remained inside her. She was afraid that in spite of his saying so, he might well be saving of his magic when he really needed it, and possibly fall into danger because of it.

Chapter 7

True to Sir John's words, they were, indeed, off with the dawn. They rode west by north to Bath, and then to the Bristol Channel, where they took ship to Caerwent. From there they took the old Roman road over to Caerleon, and northward from there, through Kenchester, Leintwardine, Roxter, and on to Warrington, Wigan, Ribchester, and Lancaster. After that, it was almost straight ahead, due north.

The scent was cold.

Aargh, the English wolf, moved upwind toward its source, silent as his own shadow, flickering on the sun-dappled forest floor and against the green small bushes, where the majestic oaks and ashes let light enough through for such smaller leaved things to grow. His nose was to the ground, his ears were upright and pricked, for the scent was not "cold" in the sense of having been laid down some time ago; rather, it had a special element of taste that came to him as a coldness.

Aargh's nose was what mouth-taste and color-sight were to human beings: it gave him access to a whole rich spectrum of information that humans passed by without ever having sensed, or to which they paid scant attention if they had. So that when he read this scent as "cold," it was only because no word existed for it in spoken language. It was as a human might describe a flavor tasted or a color seen for the first time. It was a scent that spoke to him of darkness and deep chill.

In the many years that he had held this territory against incursions by other wolves, he had never encountered this scent before; and from nose-tip to tail-end he was alert.

It was not a ground-trail of someone or something that had passed this way earlier. It was an odor riding the faint breeze that stirred the hairs of his face as he moved toward it from downwind. It grew stronger as he came closer to its source, which might be anything. Only one thing was certain. It belonged to some unknown; and he went with all a wolf's natural caution.

Caution it was, not fear. Aargh had not known fear since he was a wolf-pup; but caution he knew, and wariness. If there was something dangerous up ahead, then it was well to know what it was before it knew him.

The forest was thinning. There were more of the sunlit open patches be-tween the great trees; and without needing to check, he knew he was drawing closer to Malencontri Castle, the home of his friends Jim and Angie Eckert, the unlikely Baron and Lady of the Castle. The scent was stronger now, and he followed it more slowly, picking his cover as he went. Abruptly, he stopped, lifting his nose to get its full quality, and peering through the branches of a small bush, his ears cocked forward.

But what his ears gave him was silence, and what his eyes gave him was merely a hole in a slight rise of the ground, like the mouth of a den.

There was no sign of any living creature; but still Aargh waited. The scent, strong and close now, spoke ever more certainly of chill and an even deeper darkness—some place far removed from a forest such as this. At last he moved again—but now one slow step at a time, as he came near the hole, careful that no footfall might send a vibration through the earth to warn whatever might be in beyond that entrance.

But nothing responded, nothing emerged. He came to the very edge of the hole and explored it carefully with his nose. Some of the earth dug out and encircling its opening had been moved within the last few hours. It was still not completely dry.

It was a strange, unnatural opening in the hillside, a puzzling opening. It looked very like the mouth of a den, but it was too small for a bear, and too large to be comfortable for a wolf, who liked his den entrance to fit snugly around his shoulders like a collar, in case he might have to stand within it, the den protecting the rest of him, while only his jaws and teeth were outside. In that position, any wolf could stand his ground.

But, on the other paw, it was also too large for any badger, the next largest den-digging animal belonging to these woods—although a young boar might have used this—if it had been dug sometime since. But boars did not den in summertime like this, only in winter and bad weather.

Nor was it likely to be the den a troll might make. Trolls, also—particularly Night-trolls—denned up only under unusual conditions, such as when the females were giving birth. Nymphs, dryads, and other smaller Naturals, of course, would have no need for a den.

As far as he could tell—and he was careful not to allow his nose or any other part of himself to be silhouetted against the light at the mouth of the den, even now—whoever had dug it was not here at the moment. As if to prove this, his searching nose now told him that there was a clear, fresh trail leading off at an angle, toward Malencontri.

He followed it.

The trail led straight toward the Castle. Whatever or whoever it was went on two feet, and there was no sign of hesitation along the way—or even of caution. Aargh preserved his own caution, but followed more swiftly now—the trees did not thin out any more, but there were fewer bushes between them.

The woods were the King's, with everything in them; but common people were entitled to the fallen branches—only—for their fires. This rule had been amplified illegally by some earlier lord of the Castle—doing, like many did, anything he could get away with, by letting his serfs and tenants also take out the living shrubs and bushes for a distance from the Castle clearing, back into the wood.

This allowed them extra firewood, while leaving less cover for enemy forces and less handy material for fascines to fill up the moat so they could storm the walls.

Here, the forest was lighter. Aargh slowed. He had followed the trail now right to the edge of the wood; and he stopped to look out around a tree at the clearing itself, kept around every castle, a bowshot from its walls, to give a clear field of fire against any attacker.

It was one of those days in England when everyone had given up on the English summer after a steady diet of rain and chill, in spite of the fact that it was late June—only to have the weather play its usual trick; so that, suddenly, the sky was blue, the temperature warm, the breeze light and friendly, and all things seemed to be going well.

It was exactly the time of day and the kind of day in which Aargh would normally be taking a nap in the shade somewhere, himself. And so he would have been, if not for this strange scent and trail.

That trail led out into the open space; and looking out, Aargh saw, within the shade of one of the trees to his right, a cradle, within which he scented young Robert Falon. Not far from the child was his wet-nurse, who had found a comfortable seat on the ground with her back against the trunk of the tree and was showing a wolf-like common sense by taking a nap herself.

One of the Castle's young men-at-arms, obviously posted here as protection for the baby, was right now half-a-dozen paces away and looking in a completely different direction, absorbed in a game between the off-duty men-at-arms and the stable help.

It was a rough game, as might be expected. It bore some faint resemblance to football, except that you were not restricted to using your feet only to propel the ball, but could get it to its destination—the goal line of your opponents—in any fashion. If anyone got in the way, he could be dealt with by any means short of a knife. It was quite all right to bite, knee, kick, gouge, and wrestle around on the ground with an opponent, to take the ball. Right now the stable-lads were winning.

Aargh considered the situation.

The Unknown had clearly been interested either in Robert or the wet-nurse. Also, it had not been afraid to go out in plain view of the walls or the sentry on the tower. There might be nobody on the battlements, and the sentry might be as fascinated by the ballgame as the man-at-arms was. But going out in the open like that was not the action of any stranger who was not sure that he could get away quickly and safely, if seen.

It could be that the trail did not go all the way to the cradle or the tree where the nurse snored lightly. Aargh turned and, well inside the trees, trotted until he was level with the cradle, but still safely out of sight. Then he moved forward cautiously, using individual trees for cover, until he was less than three wolf-lengths from the cradle and about five from the sleeping nurse.

He tested the air with his nose again. It was hard to tell, at this distance, if the trail of the Unknown led right up to the cradle or the nurse. Whoever laid it could have turned off again and headed directly toward the Castle, or simply circled around it at a distance and continued on.

Happily, Robert's cradle was side-on to the tower, which meant that by keeping low, Aargh could use it for cover once he had crossed the small open space to it. Normally, when Aargh had anything to do with someone in the Castle—which meant Jim or Angie—he stayed in the woods and howled from time to time. Either Jim or Angie would hear the howl, or their attention would be drawn to it by one of the servants or men-at-arms. In either case, one of them, probably Jim, would come out to their set meeting-place.

That was a safe way. But, in this particular case, Aargh did not want to spend half a day waiting. The distance to the cradle was very short, and if he moved swiftly and silently—which he would do in any case—he should be able to reach the cradle without being spotted by anyone in the Castle.

Low to the ground, he slipped out.

In a moment he was beside the cradle, and his earlier feeling was confirmed. The trail he had been following came around this side of the cradle, close to it—and when he put his head down under the cradle, he could sniff it on the other side also. On his side, particularly, there was a spot where it was more than a passing trail, a spot where whoever it was had stopped, presumably to study Robert. From that point the trail led off at a further angle, back into the woods, and possibly back to the den.

But in any case, the baby was perfectly unharmed. When Aargh peered over the edge of the cradle, Robert's eyes were open wide and he gurgled happily at seeing the furry mask of the wolf above him. His tiny arms reached out toward Aargh's closest ear.

Wise in the ways of human as well as wolf pups, Aargh carefully furled the ear, rolling it inward until it was a tight small bundle against his head, closed his eye, and laid his head down for a moment on Robert's chest, letting the baby hands pull and tug and explore harmlessly through Aargh's coarse forehead hair—unable to touch eye or ear that might be damaged by such exploration.

After a few moments, the tugging hands gave up and he withdrew his head, looking down at a still cheerful Robert, now reaching vainly toward a butterfly that was passing some three feet above his cradle. Aargh withdrew his head and slipped back into the trees. He began to circle the Castle toward its back where the curtain-wall joined with and became part of the tower, the inner keep that would be the final stronghold to which the Castle's defenders would retreat in case an enemy got over their first defenses and into the courtyard and outbuildings of the Castle proper.

The back of the Castle was blind, having no windows and few arrow-slits, and an unbroken vertical face eighty feet high that could not be climbed and would not be practical to assault. Here the wood came close to the wall, the clearing narrowed, and it was safe for Aargh to cut across the clearing itself in the direction in which he had been headed before he had run across the scent he had followed.

As he cut close to the wall, he passed, too close to be out of sight from, an arrow-slit that he knew from the smell allowed air and some light into the Serving Room. As he passed, he heard two female voices, one obviously younger and shriller than the other, raised in argument. Aargh was fond of

Angie and Sir James, and prepared to tolerate the rest of those in the Castle; but like all their kind, all of them spent a lot of their time making noise.

It seemed to be their way, and Aargh had no time or interest in things like going around changing the world; but he disapproved. He trotted on past the Castle now toward the comfortable obscurity of the farther trees—the trees he would be re-entering in a moment. Noise never got a wolf anywhere.

Chapter 8

It was less than a week until the party led by Sir John Chandos was crossing the Low Borrow Bridge, approaching Penrith Castle, south of Carlisle. They rode into the Castle, where the three younger knights, the men, and the horses settled down for several days' rest in the stables.

In the Castle itself, Sir John, Jim, and Sir Bertram Makeworthy—the Earl of Cumberland's Seneschal, with the authority and care over the Earl's lands, mines, and fisheries in the district—settled down to dinner and a talk over a snowy tablecloth.

But first, Sir Bertram had to hear the story of Jim's first adventure in this world, from its most famous participant.

Jim had not kept count; but the Seneschal was probably the three-hundred-and-twentieth person who had to hear it for himself.

Whenever Jim told it, he tried to emphasize that it had only been with the help of his Companions, Brian, Aargh, Dafydd, Danielle, and Carolinus, plus two dragons, that he had won against the Dark Powers at the Loathly Tower.

The disclaimer seemed to make no impression on Sir Bertram, as it had not on all the others before. All those people had heard the story told before they ever met Jim, in wildly varying songs from wandering minstrels—which all made Jim the necessary, if not almost solitary, hero.

In any case, it made it special to them, hearing it directly from Jim. Having done so would make their own versions—as it would Sir Bertram's—that much more authentic to future listeners.

Finally, with the legend told, the three of them got down to business.

"You're aware of why Sir James and myself, with our men, are here—aren't you, Sir Bertram?" asked Chandos.

"I am," said Sir Bertram. He was a tall, heavy man in his late forties with a long, pale face. It was a face that looked as if it seldom found anything to smile at. "I understand you believe trouble is expected here. But where? In Carlisle itself? In the fisheries? In the mines—out on the grazing-lands?"

"I do not know," said Chandos. "Perhaps I should ask you. Have you had trouble recently in any such places? More to the point, are you having trouble with any just now?"

"Trouble!" said Sir Bertram, his face living up to its promise by turning extraordinarily grim and gloomy. "When is there not trouble? I hear of it from all sides. The Scots border-reivers have stolen away the cattle! The herring are not running! The miners *must* have an advance on the ore they have dug, or they'll starve—the ungrateful dogs know I can't permit them to starve! Who would work the mines, then? Trouble is with me all the time. Most lately, with the miners, as I say—they won't go down into the diggings, because of Piskies."

"Piskies?" asked both Jim and Sir John together.

"Yes, yes," said Sir Bertram, a little testily. "Fairies, as you might say. Earth-fairies. The miners say they can hear them digging. And when one or more say they've heard Piskies, then they all think they hear them—and they all put down tools, leave, and won't go back into the pits and drifts—the holes, trenches, and short tunnels in the earth between a couple of pits, as you might say. There's nothing to be done but wait until they have courage enough to go down again. First, one or two will go. Then the others will take heart and follow; and for a little while we will get mining done again."

"Indeed," said Sir John, "such are sore troubles, Sir Bertram. But what I am looking for is the harrying of your Lord Earl's lands and possessions. And I do not mean the occasional raids of thieving Scots, but deliberate attempts by a force of armed men to do damage and make cost for his Lordship."

"Of that, no," said Sir Bertram. His face added alarm to the other emotions visible upon it. "Are we to have that too? I knew you had come to deal with some disorder, but I did not know it was to be something that large. Armed men—men of war, no doubt—Lord save us! If it is that, I do most need your help. I do not have enough men-at-arms to set guards on all the properties."

"I am afraid guards would be of little use," said Sir John. "This will be a considerable force, with intent to damage, destroy, and cause difficulties for your overlord."

He paused to take a drink of a rather good French wine. "I had hoped that you could tell me which property or place is most likely to attract them first—mayhap one more isolated than the rest, less protected, or more vulnerable. If you can point me to such a place, then I and those with me would wait for the trouble-makers there, and engage them when they come—hopefully driving them back in such manner that they will not come again."

"Hum," said Sir Bertram, consulting the wine in his mazer. "Let me see. They could do the most mischief in the shortest time by attacking the mining areas. But there are several such, and I know not how to tell you which one is the best place to guard."

"Such is not necessary," said Sir John. "I believe Sir James would agree with me, that such a force would want to gather in some central spot—for they will surely come up here in small groups, so as not to attract attention—and then rendezvous in a convenient place."

Sir Bertram thought, frowning, for a moment.

"I think, sirs, that Skiddaw Forest might be such a place as you describe," he said. "If they gather there, they will be within striking distance of Alston, where the lead and silver mines are; and, in another direction, of Egremont, which is close to the iron mines."

"And is this Skiddaw Forest," Sir John asked, "such a place that we could move down there and set up a camp, with little notice being taken of us?"

"Without question," said Sir Bertram. "I shall send some with you who can take you to such places as you might desire. It is rising ground, most of it, with some good stands of trees. If you set up your camp well hidden and set out watchers, none will find you."

"And may I ask you," said Sir John, "to send word to the surrounding towns, and to those who might be about in the forest, to bring us word of any other armed party forming in the same woods?"

Sir Bertram nodded, and Chandos went on. "I take it," he said, "that Skiddaw Forest is not too far distant?"

"Some fifteen to twenty-five miles west," answered Sir Bertram. He sat watching them. Chandos turned to Jim.

"What think you, Sir James?" said Chandos. "Indeed, it might be wiser if we were to set off tomorrow morning, for this Skiddaw Forest. Our men can rest once they get there."

Jim understood very well that the question was merely a formality. Chandos was the man making the decisions here.

"I don't think we could do better, Sir John," he said.

"It is settled then," said Chandos, turning back to Sir Bertram. "However, because those with us have expected to have at least a few days' rest, we will not leave early in the morning. Could we pray the Castle to have a meal for us at, perhaps, mid-morning, before we start?"

"Certainly, certainly, Sir John!" said their host, his face looking almost cheerful. "It will be our happiness to do so. And I will be sending with you three or four men who know the district; and once you find where you want to stay, they can go about the area and alert those who are usually there to watch for strangers."

"Good," said Chandos.

"—The men won't be too happy about it," he told Jim later, after they had left Sir Bertram and were about to go to their separate rooms. "They've been looking forward to a few days' sleep, drink, and the local women."

"I suppose not," said Jim. "Give you good night, Sir John."

"A good night to you, Sir James."

The men-at-arms, thought Jim, as he followed a servant to his own room, would certainly not be pleased; but they would not dare to grumble. As the servant left, Jim took off his Knight's belt and wedged his sword sheath under the door-latch—which should at least delay anyone trying to open it, and cause enough noise to wake him.

The three young knights would have to look happy about it. They had no other choice. Jim himself could have used at least a couple of days without being in the saddle. He would sleep heavily tonight.

He ignored the bed, which was likely to have vermin. Beds like this were normally re-made with clean bedclothes after a guest left, out of courtesy to the next honored visitor. But servants were all too likely to sneak in and catch a nap, or to engage in some love-making "like a Lord"; and servants, like everyone else, could harbor fleas, lice, or even infectious skin diseases.

Unrolling his bedroll before the pleasantly burning fire, Jim undressed partially—not completely, of course, because the fire would die down; and in spite of the fact that it was summer, the room would be icy by morning. He unrolled his second bedroll, so as to have the extra blankets ready as needed; and pulled a single blanket over him, lying back with a sigh of contentment.

"That's that!" he told himself. "Now for a few hours of really solid slumber."

* * *

But, unreasonably, slumber did not come. He lay there, a thread of uneasiness cold within him, watching the red-hot underside of the bottom log in the fireplace. The fire had eaten much of its surface down to segmented coals that blushed—first bright, then dim—as small, wandering airs in the room blew through, then passed on; while flame-wraiths danced between them.

Something, he told himself, was wrong. It was not just his imagination. Something was very wrong.

First, there had been the change he had felt in the attitudes of his Castle servants. That had been so even before the boomp noises began. Then there had been Brian's too-quick joining in an armed action against a chief Counselor of the King—which could be read as against the King himself.

This last, apparently only because of Brian's great need for money. It was not at all like the Brian Jim had thought he knew. Brian was a chivalric idealist. He carried his passion to do what was right to almost ridiculous limits, sometimes.

Jim would have believed him willing to cut off his right hand—literally—before using it to draw a sword in any way that could be considered against the King. But Brian had embraced it almost joyfully.

And now here was Jim, himself, meekly allowing himself to be swept up in Chandos' expedition to counter the very movement that Brian had agreed to join.

Jim was not fooled. He had not been dragooned into this business because of his powers as a magician—which were actually at little more than the beginner level, though non-magicians never seemed able to believe that. He was here because he was also popularly thought to be a Paladin—a mighty warrior; and the truth was, he was even less of that than he was a magician.

He had been in a few actual, if unimportant, medieval combats, usually beside Brian. But these had been the sort of encounter people like Brian all but sneered at, refusing to dignify them with any description more weighty than "a brush," "a bicker," or "some small disturbance. . . ."

Brian, who had worked hard to train him in the proper use of sword, dagger, and lance, knew better than to speak at all highly of Jim's fighting skills. Chandos, old in war and skilled at sizing up fighting men, must have recognized Jim's lack quickly. Just last Christmas, Sir Harimore Kilinsworth, Brian's chief rival with sword and lance, had seen through Jim at a glance, and had not hesitated to tell him so. That was what had started him examining his conscience.

This was, in many ways, a cruel, primitive time. But he and Angie had made the decision to stay, after he had rescued her from the Loathly Tower—when for a short while he had owned the magic energy needed to take them home to their own time and world.

They had agreed that, when all was said and done, they liked it here. It was a time to be alive in—in many ways a noble time, when courage and loyalty to principles were acknowledged and respected above the place they had in the minds of the twentieth century. . . .

. . . Still remembering the moment of that decision, he smiled; and smiling, drifted off to sleep thinking about what had led up to it.

—He woke again, suddenly. Someone was standing over him, but it was not Angie. It was Carolinus, his Master-in-Magick, firelight making shadows from his wispy beard on the red robe that he always wore.

"Well, well," said the Mage, in a notably hoarse voice, "awake now, are we?"

"No," said Jim, annoyed at everything at the moment, and replying without thinking, "I'm asleep!"

Abruptly, everything blanked out.

Chapter 9

Jim drifted slowly, lazily, up toward wakefulness, from the deep waters of unconsciousness. It was a comfortable way of returning to the world, this effortless business of coming to. However, as he began to get near to the surface of awareness, there began to creep into him a growing feeling that something was wrong—or that something had gone wrong—immediately before he had plunged into the deep abyss from which he was now ascending.

The feeling of worry exploded inside him. He finished waking with a jerk, and sat up.

"What happened?" he said.

The Mage looked down at him.

"You put yourself to sleep," said Carolinus dryly.

"I did?" said Jim. "How did I do that?"

"I've no idea," said Carolinus. "Your methods are your methods. You used Magick, of course."

"You mean—" said Jim, "I put myself to sleep with my own magic?"

"Now, what else could I mean?" said Carolinus, an edge to his voice. "Of course you put yourself to sleep with your own Magick. Whose else could you do it with?"

"But I didn't think my own magic would work on me!" said Jim.

"Well, now you know differently," said Carolinus. "Live and learn. One of the most simple things, I should think, in the world to assume—but you evidently hadn't assumed it. Of course a Magickian's art will work on him—or her. When you transport yourself by Magick to someplace else, isn't that your Magick working on you?"

"Well . . ." said Jim, and could not think of anything more to say.

Of course, Carolinus was right. As one of this world's only three AAA+ Magickians, he should know—Jim thought of his own rank, a mere C+, and that only due to a recent promotion.

Still, there was something startling about the idea. It was a little too close to absentmindedly using magic to make yourself feel happy, or to change your mind about something, or . . . he could not think of exactly what would be a good but ridiculous example. But there was something circular about a magician being able to magic himself.

His thoughts were interrupted by the sudden realization that Carolinus had appeared here without being called. That was not a thing the Mage normally did—Jim usually had to hunt him down, if it was possible to get hold of him at all.

"Well—thank you for coming," said Jim, hastily.

"No need to thank me. I'm not here as a courtesy to you," said Carolinus. "And I haven't *come*. This is just a projection of me you're talking to. I haven't come because I couldn't."

"Why not?"

"None of your business. Or in other words, never mind," said Carolinus. "I want to talk to you about more important things."

Jim stared at Carolinus' projection. Why project, he wondered? He had always assumed his Master-in-Magick could go anywhere he wanted, anytime.

True, there had been one exception to that—a time when Carolinus had become sick. It seemed to be the case—as far as Jim knew—that in this world, magic could heal wounds, but not cure illnesses.

Now Jim scrambled to his feet, to stand there in his shorts and a light shirt—in this era everybody normally slept naked; but in spite of the clothing, he immediately felt cold. Hastily, he threw more wood into the fireplace; and the fire blazed up. He turned back to Carolinus.

"In any case," he said, putting aside with an effort his first bad temper and trying to smooth Carolinus' memory of it with cheerfulness and a friendly voice, "it's good to see you, whether you're here in the body or in a projection. I don't suppose, by the way, that you'd be able to tell me how I could send a projection of myself?"

"Haven't the slightest idea," said Carolinus.

After trying very hard almost from the start of Jim's apprenticeship with him, Carolinus had finally managed to wean him from the belief that the older man would teach him magic. Carolinus had done this mainly by leaving Jim to solve his own magical problems. And as Jim had learned more about it, the real truth of magic had dawned on him: as a fully developed ability—like music or painting—it was not something that could be taught. It could only be learned.

True magic was a creative Art; and beyond certain elementary skills and rules, every magician had to develop his or her own way of doing it—Jim woke up to the fact that Carolinus was glaring at him.

"Forgive me," said Jim hastily. "My mind wandered."

"As usual, if you don't mind my saying so," replied Carolinus. "In any case, I can't keep projecting to you here all night long. I've got something important to tell you. That's why you see me here."

"What is it?" asked Jim, feeling a sudden chill snake of worry inside him. "Nothing to do with Angie or Robert?"

"No," said Carolinus, shortly. "Never mind that now. I don't have much time, and I've got two commands to give you. One is to get in touch with KinetetE if you need help. The other is at all costs to keep the King—our King here in England—on his throne."

"Keep the King on his throne?" echoed Jim. How was he supposed to do that? He fumbled for words to explain what a wild idea it was to suggest that he could be in a position to do any such thing; but Carolinus went on speaking.

"Remember," he said, "keep your wits about you. Even in times when Magick will not work for you—you already know there are such times and places—" He paused to look sharply at Jim. Jim remembered how his powers had not worked, the time he had been marooned in the Kingdom of the Dead. But Carolinus held up a hand before he could speak.

"—even at such times," he went on, "the accomplished Magickian is not without resources. And Magick Draws."

"Carolinus," Jim said, "what—"

Carolinus blinked out. He was gone.

"Carolinus!" called Jim. There was no answer.

Jim concentrated on Carolinus, visualizing him as he had just seen him, and invoked his magic to take him to the older magician.

Nothing happened.

For the first time since Carolinus had made him acquainted with the magic he had picked up by winning at the Loathly Tower, Jim's magic had refused to work for him.

It could not have run out—not yet. He had held back from asking the Accounting Office—that strange functionary that kept track of Magickal energies—to add more magic to his account, as Carolinus had arranged that he should be able to do. He had not asked for more because Carolinus had made such a point of his hanging on to what he had—and Jim had begun to suspect that trouble might lie down the road, if he requested more magical energy to spend.

But, he had been saving. He must still have not merely a little, but a good amount of magic left. Just to check on this, however, he visualized his hand holding a rose. The feeling in his head that he got when his magic worked clicked in, at the same time that the rose appeared.

"Ouch!" he said—he had stuck himself on a thorn. He extricated himself and returned to the nearly unbelievable fact that his magic had refused to do something for him.

Perhaps Carolinus had arranged to block any attempt by Jim to join him? It was the only possibility that came readily to mind; but if Carolinus had done that, why had he? Jim returned to his bedroll and, as the fireplace light waned once more, thought over what Carolinus had said. In the past the Mage had sometimes been out of touch with Jim, but this did not feel the same.

And how could he, Jim, possibly have any say in whether the present King of England, Edward the Third, retained his throne? Baffled, his mind fell off into a tumbling whirl of questions, and scrambles for answers that only begot more questions. Faces and names and ideas seemed to tangle themselves about him in a chaotic mess.

To top it all off, Carolinus' order to seek help from KinetetE could be as wild a notion as that of his keeping King Edward on his throne. KinetetE was one of the other two greatest Magickians of this world. Jim had only seen her once from a distance, but she had looked a formidable woman—and if Carolinus was any example of AAA+ wielders of Magick, she would not be the easiest person to work with.

Both things were impossible. No one could field this mix of information, half-information, and no-information and make any sense out of it. All he could do was let himself be carried around in the whirlpool, round, round, and around . . .

Jim found sunlight lancing through the arrow-slit in the wall and hitting him right in the eyes.

And Chandos was standing over him, completely dressed, armored, and armed—and clearly ready for the saddle.

". . . And pray forgive me," he was saying, with no tone at all of real apology in his voice, "but it is time we were on our way; and I know you would not like to venture on today's ride without some food and drink. The High Table is still set for us; and if you dress and arm quickly, you may still have time for both before we need to be in the saddle. Since you do not have a squire with you, shall I send one of my men in to help you dress and arm?"

"No, no," said Jim, scrambling to his feet. "I'll be down in a moment. Just someone to get my baggage is all I need."

He became aware of Chandos staring at him, and realized that his unusual bed-wear was attracting the other knight's attention. "I must apologize," he went on hastily, "matters—a matter of magic—kept me awake most of the night."

"That's quite understandable, Sir James," said Chandos, backing away and still eyeing Jim's shorts and shirt curiously. "Well, I will be down at the High Table myself for another few minutes."

The knight went out and a Castle servant came in. Jim tumbled into his clothes and armor—with some help after all from the servant. He belted his sword around himself; and, taking his casque, hurried down to the Hall, where Chandos and Sir Bertram were sitting at the table. No one else was around, but the two looked at him with enough disapproval—mixed with interest— for a dozen.

Less than fifteen minutes after that, his food and drink a weight in his stomach, Jim found himself riding out of Penrith Castle with Sir John and his troop. Within twenty minutes more, they were riding through dense woods, where there was sometimes a road and sometimes not. But the guides sent along by Sir Bertram led them surely, occasionally skirting rises of land, until about mid-afternoon, when they were told that they had entered the Skiddaw Forest.

They passed small mountains that rose two to three thousand feet fairly abruptly. There was little difference between the trees that surrounded them— oak, ash, and birch—and the forest growth that had been with them most of the way on the ride up here. As leaders of the expedition, Sir John and Jim were informed by their guides that their route led around Blencathra and between Knott and Great Calva—these all being more mountains.

In late afternoon they came to a clearing large enough for a campground, and with a stream running nearby. The ground of the clearing sloped south-erly, and there was already a ramshackle sort of wooden structure at the upper part of it, almost beside the stream—a simple, one-room hut, possibly a hunter's cabin, or something of the kind.

This was automatically awarded to Jim and Sir John. To Jim's relief, it was quite clean-smelling and lacking in the clutter and the garbage and filth that too often was found in such chance dwellings. It was lightless but for a few cracks in the wooden walls, which themselves looked as if they would blow over in the first wind to come along; but there was a fire-pit at one end, with a smoke-hole fairly close above it, where the steeply slanted roof came down close to the end wall.

"If you will take the charge in keeping here, Sir James," said Chandos, as their possessions were being brought in, "I believe I, with a dozen of the men and one of our guides, will ride the boundaries, so to speak, of this our woodland area. Is that agreeable with you?"

"Absolutely, Sir John," said Jim, glad to be out of the saddle. A fire was already being kindled for them in the fire-pit, and some cold meat and bread were being set out on a tarpaulin-like cloth, in case those of the upper class felt hungry. Jim very much wanted to be by himself to think.

Chandos went off, taking not only his dozen men, but his three young knights. Jim stood outside the hut and watched the small party disappear into the trees, with a touch of admiration. It was like Chandos to think first of surveying the immediate terrain, just in case this was where they would have to fight.

Slowly, he turned back to the door of their shelter. Inside, the fire was doing nicely; and the man-at-arms doing duty as a personal servant to Sir John, after waiting to see if anything more was wanted, had already left. Even the smoke was being most obliging, ascending right through the smoke-hole because the breeze was blowing in the right direction to provide the needed draft.

But he stopped at the open doorway. With Chandos in a position, so to speak, of being able to breathe over his shoulder, he wanted to avoid looking amateurish as a war-leader. He turned back to the open area in the center of the clearing.

"Dagget!" he called.

"Yes, m'Lord," said a slightly hoarse baritone, behind him and just to his right. He turned his head to see a brown face made hideous by a scar that began at the man's right forehead, creased a broken nose below that, and puckered up the left cheek, still lower. How Dagget had survived such a wound was beyond Jim. Below the face, the body was stocky and compact—a man in his middle years, who now came around to face Jim.

Chandos had not brought a squire with him, either; but Dagget seemed to perform all a squire's duties, as well as be Chief man-at-arms to the accompanying troop.

"I was coming to m'Lord to see if he had commands for me," added Dagget, as he stopped, facing Jim.

"I'd like to see the men you've set on watch around us here," Jim said.

"Pray follow me, m'Lord."

It turned out there were five of them, spaced just into the woods about the open area. Having viewed all of these with what he hoped looked like a knightly interest, Jim went back to the shelter and dismissed Dagget.

Free of duty at last, Jim entered the structure and poured himself some wine. He settled himself on some of his baggage, with more of it behind him against the wall to serve as a backrest.

All the way on the ride here, he had been thinking about Carolinus' cryptic words, but he had only thought himself into circles that led nowhere, trying to understand what he could possibly have to do with the King of England, or with the Mage KinetetE.

Magick Draws—Carolinus had ended with those words. But what could they mean? Tired, his mind tried to fashion a rhyme with the words—and he suddenly remembered that old superstition his servants believed in: *Naming Calls.*

The superstition seemed to mean that if you used the name of some evil thing, it would come to you. Did that sort of thing work with Magic? How could that be?

Carolinus had also been talking about times when Magick did not work for a Magickian. So what was it that Magick could Draw when you *had* no magic?

Well, if a magician had no magic of his own, someone else could still have some . . . he remembered now that one of the things he had experienced, in his education in the Magick Art, was that peculiar feeling inside his mind that *told* him when his magic was working.

Could he also tell when the magic of someone else was at work? Maybe accomplished Magickians could sense, somehow, when Magick was being worked—would it be only near them? Or could they sense it anywhere?

He also remembered, now, times when Carolinus had warned him, in their magical conversations at some distance, that others might be listening. So Magickians could be aware of the Magickal works of others.

But what did all this have to do with anything—and with him?

Or, did it instead have to do with KinetetE, whom Carolinus had also mentioned? Jim found himself not relishing the idea of contacting her.

He had only seen her once, at a time when she had been acting as a sort of referee in a magicians' duel that Carolinus had been involved in. A duel that had come about when a certain Oriental magician had objected to Jim's use of hypnotism in his magic.

KinetetE had seemed a very formidable type.

Still, having seen her, he would be able to visualize her, and so reach her by magic—

At this point, the door to the hut suddenly opened, and Jim looked out at the red light of sunset filtering through the trees, light that was immediately blocked out by the iron figure of Chandos, who stepped in, pulling the door closed behind him.

"It is well I went out when I did," said Chandos, striding right past Jim to the fire-pit and warming his hands above it.

Chapter 10

For the first time, Jim realized that with the waning of the day the temperature had dropped enough that he was grateful for the fire, in spite of the fact that they were in the middle of summer. But they were also in the northern part of England, and at some altitude.

He followed Chandos to the warmth of the flames.

"You were saying that it was as well that you went out when you did, Sir John," he said, looking at the knight across the fire-pit.

"Indeed!" said Sir John, glancing up at him from the flicker of the flames. This was a totally different person than the courtly Chandos Jim had known before. "Our trouble-makers are already here. If I had not insisted on riding a sweep about our camp, we would never have known it. As it happened, we were able to spy them. Apparently whoever directs them thinks very much like Sir Bertram, since they have come to almost the same spot for their encampment. They are less than half a mile from us."

"How did they get here so soon?" Jim asked.

"Damned if I know!" said Chandos. "The best information I had was that they weren't even formed. But they must have begun gathering a week or more ago, from the look of their camp. Whether they have all their numbers, I do not know."

He shrugged. "It were best we move quickly," he said. "At present they are about our number, or possibly a little more. But ten of them are knights, and each will probably have at least one squire, making a leading strength of a score used to carrying the heavy lance in combat, or at least trained to. We have the two of us, three young, untried knights, and no squires whatsoever—though Dagget is as good as one."

He paused to refill his wine cup. "On the other hand," he went on, "my men-at-arms are veterans in war, and experienced ahorseback. The best can form line with us. I did not recognize any particularly worthy coats of arms among the shields I could see displayed—except for that of your friend Sir Brian."

"Brian?" said Jim. "He can't be up here yet. He visited my Castle, just the day before you reached Malencontri yourself. Did you see him?"

"No," said Chandos shortly. "They have tents, of course, and he must have been inside. But I saw that great white warhorse of his tethered with the other destriers. There is no mistaking him. A horse worth a King's ransom. I forget his name."

"Blanchard," murmured Jim, automatically, his thoughts galloping.

"It was our laggard way of coming up here!" said Chandos angrily. "I should have brought us at a better pace. We could have improved our travel time by at least two days, perhaps as much as three."

His gaze shifted a little from Jim's face, and without troubling to turn around, Chandos suddenly raised his voice.

"Dagget!"

The door creaked open almost immediately, and the dark, stocky figure, recognizable in outline against the last of the sunset, stood there.

"Sir John?"

"We sup!" said Sir John, still without turning around. "Food and drink! And place us a table in here, with somewhat for us to sit on."

"Yes, Sir John."

The door closed, Dagget and the sunset were gone again. Chandos turned, walked over to the place where the meat, bread, and wine had been laid out, and helped himself to a clumsy sandwich. He brought this back and stood again at the fire, looking across it at an angle to Jim.

"Dagget has ridden at my back for some years," he said. "He will have us to table shortly. After that, we can talk."

Sir John's recommendation of his man was not overdone. In surprisingly short time, Jim and the older knight were seated on thick, tightly-bound piles of fine branches heavy with leaves, with doubled saddle-cloths thrown over them, and were looking at each other across a short table. It had been made by elevating the building's one small bed on mounds of clay from the nearby stream; the bed had then been covered by another saddle-cloth, and then with a snowy table-cloth from Sir John's baggage.

On this white surface, in the light of the replenished fire, there was a silver spoon for each of them, two silver mazers, a silver pitcher of wine and one of water, with Sir John's coat of arms incised in its surface. There was also a stoneware bowl apiece, filled with a hot stew made largely of the beef and broth they had been given when they left Penrith Castle, but flavored with herbs from what was apparently Dagget's personal luggage.

Their main course was more of the same beef, which had been pounded to a certain amount of tenderness during the ride by being carried, wrapped in a clean cloth, between Dagget's saddle and horse-blanket. It was served up in strips, roasted to a palatable heat over one of the fires outside. The meal wound up with a sort of sweet, saffron-tasting bread pudding, also hot.

"Hear me now," said Sir John at last, pushing his empty plate away and taking one more sip of wine. He set his cup down. "You have no objection to my having the command in keeping for this whole matter? Am I right?"

"Entirely right," said Jim with real feeling. It had been strictly a courtesy question. Having anyone else but Chandos in command here would be ridiculous. But Jim appreciated being asked, nonetheless. "You've got more experience than I'll probably ever have."

"Good," said Sir John. "Because as I see it, there will be little time for dispute over who gives orders if things fall out as I expect."

He drank from his glass again, more deeply this time, and set it down with a certain amount of force.

"As I see it," he said, "we have little choice."

Jim watched him steadily. The shifting firelight played on the lines of the other man's face, making his eyes seem darker and deeper in his head. His face was remarkably calm, but not for that reason relaxed. The courtier had completely given place to the war-captain.

"From what I could see of their camp," he went on, "they could be ready to ride tomorrow to do whatever mischief they came to do. We have little choice but to assault them immediately—they may be awaiting others to add to their number, and our waiting with them would only increase our disadvantage. Even if they are not waiting, they will be a tough enough nut to crack; if, as I suspect, some at least are fighting-men of experience. There would be no point in sending to Sir Bertram for additional men—we have no time to do so; and beyond that, I would not want any of those he has been using to guard my Lord Cumberland's properties."

He paused, half-smiling at Jim.

"You were about to ask me why?"

"As a matter of fact," said Jim, "I wasn't going to ask. But I'd like to know."

"I shall tell you," said Chandos. "I know, without needing to see them, that most of Sir Bertram's men have never drawn weapons except to fight naked serfs and tenants, miners, and such. I have no great fault to find with anyone who lacks experience with the weapons of war. Indeed, very often these will die valiantly, particularly if defending their own home, family, and Lord. Some, indeed, will be much quicker and more eager into battle than a man who has been through at least one before—no experienced common soldier goes readily into conflict when he does not know whether he will win or die."

He paused, looking at Jim as if for a response. Jim nodded. This was something he could agree with.

"With those of gentle blood—like ourselves—" Chandos went on, "of course, it is different. Still, when there is a real necessity for a common soldier to fight, he may often behave in quite praiseworthy fashion, fighting with everything he has, and all the experience he may have gained before that moment. So those with experience are best. It is these, therefore, with whom I have made up my troop. If there is no way to avoid being killed unless they kill, they will go out intending to be the victor. More than that, the skills they have built from their previous fights are valuable. Lastly, they will not turn and run unless the day is clearly lost."

He paused, looking, Jim felt uncomfortably, at him.

"Nor is this really true of the common sort, alone," he went on. "You, Sir James, may well have seen this yourself. There are, God knows and present company excepted—for we both know of each other's deeds—there are cowards and traitors among even those who call themselves gentlemen. Even King Arthur had such sitting at his Round Table—in the end, you will remember, it was Sir Percival who shamed them all by living as a knight indeed should; and for that God vouchsafed him a vision of the Holy Grail. But, I fear I wander from the subject."

"Not at all, Sir John," said Jim. "We have the evening yet to talk."

"Perhaps not," said Sir John. "It might be wise to find sleep early, against a rising before daybreak tomorrow. It is my belief we have no choice in what we shall do. We must strike their camp with all our force just at daybreak, before they are ready for battle, and take what advantage we can from surprise against their possibly greater numbers."

"Can we get in position to do that, among all these trees and with loose branches and other things on the ground, without letting them know we're coming?" asked Jim. "Particularly since it'll still be dark under the trees—also, won't they have some people on watch?"

"They will have watchers," said Chandos. "But I have men who are good at finding such in the dark, cutting their throats silently, and so keeping them from sounding the alarm. My men's work will not be fool-proof, of course. They may miss a watcher, or one slain may be able to call out before he dies, so that the camp will be alarmed. In fact, it is more likely than not that something will cause our surprise to be less than it should be. It is the way things almost always go in clashes of arms—you may plan all you want, but chance will upset your plans."

"If that does happen," said Jim, "then, what do we do?"

"Merely what we have set out to do in any case," said Chandos. "The alarm being given may well mean that those who are real warriors in the camp will at least be weaponed and on their feet when we come in—though not nec-essarily in armor or ahorseback. They are indeed not so likely, any of them, to be in armor unless they are overseeing the watchers. Though there are some who can successfully sleep in their armor—it is not impossible, and I would look at someone like your friend Brian as one who might do that. But in any case, whether the camp is alarmed or not, we must carry on and make the best use of whatever advantages surprise has given us after all."

Jim nodded.

"You're right, of course," he said. "There wouldn't be any other option."

"I am overjoyed to hear it," said Chandos. He picked up his mazer and emptied its last wine down his throat. "Now, perhaps we should seek slumber before our early rising."

"I should mention," said Jim, hastily, "I'm obliged by the magic rules under which I live to sleep on a special pallet on the floor—"

"Of course," said Sir John. "I honor your obligation to duty. The table hardly seems worth disturbing, in any case."

Once more he lifted his voice without bothering to turn his head toward the door.

"Dagget!"

Immediately there was the sound of the door opening, followed by the immediate answer.

"Yes, Sir John?"

"Branches for a mattress and some horse-blankets to make me a bed! I will sleep, as will Sir James, on the floor; and we will leave the table as it is for possible use in the morning."

"Yes, Sir John." The door closed.

Sir John, in keeping with the rest of his debonair appearance, did not snore as he slept. Jim, who had been accused of snoring on certain occasions, looked across the darkness at where the knight lay on his blankets above a pile of springy birch branches, with a certain amount of annoyance at not being so quick to fall asleep, himself.

He continued to lie awake as the hours passed, the fire burned lower, and the room darkened. He found himself puzzling again over what Carolinus told him. In his time in this world, Jim felt, he had been unduly targeted by the Dark Powers. Could this be another of those occasions?

As far as Jim understood, the Dark Powers seemed to be a sort of malignant force which, by taking a hand in human affairs, hoped to drive the race either into a condition of stasis—in which no further progress of any kind could be made—or into a chaotic state of bloody anarchy and death.

Sometimes they worked through unNatural creatures, such as the Ogre, the Harpies, and the Worm he had encountered at the Loathly Tower. Sometimes their tools were twisted human beings, like Malvinne, the rogue Magician. They had even tried to use Granfer, the oldest and biggest squid in all the seas. There was no telling what tools they might use . . .

Finally, when it seemed the whole night must have gone by, still thinking about this as he lay on his pallet, Jim slipped into some much-wanted sleep.

He was not sure just how the dream started, but he was very sure of the part he remembered afterward, in which he and Angie, hand in hand, were running down some sort of corridor, or narrow way, in which there was no place to take shelter; and a tornado was coming. Suddenly, the floor rocked beneath them, and the walls closed in, and fell. He and Angie found themselves being crushed under a killing weight of debris in total darkness.

They could not move. They could not breathe. The last thing he remembered was Angie's hand, fingertips groping, reaching out and touching his; and their fingers twining together, just before what was left of life in them both was extinguished.

He woke with a jerk, choking. The hut was full of smoke, thick with smoke. He had an overwhelming desire to cough, but the smoke had filled his lungs and he did not seem to have the air. He struggled to his feet, staggered blindly in the direction of where the door should be—groped along some wall until he found the door, and half-fell into the outside, continuing in a sort of staggering run for several paces before he stopped.

He was suddenly aware that he had left the nightmare behind. He was outside in a pitch-dark forest, lit only by a small fire in the center of the clearing, at which Chandos was standing with one of his young knights. The two were in full armor, and six of the men-at-arms stood nearby. All of these were just now turning to look at Jim. The now-stiff breeze had a damp, near-to-morning smell.

"Sir James!" said Chandos. "I might have known you'd rouse without needing to be wakened. Have you noticed how the wind has just changed?"

Without waiting for Jim to answer, he turned back to the young knight, who Jim now saw was Sir William Blye.

"You see, Sir William," said Chandos, "how a knight worthy of his peers does not need to be wakened from sleep on the morning in which there is to be an exercise at arms?"

Sir William looked down at the ground. Chandos turned to Jim again. "But, Sir James!" he said. "You will catch a chill if you move around so lightly dressed. Come to the fire here, at least. And you, Dagget, take these men with you now."

Sir William went off, too; and Jim, who had already intended to approach the fire, was on his way toward it. Of the areas of warmth available to him at the moment, one was the hut behind him, which the change in wind had filled with smoke. The other, this fire out here, was not totally satisfactory, either; but the fire had been expertly banked, and while it produced little more light than they needed, it radiated a heat he could get near without giving up breathing.

Chapter 11

In fact, the fire had too much promise. The leaping flames drew him like a moth, a promise of brightness and heat; but he had not been close to them for more than a few seconds before he began to think longingly of the hut, even with its smoke—better to choke than to sizzle on one side. He looked over his shoulder in vague hope that the breeze might have shifted further, to a direction that would not fill the place with smoke blown back down the smoke hole.

It had not; but he had left the door open behind him, and evidently this had created a draft that had the smoke once more exiting the building.

What had been trapped inside was rapidly thinning out.

"By Saint George," said Chandos, turning back from watching Dagget and his men depart, "it will be a cool day."

He inhaled deeply and with satisfaction.

"—And a good day for us. I feel it in my bones. But, Sir James"—his gaze returned to Jim—"I would recommend you lose no time in dressing and arming. Meanwhile, we will see about covering this fire with earth to put it out. The sky will be light soon, and we do not want anyone in our enemy's camp to see smoke against the sky, only a half-mile or so from them. I will send a man to pack your possessions and see them safely onto your sumpter-horse, if you wish."

"I'd appreciate that," said Jim. His back, which had been away from the fire, was freezing.

He turned to all but run for the shelter and the warm clothes waiting for him there.

Along with most of the smoke, memory of his nightmare was now almost gone. It occurred to Jim, as he mounted Gorp a little later—after a hasty goblet of wine and some cold meat—that he no longer felt the chest-tearing emotion it had awakened in him. Now, his head clearing, he told himself that the cause of it had probably been an unadmitted dread of what he would be going into this morning.

He would much rather have been riding toward this armed meeting with Brian beside him—for all Chandos' ability with weapons and skill as a war-commander. Brian would at least care about how Jim might make out in the fighting. Jim felt singularly lonely and forgotten.

When Sir John had talked about the single-mindedness of veteran soldiers, Jim had been strongly and guiltily aware that he was not in their class. Unlike Chandos, unlike Brian—unlike just about every knight he had encountered so far in this world—far from relishing a fight, he was willing to go far out of his way to avoid it. Unconsciously, he had been fearing the worst; and his dreaming mind had made that fear into the worst possible dream it could produce—in which he had no chance to survive—nor did Angie.

Carefully, each horse led at its head by a man-at-arms who was picking a way through possible noisy obstacles like dead branches, they moved toward their objective. Chandos had ordered his force in three divisions. In the center, side by side, were Jim and Chandos, with the three young knights flanking them, and then those men-at-arms, who had had experience of fighting with a heavy spear.

On both flanks of their line rode mounted men-at-arms, with lighter armor and spears, whose job would be to sweep forward in an encircling movement while those in the center took the brunt of the shock of meeting opposing heavily armored men and powerful horses. Everyone in their party was here; the baggage and riding-horses had been left behind, unattended, in their camp.

Dagget and the others who had been sent ahead to take out the sentries were also to have a look at the enemy camp and report back on whether all were asleep there, or whether there was a portion of their force awake, armed, and ready to repel any unexpected assault.

Chandos had said this was unlikely—these men were here expecting to attack, not to be attacked. But the older knight clearly had no intention of taking chances.

Their advance was cautious and slow, but it seemed to Jim they were approaching the enemy camp, if anything, all too fast. He was over his first emotions about the upcoming conflict. But he was also uncomfortably aware that the wine and food he had hastily swallowed lay heavy and undigested in his stomach; and now, even under his clothes and all the padding beneath his armor, there was a coldness in him.

He had been in fights in his human shape before, but never against horsed and ready foes; and something within him grew smaller and tighter at the prospect. There was a wet wood-and-earth smell to the forest. It must have rained for a while before morning. They should be very close to the enemy camp now.

Dagget appeared suddenly at the nose of Chandos' horse. Sir John held up his hand to signal a halt. The sky was already lightening overhead to the point where, even in the trees here, they could make each other out at some little distance; and the hand-signal was passed on right and left down the advancing line so that everyone stopped.

"There were four on guard, out about half a bowshot from the camp," said Dagget to Sir John. "One of them was even sleeping. They are all now slain. We went on to the camp; and all there are asleep, as far as we could tell without looking into their tents, m'Lord."

Chandos lifted his eyes to the rapidly lightening sky.

"Best we not waste time, then," he said. "At the first true light there will be those who rise early to start fires and prepare food."

He pushed his hand forward through the air. Once more the signal went right and left along the line. They moved on.

The raw morning breeze had continued to swing, and now blew into their faces, bringing the smell of smoke from the camp before them. Jim's visor was still up; and when he looked right and left, he saw that Chandos and the other knights also had their visors up.

Curiously, this was comforting. They had at least a few more moments before the instant of meeting the enemy would come. He tried to take more comfort from the fact that he was flanked by strong, trained, and—except for the three younger knights—experienced fighters; but instead, what crept into his mind was the possibility that he might fail the rest of them by doing something outrageous, like holding back or dodging at the final moment of conflict. Even using his magic—forbidden in combat—would be criminal in their eyes.

He must not. He told himself he would not. He was just letting himself be affected by the cold, dark morning, and by the tension of the slow, steady pace of their attack on sleeping men—in which he, as well as others who were now living, could die in the next hour or so.

Now the smoke-smell was stronger. Even as he watched, Chandos reached up and snapped his visor down. The young knights followed his example, and so did Jim. He had always had a slight touch of claustrophobia; and with the shutting of the visor it seemed that his helmet became stuffy, and he had to work to breathe, smelling again the smoke from the hut. But at that moment Chandos' horse began to move faster and his voice came clearly.

"All right, messires!" he called. "We have come quietly this far, but no longer. Now, we ride!"

His horse broke into a trot. The other horses broke into a trot; and Gorp, without needing a signal from Jim, did the same just to keep up with the animals on either side of him. The men holding the bridles were gone.

The trees thinned, the ways between them opening. The trot became a canter. All of them dressed their shields, and each lifted his lance from its socket, holding it ready to drop into position for use—and the canter became a gallop.

They burst into a clearing.

For a few seconds Jim was able to register the scene before him. It was a clearing very much like their own camp, with a stream at the upslope end. Near it were tents in neat rows, with pennants now snapping before each doorway in the morning breeze. A few figures in the garb of men-at-arms, who had been moving around, stopped as if frozen, then turned.

Shouts went up from the camp. The men outside the tents drew swords and turned to face them, or spun about and ran, open to be ridden down and speared. In a split-second, it seemed, their line was upon the tents themselves. Some of them collapsed. A man erupted from one of them, unarmored but with broadsword in hand, popping up suddenly before Jim and Gorp. Gorp reared in fright and from instinct, striking out with his front hooves.

The man went down. Jim galloped around the tent, just as someone else rode directly into it, spear foremost. The tent collapsed as Jim went past the end of it. Figures were coming out of the other tents, some with a part of their armor on—a helm, perhaps a shield—some with nothing but a sword, like the first man Jim had seen. Jim's wavering spear-tip missed all of those in his path. Without warning he was out of the clearing, riding into the woods and trying to pull Gorp to a stop.

The horse took some little distance to halt. He was snorting and wild-eyed, either with excitement or fear. Jim got him turned around finally, and became aware that among the trees surrounding him, other riders were turning their mounts. Chandos was close.

"À Chandos!" shouted Sir John. Jim and the others closed on him. "To me in the clearing! Form line!"

They clustered together, forming the line that had been demanded, while going around the trees in their way. There were some collisions with each other and with tree branches, and a good deal of swearing.

"Silence!" roared Sir John. "À Chandos! À Chandos! To me, here!"

Their line began to take shape again and extend on either side. Their footmen had run around the clearing through the woods and now began to appear just behind the horses. The line moved out into the open space. The sun was above the horizon now but still invisible behind the trees. Overhead the sky was blue, but the west was full of clouds.

Chandos had lifted his visor to make his voice carry. Jim had lifted his, automatically, sometime earlier—he did not remember doing it. He saw that most visors were up, the riders' faces sweating and ruddy in the open helms.

"They form!" said the low voice of the armored rider to his left, one of the young knights. "—Those we fight!"

It was true. Somehow, in what seemed the few moments they had been re-forming their line in the trees, men from the tents had managed to don some, if not all, of their armor, and brought up their warhorses. They were forming a line on the far side of the clearing, beyond the tents.

Chandos sat his horse, giving them time to form while his party waited in plain sight, ready to ride at his signal.

The line formed by their opponents was like their own. Heavily armed and armored riders were in the center, with a number of lighter-armored men with light lances on the wings. Footmen were still bringing horses to a few fully armored men yet on the ground; and as they mounted, they found a place in the center of the line.

"Now!" shouted Chandos, as the last scrambled into their saddles. "Keep the line! At a walk, to the open ground. Go!"

They moved. They rode at a slant to the left side of the open area, where no tents had been pitched, and their opponents moved in line to match them at the opposite end of the space. It was all very slow and deliberate.

Jim took off his metal-backed glove to wipe his wet face. He could feel moisture rolling down his neck into the padding under his body armor. Gradually, the movements on either side grew less and less, until both lines were completely still, facing each other across uncluttered ground.

Chandos rode forward alone some six or eight feet and turned to look from end to end at his line.

"Keep level!" he called to the waiting horsemen. " 'Ware the slope to the right of the ground, here. Do not crowd left to make up for it!"

On the other side a thickset armored figure was shouting something to the horsemen of his line. Chandos rode back to his place beside Jim and turned about. The thickset man finished and rode back into his own line.

For a moment nothing happened, no sound or movement on either side—and in that moment, for the first time, Jim recognized Brian's coat of arms, bright in color on a shield opposite him.

For a moment his breath stopped in his lungs, for Brian looked to be directly in line with him, next to the thickset knight as Jim was next to Chandos. Then, abruptly, he realized that in fact Brian was at least three figures out of line with him, since the thickset leader was that far out of direct line with Chandos. Air rushed back into Jim, with a vast feeling of relief.

In the rush and fury of the ride into this camp, he had all but forgotten Brian's possible presence. Now there was no doubt. His closest friend was not a hundred yards away, visor down and lance held ready. But, thank God, they need not encounter with each other. Brian would take out whomever he met, almost certainly. As for Jim, he need only forget about any deliberate use of his spear and crouch behind his shield. Odds were he should survive unhurt.

But the strange moment of suspense was over.

Chandos shifted from beside Jim, taking a position several places away and more directly facing the enemy commander. He lifted his arm, then brought it down, pointing toward their opponents; and the other leader did the same.

"À Chandos! À Chandos!" he shouted; and his horse sprang forward. The line—and Gorp—jumped; after that first abrupt movement breaking quickly into a trot and even more quickly into a canter, a gallop—for the space between the lines was short in which to gain momentum with the heavy warhorses. Jim leveled his lance, crossed his fingers mentally, and found himself hurtling toward the opposite line, which was hurtling toward him—now, both at full gallop.

He had started out facing a narrow-bodied armored figure holding a spear, the point of which—even when upright—wavered slightly in the air. The figure was several bodies to the right of where Brian rode unwavering, his shield on his arm. But now the lines began to break apart as individual horses and riders made different speeds, and Jim began to find Gorp being crowded left by the horse next to him, away from the slope.

It took him a moment to realize what was happening. All the horses to his right were trying to move left—away from the slope of which Chandos had warned them.

There was no point in his reining Gorp right against that multiple push. He might as well relax and drift with the rest of them—

—and then he realized he was coming, second by second, more in line with Brian's approaching shield—and lance.

Desperately, he tried to rein Gorp to his right, but he was pinched between the horses that flanked him. Gorp tried to obey, but the weight of not merely the horse to his right but others beyond was too much for him.

At the same time, however, the lines were drawing together so quickly that Jim now saw, with relief, that it was the man next to Brian, after all, whom he would encounter. That particular warrior had spurred ahead of those around him; and Gorp's attempts to hold his position had caused him to be squeezed out ahead of Jim's line—so that the two men hurtled together almost as if in a personal duel.

Jim couched his lance, holding it loosely and waiting; then at the last moment gripped it with all his strength.

They encountered.

Jim had been in melees before; and in sports he had known the shock of opposing bodies. But this was like being thrown against the stone face of a vertical cliff. He was fleetingly aware that Brian, next to Jim's target, must have recognized his shield and was now lifting his lance, so that it could not strike Jim, even by accident.

At the moment of impact, Jim felt his lance-point slide sideways. His opponent had carried his shield slanted, to cause Jim's point to strike it at an angle and slide off—a trick Brian had tried to teach Jim. Jim's lance-point flew wide; Gorp's shoulder took the smaller opposing horse in the forward ribs, knocking it off its feet; and Jim's elbow rang against the helm of his opponent as the man fell.

But the point of Jim's lance, glancing off the tilted shield and with the full weight of Gorp and himself behind it, drove on, in behind the edge of Brian's shield and into Brian's armor and body. Brian clung to his saddle with one hand, but he and Blanchard both went down; and a split-second later, Gorp tripped over the fallen Blanchard. Jim went flying over his head.

His impact against the ground was even worse than the impact against his opponent. But for some reason it was not as important to him. The only thing in his mind was Brian.

Lifting his visor, he found himself lying on the ground just beyond Brian; and, looking back, saw the broken stub of his lance literally sticking up out of Brian's upper body. Next to the two of them, both Blanchard and Gorp were struggling to their feet. Out of the corner of his eye Jim saw another armored and mounted figure riding at him, with no spear but with a sword held high, ready to strike.

Jim's use of magic in that moment was instinctive. Ignoring all the rules of Magick and chivalry that required a magician not to take unfair advantage against a non-magician opponent, he hastily threw a ward around Brian and himself. But the on-coming figure never reached it, his horse swerving away as Blanchard lunged at it.

Blanchard, the best-trained and most powerful warhorse that Jim had ever seen, was clearly enraged. His instincts were to protect his downed master, and, as the swordsman's momentum carried him past them all, the horse turned his attention to Jim, who was all but standing over Brian.

Rising on his hind legs as a good warhorse should, the great white stallion attacked the nearest enemy to his fallen rider, with hooves and teeth. Jim, safe behind the ward, nevertheless tried to duck out of the way. Frustrated to find himself unable to make contact with his enemy, Blanchard turned his attention to Gorp, who rose also and responded in reaction. Screaming, the two stallions struck and tore at each other; and Jim, desperate to stop them quickly, reached out with his magic to separate them. He transported Blanchard back to the clearing at which they had camped last night.

Gorp, abruptly unopposed, looked about in bewilderment. Jim saw another figure on horseback charge toward him, only to be intercepted by someone else—the fight had now become a series of individual combats between mounted men who were being circled by wary men on foot, looking for openings. It seemed to Jim's hasty view only a confused series of swirls, mostly moving away downslope.

His first thought was that he had killed his friend. Brian was motionless, his eyes closed. Jim knew he had to get his friend away from here—he reached out to the campfire where he had stood near Sir John this morning, and abruptly they were there, the mound of dirt that was the covered fire still warm and smoking slightly. Blanchard, already there, turned to charge at Jim once more; but Jim's ward still protected Brian and himself.

Beyond Blanchard Jim could see, tethered to a line running through the trees, the spare horses that had been left behind when their line moved out to the attack earlier this morning. That reminded him to reach back to the battlefield for his own warhorse, Gorp.

Throwing his helmet down, Jim turned his attention now to Brian. But Brian lay still, and did not answer when Jim spoke to him.

Jim did not know if he had the strength to pull the end of the broken lance from Brian's body—his brain seemed jangled, and he was not even able to remember if the spear had been barbed, or not. . . . He was fairly sure a knight's lance would not be, but—his guts seemed to turn over at the thought of physically pulling it out of Brian's body. Like an echo came Carolinus' voice in the back of his head, reminding him to hoard his magic.

"The hell with that!" he said. Pulling out the lance fragment by hand, he might do even more damage to Brian than he had already. He set about visualizing a process for magical removal of the lance-point.

The tension still in him made this, too, difficult; but eventually the image in his mind took solid shape. He saw the lance point and shaft dissolving where it was—everything it might have carried into the wound with it evaporating, disintegrating the smallest source of infection—and finding its shape again outside Brian's body. He saw the bleeding stop and the wound closing. And, as it became clear in his head, so it happened—suddenly the broken piece of blood-stained lance was lying on the ground beside Brian's still body.

He used the same technique to remove Brian's armor, then cut open his clothing with his dagger. The wound was now a pink line against Brian's chest. It was no longer bleeding, but large amounts of blood had soaked the padding under the armor, and even made a small pool on the ground.

Jim put his ear to Brian's chest. Brian's heart was beating, slowly but strongly. He was still unconscious, but that could be from shock. Jim had done all the healing that he could with his limited knowledge of magic.

He remembered when Dafydd had lost so much blood at the time when they had met the pirate called Bloody Boots, on their return to England from France. Carolinus had been able to heal the archer in other respects; but there was nothing even he could do about the loss of blood. But then Jim had found a way to roughly type Dafydd's blood and find a match; so that Carolinus was able to use magic to transfuse some blood into Dafydd after all.

Jim might be able magically to manage the transfusion, now. But they were far from Malencontri, the only place where the care a badly weakened Brian would need could be found.

Jim tried to think now, but he found himself exhausted, not so much physically as mentally. Use of magic took a physical toll on the body, and maybe a mental one, for all he knew—he had never before done so much in so intense a state. He tried to force himself to concentrate on what he absolutely had to do next. He could think of nothing. His head whirled.

He was too worn-out to do anything more. He crouched once more to lay his ear against Brian's chest. It beat the same as before, a reassurance he badly needed.

Still trying to think of how he might get Brian to safety, he fell asleep, one arm thrown across Brian's chest to wake him if Brian should suddenly move or appear to need help.

Chapter 12

The distant rolling of drums, thundering at a military beat and approaching, in the dream he was having, got mixed into something about having bought a hot dog from a street vendor and being just about to bite into it.

It was a hot dog drowned in mustard, a delicious taste he had not experienced for some years now, since he and Angie had come to this world. Gradually the mouth-watering prospect faded away and vanished. The drums turned into a different sort of drumming: a steady hammering ring of rain against the ward Jim had set up to protect Brian and himself. He came all the way to wakefulness.

The day was almost down to a twilight darkness. Sullen dark clouds, obscured by the rain, covered the sky in every direction; and the rain came without pause.

If fell on the lowered head of Blanchard, standing just outside the ward, as close as it would let him come to his master. The horse no longer seemed to think of Jim as his rider's enemy. He snorted and shook his head, drops of water flying.

"Stop raining!" grumbled Jim, half-awake, making a magical command of it.

He wanted to get back to sleep—and he had not even had one bite of that hot dog. But the rain kept falling; and Jim became alert enough to remember that the weather, like sickness and a few other larger things, did not respond to a magician's command. At least, not his.

Awake now, he turned to check on Brian. But Brian was still and very pale. Jim hastily put his hand up to Brian's lips and felt a movement of breath. He was alive, then; and the lack of blood showing at his lips should mean the lance had not pierced a lung. He felt the skin of Brian's chest.

Brian's skin was cold.

He looked up into the rainy sky, but it told him nothing. He could not tell just how long he had been asleep—it had been morning, and the sky cloudy, the last time he had noticed it. Now that he looked at the gray sky overhead, he made a wild guess that behind the cloud cover it was noon or later. But the rain had brought a distinct chill to the air, and he needed to get Brian warm as quickly as possible.

He looked back at the great white warhorse. Blanchard continued to look at Brian. *Faithful unto death*—of course, Jim thought. He might have expected it of Blanchard.

Jim broke the ward and got up, finding his joints rather creaky. The clearing was empty, silent. Even the wind had stopped blowing. The rain was lessening, but everything was wet. He thought of taking Brian over to the hut, where it would be dry enough to build a fire. And perhaps he could find, in the belongings on the sumpter-horse, some of his own dry clothing to cover and warm Brian.

Something had to be done. They could not stay here indefinitely. Brian badly needed the best care that could be given him. That could only be Malencontri, with its servants, and particularly with Angie.

But they were more than half of England away from Malencontri. Even if the distance had been only a few miles, rather than several hundred, there was no non-magical way to get Brian there in less than ten days or more of carrying him slowly and carefully, possibly slung between two horses—that is, if he would survive the trip.

The only alternative was to use his magic again. This supply that Carolinus, only a short time back, had emphatically warned him to hoard, was being squandered right and left. Moving himself, Brian, and the horses back to proper care would be a prodigal use of it. But he could not let Brian stay here and die.

Nor could he leave the horses behind. Horses were valuable—those like Gorp were more than valuable; they were necessary for someone like himself. And Brian would never forgive him if he lost or left Blanchard.

He concentrated on Malencontri and two places in it: the stable-yard for the horses, and the Solar for himself and Brian. He closed his eyes with the effort of getting it all plain and clear in his mind. It did not matter that Blanchard, Gorp, his riding-horse, and the sumpter-horse were now separated—he visualized them standing side by side, at the entrance to the stables—and sent them on their way. They disappeared.

He concentrated now on the Solar room, in the Castle tower; and— abruptly—he and Brian were there, on the Spanish rug by the side of the bed. Angie was not there; but looking right at them was one of the female servants, who was in the process of tidying up the room.

"Eeek!" cried the servant, for once in very real alarm, rather than in the ritual polite scream. She ran out of the room.

Jim dismissed her from his mind. She would tell Angie he was here; and since she would not have been any help with Brian, there had been no reason to keep her. He turned back to Brian, grateful the rug was there, to keep him off the stone floor.

There were no such rugs made in England at this period in history, but they were just starting to make rugs in Spain. Jim and Angie had gotten this, with Carolinus' help, through a magician in Castile. Jim realized now he should have transported Brian to the bed, bloody clothes and all; and he was still trying to figure out a way of physically lifting him onto the bed without doing any more damage to him—like all unconscious people, Brian seemed to weigh a ton—when Angie herself burst into the room.

"Jim—" she began; but Jim interrupted her.

"Brian's in bad shape!" he said. "He's had a lance through him and lost a lot of blood. I took out the piece of lance and healed the wound; but he's still unconscious. Order a bedroom cleaned for him, will you? And some men up here with a stretcher to carry him to it? As quick as possible!"

The color had drained from Angie's face as she stared at him.

"As quick as—" she began, staring at Brian. "Oh, of course! I'll take care of it!"

She turned and ran out the door of the Solar.

Jim turned his attention back to the motionless Brian. The carrying would have to be done carefully. Even though theoretically the magic had healed his wound, it might not be the smartest idea in the world to manhandle his limp body. It would be best to wait for the stretcher to show up. While waiting, he searched his mind once more for first-aid procedures.

There was the business of the pulses in various parts of the body. If a pulse could be felt in the carotid artery, then the heart was beating more than forty beats a minute. He felt around Brian's neck under the back angle of his jaw, found the carotid, and felt the pulse. His fingertips pressed in and he counted to the time of one-Mississippi two-Mississippi three-Mississippi—his counting was inexact. Brian's heart might be beating even faster than that. The next point to check was the femoral artery, in the inside of the upper leg.

He felt around for some time; and when he finally did find the correct spot, he was barely sure he was not imagining a pulse. Brian was unconscious, and that worried Jim. It was impossible to believe in Brian's dying. He was always so boundingly alive—Angie came striding back into the room with four of their older men-at-arms.

They were carrying a stretcher, which had been one of Angie's innovations, the result of having to take care of a steady stream of accidents or sickness among the servants. The stretcher was no more than two wooden poles threaded through the folded-over edges of a strip of stout cloth; but it was surprisingly useful for carrying someone, as long as the bearers were careful.

Almost on their heels came Ellen Cinders, Room-Mistress at Malencontri. She was a somewhat raw-boned, severe-faced, lean woman, remarkably tall for this period in time, towering several inches even above Angie.

"M'Lord, m'Lady," she said, curtsying. "The room with the new shutter, just below the Solar here, is almost readied. We can move the good knight down right away. There are already fresh bed-stuffs on the bed there, the chamber-pot is clean, the floor dusted, and a fire is lit. Are there other needs for Sir Brian?"

"There will be," said Angie. "I'll be down shortly. You go with the men and wait for me there. All right, all four of you lift him together—carefully. That's right. Now, lay him on the stretcher—carefully—and carry him carefully down the stairs and move him carefully off the stretcher to the bed. You understand?"

There was a chorus of "Yes, m'Lady"s.

Jim and Angie watched as they carried Brian out; and, with Ellen following closely behind them, they went out the door and it closed behind them. Angie turned back to Jim.

"Angie—" began Jim hastily.

"No, you listen to me!" said Angie. "Brian's taken care of now; and this is more important than anything you've got to say to me. Jim! We've lost Robert! Robert's been taken—"

Her face suddenly crumpled, and she began to cry. After staring for one astonished split second, Jim stepped to her and put his arms around her. She was as rigid as a statue. Angie did not cry often or easily; and the tears forcing themselves from her eyes now had to fight against her will to keep them repressed.

Jim had some experience with her under such conditions; and he continued simply to hold her. After a few minutes, the stiffness went out of her, and she sagged against him and finished her tears off in a very normal manner.

"I'm sorry," she said, wiping her eyes and standing back.

"Not at all!" said Jim, gruffly. "Perfectly normal!"

Angie hugged and kissed him.

"I love you," she said.

"Well, so do I," said Jim, "—I mean, *I* love *you!*"

Angie patted him gently on the arm.

"Anyway, it's all right now," she said. "Let's sit down, and I'll tell you about it."

Angie sat down on the edge of the bed, half-turned to face Jim; and he sat down also, facing her. She sounded perfectly calm and reasonable now, but he knew that this simply meant her self-control had taken over.

The baby Robert Falon, who was Jim's ward by order of the King, was really much more Angie's. It was Angie who loved him fiercely and had wanted him from the first moment she had found him, left alone and crying in the snow, the only survivor of the party that had contained his father and mother, who had been—like Jim and Angie—on their way to the annual Christmas Party of the Earl of Somerset.

Jim had a strong impulse to put his arm around her; but right now that might be counter-productive. He sat and waited for her to speak.

When she did, her voice was perfectly level, but hard.

"A few days after you left," she said, "I heard Aargh howling, and I went out to meet him. He said that the day before, he had been passing by Malencontri and found a deep hole in the ground. There was a scent of some creature he'd never smelled before. The hole was back in the trees, just a little bit beyond the cleared space. Aargh had done what he usually does—gone to find Carolinus and tell him about it first. But Carolinus wasn't there; and he hadn't been in his cottage the last couple of times Aargh had tried to find him; so Aargh came to tell me directly about it."

"I'm surprised he'd be that concerned—about just a hole in the ground, I mean," said Jim.

"I was, too—then," said Angie. "But, just to be on the safe side, I invited Aargh in to see if he could smell anything inside the walls. But he wouldn't. You know how he is about going into a human building. But he said he'd watch the hole and see if the scent was freshened, which would mean whatever'd made it had been back. The hole was big enough that a small bear could have dug it, he said, but no bear would dig straight down. He said he'd be close to the Castle in case I needed him."

She stopped, looking fiercely at Jim.

"But just today, Robert was gone. No sound—but there was a hole in a stone wall, Jim! The nurse said she knew nothing about it. I think she told the truth. She was terrified of the hole, and of what I might do to her for losing Robert. She begged for a cross, and when she got it, she swore on it Robert'd been there when she went down to bring up her lunch to eat in his room; but when she came back in just minutes, the hole was there and Robert was gone."

Angie stared at Jim.

"A hole in a stone wall?" said Jim. "And nobody heard anything? Nothing at all?"

"I was out of the Solar—out of the tower, completely. The man on watch on the tower-top, just over our heads, said he heard nothing. But the hole went down through the thickness of the wall out of sight! I had them put a weight on the end of a rope and lower it down the hole. It went down and down until it reached the end of the rope. There was nothing there, and no way out."

"Angie!" said Jim, with a dry throat. This time he did reach out to put his arms around her after all. But she was once again like a stone statue; and she shook her head.

"No!" she said. "The way I feel doesn't matter. We've got to find him and get him back. Do you know of any magician, or Natural, or creature that could make a hole in the wall like that and dig straight down—or up—and carry a baby away?"

"No," said Jim, "I don't—but, Angie, I'm sure if whoever-it-was took Robert, they didn't take him with the idea of doing any harm to him. Otherwise, they wouldn't have gone to so much trouble to get him. I'm not surprised Aargh couldn't find Carolinus. The last time I saw him, myself, he sent a projection of himself. He's someplace else; and I can't contact him at all."

They stared at each other.

"It's never been like this!" said Angie. "Magicians, trolls, sea serpents—never anything like this!"

"Well," said Jim, "you're right, we're going to have to put our heads together. Now, how long ago was this?"

"Just a couple hours, that's all," said Angie. "It seems like a million years already. But I didn't know whether I'd see you again for months or when—I might even not see you at all! And Carolinus—I tried to call him myself, the way you do. When he didn't come I sent a man on our fastest horse to the Tinkling Water."

"He's not there," said Jim. "But he told me I could call KinetetE—she's one of the other AAA+ Magicians. I'll call her now."

He tried. No voice replied. No magician appeared.

"I guess I'll have to go to her, wherever she is," said Jim. "I'll have to figure a way to do it—and that means sticking the problem in the back of my mind and letting it work itself out. It's this business of each magician having to invent his ways of working magic."

He looked at her, sitting bolt-upright beside him.

"I'm sorry," he said.

"How long will that take?" she asked.

"Oh . . . a day or two at most."

"Two days!"

"I'm sorry," said Jim again. "I'll be as fast as I can. You know I will!"

Angie sat unmoving for another moment, then stood up.

"All right," she said, in a voice with no emotion in it at all, only her usual, businesslike tones. "Now, what needs to be done with Brian?"

"Are you sure you—"

"Certainly. I'm going to be right beside you, day and night, to hear when you've worked it out; so we might as well be doing what else needs to be done. What does he need?"

"The same as Dafydd that time we'd been in that fight with the pirate. Blood. That time Carolinus had to do the transfusion with his magic. But I think I know how to do it myself now."

"Then we'll get busy." She stood up, Jim rising with her, and started to turn away from him toward the door. Abruptly, she checked and turned back, to stare closely into his face. "There's something important you're not telling me. What is it?"

"It'll keep," said Jim.

"No, it won't. I want to know. Now!"

"All right," said Jim. He had been tired—exhausted, he had thought—from the moment he had awakened alone with Brian in the rain. But now he was wide-awake. He looked out one of the Solar windows and guessed from the sunlight that it was no more than early afternoon.

"Actually," he said, "I'm back earlier than I would have been, because of Brian. He was one of the raiding party Chandos and I went up there to fight. I had to get him back here as soon as possible, after he got that lance in him."

"He'll be all right," said Angie. "Remember how he's recovered from things before. He practically springs back to life before your eyes. But you fought those he was with?"

"Yes," said Jim, somberly.

"You ended up fighting together after all, then?"

"No," said Jim. Suddenly he felt exhausted again. His knees gave and he sat down on the bed again.

"It was my lance that went into him."

Angie stared back.

"Oh, Jim!" She took his closest hand in both of hers.

"I couldn't help it," said Jim in a voice that sounded dead even in his own ears. "We were charging in a line. The horses started crowding Gorp over to where I was opposite Brian. Then my lance slid off the shield of the man I was facing and went into Brian. Brian was next to him."

Angie's grip tightened on his hand.

"Did he recognize you?" she asked.

"He must have," said Jim. "He would have recognized my shield long before I recognized his—and he lifted his lance point so he wouldn't hit me. Gorp's weight and my lance knocked him and Blanchard down; and Gorp fell with me, too. When I crawled to Brian, he was already unconscious."

"Jim . . ." said Angie, gently.

Jim nodded, and squeezed her hand back. Then he got to his feet.

"Well, that was it!" he said. "But I'll have to face him as soon as he's conscious again. In any case, as you said, let's do what needs to be done, now. Carolinus might have helped, but he can't as things stand. Dafydd's nowhere near us—"

"Oh, but he is!" said Angie. "He's on his way. I sent a messenger-pigeon to the Giles-o'-the-Wold pigeon-cote, a few days after you left—I thought I'd feel better if they were around while you were gone. He and Danielle were there with their children, and sent an answer back saying they'd start right away."

"Well, thank God for that," said Jim. "We've got one friend."

"We've got Rrrnlf, too," said Angie, "if that's any help."

"Rrrnlf?" said Jim, staring at her. "The Sea Devil? What's he doing back here?"

"I don't understand it," said Angie. "It's something about that little man— or whatever—he's carrying around. Anyway, he was ready to wait for you; and I thought he might be useful, so I didn't object. He's in the courtyard as usual."

Of course, Jim thought. *Where else could he be?* Rrrnlf, unusually large even in proportion to his thirty-foot height, could not possibly come in through any Castle entrance, large as they were by human standards.

"Well," said Jim. "I'll look at Brian now; and we'd probably better get the signal out for Aargh right away, so he can show me the hole outside. And I should look at the hole in the Castle. Then I'll try getting in touch with KinetetE again, or moving myself to her. But Brian first. . . ."

He leaned back on his elbows on the bed and blinked. He was suddenly dizzy, and his head swam.

"Jim, are you all right?"

He heard Angie's voice as if from some distance away.

"All right, I think. Yes," he said, sitting up. His head was clear again.

Just a momentary unsteadiness, he thought. Things had been coming at him too fast.

"I'm fine," he said. "Come to think of it though, it's probably just as well I can't talk to Brian and disturb him right now. Maybe I need to hear Aargh's story first—"

He was babbling, and he knew it. Happily, he was interrupted just then by the hasty opening of the Solar door, with no preliminary scratching or other warning, and Ellen Cinders was back with them.

"Beg pardon, m'Lord, m'Lady—" she said breathlessly, "but I thought you'd like to know. Sir Brian's no longer unconscious. It's sleeping he is."

"Fine, Mistress!" said Angie. "Now you go back down and stay with him. Next time send one of the men up here with any message. I'll be down shortly. Let us know if anything changes about the way Sir Brian is feeling or acting, or if his wound's giving him trouble."

"Yes, m'Lady."

Ellen Cinders was gone again.

"When did you eat last?" said Angie. She had been eyeing Jim narrowly ever since he had leaned back on his elbows for a moment.

"Oh," said Jim. "I've had some meat and bread, wine this morning; I'm not really hungry . . . maybe a hot dog in its bun, with lots of mustard . . ."

"What?"

Jim came back to his present world with a thump.

"Just daydreaming," he said. "I meant—I think what I'd really like right now is a good, strong, hot cup of tea."

"Ah!" said Angie, turning to the fireplace, where a kettle swung just outside the heat of the fire, on a metal arm that could be rotated to put it right over the blaze. Angie swung it over now.

"Coming right up!" she said.

Meanwhile, Jim's body had reminded him of another need. He was already halfway to what he and Angie called the bathroom, but which their neighbors would have simply called a privy, for all its luxury. True, that luxury consisted of running water from a cistern on the open top of the tower, and lead plumbing down the outside of the tower that bridged over the moat to an underground gravel-layer septic field.

The room also had a marble bathtub, taken from an old ruin of the centuries when Rome had ruled in England—but the water to fill it now had to be heated and brought in buckets.

"Be right back," he said as he disappeared. When he returned, Angie was at the open door of the Solar, speaking to the man-at-arms currently on duty outside there.

"—down to the Serving Room immediately. Tell Mistress Plyseth—for your Lord we want bacon, hot breads—" (some weird foods had appeared when they had asked before this for toast) "—and four eggs in an omelet; milk, honey, butter, and some fruit preserves. Mistress Plyseth knows what I want. You stay with her until she sends it back up. Now let me hear you repeat what I told you!"

Jim heard the man's voice faithfully repeating each item Angie had mentioned, and almost with her intonations. One of the blessings in their situation here was the medieval memory; which had to remember things, since nobody except clerics and other particularly trained people could write. Angie closed the door and came back. Jim flopped on the bed again, while Angie busied herself with the tea.

What Jim really yearned for at this moment was coffee. But Carolinus had never been interested in coffee, or in getting Jim or Angie any. He was interested in black teas, and so he had gotten Jim and Angie some of that through his magical connections in the Orient.

"Here," said Angie, bringing him a cup. "The milk and other things should be up in a moment; I had some honey here, so this cup is the way you like it as far as that goes. Maybe you'd like to start on that."

Jim did. He sat sipping the scalding tea, his mind clearing. Before he had gotten more than half the cup down, the man-at-arms and a servant showed up with the food. Jim had not thought he was hungry, but once he smelled the food, he realized it was at least one of the things he had wanted.

Angie had been right. Even as he ate, his mind finished clearing. Not until he had stuffed himself, however, did he sit back in one of the special padded-back and padded-arm chairs that had been made for the Solar, to look at Angie and come to the point of what should be done.

"All right now," he said. "Now I'll go look at Brian."

"If he's really sleeping, there's no hurry—unless there's something you can do for him," said Angie. "With a wound like that, he should be left to rest, don't you think? Ellen said he was sleeping now, and he'll need it."

His enjoyment of the omelet, dreams of hot dogs past, and his pleasure at being home all dropped away from Jim at once, leaving him hollow inside. The moment when the armored lines had met returned to him again, with fresh force, and in his memory he saw once more, Brian falling.

He turned his head a little away from Angie, so that he was staring at nothing but the white-painted, mortared wall of two-foot-thick stone blocks that had been built there just this year to divide off the small room for Robert and his nurse. He looked back at Angie.

They gazed at each other, and he felt one of her hands close tightly on his, again, where it lay on the table between them.

"Oh, Jim!" he heard her say. For a long moment they continued to sit so. But then Angie managed a smile. He smiled back.

"You're brave," he said.

"So are you." Angie let go of his hand and stood up.

"I'll go down," she said, "and see if Brian's actually sleeping. If he is, I'll come back up and tell you. You can decide then if you want to see him today, or whether you'd better let him rest as much as possible before you do anything for him, yourself."

She was out of the room before Jim could think of anything pertinent to say. He sat where he was, remembering. In a very few minutes, she was back.

"He's sleeping," she said, sitting down at the table. "And he even looks better. If I were you, I'd just let him sleep for at least another day or so. There's no reason to put any more stress on him than he's already had. I'll send a pigeon to Geronde to tell her he's here; and why don't you go out and put the signal-cloth on Aargh's stake? I think your healing Brian when you did was all he needed. If there're no complications, he ought to be up and around in just a few days."

"You think so?" asked Jim, suddenly, unreasonably reassured by the matter-of-factness of her voice.

"I do," said Angie. "You can check him yourself tomorrow, and see what you think. By that time, knowing Brian, you might want to put a spell on him to keep him from getting out of bed."

Chapter 13

N o," said Jim, as they went down the stairs. He had been thinking about Angie's idea to keep Brian in bed by putting a spell on him. "I don't think I ought to. It wouldn't be right to put a spell on him without telling him; and he'd resent it if I did—as if his word wasn't good enough. I wouldn't blame him, either. Even more here in the fourteenth century, than in our own time, you've got to watch what you say to people."

"I suppose so," said Angie, "But it'd certainly help."

"I know," said Jim. They were halfway down the stairs now. "I really wish I could do something with magic to get him better faster; but I don't know what to do."

"Like when Carolinus got sick and couldn't heal himself?" Angie said.

"That's right," said Jim. "Magic can be powerless in some places—like in the Kingdom of the Dead—or in some situations. You know that magic won't work where someone who's a legitimate practitioner of his religion—a holy man of any kind—has forbidden it. The blessing has to be renewed every twenty-four hours, of course; but you remember how much trouble I had with that last Christmas at the Earl's castle—that blasted Bishop—"

"You don't have to blast him," said Angie. "Remember how helpful he was in making the King give us Robert."

"You're right, of course," said Jim. "—that blessed Bishop had blessed the place before we got there. I couldn't magic anything—"

He broke off.

"Why are you looking at me like that?" said Angie.

"I just remembered—Carolinus moved himself and me, magically, around in the castle, as if there'd never been any blessing at all."

"After all, he's one of the world's top magicians," said Angie.

"But that shouldn't affect something like . . . but you're right, he's done that before—given me the idea magic wouldn't work for something, and then used his to do it, himself—" He was interrupted suddenly by a long, wavering howl, distant, but clear, somewhere outside the Castle.

"Aargh!" said Angie. "We don't need to put out the signal after all!" She began to hurry down the steps. Jim hurried also, but carefully; staying behind her. There was no handrail or other protection to keep anyone who slipped off the open side of the steps from plunging to the floor-level of the tower, a murderous distance below.

The sound of Aargh's howl had penetrated and been heard all over the Castle. A wolf howling in daylight was considered the worst sort of bad omen, even though the staff at Malencontri were now used to Aargh announcing his presence this way. Faces about the stable and the courtyard were somber as the two rode toward the great gate in the curtain-wall. Occupying nearly all one side of the courtyard was the massive, leather-clothed figure of Rrrnlf, the Sea Devil, slumbering on one side with his face to the wall.

"Good," said Jim. "With luck we can get out and back in again without having to talk to him."

The distance to where Aargh should be waiting was nothing at all. They could have walked it in three minutes; but being Lord and Lady of the Castle, of course, they had to ride. This was something the servants silently insisted on. It was only fair. As servitors, the Castle people did their duties properly; and it was up to their superiors to do theirs with a matching correctness.

Unfortunately, this instance of propriety meant that the horses they rode had to be tethered some distance from the meeting place—horses did not like wolves any more than the Castle staff did; and unlike the servants, horses did not even have the comfort of being sure that this was not any savage wolf, but a friend of the family. Jim and Angie had to walk the last forty yards to reach the naked stake. Aargh, of course, was nowhere in sight.

"I think he just likes to surprise us," whispered Angie to Jim as they waited.

"No such pup-like foolishness!" said a familiar, harsh voice behind them.

They turned. There he was: a massive, grey-furred, golden-eyed, wicked-toothed, feral shape, the size of a small pony. "It's that he doesn't want any surprises himself. You've got Brian in that place of yours now, haven't you?"

"How did you know?" asked Jim.

"I went around the Castle a few moments ago," said Aargh. "I heard his stallion in the stables, challenging yours—safe enough, of course, with each in a different stall. Just talk, actually—but all horses are fools."

"You shouldn't say that," Angie told him.

"I say what I please!" answered Aargh. "Horses *are* fools. All grass-eaters are fools. But if the horse is there, Brian's there. What kept him from coming out with the two of you?"

"He's been wounded," said Jim, "and he's going to have to stay in bed and rest until he gets back all the blood he's lost."

"Wounded?" said Aargh. "A great help. First Carolinus can't be found, then Brian gets himself wounded. All we need is for Dafydd to break a leg. You two-legs can't get around with one of those out of order, the way we wolves can. One of the reasons why deciding to stand up on your hind limbs wasn't so smart, after all. That puts the trouble all on me, I suppose."

"Have you forgotten Jim?" said Angie sharply.

"Forgot him? No," said Aargh to her. "He's helpful as long as he doesn't break a leg, too. But he can't wield a sword like Brian, or shoot an arrow like Dafydd. Useful to be able to do things like that, if you're born with teeth that wouldn't frighten a mouse."

"As a dragon—" Angie was beginning heatedly, when Jim interrupted.

"It's all right, Angie," he said. "Aargh's not being insulting, just practical. We do need Brian—to say nothing of Carolinus. But the main thing right now, Aargh, is finding Robert, regardless of how many there are of us, or how we have to do it."

"You can count on me in any case," growled Aargh. He stared at Jim. "I suppose you want to see that hole, now?"

"Yes," said Jim.

"Well then, come along," said Aargh. He turned his back on them and trotted off.

They followed.

The hole was less than three minutes' walk away. It made a dark circle in a small bank among the trees, only yards from where the clearing around the Castle began. Aargh was standing over it as they came up. He waited while Jim got down on his hands and knees and sniffed at the hole himself.

"Any scent?" asked Aargh ironically.

"No," said Jim, getting to his feet. "None I can smell, anyway."

"A good choice of words," said Aargh. He stretched his neck out so his nose was over the hole, and his nostrils widened for a second. "If you had any nose at all, you couldn't miss the smell of meat—meat being cooked."

"Meat?" Jim said.

"That's what I said," said Aargh. "Meat. When I first came across this hole there wasn't any such scent from it. The hole ended here."

"How could you tell, if it goes straight down farther than you could tell?"

"It doesn't," said Aargh. "I don't know about that hole in your Castle, but this goes down about six feet. I didn't go into it. But I put my head in far enough to get the sunlight out of my eyes; and after they were used to the dark, I could see where it turned into a level underground-digging, going off to where the sun sets. Now, there's a digging in the other direction, too. The level part may go on forever. But it's the way I'd say whoever took your Robert carried him off when he went."

"Then what's all this about cooked meat?" asked Jim.

"It could only be coming from our Castle, Jim!" said Angie.

"So," Jim said, "this hole was dug first, and then another one was dug later from it, into the Castle to take Robert?" Angie looked at him.

"I don't understand what's going on," said Jim. "But whatever dug these holes certainly can dig. Like a large mole."

"There aren't any large moles," said Aargh.

"Well, we won't worry about that part of it now," said Jim. "It tells us more than we knew before, anyway. I'm grateful to you for noticing it. Now, though, we need to decide how we're going to start looking for Robert—maybe tomorrow would be best: Dafydd will have gotten here by that time; and Brian may be strong enough to sit up in the Great Hall. That'll be the place to meet; and, meanwhile, I'll see what I can find out at Carolinus' cottage."

"Better we meet outside here!" said Aargh, with a snap of his jaws.

Jim looked at the wolf. He had forgotten.

"I know you don't like to be inside buildings," he said, "but you've been with us in the Great Hall before—"

"Not happily!" said Aargh. "A wolf could get trapped in a place like that!"

"Can't you come in one more time, considering the circumstances?" Angie asked. "Brian might be well enough to be carried down to the Great Hall, but he won't be up to being carried out here; and it was you who said how useful he was to us. Even if he can't swing a sword, his advice is worth listening to. Don't you think?"

Aargh growled briefly.

"I'll come in one more time," he said.

With that, in his usual sudden way, he disappeared among the surrounding trees.

"He'll come in," said Angie, as they rode back to the Castle. "He'll come in as many times as we need him, actually."

"I know," said Jim. "He argues a lot, but he's always there when you need him. I'd better go back with you to the Solar. But I think from there I'll just keep on to the top of the tower and head off from there to the Tinkling Water, to see what I can learn."

"We hope," said Angie.

They rode back into the courtyard. Rrrnlf, Jim noted with relief, was still sleeping. It was a good thing that Sea Devils did not snore. Or, at least Rrrnlf didn't. You wouldn't have been able to hear yourself think in the Castle if he did—Jim became conscious that Angie was silently looking very unhappy again.

"We'll get him back all right," he said.

"It's just that he's so little," she answered, blinking.

She changed the expression on her face and sat up straighter in her saddle as they came close to the stables.

"You'll fly there as a dragon, of course?" she said.

"That's what I had in mind."

"Yes," said Angie, thoughtfully. "You know, in some ways I worry less about you when you're in your dragon body than I do when you're in your human body."

"You shouldn't ever worry about me. I can always put a ward around me to protect myself."

Angie said nothing.

They left their horses to the stable workers and climbed the stairs in silence. At the Solar door he left her and mounted the last flight of stairs to the tower-top.

Under the cloud-flecked blue sky there was no one but the man-at-arms on duty, with his spear and sword. He had been leaning on the battlements, looking down at what was going on in the courtyard. But at the sight of Jim, he hastily straightened up and looked watchful.

"Geoffrey," said Jim, "go down and ask if my Lady will give you audience. Stay at her orders until she sends you back up here."

"Yes, m'Lord."

Geoffrey put his spear on his shoulder and headed immediately toward the staircase. He was one of the veteran men-at-arms, in his late twenties at least, his black hair already retreating from his forehead and his square-jawed face weather-beaten and tanned. Jim knew that Geoffrey knew Jim was about to change into his dragon body; but like all good and experienced Castle people, he was perfectly capable of pretending that he knew no such thing. He disappeared down the stairs.

Jim was not quite sure why he preferred to change into his dragon-shape when none of the servants were watching; but something like instinct told him that it would be better if they saw as little as possible of his actually working magic. At any rate, once Geoffrey was gone, Jim concentrated on turning into a dragon, with his clothes magically removed at the same time— so that they would not be destroyed, but still be with him when he wanted to turn back into a human.

Immediately he was a dragon; and with the change came the inevitable difference, that he was now in touch with a dragon's way of thinking and a dragon's way of feeling. This was more than a little different from that of a human.

For one thing, dragons were not generally given to prolonged worrying. Some of his concern about Robert, Carolinus, and the servants, was abruptly gone—although as a conscious problem it was still there in the back of his mind. But the change, together with the sense of now being very healthy, very large, and very powerful—a sensation that could only be described as being very Dragonly—took possession of him. In spite of the current situation his spirits rose.

He looked around himself to make sure he had room to spread his wings clear of the top of the battlements, and then made a leap into the air, beating downward with his wings and immediately flying up at a steep angle, making as much noise as possible, for Angie to hear.

In a moment, or so it seemed—such was the wing power of a large adult dragon—he was out over the trees and far enough from Malencontri so that had Geoffrey been back on watch, the man-at-arms could have mistaken him for nothing more than a large but distant bird.

He had already caught a thermal; he relaxed on outstretched wings, letting it life him in an ascending spiral, up and up until he reached about fifteen hundred feet. At that elevation, the thermal became too weak to carry him much farther. He slanted off, taking advantage of the moving air up here as a ship might set its sails to take advantage of a wind. He headed southeast toward Carolinus' cottage.

As usual, the sheer joy of being air-borne seduced him. He was tempted to prolong the simple pleasure of soaring; but matters were too grave for him to indulge himself. Shortly, he landed on the gravel walk to Carolinus' small, fairy-tale-like cottage; it stood in a lush clearing, walled about by enormous, ancient trees, and carpeted with heavy grass right up to the flower beds with which Carolinus had surrounded the cottage.

Everything looked as usual. In the little pool from which a fountain rose, one of the small water-creatures—either a fish or a minuscule golden mermaid, it or she was always too fast for him—leaped, arced over, and re-entered the water before his eyes could properly focus. The feeling of peace in the clearing was overwhelming. He pushed it aside and went up to the green-painted front door of the cottage.

As he had expected, it was closed. Further, as he had also expected, when he tentatively tried to open it, it did not budge. He did not put any effort into trying to push it open; it and all the rest of the cottage—in fact all the clearing—were under the impenetrable spell of Carolinus.

He knocked, on the odd chance that Carolinus might actually be there. But there was no answer.

Now that he was here, it was a question of what he could actually accomplish. His magic was limited, and there was absolutely no hope that any force he might summon could break through a ward put up by a magician of Carolinus' powers. While he was mulling over the matter, he changed himself back into his human form, clothes and all. For want of anything else to do, he knocked again.

"Carolinus!" he called. "If you're in there, but can't answer, give me some signal, if you can."

He waited. He listened. But nothing changed. The tinkling water of the fountain, from which the clearing got its name, went on. He pressed his head against the door and listened closely.

At first he heard nothing. Then an inspiration came to him.

He visualized himself as having the sensitive hearing of a bird who could hear an insect moving in the grass. He listened again.

This time, he did hear something—a sort of breathy singing, like that of a kettle on the hob, over a fire, just about to break into a boil.

Of course, he told himself, it would be Carolinus' kettle, which he had ordered magically to be always "on-the-boil," so that he could have his hot cup of tea without delay any time he wanted it. The same kettle that had once nearly worn its bottom through, sliding all the way to Malencontri to bring word that Carolinus needed help.

The local people all believed that the kettle, as well as the other utensils and appurtenances in Carolinus's cottage, had a life of its own. Certainly, the kettle had given some evidence of this—though it was limited in what it could do. It occurred to Jim that it could be worth trying, at least, to speak to the kettle now.

"Kettle!" he shouted through the door. "This is Jim Eckert, just outside. Carolinus' ward is keeping me out, but I need to talk to you. Is there any way I can get in? Or can you come out?"

He pressed his ear to the door again, to hear if there was any change in the kettle's noise—and there was.

Suddenly the kettle was singing recognizable words.

> *"Jim, Carolinus said you might*
> *Come, if anything's not right.*
> *Give two knocks, then a third*
> *And simply say the magic word."*

Jim took his head from the door and stood there, thinking. Magic word. What magic word? It was just like Carolinus to turn something simple into a lesson in magic. But no one had ever mentioned magic words before.

Jim checked himself from getting really angry. Emotion would get him nowhere. There was a puzzle here. Obviously it was meant to baffle anyone else who might hear the song; but Carolinus had assumed it would be solvable by him. That would mean . . .

Of course. The magic words would have to be some that no fourteenth-century person would know. No sooner had this thought occurred to him than Jim almost lost his temper again, as a particular magic word suggested itself to him. Oh, no, he told himself. Carolinus couldn't be that obvious and ridiculous . . . but maybe he could.

Jim took a deep breath, knocked, and addressed the door.

"Open, Sesame," he said.

The door swung open. Jim walked in. The door closed behind him; and in the dimmer, but still adequate light from the windows, he saw the kettle on the hob and heard it singing to him. Now it was singing something that sounded like a chorus.

> *"Welcome, good Jim Eckert!*
> *Welcome . . ."*

It kept on singing until Jim spoke.

"I'm happy to see you again, too, good kettle," he said. "I don't suppose you know where Carolinus is?"

The kettle rocked itself a little above the fire and gave vent to a long, slow whistle, quavering down on a sad descending note.

"You don't, then?" asked Jim.

The kettle gave a short, sharp whistle.

Jim nodded.

"I understand," he said. "Well, if you don't and I don't, there's no guessing where he might be. But it occurs to me that wherever he is, he may think of having tea; and the kind of tea he'll want is the kind you give him back here at his cottage. So, maybe he'll come back just long enough for a cup of tea, or maybe he'll just sort of reach in here magically to tell you to make him a cup of tea and then get it from you magically and drink it where he is—or something like that. In any case, what I thought was I might give you a little rhyme you could sing to him if he does anything like that, to give him a message. Would you do that for me?"

Another short, sharp, affirmative whistle from the kettle.

"Fine," said Jim. "Give me a minute, now. I'll have to think the rhyme out. . . ."

Indeed, he had. He was not really any good with poetry of any kind, and probably no better at making up a snatch of song. Happily, he knew the melody that the kettle sang everything to, so he could put the words to that. He pondered a moment; and after some struggle, came up with:

> *"Robert's stolen, Angie's said.*
> *All of us are very mad.*
> *Advise us, Carolinus!"*

It sounded very bad in his own ears, even as he sang it to the kettle. But when the kettle sang it back in its own plaintive, breathy little voice, it sounded a little better.

"Well," said Jim to the kettle, "maybe it'll help. Thank you, kettle."

The kettle gave a short, sharp whistle.

"And the best to you, too," said Jim. He went out the door, which closed firmly behind him. Just for fun, he tried it and it was as firmly locked as it had been originally.

He changed back into his dragon form and flew somberly home to Malencontri.

C h a p t e r **14**

Jim was still somber the next morning. He had slept well, but he woke to worry. It stayed with him all through breakfast—which, mercifully, the servants did not object to him taking in the Solar, unlike dinner and supper, which must always be taken in state, in the Great Hall. Angie had already left before he woke; and Jim ate with only his own thoughts for company. But there were plenty of these.

Carolinus being out of touch just when they needed him was bad, but that problem had to be put aside for the moment. On a chance, he tried calling KinetetE; but again there was no answer. He tried moving himself to her, but he had never been able to do that without envisioning where he was trying to go, and he did not believe it would work. It did not. He put thoughts of her aside.

Right away, first, he had to do what he had been dreading—it had to be done—talk to an at least conscious Brian about how he had come to be wounded. Still lost in his thoughts, he went out the door and literally bumped into two women just about to come in through it.

"My Lady's not here—" he began.

"We know," said the shorter woman sharply. "She's meeting us here in a few moments and sent us on ahead." Jim blinked and came back out of his thoughts.

"Oh, hello," he said, recognizing the two. "Geronde! Danielle!"

"I have just seen Brian," said Geronde, the shorter of the two. "You don't suppose I'd stay at Malvern Castle with Brian sore hurt?"

"No, of course not—" said Jim. "Of course not. It's just that I wasn't expecting . . ." Jim let himself run down rather than get into trouble.

"I expect you'll find Dafydd in the Great Hall," said the tall young wife of the Welsh bowman, still strikingly beautiful even after two children.

"Of course. Good to see you both. I went to try to get in touch with Carolinus last night; but I didn't have any luck," said Jim, realizing even before the words were all out of his mouth that they already knew about this.

"Oh?" said Danielle.

"Ah, yes," said Geronde.

Geronde opened the Solar door. The two swept by him, went in, and closed the door behind them. He was left in the corridor, feeling as if he had suddenly become unwashed, unshaven, and generally disreputable-looking.

The encounter had not done anything to make him eager to see Brian. Nonetheless, he went on down to the room to which Brian had been taken the day before.

"James!" said Brian, sitting up in bed and looking far less pale. "I have been hoping someone would come by—most of all you! It's a damned dull life, lying here. Particularly when I know I could be up and about."

"Not quite yet, Brian, I don't think," said Jim. He looked at the serving-woman on duty, seated on the stool in a corner of the room. "Bet, step outside and close the door behind you firmly. Wait in the hall until I call you."

"Yes, m'Lord."

"Sit down! Sit down!" said Brian. Jim pushed Bet's stool closer to the bed and sat down. "The last thing I remember," Brian went on, "I was up in Cumberland; and you were down here in Somerset."

"Not exactly," said Jim. "The fact was, I was up there in Cumberland at the same place you were."

"Were you!" said Brian. "Be hung, drawn, and quartered if I can remember a thing about that!"

"Well," said Jim, "do you remember the people you were with being attacked by another group when you were in the Skiddaw Forest?"

Brian rubbed his forehead.

"I do seem to recall something of the kind. But I do not remember your being there, James."

"I was on the other side," said Jim.

"Were you, by God!"

"Yes," said Jim. "In fact, when our line rode against yours, I was almost opposite you. Not really opposite, but a little off to one side—two or three riders away from coming directly at you—so that I didn't think we'd encounter when the lines met. But as it happened, Gorp was crowded over by the other horses, in your direction, and I found myself riding at the man right next to you."

"Did you, now!" said Brian. "I hope you remembered to keep your shield up and a loose grip on your lance, as I've taught you. Did you unhorse the man you were riding at?"

"Well—as a matter of fact," said Jim, and coughed awkwardly. "—you see, I was concentrating on you. You saw me, too, just about that time, and you lifted your lance so that you couldn't possibly strike me with it, even if you were crowded in my direction."

"Quite right. Naturally," said Brian. "But then what?"

"Well, to tell you the truth, Brian," said Jim, "the rider I was encountering tilted his shield sideways, the way you've tried to teach me to do; and the tip of my lance glanced off it; and—well, to make a long story short, Brian, I was the one who put the lance into you."

"Were you!" Brian stared at Jim. "Well, of course. Only right that you should choose the next possible opponent—"

"Brian, I didn't do it on purpose!" said Jim. "Believe me, it was just an accident. My lance-point simply slid in your direction; and since we happened to be moving toward each other—you know how it is—my point took you behind your shield's edge and gave you the wound that's got you in bed right now. It was all my doing."

"Ah, that explains it," said Brian. "Nonetheless, James, you must remember this. If duty calls upon you to ride against foes, you should not hesitate to encounter whoever might be riding against you. At such times, duty comes first."

"I should have raised my lance-point, like you did," said Jim miserably. "But there just wasn't time. It was all over in a flash. I can't tell you how sorry I am, Brian."

"Sorry?" said Brian, frowning. "Why should you be sorry, James? Certes, your lance-point in me is no different from that of any other man."

"But it's the last thing I'd ever want to do to you," said Jim. "Only, I couldn't avoid doing it."

"Well then, how could things have been different?" said Brian. "I thank you for your friendship and courtesy in rescuing me after I was wounded; and, in

any case, here I am, healing merrily and due to be up—possibly this evening
for supper?"

"It's still a little early. Just a little early," said Jim. "You must remember—"

"I know!" said Brian. "I've got to lie here and make blood for myself! Angela
told me so when she brought Geronde by, earlier this morning. A healthy
man ought to be able to replace his own blood in an hour or so, you'd think.
But no, apparently it takes days. I tell you, James, I feel ready to ride a course
against anyone right now."

"I don't doubt you do," said Jim. "But I'd feel better, Angie'd feel better,
Geronde'd feel better, if you just kept to your bed for a little while longer."

"Well, no help for it," said Brian. "I will even endure it, then. But, James,
tell me of the fight—if it could be dignified by such a name. Who won?"

"I don't know," said Jim. "When I struck you, I was thrown from my own
horse as well. Blanchard started to attack me, and the fight was likely to
trample us both into the ground; so I took us both away from there."

"Blanchard!" cried Brian, coming bolt upright in the bed. "What of Blanchard? Have any idea what happened to him? There are many who would
like to have him, no doubt about that—"

"It's all right—it's all right! Blanchard's right here in my stable," said Jim. "I
brought him back with us."

Brian let out a long sigh and slumped back against the headboard.

"You have saved life and soul for me at once, James!" he said. "I had rather
lose a limb than Blanchard. Rather anything than that. You know how much
he means to me—and, to say truth, it is no less than his true worth."

"I know," said Jim. "Actually, just before our encounter with your group, Sir
John Chandos had told me that he knew you were there—he had seen Blan-
chard, and recognized him at once. He spoke of Blanchard being worth a
King's ransom."

"A ransom for all the Kings that ever were!" said Brian fiercely. "And still I
would not sell him for such price! But James—now you are here, shall we not
spend a little time pleasantly? I know there is no asking you if I may have
wine, but there is no lack of this small beer and perhaps we might play a
game of chess?"

Jim stared at his friend for a moment. But Brian was not showing off. That
wound in his shoulder might be healed, but the body would be remembering,
with pain, the insult it had taken. Jim had no way of relieving that pain. He
could to some extent short-circuit his own pains magically, but the only available help for Brian in this time was the alcohol in the wine he would have
liked to drink; and Jim did not want to risk it on a blood-depleted body. But
the only complaint Brian was making was of boredom.

Brian was not being stoic. He was simply ignoring pain he could do nothing about. *Could I ever do that to such a degree?* Jim asked himself—and knew the answer was *No.*

"Chess, by all means," he said humbly.

It was the least he could do, under the circumstances, for the man he had nearly killed. He was not particularly overjoyed at the idea, however. In the twentieth century he had considered himself a rather good chess player; but the rules Brian had been brought up with had never heard of castling; and the Queen, instead of being the most powerful, was one of the weakest pieces on the board, being only able to move diagonally, one square at a time.

The changes were not so large that Jim could not play; but they threw his whole portfolio of tactics into disarray, and he was forced to either adapt what he would normally do, or come up with something fresh. And in the latter case, he was in the position of playing the game as if for the first time.

Nonetheless, they played. Brian won three games quite easily, which cheered him up immensely; and, following his last defeat, Jim was able to plead that he had things to do; and leave a more contented Brian than the one he had encountered coming in, even though the other man knew the whole truth now.

Once outside Brian's room, he turned automatically back up the stairs to the Solar. But the sound of women's voices checked him before he opened its door.

This might not be the best time in the world for him to show up. There had been a touchiness in both Geronde and Danielle when he had met them on the way out. Until he knew the cause of it, the best plan would be to stay clear. Angie would handle it much better alone.

He turned and went downstairs. He found Dafydd at the High Table in the Great Hall, as usual working on one of his arrows. Dafydd was one of those people who had to be doing something with his hands most of the time.

"My Lord," he said formally as Jim sat down at the table with him.

"James," Jim corrected him. "After these years of knowing each other, how can we be anything but 'James' and 'Dafydd' to each other?"

Nonetheless, he looked closely at Dafydd as he said it. Dafydd had a way of speaking formally when he was about to disagree with Jim about something. A sort of warning flag that said, "Take me seriously, now!"

"James, then, it shall be," said Dafydd, his regular features and tall slim body relaxed and calm as always. "Good it is to see you well; and will you tell me of Brian, how he is now, and how he came to be wounded?"

Jim told him.

The only part he avoided was the matter of Brian being approached to fight for those opposed to the King's taxes. Brian had certainly told him this in confidence; and he was not really free to share it with even as old and good a friend of Brian's as Dafydd, without permission.

"—So," he wound up, when he got to the point of the two forces being opposed in Skiddaw Forest, "I was not expecting to find Brian facing me in the battle. I tried to avoid him—he saw me, and lifted his lance to miss me. But with the press of horses and men, I was pushed into him . . . and, well, I ended by putting my lance into him, even though I tried not to. That's why he's still in bed, upstairs. He doesn't like it, but he's got to rest while he makes back some of the blood he lost."

"That is sad, now," said Dafydd. "But such haps will be, when men fight. I looked over my arrow-point once and saw my cousin, less than two hundred yards away, his own bow bent, but not at me. Indeed, he had not seen me. He was part turned from me, but I knew him by the way he stood. Yet, since those around me should not wonder, I let the arrow go, but so that it missed. Then I went back through the lines before he could see me. An archer less known would not have found it easy to so desert the front line. But I had some small reputation for skill and courage. Therefore, no man questioned my leaving. Which was well; for then I must needs have killed him; and I mislike the killing of any man or beast for small reason."

As he spoke his fingers had been finishing whatever he had been doing with the arrow before him, and he now laid it down on the table. Jim looked at it curiously. Its point was about six inches long, and of metal, narrow and six-sided, tapering to a needle point.

"That looks like the arrow you made to deal with the Hollow Men, when we were up on the Scottish border with Giles de Mer and his family," Jim said.

"It is like," said Dafydd. "But it is not as the ones I made then, but of a somewhat newer fashion. I find other archers have been making these, to deal with the armor of steel plate that is becoming more common now. This is called a bodkin point."

"If you were able to put a broad-point war arrow through the thick top of a heavy table, as I saw you do, there in Giles de Mer's Castle," said Jim, "what will you be able to do with this?"

"Indeed, I have a strong wish to know that myself," said Dafydd. "But we must wait the event. Meanwhile, the Lady Angela tells me there is a hole in the wall of this Castle."

"Yes, in Robert's room."

"And it goes down beyond reach in the walls."

"That's right, too," said Jim.

Dafydd looked squarely into Jim's eyes.

"I do not think, look you," he said, "that this is any common taking of a child. Nor is it Magick, for Magick has no need to break walls or dig holes. No beast that I know of acts in this manner. I can think of only one other direction we may look for what took Robert."

"And that is?" asked Jim; for Dafydd had paused in a meaningful manner, while still keeping his eyes on Jim's.

"There is the sea," said Dafydd. "The sea is vast, possibly as vast as the land, and there may well be many creatures in it we cannot imagine, let alone ones we have seen. It could be such which came and took Robert."

"You really think so?" said Jim. He found himself at a sudden loss for words. "But what would something from the sea—deep in the sea, it would have to be to never have been seen—want, to dig its way inland and take a child?"

"I do not know," said Dafydd. "I do not even know there is such a creature. I only know that is the only other place I can think of to look. As for whether the sea holds such, you have one in your courtyard right now who can answer that question."

"Of course," said Jim. "Rrrnlf!"

"He may be able to tell us a direction we can go in, at least," said Dafydd. "Without that, how can we even start looking for the boy?"

"We've certainly got nothing to lose," said Jim, half to himself. He became aware that Dafydd was still looking at him and that reminded him of something. "You will be able to help me look for Robert, then, Dafydd?"

"What made you think I would not?"

"Well, I—" He found it difficult to put into words the almost antagonistic attitude that Danielle had shown when he had bumped into her and Geronde at the door to the Solar. "I thought maybe, Danielle being here with you . . ."

"Danielle will fight to keep her husband and the father of her children safe," said Dafydd. "Yet she will come to understand we must all help each other when need arises. She may indeed not be best pleased that I engage myself in this; but, at the last, she will not be standing in my way."

"Well, I hate to take you from her," Jim said, "but I'm going to feel a lot more certain with you at hand. A pity Brian's still so weak—"

"Do not concern yourself about Brian," said Dafydd. "If it is what he will do, he will do it, though the whole world stand in the way. It is how he is made. Now, should we step out and speak to the Sea Devil?"

"Right!" said Jim, getting to his feet. Dafydd rose too. "What do you think about having him take a look at the hole in the woods, as well? There's no hope of him getting into any place as small as Robert's room."

"I think well of it," said Dafydd.

They were already headed down between the two long tables toward the front door of the Great Hall. Dafydd had picked up his bow, quiver, and the arrow he had been working on almost with one sweep of his hand, and now had the quiver slung over one shoulder and the bow on the other.

"When I last saw him, he was asleep," said Jim as they went through the door. "—Ah, he's awake now."

Rrrnlf was not only awake, but sitting up cross-legged on the ground of the courtyard, his head only a few feet short of the catwalk inside the curtain-wall.

He seemed to be moodily tossing something from hand to hand. Jim stared when he saw that the tossed object was in fact the same ugly little man who had been with Rrrnlf on his last visit here. The manling was as silent as ever, as his companion lofted him into the air and caught him, as he came down, in the other massive hand.

It was as if the little man was nothing more than a juggler's toy—nor did he seem to object to the treatment.

His oversize clothes seemed almost to have grown on his body—whatever it might look like underneath them—and not even the expression on his face changed as he was sent flying up into the air and caught again. Like a weighted toy, he stood upright, arms nearly at his sides, until he was tossed upward; and at the highest point of each toss he rotated neatly in a complete turn, without bending his body, so that he descended feet-down, to be caught in Rrrnlf's other hand. The same blank, open-mouthed expression Jim had always seen on his face before, remained throughout.

It occurred to Jim crazily that possibly the little man might even be enjoying being tossed back and forth like this. Though why he should be stretched Jim's imagination beyond its limits to answer.

Rrrnlf, on the other hand, was looking somewhat out of sorts. However, he cheered up at the sight of Jim and almost absently tucked the manling out of sight inside his shirt.

"Ah, wee Mage," he boomed. "Here you are again!"

Jim was tempted to point out that *here* was his own proper territory and base, the place where he belonged. It was Rrrnlf who came and went from it. He did not, however. It was always easy to get sidetracked when talking with the Sea Devil.

"Rrrnlf," he said, "there is a strange hole in the forest, and Dafydd and I would like to go out with you and have you take a look at it."

"Me?" said Rrrnlf. "Look at a hole? What's in the hole?"

"We don't know," said Jim. "That's why we want you to look, and maybe sniff at it, and tell us what you think. Maybe you will see or understand more about it than we do."

"Certainly, wee Mage," said Rrrnlf, standing up. Towering over them, he added, "But I wouldn't worry. Holes very seldom bother wee folk like you. In over ten thousand years, I can't ever think of a hole bothering a wee person."

"Do they bother sea devils or others in the sea?" asked Jim.

Rrrnlf laughed.

"Nothing bothers a sea devil, wee Mage," he said. "You know that. As for other sea-folk, it would depend on what the sea-person said or did to the hole. Though . . ." Rrrnlf scratched his head thoughtfully, "I can't really think of anyone in the sea being bothered by a hole, either. Where is this hole?"

"You had best follow us," said Dafydd.

"Run along ahead then," said Rrrnlf.

He stood with a friendly smile as Jim and Dafydd walked out through the gate and across the open ground. There was neither sight nor sound of Rrrnlf until they were into the forest—when there was a loud sound of breaking branches just behind them, and Rrrnlf's voice making noises that sounded as if he was swearing in what might, Jim thought, be Anglo-Saxon—at any rate, he could make no sense out of it.

"Wee Mage!" roared Rrrnlf's voice almost over their heads, somewhere out of sight beyond the leafy branches. "Where are you?"

"Down here!" Jim called back. "Just follow the sound of my voice. I'm . . . going . . . in . . . this . . . direction. . . ."

He continued, walking and shouting at the same time, until he came to the hole. Then he stopped.

"Here it is!" he called.

There was a final rending of wood. Branches and leaves rained down. Rrrnlf's face peered down at them.

"But where's the hole?" Rrrnlf said.

"Right at my feet!" answered Jim. "If I took another step I'd fall into it."

"Oh," said Rrrnlf. There was some more tearing of branches, and a moment later Rrrnlf was on hands and knees beside Jim and Dafydd, looming only about a dozen feet above them in that position and peering at the hole. Jim and Dafydd had to back away so that the Sea Devil's massive face could get right down to ground level. Undoubtedly, thought Jim, he was positioning one eye directly over the opening of the hole, but it was impossible to see from where they were standing.

After a long moment, Rrrnlf grunted, lifted his head, wiped a certain amount of dirt and grass from around his eye, and peered at Jim and Dafydd.

"It's a hole, all right," he said.

"Yes," said Jim, hanging on to his patience. "But it seems to go someplace. Aargh looked into it and said it goes down about a distance as tall as I am, and then tunnels off at an angle to your left there, Rrrnlf."

"Aargh?" said Rrrnlf. "Oh, the wee wolf."

"That is so," said Dafydd. "Would you be having any idea, Rrrnlf, where that tunnel leads?"

"Why, where else could it lead?" said Rrrnlf. "It runs south and west of here to where you wee folk dig in the earth for lead and tin and silver."

Jim and Dafydd looked at each other.

"Cornwall," said Dafydd. "To the mines, there."

"—And then, of course," said Rrrnlf cheerfully, "it goes to the sea, of course."

Jim felt a sudden happiness.

"Dafydd!" he said. "You were right!"

"How could he not be right?" said Rrrnlf. "Do not all things finally go to the sea?"

Chapter 15

Not everything, Rrrnlf," said Jim.

"Why, of course everything," said Rrrnlf, standing up to look down through the hole he had torn in the foliage. "If you go anywhere on or in this land of yours, wee Mage, you end up at the Sea. How could it be otherwise?"

"But you don't know for sure that this hole leads to the sea," said Jim.

"But it does," said Rrrnlf. "Can't you smell it? You people on land are great for smelling things."

"Not all of them!" said a harsh voice, and a furry nose slid into Jim's field of vision, dipping down into the hole. "I have the best nose there is; and I smell no sea."

"Well, there you are, Rrrnlf," said Jim. "But you say you smell it?"

"No," said Rrrnlf. "I never bother smelling things. I . . ."

He stood for a moment, frowning and gazing past them at nothing.

"I *feel* it!" he said, returning his gaze to Jim's.

"How do you feel it, then?" asked Dafydd.

"I just feel it," said Rrrnlf. "I feel this tunnel runs on and on, past the place where you wee people dig and then it runs into other tunnels and they into other tunnels, and they into a place under-the-hill with an underground river running through it and down the river to the Sea."

"And where is this place under the hill?" asked Dafydd, almost sharply for him.

"Oh, it's under the Sea—out there—"

He pointed generally southwest, not quite in the tunnel's direction but almost.

"One of the Drowned Lands?" said Dafydd, still sharply. Jim looked at him.

"I suppose you could call it that," said Rrrnlf, after scratching his head again for a moment. "Like here, but middling deep in the ocean."

"Would you tell me then which one it might be?"

"Are they different?" asked Rrrnlf doubtfully. "We sea devils aren't allowed into places like that; and they all look alike from the sea-bottom alongside."

"James, Aargh," said Dafydd, once more with the different edge in his voice. "I think we should talk together of this as soon as possible."

"What's there to talk of?" said Aargh. He dipped his nose at the hole, indicating it. "Let James make the way down there wide enough for all of us to go side by side, and follow the hole to its end."

"I do not think it will be that simple," said Dafydd. "And the reason for that, look you, will have to come out when we sit in the Great Hall and talk."

He paused and looked at Aargh.

"Or is it that you will not come in with us?"

"I told Jim I will, and I will," growled Aargh. "But I see no sense to it. Why not talk here?"

"Brian might be able to be carried down to the Great Hall," said Jim. "But he could probably not be carried out here."

Aargh gave a small growl but otherwise said nothing. Knowing Aargh, Jim took this for a reluctant "yes."

"That little place you talk in," said Rrrnlf over their heads, "it's too small for me to come into. I'll be out in your courtyard if I can be of any help."

"Thank you, Rrrnlf," said Jim, mentally uncrossing his fingers. He had already been trying to think of reasons that would persuade Rrrnlf not to want to attend the meeting in the Great Hall.

It seemed to Jim to be a typical situation for him lately: trying to get a sort of war council organized while the desires of others pulled in many directions—as Brian, for instance, would certainly demand to be there, even though he should not get up.

Brian would have to be told of the meeting—otherwise he would be mortally offended. But once he knew, it would be hard to talk him into staying in bed upstairs. Perhaps impossible.

Impossible it was, but that turned out to be the least of the complications. Not only was Brian there—having been carried down by servants and propped up in a barrel chair with padding all around to keep him comfortably upright, his legs resting on a backless seat doing duty as a footstool—but Geronde, Danielle, and Angie had made themselves members of the meeting.

Aargh was not complaining; but Jim was more than sure that he was not exactly pleased to be there. He was lying on a bench at one end of the table, his rear legs out to one side and the front of his body upright, facing forward with the paws out front. This put his head very close to being on a level with the heads of the rest of them seated at the table.

All having been arranged, Jim sat down. Brian looked at him sternly, his face still pale. He had managed to bully the servants into dressing him; they had even slung his sword-belt around his waist.

The presence of the sword was improper for a guest in a friendly house. Jim doubted that Brian had the strength to draw, let alone wield, it for the moment; he suspected it was there, essentially, as a statement that he was ready for anything, whether they liked it or not.

At first there was a rather ominous silence around the table. Happily, however, now that everyone was seated, more servants appeared with wine-jugs, water-jugs, mazers, and several plates of small finger food.

Then they left. It was clearly up to Jim to get things started.

He cleared his throat.

"Dafydd, Aargh, Rrrnlf, and I all looked at the hole in the woods together, just now," he said, in what he hoped was a tone of voice that would encourage discussion. "Rrrnlf says it leads at last to the sea. Dafydd, however—" he suddenly realized he might be getting into dangerous territory. Dafydd might not have envisioned the three women being present; and neither Danielle nor Geronde looked as if she was about to agree happily to their men being involved in whatever action might be discussed.

"—Dafydd," Jim hastily changed his direction in mid-sentence, "thought we should all sit down and talk it over before we decided on anything, though."

The expressions around the table did not change. Jim looked at Aargh, to see if the wolf could help him by saying something. But Aargh stayed true to his sphinx-like pose. He said nothing at all. Dafydd, however, spoke up.

"Ah, well now," said Dafydd, "it seems to me there may be a better way for us to travel and a quicker. We—"

"You're not going!" Danielle interrupted him.

Dafydd turned to look at her.

"Am I not, then?" he said.

"No!" said Danielle.

Dafydd nodded his head slightly several times, with the absent-minded motion of someone who is still considering a situation and would make up his mind later.

Jim felt the pressure of someone looking at him; and turning his head slightly, saw it was Brian. One of the servants had made the mistake of putting a mazer in front of him and pouring some wine into it. Brian was now lifting it—a little shakily, to be sure—but with a look of triumph on his face as he met Jim's gaze.

Jim said nothing. He watched as Brian put the mazer to his lips; and the expression on Brian's face suddenly changed. He took the mazer from his mouth and stared into its contents with some surprise, then put it down on the table again.

"Quite right!" said Geronde. "Far too strong a wine." She took a pitcher from the table and filled Brian's mazer to the brim with water—a mazer whose wine Jim had already changed to half-water, even as Brian was lifting it to his lips. After Geronde's pouring, the liquid was only faintly pink.

Brian turned his head and smiled at her grimly.

"Is this talk to go on all day?" said Aargh. "It's like you people. You talk and nothing happens. Now, if Carolinus were here—"

"I am here!" interrupted the cross and unusually hoarse voice of Carolinus. They looked to see him standing—and wavering around his edges—between the two long tables. It was clear to Jim, at least, that Carolinus had once more appeared only as a projection. "You left a message with my kettle, Jim? I haven't but a moment or two. What is it?"

Jim got hastily to his feet.

"Carolinus!" he said. "I can't tell you how glad I am to see you. Can I speak to you for a moment privately—I mean privily?"

"That's all right," said Carolinus sourly. "We AAA+ Magickians can just manage to understand the word 'privately' from—well, come along, then."

His projection slid off in the direction of the Serving Room. Jim pushed his chair back and hastily followed.

They left the others behind and stepped into the Serving Room, which, Jim was surprised to see, had no servant in sight. Then understanding came: the Castle staff might be used to Jim's magic, but Carolinus was another kettle of fish. None of them were going to take the risk of offending or bothering the Mage. They would all now be out of earshot.

"The thing is—" Jim began; but Carolinus cut him short, as they stopped before the fireplace.

"Never mind, never mind," the elderly magician said. "I don't have time, I tell you! Now, let Dafydd guide you where to go; and follow him into Lyonesse, then across it to the entrance to Overhill-Underhill. But you cannot take Aargh along on this journey."

"What's Overhill-Underhill?" Jim asked. "Why not?"

"Never mind. You'll find out when you get there," said Carolinus. "And Aargh's presence would have a bad effect. Never mind that now!" He shook his head.

"But pay attention to what's written in the stone over the entrance before you go in. Now, my time is short. I must tell you, some days back you lost your unlimited drawing-account. Your old antagonist, Son Won Phon, got active as soon as I was tied up as I am now, and the result is your Account's been put on hold. I don't know how much you had in it—and since you still technically *are* an Apprentice, the Accounting Office won't tell you. So use as little of the magick you've in it as possible—stretch it. But above all, remember! The King and Prince Edward must be preserved at all cost. I have to go—"

"King? Prince Edward?" echoed Jim.

But Carolinus was no longer there. Jim stared at the place where the Mage had been. This was the second time Carolinus had made a cryptic reference to the need to protect the King of England and its Crown Prince.

"But I'm out to get Robert back, damn it!" Jim said to the empty air. He went slowly back to the High Table.

"Well," he said, sitting down and looking into the questioning faces of the others, "Carolinus is gone—just vanished. You probably noticed it wasn't him in the body, just an image of himself. But Dafydd, he said you'd know how to show us where we need to go. We're going to have to cross part of . . ." He ran down and, for a desperate moment, stared past everyone at the long side wall of the room, with its two great fireplaces, before turning to Angie.

"Damn it, now!" he said. "I know the name of the place perfectly well, but it's slipped clean out of my mind. Angie, what're the lines about an older land, from that poem I like about where King Arthur died?"

"Oh, you mean *The Passing of Arthur*, by Alfred, Lord Tennyson? Arthur didn't die, you know," said Angie of Infallible Memory, "He was carried off to Avalon by the three Queens. But the lines you want—"

She quoted them:

> *"Then rose the King, and moved his Host by night,*
> *And ever pushed Sir Modred, league by league,*
> *Back to the sunset bound of Lyonesse—*
> *A land of old upheaven from the Abyss*
> *by fire, to sink into the Abyss again—"*

She broke off.

"That's it!" said Jim. "We go across part of Lyonesse to the entrance to the entrance to a place called Overhill-Underhill."

The others all stared at him. Then Dafydd spoke.

"Lyonesse has been under the sea these many centuries," said Dafydd, his quiet voice strange in the silence. "It is no longer mostly bare rock and empty waste. Now it is thick with magicks, beasts, and trees and other plants that talk and act."

"By all the Saints!" said Brian in a voice as excited as his weakness would permit it to be. "Is that how it is? It has been thought that all memory of its place and likeness was lost."

"Not in my country," said Dafydd. "But since it is Lyonesse that you must reach, you will need my help to reach it—no, my Golden Bird—" he said, turning to Danielle as she began to speak again, "I pray you, wait. You and I will talk this over afterward, and if you do not agree, I will not go. James, did Carolinus not say anything more except to mention that you had to go through Lyonesse?"

"Not about getting to where we need to go," said Jim. For some reason he was reluctant to mention the entrance to Overhill-Underhill with the message over it. "He did say something about how it was all-important that King Edward and the Prince be preserved—"

"But James!" burst out Brian. "This could be serious. What threatens the King and the Prince?"

"Carolinus didn't say—nothing but what I've told you," said Jim. Out of the corner of his eye he saw Angie, battling to keep from showing her outrage at the idea that any threat to the King could be more important than the recovery of Robert.

"Well, then you should use your magick and take us to Lyonesse immediately!" said Brian.

"You cannot go!" said Geronde fiercely, looking ready to spring from her chair upon Brian. "You are in no shape to go anywhere on two legs—or four. In no shape to be of any use, even if you go."

"Dammit all to Hell, Geronde!" said Brian. "I may be a bit weak today. Perhaps I need another good night's rest. But I'll be ready for a horse tomorrow, and in two days I'll outride everybody. Besides, I have no choice. It is in my vows."

"Your vows be—" Geronde checked herself just in time, on the edge of what Brian would surely consider out-and-out blasphemy. She turned her gaze on Angie. "Angela, you know he is not fit to go!"

"Well, he's very weak—" Angie was obviously wavering between an outright lie and her own desire to support Jim, who she knew would need Brian's combat-wise mind, even if it had to be carried along on a stretcher.

"My vows," said Brian, slowly and heavily. His face was pale to the verge of pure whiteness, but his voice was stronger than it had been. "My vows are that I will do no hurt to women, children, or members of Holy Church, but will otherwise offer them aid and succor if they are in need."

"The part about children is not in them!" said Geronde, fiercely.

"There are some knights," said Brian in the same hard, measured tones, "who leave it out, feeling that aiding and succoring children is beneath the dignity of a knight. I left it in, and those words were heard by God."

"Angela, James!" Geronde appealed. "Tell him you do not ask his help. Think! You have no right to ask. God knows I would wish well for the child for your sake, if for no other reason. But remember something. He is not a blood-son! Your house will not rise or fall on whether he lives or dies!"

"I want him back," Angie said. Jim kept his mouth closed.

"Then I will ride when you ride," said Brian, in the same tone of unalterable determination.

"In any case, that won't be before tomorrow morning," added Angie quickly, to try to bring the situation to a generally acceptable conclusion.

"Tomorrow morning it is," said Brian, inflexibly. "But by then, you will be ready to Magick us down to Lyonesse, will you not, James?"

"Well," said Jim, "as a matter of fact . . ." His mind was busily hunting for an alternative after what Carolinus had said about saving his magic energy. "—Actually, if Rrrnlf could just carry us down through the sea as he did that time when we went to face the Kraken, Granfer, he could get us to the undersea edge of Lyonesse. It might be a wiser way of going."

Everyone but Angie and Aargh was looking at him with puzzled expressions. Surely a trip like that was nothing to a Magickian?

"You see," Jim went on rapidly, suddenly remembering Carolinus' words to him in Cumberland, "I believe Lyonesse is another Kingdom where my magic won't work—as it didn't work when we all went by mistake into the Kingdom of the Dead below Malvinne's Castle—you remember, Brian?"

"I do," said Brian.

"So," said Jim, "there may be strong magical reasons why we shouldn't go there by magic, but by some other way. Why don't I just have Rrrnlf in to talk to us here and see what he has to say about it?"

Jim's mind had been galloping as he talked—not so much to find the right words, as to keep the floor, so no one else could begin to argue. He had quickly worked up a visualization to bring Rrrnlf into the Great Hall. Once the Sea Devil was with them, argument would be foreclosed.

"Rrrnlf—" he said out loud—purely to impress his audience, since it was not necessary for the magic—"I summon you to me, now!"

Everybody looked suitably impressed, except Angie—but then their expressions changed. Overhead there was a sudden splintering crash. Three-quarters of Rrrnlf filled the space between the two tables less than a dozen feet from where they sat, and above them his enormous voice roared, unseen.

"Who does this to me?" it roared.

"Hell's bells!" said Jim under his breath. "I forgot again how tall he was, compared to the roof in here!"

There was another splintering crash and one of Rrrnlf's enormous hands smashed through the ceiling next to the hole through which his body up to the middle of his chest was visible.

"Stop that, Rrrnlf!" shouted Jim. "I'll take care of everything for you in a moment! Damned if I'll mend the roof by magic, though," he ended up, muttering the last few words to himself. "The Carpenter can mend it. It's nice, dry weather."

He wavered for a second between shrinking Rrrnlf or moving them all magically outdoors. He settled for making Rrrnlf about ten feet shorter—and abruptly, all of the Sea Devil was visible, blinking down at them now in the relative dimness of the Hall—a dimness somewhat alleviated by the sunlight beaming through the holes in the ceiling.

"Wee Mage!" said the shortened Rrrnlf. "What happened? You are bigger than you usually are. So are those with you!"

"It's just one of those things that happen with magic, occasionally," said Jim. "We'll go back to being as small as we ordinarily are the next time you see us. I wanted to ask you something. I'd like you to carry Brian and Dafydd and myself to Lyonesse."

"Not to Lyonesse, wee Mage," said Rrrnlf earnestly. "I can't come to it. Didn't I tell you that?"

"I only want you to take us to the edge of it—" Jim was beginning, when Dafydd interrupted.

"James," he said, "best you let me explain. Rrrnlf is quite right. He can't come to the edge of it unless he burrowed into another Kingdom or walked across one—and those Kingdoms are shut to such as he. What Rrrnlf can do is take us to the edge of the Drowned Land. From there, we can make our own way."

"Are you sure I can do that, wee Bowman?" said Rrrnlf doubtfully. "Maybe it's not possible."

"It is," said Dafydd.

"In any case," said Jim, "you don't have to take us *into* it. Just carry us down through the water to the edge of it; and maybe then I'll use just a little magic to go the last few feet into wherever this place is; but I'll leave you behind. I could go all the way by magic myself, true. But I'd have to visualize it first. Since I haven't been there, I can't do that."

I should have thought of that excuse sooner, for not using magic to take us into Lyonesse, he told himself annoyedly. He had only just bumped his nose into it when trying to reach KinetetE, after all.

"Is that what you do, wee Mage?" asked Rrrnlf. "Vizzle things?"

"Well, yes," said Jim. "But that's something that's hard to explain to someone who isn't another magician. Now, you're sure you can take us right to the edge of this Drowned Land, are you?"

"I wish I could vizzle things," said Rrrnlf wistfully.

"I wish I were thirty feet tall and as strong as a sea devil," said Jim. "But I'm not. We each do what we can in our own way."

"The most practical thing I ever heard you say, James," said Aargh approvingly.

"I suppose you're right," said Rrrnlf, sadly. "You wee people—"

He broke off, suddenly reaching under his shirt.

"That reminds me," he said. He brought his hand out holding the ugly Little Man with the tied sleeves, and set him on the table in the midst of them, as if he was an ornament. The eyes of the little man were fastened on Jim.

They stared at each other across some three and a half feet of polished table-surface. The other had been shrunken, proportionately, along with Rrrnlf, Jim noticed.

He was really not ugly, Jim told himself, distractedly. For that matter, he was not a man—that is, he was not human. He was—he had to be—a Natural. Not only his various oddities of person, but some deep instinct, told Jim that he was exchanging stares with someone not of the Human family.

Not that that made a lot of difference. A great many Naturals, like Rrrnlf, were a case of pure walking goodness and kindness—if perhaps a little short on what humans would call common sense. Others could be as terrible as the Earl of Somerset's ancient Castle Troll, who nevertheless had not only a surprisingly good side, but an emotionally vulnerable one. And some could be as inhuman as Melusine, the Elemental from France whose mercurial temperament and unthinking selfishness endangered all dragons and every human male she laid eyes upon.

There was something, some indefinable feel, about a non-human that humans somehow picked up on.

Nonetheless, he had been wrong about the small creature being ugly—he was really not so much ugly as odd. His face was a little longer than normal human proportions, and his thick brows and black, lank, very coarse hair seemed to give him a primitive look. But if you focused on his continually open mouth and large blue, wide-open, eyes, he seemed like one just beginning to discover the world around him.

The unhuman impression was certainly reinforced by his shortness, and the fact that his arms—unseen under those wide and over-long sleeves—appeared much longer than was natural. It was as if no part of them should be seen by ordinary eyes.

Of course, it was possible that the shirt had originally belonged to somebody double his size. It hung oddly upon him, bulging up in unusual places as if his body were lumpy or angular underneath it.

"He's glad to see you again," said Rrrnlf, interrupting Jim's thoughts.

Jim continued to stare at the small man. "How do you know?" he asked. "Has he started talking, then? The last time you brought him here, you told me he'd never said a word."

Rrrnlf wound up scratching his left ear with his right thumb, dropped his arm, and stared at the small man, who was now paying no attention to him at all.

"Yes," he said. "He's doing it now. He's happy to see you again . . . or is it 'happy' he means? Maybe he's just happy he's looking at you again."

This, Jim thought, was the first instance of voiceless communication among this world's Naturals that he had ever run across. In an odd way, it seemed like something that did not belong even here, in this world of Naturals and magic.

However, he thought, catching himself up sharply, there was no point in wondering about all this.

"I'm sorry, Rrrnlf," he said. "I don't see how I can—"

"—No, I was wrong," Rrrnlf interrupted him. "What he's saying is, he wants to stay with you."

"Me?" said Jim.

"You," said Rrrnlf solemnly, nodding. "I understand him, now. He's saying you're his Luck; and he's got to keep you with him. If he keeps you with him, you're going to have to keep him with you."

This might be perfectly good logic to Rrrnlf, but it was a complication Jim did not need just now. He hardened his heart and spoke harshly.

"I can't keep him here," he said, "no matter what he thinks of me. You'll have to take him when you go."

Without warning the small man stretched out his strange arms to Jim, in the exact gesture of a very young child begging to be picked up and held. Jim's deliberately hardened heart melted like an ice cube on a hot stove.

"—Well, maybe . . ." he said, with a guilty glance at Angie, "for a while, anyway. . . ."

"Well, that's that, then, wee Mage," said Rrrnlf. "I'll take a nap until you're ready to have me take you, the wee knight, and the wee bowman wherever I'm allowed to."

"All right," said Jim, interpreting that as a desire to be returned to the courtyard. He returned Rrrnlf and the Little Man to their ordinary sizes; and Rrrnlf was abruptly back to being two-thirds in the Hall and one-third up through the hole in the ceiling.

"I'll have to jump," they heard his voice booming, beyond the roof, before Jim could visualize him back to the courtyard; and—amazingly, considering his size and weight—his knees flexed and he shot upward like a rocket, out of sight. There was a tremendous thud in the courtyard and a few entirely honest screams from people who must have been there watching—hopefully, from a distance.

The group around the High Table had already begun to break up. Aargh was already gone, somehow unnoticed. Danielle was going off with Dafydd, a hard look in her eyes. Geronde was supervising the servants who were to carry Brian back upstairs.

"—Can I help?" Angie was asking Geronde.

"It is not necessary," said Geronde, not looking at her.

Jim and Angie were left, still sitting in their chairs. They both looked at the small man.

"Well," said Jim, looking uneasily at her. "It looks like we're stuck with him for a while, at least."

"That's all right," said Angie, "as long as he doesn't get underfoot."

"Of course," said Jim, hastily. It had never entered his mind that he would have to take in the small stranger. There might be a problem of feeding him— but it was impossible to tell what that might involve. Some Naturals did not seem to need to eat at all. Others ate and drank, like Hob—but only when they felt like doing it, not because they needed to. Then, of course, there were some like the several different kinds of trolls, who were like all predatory creatures and had to kill and eat regularly.

As far as Jim knew, Rrrnlf did not need to eat; and if that was true, and if this little fellow had traveled with him all this time, the small man probably did not need to eat either, because Rrrnlf would certainly never have thought of feeding him.

An inspiration kindled in Jim. The thought of Hob, their Castle Hobgoblin, had sparked it.

"Maybe—" said Jim, and broke off. He lifted his voice and directed it to the nearest fireplace. "Hob!" he shouted. The answer, as he had expected, was immediate. But not the words that made it up.

"I don't like him!" came back the answer from the fireplace in a small hobgoblin voice, but with no portion of Hob himself showing. "I don't like him at all!"

Chapter 16

D on't be an idiot, Hob!" said Jim.
"He won't hurt you. If you like, I'll put a magic ward around you, so nothing can get at you while you're out here."

"I'm not afraid!" said Hob's voice. "I just don't like him."

"Well, then, come on out here and join Lady Angela and me."

"Well . . ." Hob's voice came back, "if you're going to go on being there . . ."

His narrow brown figure emerged from the top of the fireplace head-first, turning itself rightside-up in mid-air as it emerged, and leaped to the end of the High Table between Angie and Jim.

"I'm not afraid of him at all," he said. "But he doesn't belong here—and you like him better than you like me!"

"Hob!" said Angie. "You know we couldn't possibly like anybody better than we like you."

"Really?" said Hob, looking up at her.

She took his small hand in hers.

"Never!"

"Oh," said Hob. He squared his shoulders and grew a fraction of an inch in height.

"Well," he said, looking at the Little Man. "What are you going to do with him, then?"

"It's not what I'm going to do with him, or the Lady Angela is going to do with him. It's what I want you to do with him," said Jim.

Hob's face dropped, and he shrank back to his usual height. Jim went on. "I'm not sure he knows how to take care of himself in a place like this, so I'd like you to take charge of him—for tonight, at least—and find him someplace to stay where you can keep an eye on him. He's a Natural, just like you, you know."

"So's a troll," said Hob, "but a troll'd as soon eat me as look at me."

"I don't think this fellow will eat you," Jim said.

"Well, maybe not. I wouldn't let him, anyway," said Hob. "I don't want him in one of my chimneys, and what if he doesn't want to be there, anyway. Maybe I can put him just up under the roof with the bats, or something like that."

"Bats?" said Jim. He looked at Angie. "We've got bats?"

"Of course," said Angie. "Just about any castle or cathedral or any permanent structure has them."

"They're nice, friendly bats," said Hob, earnestly.

"Well, I'll take your word for it." Jim looked at the Little Man. His eyes were on Hob, now, but his expression was as unvarying as ever: open-mouthed fascination. "As long as he doesn't object."

"No, he says that'll be all right," said Hob.

"He does? How do you—are you telling me you can hear him talking, Hob? How do you do that?"

"I don't know. I just do," said Hob.

"I can't hear a thing," said Angie.

"Me either," said Jim. "Hob, if you can get an answer out of him, ask him what his name is."

"What's your name?" Hob said, turning to the small man. "Oh, is that so? Well, they're *my* Lord and Lady! and this is *my* Castle. You're just a strange varlet—what's your name, I said?"—pause—"He says his name's Hill," wound up Hob, looking back at Jim.

"Hill?"

"That's what he says," said Hob. "I don't think he's very wise. He's the most witless of—of us Folk you call Natural, m'Lord—I ever met. I think."

"He can hear you when you talk to him out loud, then," said Jim, thinking he had been very smart to agree quickly with Angie when she said that the Little Man wasn't wanted within the Solar. "Ask him why he wanted to come with me, instead of staying with Rrrnlf?"

"He says—that's no reason!" said Hob, addressing his last words once more to the Little Man. Then he turned back to Jim again. "All he'll say now is 'He's my Luck!' And now he won't talk at all."

"Well," said Jim. "Take him up to the bats. If he wants to come along with me wherever I'm going, he's going to be in for a more exciting time than he probably thinks. You'll have him as a guest for tonight, anyway, and maybe a little longer than that. It depends on how soon Sir Brian is ready to ride with us."

Hob stood on one leg, looking reluctant. "Yes, m'Lord," he said after a moment, and turned away. "Come on, Hill."

"And, Hob!" Jim called after him. "He may not like being here any more than you like him. Be kind to him."

Hob stopped. So did Hill. Hob turned back. So did Hill.

"Kind, m'Lord?" Hob stared at Jim.

"You know," said Jim. "Kind is what you are when you do things like taking the young children for rides on the smoke."

"But he's not a young person," said Hob, who was about half the height of the Little Man. "He's big!"

"So was I, and you took me."

"Oh, you're different, m'Lord," said Hob. "I like you."

"Well, let's say that's what being kind is; being kind is doing something nice for someone, but there's no reason why you have to like someone first before you do something kind for them. You could do something kind for them first, and then find out you like them—and they like you."

"Oh?" said Hob. Shaking his head confusedly, he turned again and led Hill into the fireplace. A waft of smoke carried them both up the chimney, and they were gone.

"Maybe I can leave Hill behind, accidentally," said Jim to Angie. "Particularly if Brian's ready to ride tomorrow, and we can get off in what looks like a hurry, so I've got an excuse to not take him."

"Lots of luck," said Angie.

"Luck is my middle name, according to Hill," said Jim. But the joke fell flat.

In the middle of the night Jim woke up with a solution to a problem he had been mulling over. Even though Brian seemed to be healing, Jim knew his friend had suffered a severe loss of blood. Jim had been able to heal the wound that caused it, but Brian was still very much short of the blood he needed to be healthy. Jim did not really know how dangerous that could be.

When that had happened before to Dafydd, Carolinus had been able to use magic to effect a transfusion, once Jim had figured out a way to match blood types.

Jim had fallen asleep thinking about how to go about the magic that Carolinus had once arranged, but in the middle of the night, he woke up from a dream in which he had found a way to do it. He lay there, half-awake, slowly realizing that what he had dreamed would work: his own heart acting as a miniature pump, regulated by heartbeats.

Careful not to wake Angie, he slipped out of the bed, parting the curtains only enough to let himself out, dressed, and went downstairs quietly.

A man-at-arms was on duty at Brian's door. A purely formal duty, but the guard was equipped with sword, spear, and helm—just as if it had been something like active duty.

Jim rounded the curve of the corridor just in time to see the man yawning hugely. He caught sight of Jim at the same time and closed his jaws with a snap, straightening up and striving to look bright-eyed and alert as Jim approached.

"Quiet this time of night, Bartholomew," said Jim.

"It is, m'Lord," said the man-at-arms. "Sir Brian's been sleeping steady. I've heard no sound from him there, bar a snore or two."

"Good," said Jim. "I'm going in just to take a look at him. Be quiet opening the door, and closing it after me. Is there light within?"

"Fire still burning, m'Lord," said the guard.

"Make sure it burns all night long," said Jim. "Now open the door."

Jim went in, and the door closed softly behind him. It took a moment for his eyes to adjust to the dim illumination of the low-burning fire, but then he saw Brian sleeping peacefully on his side—not snoring at all.

Jim stepped softly over to him. For a moment, he stood, just looking down at his friend. It might be an illusion caused by the ruddy light of the fire, but Brian looked more healthy now, relaxed and slumbering. Jim softly closed his fingertips on Brian's wrist. There was a chance he might wake if touched, but Brian had always been a very sound sleeper—unless there was some kind of alarm, like the sound of metal striking metal, shouting, or a gong or drum, no matter how distant.

"Dammit to hell . . ." muttered Brian without opening his eyes. He snored once, and went back to sleeping quietly. Jim gently searched the wrist until his third finger found the pulse there, pressing only enough to be able to count the heartbeats.

Jim, with no wristwatch here in this fourteenth century, had learned to run a clock in his own mind. He timed Brian out at fifty-two beats to the minute, now, averaging two readings.

That was all right, then. His own heartbeat had always been slow, perhaps because of his genetic makeup, or maybe his years of sports—he paused to check his own pulse. Standing, as he was right now, his own heartbeat was about fifty-four. Sleeping, he probably would have dropped to about forty-eight or possibly a little lower.

In any case, their heart-rates were close enough.

Using the same technique by which he magically moved wine around, he took a drop of blood from Brian's body, putting it on the flat of the blade of his knife. Then he put a drop of his own blood near it. When he commanded that the two drops would refuse to mix if they were not of the same type, they flowed together silently. Jim could not be sure if he was a universal donor, or just the same type as Brian, but it made no difference: Brian could take Jim's blood.

Jim paused to squint slightly at Brian and concentrate on the vision he was building in his mind. When his mind's image of Brian clicked firmly into mental lock, he imagined blood being propelled by the pump that was his heart, down his arm and through the end of the same finger that touched Brian's pulse—and into the blood vessel it felt. Flowing slowly, a twentieth of an ounce with every heartbeat.

That surely should not be too quick a dumping of extra blood into Brian's venous system; it should work effectively enough to transfuse at least a pint of his blood into Brian—putting him in stronger condition if he did insist on riding tomorrow. Jim counted his own pulse-beats until enough ounces had been transferred.

He moved toward the door, but stopped as he caught the murmur of muted voices beyond it. One of the voices was that of the guard. He was speaking with another man-at-arms, using the common local dialect rather than the more formal language in which they spoke to Jim and Angie.

"Thee broughten somat to wet my mouth, then, Nick?"

"Aye. Here 'tis. Small-beer, Bart. All I could get thee."

"For all that, it goes down grateful. I was sad parched, Nick." There was a pause, then the voice of the guard went on. "What's new downstairs?"

" 'Ee's growing, and 'ee's willing. Never fret, Bart. Thy silver's safe."

"We'm bound to win on him. Agin natur otherwise. Mark my words, Nick . . ." The murmurs dropped to an unintelligible level. Jim felt a sudden uneasiness, triggered off by his recent worry over how the Castle's people really felt toward him.

Ridiculously, at the same time, a slight feeling of guilt began to creep over him. Manners were different in this earlier century, but he had been brought up to think it was not right to eavesdrop. Somehow, he now felt almost trapped inside this room, like a thief in a house with the police outside. He did not really want to catch the two outside breaking all the rules of sentry duty. But this was no way for the Lord of a Castle to feel.

He squared his shoulders, put his hand on the latch, and opened the door, slipping through and closing it gently behind him. But, soft as he went, it gave adequate warning: when he stepped through, he found only Bart, standing at his post. Glancing down the corridor as far as the curving stone-walled passage would let him, Jim saw nothing. When he turned back, he noticed a leathern jug, or "jack," hidden between Bartholomew's legs and the wall. He carefully ignored it and started off toward the stairs himself.

"Good night, Bartholomew," he said.

"Good night, m'Lord," he heard behind him.

He went on up the stairs, pondering once more on the conflicting mores of different centuries. Strictly speaking, he should not have felt any hesitation about listening to what was being said on the other side of the door—no other Lord in this century would have. But even after some years here, these little conflicts-in-social-training rose to bother him. Someday, someday, he would find time to sit down and sort them all out.

A fourteenth-century Knight and Lord of a Castle in his position would, he told himself now, have listened to the cryptic interchange between the guard and his friend for the reason that he wanted to know what they were up to—but he would never have listened, as Jim had, with what was essentially a personal interest in their lives.

Who was the "he" they had been talking about. Could it have been himself? Nonsense. He was older than either one of them!

But he was still growing and changing in the sense of fitting into their medieval ways.

Forget it, he told himself.

Now, Brian would be stronger tomorrow, and possibly well enough to ride, the day after that. That was the only thing of importance.

He made his way quietly back into the Solar. Angie was still asleep. He crawled cautiously into the bed, pulling the curtains and sliding under the covers without waking her. The bed was warm and brought him a comfortable feeling of everything else being shut out. Angie was there. The worries of the day slipped away and sleep claimed him.

He woke to hear her shouting. Lifting his head, he saw her leaning out one of the windows, calling commandingly to the courtyard just below the tower.

"—And pull those two apart!" she was ordering at the top of her voice. "The rest of you get back to work! You've all got work to do, haven't you?"

There was a pause, during which Jim went on with the job of coming awake.

"That's better!" called Angie. She shut the window and came back toward the bed. Jim, now half-sitting up in it, watched her through the opened curtains on that side, as she came toward him.

"Oh! Good. You're up," she said, reaching the bed. "I was just about to wake you."

"You did," said Jim, still groggy, still not so far from sleep that he could not hear the siren call of covers and mattress.

"Well, it's time you were dressed, anyway," Angie said.

"What was all that, down in the courtyard?"

"It's over now," said Angie. "It was May Heather and her friend Tom from the Kitchen. They were fighting again."

"Again?"

"I can't understand it—I've asked both the Kitchen-Mistress and the Serving Room–Mistress to find out why they keep doing it; they're supposed to be the best of friends. Inseparable. As twins. But five percent of the time it seems they're trying to kill each other over some minor point of argument. They're both thirteen, you know."

"Is Tom thirteen?" asked Jim. "He's small for his age, then."

"Not in this century. It's a matter of nourishment, remember," answered Angie. "Children just don't grow as big as in our time because of the lack of food in the winter, and a poorly balanced diet most of the rest of the year. Besides, right now May Heather's at the age where she's grown bigger than he is. Girls take a spurt, you know, just about this time of their lives."

"Oh?" said Jim. "I guess that's right."

Fully awake now, he could see it was full daylight, judging by the sunlight coming through the windows. Ordinarily, he would have been awake at dawn, following the medieval sleeping habits to which they had become adjusted.

"Well, I'm up now," he said, scrambling out of the bed. "Could you order breakfast?"

"I already have," said Angie. "—In fact, here it is."

The door had swung open, without even the courtesy of a scratch to ask admission, and three of the women from the Serving Room came in, carrying food and catching Jim with no clothes on—he and Angie having come to follow the other medieval custom of sleeping naked, at least at home. Completely unperturbed by his undress, they set the table, curtsied, and went out again.

"I wish they'd learn to knock!" said Jim.

"Give up," said Angie, "and eat your breakfast. You ought to be used to things by this time. Put something on now, sit down, and eat."

"They run us," grumbled Jim, hastily dressing. "We don't run them."

"Well," said Angie, already busy with some of the hard-boiled eggs and bacon, "they're the way they are, and we're not going to change them. Hurry up before the food gets cold."

Jim joined her; and the breakfast brought new life into him. It also started his mind to working on some thoughts that had been spinning around in the back of it ever since his private talk with Carolinus. The food tasted very good indeed; and by the time he finished, his mind was made up.

"I'm going to try something," he told Angie, pushing his chair back. "Stay where you are. I'm going to call up the Accounting Office and check on my balance."

"Oh?" said Angie. "You're always doing that when I'm not around. You don't mean I can watch, this time?"

"*Listen*, is more like it," said Jim. He took a step away from the table, stared into the air before him, and spoke very loudly.

"ACCOUNTING OFFICE!"

"Yes, James Eckert?" instantly answered the bass voice of the always invisible, possibly bodiless, and always prompt functionary, some four feet above the ground and directly in front of him.

"I'd like three times the magical energy I earned at the Loathly Tower added to my account, if you don't mind," said Jim, as strongly and authoritatively as he could.

"I regret, James Eckert," said the Accounting Office. "No further overdrafts are permitted to your account."

So, Carolinus had been right.

"Well, this is a fine thing!" said Jim. "At least, then, you can tell me how much I have left at the moment."

"I regret, James Eckert."

"Don't tell me you can't do that either?"

"It cannot be done for anyone still within the Apprentice Ranks."

Jim sighed internally. Carolinus had told him it would do no good to ask. But it was always worth trying.

"Here I am, just about to start off on a trip, and I can't find out how much magic I'll have with me. Even if I'm only a C+ class Magician," said Jim, "it seems to me you owe it to me to let me know, roughly at least, how much magic I can have the energy for."

There was a slight pause. If it had been anything else but the Accounting Office, Jim would have been sure the other was hesitating. It spoke, however, a moment later.

"Approximately," said the Accounting Office, "you have the equivalent of a full drawing-account of a B+ Magickian still available to you. But no more can be added once that is gone."

"Thank you," said Jim. There was no answer from the Accounting Office. Apparently, it had already left, in its usual abrupt manner.

Seated at the table, Angie was looking distressed.

"Is that going to be enough?" she asked.

"I don't know, that's the trouble," said Jim. "There's no way of telling. I don't even know what the full account of a B+ Class magician adds up to. It ought to be plenty of magic for ordinary uses. But if I'm going to be taking Brian and Dafydd along with me—with horses for all of us and a sumpter-horse for our baggage, moving all that by magic—it could get eaten up in a hurry."

"Do you have to take that much?" said Angie. "I mean, horses and such?" She got up from the table and came around it, toward him.

"If I do suddenly run out of magic, then what are we going to do for transportation—to say nothing of the heavy armor and weapons and other stuff we may need?" Jim said.

"Oh," said Angie, stopping. But then she smiled down at him. "It'll be all right, though. I just have a feeling it'll all be all right."

"I hope," said Jim, slowly getting to his feet. But then he, too, brightened. "But anyway, thank God for you!"

They wrapped themselves up in each other.

"Now," said Jim, as they both let go, "let's go find out whether there's a chance Brian can ride tomorrow."

Brian was absolutely certain that he could ride—not merely tomorrow or the day after, but this particular day itself. Furthermore—he began unthinkingly to take charge and issue orders—they should start getting the horses groomed and packed immediately. Jim would have to lend him a few things. What had happened to the helm and body-armor that he had been wearing up in Cumberland when he got wounded? What about his weapons? And he would need some changes of linen and other things.

"I've got them all," said Jim.

"Oh?" said Brian. "But we must certainly take them—and you will need the like."

"I only planned to take one sumpter-horse," said Jim.

"I think we can put it all on one without straining the animal," said Brian, a little impatiently. "We can ride with the spears, harkye."

"I know," said Jim. "I guess one horse can manage everything."

He put his quill pen back into the inkhorn he had clipped to his doublet before coming down, and folded up the sheets of greyish paper he had been noting on.

"Must you write everything down?" said Brian, who could barely sign his name. He instantly checked himself, smiling awkwardly. "I pray you forgive me, James. I am ill-mannered. It is this impatience in me to be ahorse."

"That's all right, Brian," said Jim. "As for writing it down, it helps me be sure that I've remembered everything."

"But I gave you such a small list of things needed!" said Brian, out of the innocence of a memory which life had trained early, late, and often, to remember word-perfect what was said to it, and to repeat it again, word-perfect, some days afterward if necessary.

"We magicians are like that," said Jim. "I'll send up some servants and you can start getting yourself ready to go. Did you have breakfast?"

"Hours past," said Brian.

The sunlight coming through the arrow-slit in Brian's room agreed with the same sunlight Jim had just seen coming through the Solar windows, to indicate that the sun had not been up much more than an hour. But he did not put it past Brian to wake and breakfast two hours before that.

"Well, we'll get together downstairs, then, soon," said Jim, and went out.

He made his way down to the Great Hall, meaning to ask for Dafydd. But he found the archer already at the High Table, by himself and once more at the never-ending work of a fletcher, carefully balancing and trimming his arrows.

"Good morning to you, Dafydd," Jim said, sitting down across the table from him.

"Good morning, Sir James," said Dafydd. He leaned across the white table-cloth and his voice lowered until it was barely a murmur, while his hands went on with their work.

"James, I have been thinking, look you now. There are some things I would wish to tell you from what I have been told about Lyonesse. Would to it that the good Carolinus appear to us once more to speak of this; but we cannot hope for it. It was in my mind to speak to you when I should first see you this morning. But since I have thought it will be best if we wait until we are away from the Castle."

Jim also lowered his voice.

"If you think it's something really important, Dafydd," he said, "we had probably better talk about it here and now, just you and me. Away from here, we will not only have Brian, we will have Rrrnlf with us; and for all I know, his hearing may be so good that he can hear, no matter how secretly we try to talk. I assume it's something secret?"

"That is even so," murmured Dafydd. "Can we speak here without any overhearing?"

"Yes," said Jim. "I can take care of that."

He lifted his voice.

"John Steward!"

He waited. Dafydd waited. But John Steward did not appear. After a little while, however, May Heather came out of the Serving Room.

"Please you, m'Lord," she said. Her jaw was slightly swollen on the left side and there was a bad scratch on her nose, but otherwise she looked her usual cheerful, energetic self. "Mistress is gone from the Serving Room and there's no one there but me. Can I do summat for you, m'Lord?"

"Well, you'll have to take over John Steward's duty for the moment," said Jim; and he was ready to swear that at the words, May Heather grew two inches.

"It's an honor to me, m'Lord!"

"Tell everyone else in the Castle except Sir Brian or my Lady that I'm discussing a magic matter with Dafydd ap Hywel. I want none of the servants going blind or deaf on me. So tell them all I've magicked the Hall here and they've got to stay out of sight and hearing of the two of us here to be safe. I charge you—see everyone stays at a distance—and guard yourself also."

May Heather gulped.

"Yes, m'Lord, I will tell it so. I will say everything as you order."

"When I'm ready to have you all come back," Jim went on, "I'll go into the Serving Room and bang on one of the pans or pots there with the handle of my dagger. When that's heard, it'll be safe to return."

"Yes, m'Lord. I'll go right away and make sure everyone's at distance!"

May Heather turned and bolted off into the Serving Room, turning just before she was out of sight, toward the passage along the other side of one of the two long walls of the Great Hall.

Jim watched her go, waited to give her time to go up and down the passage, herding anyone there out, and then gave his attention back to the tall bowman.

"Now, Dafydd," he said in a low voice, but not as quietly as they had been speaking before May had come in. "What did you want to tell me?"

"It is of a danger into which we may go," said Dafydd. "For, as we of the Old Blood know, any whosoever enter Lyonesse as Carolinus bid us do, must face the chance of never again being permitted to return to land above the waves."

Chapter 17

Jim stared at the bowman.

"You see why I did not wish to mention it aloud," said Dafydd quietly, finally. "Our wives are not much of a mind to see us go, even now. If they could think that the return of any one of us might be decided not by our skill or luck, or even the favor of God, but by chance as at a dice table, I think perhaps their words would be stronger yet."

Jim nodded.

"You're right," he said in a voice as low as Dafydd's. "But are you saying it's really a matter of pure chance—it's nothing that anyone can control in any way?"

"So far as I know," said Dafydd. "That was why I wished to discuss it well away from the Castle. Those of us who go should do so knowing that risk is there. It may well be that Carolinus knows means by which this can be avoided, but he did not tell us, and I have only what I have known since childhood. Not that the people who told me had been to Lyonesse, but the story had been known of for many years; and the names remembered of some who have never been permitted to come back."

"But they could have met with an accident, or something?" said Jim.

Even if what Dafydd told him was merely an ancient tale, rooted in someone's imagination, in the fourteenth-century minds of Dafydd and Brian it could raise havoc. Also, he most thoroughly agreed that "havoc" alone was not the word for what the tale could give rise to in the equally fourteenth-century minds of Geronde and Danielle.

Come to think of it, Angie also would be disturbed. Not from a superstitious point of view, probably, but simply because of the rumor of some unknown danger in the place to which he must go.

"You must know something more about this, Dafydd," he said. "Who would not permit one or more of us to come back?"

"I know nothing more," said Dafydd. "But I know it to be true. The story of a Companion left behind has been told too many centuries, about too many people. We of the Old Blood Under the Waters do not willingly go into Lyonesse, look you."

Jim stared at him, but Dafydd's expression did not change.

"With what you've told me," he said, "I can't do a thing. I don't have any idea what kind of protection even magic might give us in this instance."

"As for your magick, now," said Dafydd. "It will work in the Drowned Land of my people, I have been told, because we are men and women there. But the tales also say that the Art of human magickians will not avail in Lyonesse. For though those there seem to be human—yet there is a difference. It is a Kingdom apart."

Jim nodded slowly.

"I believe you," he said. "And I don't know of anything I can do to protect us."

"Nor can I think of anything you can do, and I did not expect you to," said Dafydd. "But, in fairness, you must needs be told, as will Brian when he goes with us." He paused, looking at Jim. "There is another matter," he said.

"What are you trying to tell me, Dafydd?"

"There are old stories," said Dafydd, "of changelings. Babes who have been taken by the Fairies and Fairy babies put in their place. There was no other sort of child left in Robert's cradle when he was taken; nor have I ever myself seen such, or seen unmistakable sign of any such things as Fairies."

He looked seriously at Jim, who nodded understanding.

"Yet it can be that such exist," he continued, "and that there was some reason a changeling was not left in Robert's place. Others have sworn they had clear evidence that such creatures exist. What such creatures are, and why it is they wish for doing such a thing, I know not. I only say what has been told to me, that those who do this are powerful, and evil in their designs."

"Hmm," said Jim. He felt the pressure of questions that would not quite formulate themselves. He was still busy deciding how to ask them of Dafydd, when the bowman went on.

"The second matter I wish to tell you of," he said, "is that early this day, before you were down stairs—a man in chain armor over-dressed with a green tabard and a dark-green hat with a feather, rode to your gate, with three men-at-arms.

"All bore what seemed to be something not too different from the Royal arms—yet it was not the Royal arms. The men-at-arms wore helmets, carried swords at their sides, and rode horses almost as well as the Gentleman in the tabard."

He paused to drink, and so did Jim; then Dafydd went on. "They were challenged at the gate, but claimed to have a message for you, and asked for you. On being refused, they left the message with the Lady Angela, and rode off to the east. You have not mentioned this, so I thought I would."

Jim stared at him.

"I didn't know anything about it!" he said. Then, suddenly realizing this might sound as if he felt Angie had acted improperly, he quickly added, "—But I'm sure if it was something important, she would've told me. Maybe, I'd better go and ask her about it—"

He broke off suddenly.

Somewhere in the courtyard out beyond the front door of the Hall, a voice had been raised. A very angry voice, and a very familiar one. Brian's voice. It was impossible to make out what the voice was saying. Jim had not wanted Brian on his feet so soon; and the last thing he wanted was for any of the people of the Castle to upset him.

"Maybe we better go out and see what's bothering Brian, first," he said, getting to his feet. Dafydd was already on his, his unstrung bow over one shoulder and his quiver full of arrows over the other.

Brian's voice grew louder and more intelligible as they approached the door. Once outside, they could see him plainly at the entrance to the stables, with Blanchard standing beside him, and the Stable-Master apologetically facing him with hat in hand. Other stable-hands stood by behind the Stable-Master—a good distance behind—and the Castle Blacksmith was just reaching them.

"James!" said Brian, as Jim and Dafydd reached him—not merely here at the stables on his feet, but acting as if he had never had any reason to be off them. "Here's a pretty thing! Blanchard was ready to throw a shoe, and no one did anything about it until I led him out from his stall!"

"Crave your pardon, m'Lord," said the Master of the Stables, turning to Jim with relief on his face. "But the great horse being so savage to footmen—as is only right, of course—none of the lads wanted to go into his stall, so they did no more than put fodder over the wall from the next stall for him. I would have taken him out myself, today, for exercise; but what with other matters—"

"There should have been no other matters!" thundered Brian. "Blanchard should be your first and only care, when he is here, outranking as he does all other horseflesh—"

He broke off abruptly, glancing at Jim in sudden embarrassment.

"—With the exception of your good Lord's warhorse, Gorp, of course!" he said, loudly. "The shoe must have loosened in that bicker of ours up in Cumberland. But now—it must be fixed immediately. Immediately!"

"It's no use, m'Lords," grunted the Blacksmith, now standing bent-kneed with Blanchard's right front hoof up between his knees; and working on it, knife in hand. "He's cracked a hoof, that's what he's done. Not a great crack, Sir Brian. I'm paring it back now; but I have to go cautious so I don't do harm rather than good. Some things cannot be rushed, m'Lords. Until I shape this hoof with a knife, we cannot think of putting a shoe on it."

"The Saints give me patience!" said Brian. But he turned away from Blanchard, who was standing unconcerned on three legs while the Blacksmith worked. "Oh, it seems a messenger came for you, James."

"So I was just told," Jim answered. "Who's got the message?"

"The Lady Angela has it—I believe, up in your Solar," said Brian. He lowered his voice, "A *written* message, James!"

"I see," said Jim. "I'd better get up there right away. Brian, shouldn't you be sitting down, back in the Great Hall, saving your strength for the trip?"

"*If* we have a trip," said Brian gloomily. "If we ever get off before sunset."

Jim glanced at the sun. It was no more than three hours into a long summer day.

"Well, I'll go up to the Solar," Jim said. "I ought to be down in a few moments. Brian, you can't do anything here to hurry things up. Go to the Great Hall, sit down at the High Table, have a cup of wine, and see if you don't feel better."

"I can drink wine now, can I?" Brian said, lighting up.

"You can," said Jim. "Not much, though! Magically, I gave you some extra blood while you were sleeping last night, but you're still short of what you should have."

"May Saint Brian, my name-sake, ever remember you!" said Brian, and started toward the Castle. Dafydd went with him while Jim hurried on ahead, in through the long Hall, through the Serving Room—where he remembered to stop and bang on a large pot a couple of times—and up the stairs—the long, long, winding stairs—until he came panting to the door of the Solar.

He leaned against it for a second getting his breath back, then opened it and went in. Angie was sitting at the table with her elbow on its surface and her chin supported on her hand, looking out the window, thoughtfully.

"Angie, you've got a message?" Jim dropped into the chair opposite hers. Her gaze came back from the window.

"Yes, dear." She pushed what appeared to be several pages of parchment across the table-top toward him. "Do you want to try reading it?"

Chapter 18

Jim snatched up the parchment, which turned out to be a single large page, folded accordion-style.

Centered on it was a single paragraph, small by comparison, written in an unsure hand. At the bottom was a seal in red wax.

Jim stared at it. He might not recognize most coats of arms, but this was the crest of a member of the Royal family—the lions *statant gardant* (crowned), plus the fleurs-de-lys which Edward III had added to his arms when he had begun laying claim to the throne of France—both of these were immediately recognizable.

Certainly, however, it was not the Great Seal, used for important and historic occasions; nor even the lesser Seal, for official purposes. Still, it was similar enough that it could only be the arms of a member of the Royal family.

He went back to trying to read the writing. As done by the scribes of this time, the letters with their ornate club ascenders and other flourishes were difficult enough for him, particularly in Latin. This, however, was in English; and by someone who had been trained to write, but not well. It was still what would be considered a readable hand for the time. But when Jim tried to make out the words, the letters seemed to form one long unintelligible chain before his eyes.

"Angie?" he said, handing the paper to her, "can you read it?"

"I already have," said Angie. She took the paper and read aloud.

" '*To our loyal and good friend, Sir James le Dragon de Malencontri, my dear and continued love for you, Sir James, and my wish that in God's name all is well for you. For me it is otherwise. For the love you bear me, come immediately to me at Windsor, that together we may frustrate that wicked woman, Agatha Falon, who puts me in dire straits, and from which no one but yourself can save me. As you love me, bring your closest friends and come at once.*' "

Angie stopped reading. Jim stared at her.

"Is that all?" he said. "It looked like there was a lot more written there than that."

"There is," said Angie. "But it's pretty much the same message, over and over again."

She laid the parchment down exactly at mid-point between them on the table, and her eyes met Jim's.

"Did the messenger have anything to say to you?"

"No," said Angie. "I told him you had already left, with a sumpter-horse, before daylight. I said I didn't know where you were going. I didn't tell him about Robert or about anything else."

"You didn't write any kind of an answer, then?"

"The Prince would've considered my writing an answer presumptuous—an unauthorized prying into his private affairs—you know that," said Angie. "But in any case, I didn't want to put anything on paper; just in case you wanted to ride after him and tell him I had been mistaken—or you'd come back unexpectedly—or something like that."

"I wouldn't want to do that," said Jim. "And you did the right thing, of course. I can't help him, now; we've got to find Robert first."

Angie breathed out slowly.

"I knew you'd say that!" she said. "But I wanted to hear you say it. Do you think this business of the Prince will get us in more trouble?"

"How can I tell?" said Jim, gloomily. "I don't even know what he's upset about. But you think the messenger believed what you told him?"

"Why shouldn't he?" said Angie. "I don't think he knew what was in the letter. He was one of the Prince's own men—not a real, official Royal Herald—he told me that. He did say he'd been expecting you'd be going back with him to Windsor—the Prince is evidently staying away from Court. But it's not unusual for somebody who's as far out in the country as we are, not to be at home when a messenger gets there. Anyway, Geronde and Danielle were with me in the Great Hall when I opened the letter and read it."

She giggled, an unusual sound from Angie.

"They were impressed," she said.

"Why?"

"Because I had the nerve to open a Royal letter addressed to you, but more because they could see me reading it right through without trouble."

"You didn't tell them what it said?" Jim asked.

"Of course not," she answered, "but they backed me up when I told the messenger you'd left."

"That was good of them," said Jim.

"But you know they couldn't do anything else," answered Angie.

It was true, he thought. At the present moment Geronde and Danielle might not be feeling exactly happy with him and Angie, but—even aside from friendship—it would be instinct in almost anyone, at this time in history, to back up anything said by a known person to a stranger—unless asked to swear on it, which would put their souls in peril.

"But," Jim said, a new thought striking him, "I'm surprised the messenger didn't ask you which way I'd gone, and start out to try to catch up with me."

"I said I wasn't awake when you left, and only learned about your leaving from the servants."

"Well, you did marvelously," said Jim, looking at her gratefully. "But what I wanted to tell you is, Brian is feeling much better. I managed to give him some blood last night, and he says he's determined to leave as soon as possible."

"Rrrnlf will be taking you?"

"Yes," said Jim. "You remember—he isn't allowed into the Drowned Land; but he can take us most of the way faster than any other way I can think of."

"You're going right away, then?" said Angie.

Jim nodded.

"We'd better say good-bye up here now, then," said Angie. "The courtyard is going to be full of people—as public as you can get."

"You're right," said Jim.

The courtyard was indeed full when the two of them got down there a little while later. Every servant who had the slightest excuse to be there, or to be passing through, was present.

The two other couples were there. Danielle was standing very close to Dafydd and talking to him urgently in too low a voice to be overheard. Dafydd was looking as calm and unconcerned as ever, with his quiver of arrows and his bow already slung from his shoulders.

Geronde and Brian were also standing close, but saying nothing—merely concentrating silently and completely on each other, bound by the conventions of their rank which inhibited public display of great emotion on the part of either simply because Brian was going off on a risky journey from which he might not return.

The four horses were also there—Gorp, Blanchard, and Dafydd's mount saddled and bridled, swords scabbarded on the saddles and the tall spears in their sockets on the other side of the animal. Stablemen were holding the warhorses by their bridles, but at a good distance apart.

Nobody was bothering to hold the sumpter-horse, which had evidently been standing around loaded for some time, with a thick cloth of felted, uncombed wool doing the duty of a tarp as an outer cover over its burden. The sumpter-horse looked disgusted but resigned.

Rrrnlf was still sleeping.

"Hatpin?" Angie asked Jim, producing the instrument and looking at Rrrnlf's big toe, which was protruding from the sandal on his right foot in easily available position.

Jim winced.

"No," he said. "On second thought, I can spare a little magic and wake him that way."

He pointed at Rrrnlf.

"Wake!"

"Wha? Whoop?" roared Rrrnlf, sitting up suddenly. He said something very loudly in what was probably Anglo-Saxon.

"No, no, Rrrnlf," said Jim, "this is the fourteenth century!"

"Oh, that's right," said Rrrnlf. "There you are, wee Mage." He looked around. "And there is wee everyone else, including the wee beasts you all ride on."

"Yes, I'll be wanting you to take them along with us, too," said Jim. "But first I'll have to make some magic to put a sort of invisible wall around us so that you can hold us as tightly as you need to without crushing us. I think the three of us and the horses are too much for one hand; and you probably won't want to have both hands full when you're traveling—"

Jim broke off. Blanchard, who had frozen with startlement when Rrrnlf suddenly came to life to loom over him, now decided to express his feelings. Whinnying, rearing, showing the whites of his eyes and threatening to foam at the mouth, he fought the reins with which his stable-hand was trying to hold him; and several others of the stable crew, including the Stable-Master, came running to help.

But it was Brian who saved the situation, catching the reins and starting to

soothe the warhorse. He put one forearm across Blanchard's eyes to temporarily shut out sight of Rrrnlf; and with that horrifying vision blotted out, plus
Brian's voice—the only one he ever really listened to, anyway—murmuring
soothing and flattering words in his ears, the great horse calmed down.

Gorp jerked his head about a little as if he would like to throw the same
kind of tantrum. But he was somewhat inexperienced in doing so; and when
no one paid attention, he stopped. The sumpter-horse looked at them both
with what was now utter and simple disgust.

"All right now," said Jim, when peace had been restored and Blanchard,
with Brian's forearm removed, was able to look right at Rrrnlf without going
into a frenzy. "If you'll lead all the horses over here to me, facing me, but a
little bit apart—that's right."

It was indeed right, although none of the stable-hands wanted to get too
close to warhorses in such proximity. But Brian did it with a no-nonsense
attitude. Things were quiet now, and the steeds were content to have them
that way.

"All right," said Jim. "Now I'm going to enclose each one of the horses in
a ward, and then all of them in one other big ward, so that they'll be protected,
but safe from each other at the same time—Brian, you'd better step back from
Blanchard for a minute—will he stand if you let go of the reins?"

"Stand!" ordered Brian, dropping the reins to the ground. He backed away
with the healthy respect always accorded a Magickian at his work.

"Fine," said Jim. "Now, you stable-men let go of Gorp and the other horses,
and stand back too. Right. Now—"

"One moment, James," said Brian. "Are you going to leave that little Hobgoblin of yours and that whatever-he-is here with the horses? Or what else
are we to do with them?"

"They aren't even here," said Jim.

"Of course they are!" said Brian. "They're under the cover on the sumpter-
horse, with everything else. I thought you wanted them there, for reasons of
your own."

"Certainly not!" said Jim, staring at the sumpter-horse. "Under the cover?
Hob!"

Something stirred under the cover, near one of its edges. "Come on out
here, Hob! Bring what's-his-name with you."

The small man and Hob crawled out from under the cover at the back. But
instead of getting down on the ground, they stood up on top of the sumpter-
horse, which stood as indifferently steady as a half-buried rock.

"Hob," said Jim, striving for calmness, "how do you happen to be here, and
what is this other Natural doing with you?"

Hob stood on one leg.

"*He,*" said Hob, looking up at the small man to his right, "said he was going to crawl in under the cover all by himself." There was a clear note of jealousy in Hob's voice. "So I brought us here on the smoke—it makes us light for the horse; he likes that. Besides, if he came and I didn't, how would you be able to talk to him?"

"I didn't plan to talk to him," said Jim, trying to sort through Hob's explanation, "because he's not supposed to be there in the first place. He came without asking. You—what's his name again, Hob?"

"He says to call him Hill," said Hob.

"Hill?" said Jim, still striving to sound calm and reasonable. "Hill, this is nothing against you; but you and Hob have to stay here. I don't want you with us."

The small man continued to stare at Jim with no change of expression at all; but Jim suddenly found himself feeling vaguely uncomfortable. That steady gaze had something of deep reproach in it.

"Oh!" said Hob suddenly. "He's crying!"

Hob reached and put both hands on one of Hill's arms, but Hill paid no attention to him, only staring at Jim.

Jim stared back. The face he looked into, with its blank, childish stare, the mouth still half-open, had not changed at all. There were no tears in the blue eyes.

"Crying?" said Jim. "He's not crying. Why should he cry, Hob?"

"He's crying inside; and he says it's because you're his Luck!" said Hob. He touched the other's arm, but was still ignored. "It's all right, Hill. I'll be here with you; and how would you like to go for a ride on the smoke?"

Hill did not answer.

Jim felt the beginning of a strange uneasiness. Back in his own century he would have ignored all this talk about "Luck" and Hill having to be with him. But here in this world he had developed a sensitivity to the unknown and the strange; and in spite of his common sense, there was a feeling inside him that somehow he would be doing wrong if he made the small Natural stay at Malencontri.

"Oh, all right!" he said, angrily. "The two of you can come. But don't either one of you get in our way!"

"Huzzay!" cried Hob. Hill was already burrowing back under the cover on the horse's back. Hob followed him.

"All right, here we go, then," said Jim.

He pointed his right index finger first at Gorp, then at the sumpter-horse which was between the two stallions, then at Blanchard, and finally at Dafydd's horse—the one he had ridden to Malencontri. Then he swung his finger back and forth, pointing from one to the other.

"There," he said. "That takes care of that." Gorp started to move restlessly, bumped his nose against something invisible between him and the sumpter-horse, and stopped, looking surprised. Blanchard was still being obedient to Brian and standing with his reins on the ground.

"Now," said Jim, "if you'll both come over here, Brian and Dafydd, and stand in front of your horses. I'll join you." The two men came over promptly enough, but somewhat stiffly, like a couple of patients just told the dentists were ready for them, now.

As soon as they were in place, Jim stepped forward, turned around, and stood with the other two. He half closed his eyes to visualize; and a moment later that part of his mind that had become sensitized to his magic when it worked gave him the sensation that the wards were around him and around the other two, as well as the horses.

"I think we're ready, then—" he broke off. "No, wait a minute. Rrrnlf, will you bend down and lay your hand open on the ground, so I can see how we're going to fit into it, the horses and all?"

Rrrnlf did so. It was perfectly clear that they would make a handful that Rrrnlf could get his massive fingers under, but it would be a clumsy handful.

"I think I'll make all of us half-size. Brian, Dafydd—will you remind me to make us full-size again, once we've gotten where we're going?"

"Assuredly," said Dafydd, before Brian could say anything.

It took only a moment's visualization. Jim himself felt no change and was sure from the silence of Brian, Dafydd, and the horses that none of them had, either. But Rrrnlf's hand, still open and waiting for them on the ground, now looked ample to hold them.

"Yes, we can be carried easily." He looked out into the crowd. "I'll be back as soon as I can," he said.

"Farewell, my Lady," said Brian to Geronde with surprising feeling in his voice, considering the publicness of the scene.

"I will be back, my Golden Bird," said Dafydd at the same moment, softly, but with sufficient voice to carry to Danielle, who was—after all—not that far away from him.

"Now, Rrrnlf," said Jim. "Carry us to the border of the Drowned Land."

"Very well, wee Mage," said Rrrnlf. "Do the wee riding-beasts come all the way there, too?"

"You'll find we're all one piece when you pick us up," said Jim.

"And harkye, Sea Devil," Brian rapped out before Jim had barely got the words out of his mouth. "—Carefully! Particularly with Blan—with the horses!"

"Certainly, wee Knight," said Rrrnlf agreeably; and the huge hand closed around them so that they were looking out between Rrrnlf's massive fingers at the Great Hall behind the Sea Devil's back.

They were lifted with a jerk—the horses all neighed in alarm and protest. There was a swinging movement, followed immediately by a clearly heard thud that jarred them as they stood; and they were looking back at the outside of the curtain wall. Rrrnlf was carrying them in his right fist, hanging at his side, with the knuckles facing back so that they could see between his fingers what they were leaving, but not where they were going. All three men peered out.

A steady, swinging motion began. Malencontri was one size smaller with each swing; and abruptly there were trees between them and it.

The glimpses of the Castle shrank more with every swing, as they moved with what must be surprising, enormous strides—even for someone as tall as Rrrnlf. At last, Malencontri was lost to sight; gone, with Angie, Geronde, and Danielle and everyone else there. The glimpses of the familiar part of the forest dwindled, dwindled, until there was nothing but the tree-trunks and the leaves.

Finally there was only the forest and movement.

Chapter 19

Something more than Rrrnlf's length of stride had to be at work. Because it was not more than a matter of a few minutes before his voice could be heard booming above them.

"Ah, sea!"

The long, repeated swings at the end of Rrrnlf's arm as he strode, that might have made them queasy if Jim had not silently suggested magically that it made them sleepy instead, ceased suddenly; and Brian exploded into speech with the suddenness of someone just woken up.

"It cannot be possible!" he burst out. "We are a full day's ride from the sea— well, maybe something less than a full day's ride, but too large a space to be covered in this short length of time!"

"Natural magic," explained Jim glibly; and as suddenly as Brian had spoken they were enclosed in a watery greenness. All three were experiencing an unnerving sensation which only Jim could recognize as like being in a swiftly dropping elevator—the feeling of having left his stomach up behind there somewhere.

Jim stole a glance at his two friends. They were both expressionless. Too expressionless. Jim suspected that each thought the sensation was happening to him, alone, and was determined not to show a reaction. Jim opened his mouth to explain, then closed it again. That could not be done easily in fourteenth-century terms—and anyway, the sensation had ceased now and the reason for it did not matter.

In moments, it seemed, they were looking through what seemed to be about a three-foot thickness of water, at a sandy plain, beyond which they could see a green land, cheerfully lit by some unseen sun, and rising to rocky heights and valleys farther in.

"There were some wee people there, just a few moments ago," said Rrrnlf, "but they all turned and ran off, and they're lying down in the grass now, so you can't see them." His hand unfolded from around them and his voice took on a less happy tone. "Wee Mage, why is it all these wee people always run from me?"

"Because they have guilty consciences," said Jim, before either Dafydd or Brian could answer.

"Ah." Jim, looking up, saw Rrrnlf with a puzzled expression on his face. "So that is it. Why do so many of you wee people have 'guilty consciences'?"

"We don't," said Jim, still talking fast before anyone else could say the wrong thing. "It just happens that you've most often seen my friends and me at times when people with guilty consciences have been chasing or lying in wait for us."

"Ah, now I understand," said Rrrnlf.

"Dafydd," went on Jim, still quickly, "is this the Drowned Land you were talking about?"

"It is," said Dafydd. "Shall you take us through the last piece of water here to the land itself, then, James?"

"Yes," said Jim. "Just stay as you are—"

"Do I pass the wee beasts in to you, after you've gone?" interrupted Rrrnlf, a little anxiously. "What must I do if you leave them with me?"

"We take them!" rapped out Brian, before Jim had a chance to speak. "And Rrrnlf—carefully!"

"Yes, wee Knight!"

"We'll all be careful, Brian," said Jim. "Thank you very much for bringing us here, Rrrnlf."

"Indeed," said Dafydd, "I thank you also, Rrrnlf."

"Thankee, Sea Devil," said Brian, a little stiffly and obviously unsure about the proper form of address when someone like himself was thanking a mere Natural, but one thirty feet tall, who had just whisked them over distances and down into the ocean deeps with no apparent trouble at all. He added: "A great task. Well done!"

"Oh, I like doing things for you wee folk," said Rrrnlf. "Can I watch you move everyone in by magick, then, wee Mage?"

"Of course," said Jim. He made the ward a single large enclosure. He had had time to work out the type of visualization he wanted, for a sort of magical tunnel through the water and into the air and land before them. He envisaged it now. It appeared, and he started walking forward into it, leading Gorp while removing the wards around the horses in sequence. His friends followed in turn, with their own horses. The sumpter horse plodded along behind as if this was the normal way to act.

They emerged on a sandy shore. It would have been happy if Blanchard had continued to follow docilely along. Unfortunately, the great horse seemed to come abruptly out of shock at finding himself no longer held in a tight invisible stall, surrounded by a massive hand; he reared and whinnied. Brian leaped to catch his reins near the bit, pulled his head down, and began talking to him, petting and calming him. Slowly, Blanchard yielded himself grudgingly to calmness—still snorting from time to time as if to express how hard this sort of thing was on his nerves.

Gorp regarded him for a second, and then started nuzzling the sand at his feet, as if looking for a blade of grass. There was none, and he gave up, raised his head, and stood, merely staring straight ahead. Dafydd's quiet mount had ignored the whole matter; and the sumpter horse, carefully looking away from Blanchard so that the warhorse should not see, sneered. It had never been a particularly good-natured sumpter horse.

"Dafydd," said Jim, "are we free to just walk across this land of yours, now?"

"I see no reason why not," said Dafydd calmly. "Also, you must not call it 'my land,' Sir James. I am of Wales. It is true that I have ties to some who dwell in the country before us there, but that is another matter."

Too late, Jim remembered that Dafydd had sworn Brian and him to secrecy about his being heir to a title from this Drowned Land—the *"Prince of the Sea-Washed Cliffs,"* they had learned it meant, translated into English. Implied in that request was a desire that his title down here not be mentioned to anyone in the world above.

"Farewell, Rrrnlf, now, and thank you," said Dafydd; and, leading the sumpter horse as well as his own, he moved on toward the soft green of the grassland beyond the shore.

"Certainly, wee Bowman," said Rrrnlf—and disappeared.

Jim had paused at the land's edge to express somewhat more extensive thanks than Dafydd had given, and this was a more abrupt departure than he had expected. It made him wonder for a moment if he had offended the Sea Devil in some subtle way.

However, Gorp was tugging at his reins, wanting to follow after the other horses. Jim, with Brian and Blanchard following, passed into the green land.

"Oh! Look, Hill!" cried a small voice that Jim knew only too well. He looked to see two faces peering out from under the raincover on the sumpter horse's load. He swore, not quite enough under his breath, as it turned out.

"Well now, damn it—" Jim was beginning, when Brian interrupted.

"You did say, James," said Brian severely, behind him, "that they could come with us. You said nothing about them keeping silence; and you know that the Hob, at least, must be talking. Your people will never know where they are with you if you do not stay with your decisions. A knight—"

"I know, I know," said Jim, holding up his hand to stop Brian. "I just forgot they were with us for the moment."

That answer and his upraised hand effectively stopped what Brian had obviously been about to begin, an educational lecture on the management of servitors and followers. Jim had had enough lately of his own conscience questioning his handling of the folk of Malencontri. That conscience needed no help from other people. They went on together without any more words.

"M'Lord," Hob's tiny voice came piping back to him from the back of the sumpter horse.

"What is it now?" Jim was aware of the irritation in his voice.

"Very sorry, m'Lord, but you wanted to be reminded to make us all the right size again," Hob said timidly.

Jim had time to note that a stunned look had come to Brian's face, and all of them stopped abruptly. Before the others could say a word, Jim undid that particular piece of his magic.

"Thank you, Hob," Jim said.

Silent by mutual unspoken agreement, they continued on.

To begin with, they only led the horses across an open meadow of long grass; but after a short way, they mounted and rode on across this open land, stretching away into the distance, and began to climb the lower heights they had seen at the horizon. In time, they came upon a track, or trail, which led them into a dirt road of wagon width, somewhat dusty, but with hoof and shoe marks of many passers-by.

As they rode it grew in width; and eventually the bare earth thinned to reveal an underlayer of blocks of white stone; and it was not long before they were completely out of the dust and dirt, walking the horses on the white stones of a Roman road.

"If I may pray forgiveness of you both," said Dafydd, "it were best I rode first while we are in this Land."

"Certes," said Brian, agreeing with a readiness that surprised Jim, until his next words explained it. "Are you not of rank in this country?"

"I am that," said Dafydd. "But I thank you for your courtesy, nonetheless." And with the words there came an undeniable change in his voice and manner.

He took the lead, and they went on. Soon they began to meet people going on foot the other way, ordinary-looking people by their clothes: artisans, farmers, and the like. These all spoke to them cheerfully, in a language that Jim was pretty sure was not Cornish, and might not even be Welsh, although it had some of the singing quality that Welsh had to the ear of an English-speaker.

Dafydd answered in the same tongue. He made no attempt to translate; and Jim assumed that it was merely wayside greetings being exchanged.

As they proceeded, however, the traffic increased, both coming toward them and catching up from behind and passing them—for they were only walking the horses at a leisurely pace. It was all foot traffic, all people who beamed and called out as they passed; and finally Dafydd was reduced merely to waving and saying a single word in answer.

It was about this time that Jim began to notice that in addition to the traffic on the road, people were coming to the road from the green areas on either side, as if from farms out of sight from the road.

He turned about in his saddle and looked behind him. Beyond Blanchard's rump, he saw more people coming to the roadway from all points of the compass.

Gradually, they were being surrounded. This crowd thickened, and moved with them, not on the road but parallel to it in the grass on either side; and all beaming. The greetings were scarcer now, but the people waved at Dafydd, who was now down to merely smiling back, so many were the signals from the crowd to him. Thick as the multitude became, however, it was careful to leave the full width of the roadway open to the three men and their horses.

But then there came a different rhythm to Blanchard's hooves on the stone roadway behind Jim, and Brian drew up level with him.

"What think you, James?" he said, in a low voice, leaning toward Jim, their conversation quite lost in the polite, low-voiced murmuring of the crowd and the noises of the horses' hooves against the stone. "Is there some matter here we should know about? Perhaps we should ask Dafydd. What think you?"

"I don't know, Brian," Jim said. "Let me think about it a few moments longer."

Brian waited. Jim looked closely at the people around them. They were all long-limbed like Dafydd, but otherwise had little in common, except that they were all suntanned, with the look of having spent years of their lives in active physical work.

They did not quite have the bony, hard-muscled, near-starved look of many who worked the land above the waves. These people looked instead as if they had never suffered from lack of either sleep or food; and they all had an extraordinarily merry look about them—as if they had found a happiness in simply being alive.

Now that they had stopped talking directly to Dafydd—perhaps out of a realization that he could not acknowledge everything said to him by so many— they were talking among themselves. The tones of their voices were joyous and laughter skipped back and forth—a delighted sort of laughter, however, not the kind of throaty explosion that enjoys a joke at someone's expense, only an acknowledgment of something worth enjoying and laughing about.

"I've no idea how they all heard about us so fast," Jim said in a low voice to Brian, "but clearly it's Dafydd they've all come to see. Why don't I ride forward and speak to him, and you come behind me? We can both avoid jostling him too closely, but let me do the talking."

"That is well thought of," said Brian. They moved their horses forward and Jim stopped about half a horse-length behind Dafydd and spoke to him from behind.

"Dafydd," he said, "can you tell us what's going on here?"

Dafydd answered without turning his head.

"It is that they are glad to see me, for what I am in this land, only that," he said. "I chose this road, hoping to avoid just this. But it has come about regardless."

"Should we take another road?" Jim asked.

"This should still cause no problem, look you," went on Dafydd. "This is the way that will take us most shortly to Lyonesse; and without coming to any of the old cities, which are important places where people of rank dwell. It will not matter that those of the farm and countryside come around me in this manner. We will keep moving, and soon be gone; and they will have perhaps a memory to talk about—but no more."

He paused, but did not point. "Do you see where the ground ahead rises and the road is cut through for some distance along the base of the mountains? From there on, there will not be room for large crowds on either hand. That cut will last for some miles, and these with us now will not follow. Then we will pass into a forest; and at its far end we will come to the border of Lyonesse."

"What do you want us to do, then?" Jim asked.

"Only to ride on as you are now," said Dafydd, now turning to look back at his companions for the first time. "Though I pray you favor me by staying back, that the people watching may be happier."

"Certainly," said Jim. Dafydd's face was strangely serious, his mouth a thin, straight line, his eyes looking at them with an unusual authority. Brian's own gaze sharpened. But Jim and Brian fell back without a word, and went on side by side.

"We might as well have each other for company, Brian," Jim murmured. "Chances are these people can't understand us anyway."

"There is that, James," said Brian.

Yet they rode in silence until they came to the cut, and the ground began to rise on either side of them.

There, in spite of Dafydd's prediction, the hillsides were still clustered with people, particularly on the less steep lower slopes. Meanwhile, in the open land they had left behind them, the people were dispersing; then were lost completely to sight as the hitherto ruler-straight road began to wind between the hills, and it was only possible to see for short distances ahead of them.

The sun still shone brightly, however. It and the good humor of the crowd seemed to have infected even the sumpter-horse, now following after Dafydd with its head-rope dragging forgotten on the ground—as if it would trail him like a loving dog, wherever he might choose to go.

The slopes grew steeper and less hospitable, their tops seeming closer; yet they remained crowded with standing, waving people. The road curved more and more frequently—and, without warning, around a curve ahead of them came four men, two abreast, on beautiful horses much lighter of bone than either Gorp or Blanchard.

The men seemed to be warriors of some old-fashioned kind, clad in armor of boiled leather, reinforced by plates of metal, and wearing antique helmets with only a nasal bar to cover an open face area. Each carried a spear, and swords hung at their sides. All their horses were white.

Just behind them came two more pairs of white horses, a team pulling at a trot an open carriage, like a barouche, with the driver's seat outside and facing seats within. Only one person sat in it: an old man, clean-shaven, erect in the middle of the backseat. The carriage itself was golden, glittering as if it had been covered with the precious metal itself. Behind it came, two by two, more mounted and armored spearmen.

Dafydd reined in his horse. It stopped, the sumpter-horse stopped; and both Jim and Brian reined in their own mounts. They sat waiting, until the leading riders came almost up to Dafydd before swinging out to take station on each side, facing inward to the road. The horses of the carriage pulled it right to Dafydd, who dismounted and walked slowly to the barouche, and spoke in the same tongue that Jim and Brian had been listening to for some time now.

"Perhaps," said Brian softly out of the corner of his mouth to Jim, while keeping his face straight forward, "this is somewhat in which we also should be concerned?"

"Maybe we ought to wait a few minutes," Jim was answering, in the same fashion, when Dafydd turned, looked at them, and waved them forward.

Brian swung out of his saddle, and Jim imitated him, getting down from Gorp. Both warhorses were used to standing ground-hitched, with their reins dangling in front of them, without moving; and both Brian and Jim left them without concern, going forward to join Dafydd at the carriage.

"You will be leaving with—" To Jim's astonishment, the old man in the carriage spoke in perfectly comprehensible English, except that his last word, or words, were Dafydd's ancient title, in their ancient tongue, "—I would wish you to hear this."

"My Lord King of this Land," said Dafydd, speaking to the old man, but also in English, "may I make known to you my Lord Sir James Eckert, Baron de Bois de Malencontri et Riveroak, and Sir Brian Neville-Smythe of Castle Smythe, both of the Saxon lands."

"I am pleased to lay eyes upon them," said the King to Dafydd; and turned back to Jim and Brian.

"Something of your names and deeds have sunk down to us even here in our special Kingdom," he went on. "From what I have heard, and from what Dafydd has said, you are good men and true. I would that you understand that, although no doubt you came here with no harm intended, your coming has created a problem; and I must speak with—" Once more, he pronounced the title that Dafydd held among these people. "I trust you to believe me when I say we bear you no ill-will, nor is there any ill-will toward he to whom I am now about to speak. Will you favor me, gentlemen, by waiting here, while the two of us discuss this privately?"

"Sire," said Brian, "I will be glad to."

"So will I," said Jim.

"Good."

Jim heard no order given, but a horseman behind the carriage leaped down and ran forward to open a door in its side. He took the arm of the older man as the latter pulled himself to his feet and came slowly down steps that had emerged from the side of the carriage. He kept his hold as the old King stepped unsteadily down to the earth.

Beside the road, for a short space the slope was gentle before rising more steeply to the hilltop. The hillside was now empty, clear of people to the point where the green crest of the hill was sharp against the cloudless, seemingly infinite, sky. On the gentle slope, Dafydd and the King walked off a little distance, and began to pace backward and forward in unheard conversation.

The old man stepped slowly and uncertainly; and occasionally, Dafydd's hand closed on his elbow to steady him. Clearly, the King had been a tall man once—possibly even a little taller than Dafydd—but age had stolen the stoutness of his bones and bent him, to the point where he seemed half-a-head shorter than the younger man. Nonetheless, it was clear which one was the King, as the two walked together.

Brian and Jim stood and waited, as did the horses, the armored riders, and the people on the other hillsides; and a hush was over everything, in which it was barely possible to hear that Dafydd and the King were speaking, like the murmuring of a running stream, around a corner and just out of sight.

As he and Brian stood, watching and waiting, a movement above caught Jim's attention. He lifted his gaze to the crest of the open slope, where a man had appeared and was now outlined against the sky—a man as tall as Dafydd and also with a bow-stave slung over his shoulder. He was dressed in a cap, jacket, and hose, all of a light blue. He stood motionless, merely looking down at the two walking below; but at the same moment some twenty or so of the mounted spearmen galloped from behind the carriage to form a semicircle about the space where the King and Dafydd had walked, facing up against the slope.

The man in light blue made no move, but after a moment he was joined, a little to his left, by another bow-carrying figure—and, one by one, more and more figures identically dressed and armed appeared along the crest of the hill.

The spearmen on horseback waited without moving. The archers in blue on the crest of the hill waited, looking down. Dafydd, with the aged King, continued a slow walk back and forth, and their talk.

Chapter 20

The two of them—King and Bowman-Prince—continued to talk. Brian and Jim waited. The guard of the King's spearmen waited. The archers on the hill waited. In the farther distance waited the people who had flocked from so far around to be close to Dafydd.

Now there came moments when the King began to walk with a longer stride, like one used to covering long distances on foot, vigorously and in his full strength. But then his step would falter again; and once more Jim would see Dafydd's hand steadying the older man.

Finally, they stopped. They stood talking in place a moment longer before Dafydd turned to beckon Jim and Brian.

They two had returned to their horses—Brian, with a warrior's instinct, had remounted when the spearmen moved out, and Jim had followed without thinking much about it. Now they dismounted once more and walked to Dafydd and the King. Close up, the King's face was grey with tiredness. But it was he who spoke, however, and his voice was still firm, if low-pitched, as if to keep the conversation private even from his guards.

"Dafydd tells me," he said, "the three of you are only passing through our

Land to the border of Lyonesse; you, Sir James, hoping there to find your lost ward."

"That's right," answered Jim.

"I have delayed you in your search this long," said the King, in a voice that began to have a hoarseness in it, "to entreat"—again came Dafydd's title—"not go on with you, but stay with us, here on the earth that has been that of his elder family since time immemorial. But he says he cannot, that he must go on with you." He paused to cough lightly.

"I would ordinarily entreat you also, my Lord James Eckert," he went on, "to free him from any duty he has to accompany you, so that he could stay—except that I understand that there is something more than duty here involved. Therefore, I will importune him no more, but stand aside to let you all pass, wishing that God may be with you once you have crossed into Lyonesse."

The last words came out noticeably ragged with emotion.

"I'm sorry—" Jim began—but saw Dafydd, standing back a little from the King, shaking his head. "But certainly Sir Brian and I must go on, and Dafydd must come with us if that's his choice. You speak as if our going into Lyonesse were something with a good deal of danger in it."

"Whether you will find your ward there, I do not know," said the King. "It is a land of old Magicks, and some that may not be magick. The strangest of all the Other Kingdoms. Whether it is an old land of Faery—as some say—or not, I do not know. But I do know there are perils, other than weapons and foes."

He stopped for a moment, as if catching his breath.

"We do not cross that border. It is forbidden; and the few who have defied that rule have either never come back, or come back only briefly—changed or under strange circumstance. There was one man who entered Lyonesse. Since then he has returned only once every hundred years to his family. Each time it is only for moments. He does not seem to know or be able to speak to his descendants; and each time, his clothing is more ragged, his beard is longer and more wild, and he himself looks more like a soul in pain. Then he vanishes again. I would warn you what to guard against if I knew what might be there. But I know not."

"I appreciate your thinking of warning us, though," said Jim. "All the more since you'd like Dafydd to stay with you and be safe from whatever happened to that other man you just told us about. But in any case, I have to go on—"

"And I!" interrupted Brian.

"—And," said Jim, "I, of course."

"Then," said the King, "there is no more to say. In my heart I knew it. I ask you only one thing as gentlemen—for that you are such I know by the fact that Dafydd is with you—if you return safely, do not speak of our Land anywhere, even to those of the Wales of which we used to be part. I ask that if any ask you questions, you do not answer them. Will you do that much for me?"

Both Jim and Brian murmured agreement.

"Then," said the King, turning toward his carriage, "I will leave you now—"

He shook off Dafydd's light grip on his arm. "I will go by myself, unaided. Dafydd, the people of your household will want a last touch of you—that, at least."

"I had intended they should have it," said Dafydd.

The King nodded, turned, and with his long if uncertain stride, went the short distance back to his carriage. He was helped in, said something in his own language, and the carriage turned; his spearmen surrounded him, and they all began to move away, back down the road they had come.

Meanwhile, Dafydd had turned to face the blue-coated bowmen. Beginning with those closest to him, one at a time they came off the crest and down the slope to him, each a little distance after the one before, almost in a line.

"Sir James, Sir Brian," said Dafydd, without turning to look at them, "you will favor me, if you go back to your horses."

"Certainly, Dafydd," said Jim.

He and Brian remounted and sat watching. They were still only twenty yards from Dafydd; and as they watched the sky-blue-clad bowmen came to Dafydd, one by one.

Each, as he approached, took off his small cloth hat when he was about three paces from Dafydd, took the last few steps, and knelt on one knee, with his head bowed. Dafydd reached out with his left hand, closing it on each right shoulder, and pressed gently. No words were said. Dafydd let go, the bowman stood up, put the cloth cap back on, took a step back, turned, and went—and another came.

One by one they came. Jim had not thought to count when they first started, but when he did, he stopped at a little over a hundred. There were only a few more blue-clad figures yet to come by that time, and then Dafydd would be alone once more. Those who had knelt before him had gone back over the crest and vanished. The thought reminded Jim of the crowds that had walked with them earlier, but withdrawn when the King's troop approached. He looked. They, also, were gone now.

As Jim turned back, the last archer put his cap on, turned, and left. As he vanished over the crest, Dafydd came back to Jim and Brian, mounting without a word but with a set face.

"Let us on!" said Brian.

Above them the improbable sun, that should not shine under hundreds of fathoms of seawater, was lowering toward the west.

They lifted their reins and moved together up the road, Jim and Brian moving forward to ride one on each side of Dafydd. He himself was sitting his horse like a man in deep thought, his eyes unfocused on the road ahead.

The silence was complete. Jim found some obstinate twentieth-century part of him rebelling against the King's almost unnatural horror of Lyonesse. He knew magic existed in this world—who better? But none of it cold be so terrible as to be beyond explanation—

"Thank you, Sir Brian, Sir James," Dafydd unexpectedly said.

"Hah!" said Brian—that convenient, one-syllable sound for dealing with moments of high emotion or tension.

"No need for thanks, Dafydd," said Jim.

Dafydd became silent again, and they rode along with no further words until they had rounded the next curve in the road. Then, unexpectedly, Dafydd spoke again.

"It is only right," he said, "that you should know what the King said to me, now that you have promised not to speak to anyone else of what you have seen and heard here."

"Not necessary, dammit!" said Brian.

"Nonetheless, it would please me to tell you. You do not mind hearing?"

"Of course not," said Jim.

"The way of it is," said Dafydd, looking down at his horse's ears, "that he mentioned many things to do with my ancient lineage here, and those of my blood who still exist—as you saw. But there was more than that. He is this land's King, of a direct line of the Kingship as long as folk can remember. But that line has dwindled—"

Without warning, it was as if they passed through an invisible, impalpable wall. Nothing around them seemed changed. The sun shone as bright as ever from the same sky. But—

"We approach our border with Lyonesse," said Dafydd, with no change in his voice. "To continue. His line dwindled with his children. His three sons all died, two before they were yet men; and his two daughters sickened of an illness that no one in the land could understand, and died also, less than a dozen winters ago. No grandchild was born.

"He is an old man; and he sees this Land, which we both love, he and I, left Kingless. My family is closest to the throne. I am its head—insofar as it has a head, since I live not here, but elsewhere. So he wished me to stay, bringing my wife and children here, and to take up the duties of King after he was gone."

Neither Brian nor Jim said anything. There was nothing to say.

"I told him," said Dafydd, looking straight ahead at the white road that now ran into a crowded forest of dark trees, whose leafless branches, tangled together, coated both slopes so thickly that the earth beneath was lost to sight in deep shadow within a few steps.

"I said to him that while I felt the pull of a duty here, I felt the pull of a stronger one elsewhere. My life is not in this Land; it is above, in the world we know, with my wife and children, as Dafydd the Master Bowman, not Dafydd the King. For me, being a Master Bowman is more than being King, and I would not want to bring up my sons and my daughters in this lost and drowned land, but in the world where life and history go forward."

The road narrowed, and the branches of trees on either side began to meet above.

"A man must choose," said Brian, after a while. "That is the way God ordained life to be for us. There can be no hesitation in such choosing."

They rode into the full shadow of the forest; and while there was nothing fearful or strange about that shadow, yet in some way it seemed to come between them. So that they each rode on, isolated, talking no more and, in Jim's case, deeply immersed in thought.

The stone road they had been following had some time back given way to a smaller road of white dust, which had narrowed from there to the width of a simple path, so that they had come to ride separately. Brian had moved to the front at that point, without discussion; Jim came next, and Dafydd third, with the sumpter-horse.

Their road dwindled further, to the point where it was scarcely more than a trail that faded out from time to time, so that they had to remain alert as they went—although the horses seemed perfectly confident that they were traveling straight ahead, as if on a familiar road, and Brian also did not seem to feel any doubt about how they were going.

The black, sparsely leaved trees, meanwhile, had closed in around them, almost as if they would like to reach down and hold anyone passing. Silver light filtered through the intertwined branches and illuminated their way dimly, but well enough, as their eyes adjusted, that they had no trouble seeing where they went.

Jim's mind was occupied by the last words Dafydd had spoken about his decision not to be a King—and Brian's immediate agreement with them. When he and Angie had decided to stay here in the fourteenth century rather than return to their own native twentieth century, Jim had never thought he could have any serious difficulty handling whatever problems might come up: if he did not know how to deal with one to start with, he could easily learn how—after all, learning had been his life from his earliest childhood.

But lately, there had come this problem of the changed attitude of the Malencontri servants. It was a problem that involved all sorts of things that the people of this time took for granted—one of the strongest being that the way things always had been, so they must go on being forever.

"It stands not different in the memory of man!" his tenants would quote to him, when he wanted them to try a new way of doing anything at all. Theirs was the way they had done it all their lives.

It was an argument against which nothing he could say had any force. Any change, to them, would be turning the world upside-down.

It was, he thought now, simply Reality slapping him in the face for not paying proper attention. Only when he recognized how greatly he had to adjust to be at home in this earlier culture, had he finally realized how badly suited he was for life in this era.

It was probably not surprising that it had taken him this long to figure it out: he had never been a person given to self-doubt. In his own way, he was almost as brash as Brian, who never seemed to have a doubt in the world.

Needing to raise money to pay the bride-price demanded by Geronde's father, Brian had cheerfully joined what amounted to an insurrection against his King—in spite of his feeling of utter and complete loyalty to that King. How he had justified it to himself Jim still did not understand; but undoubtedly, knowing Brian, the conscience that had to deal with it was at rest.

Now, for the first time, Jim had begun to feel doubt creeping out into other areas. Perhaps he was not up to this business of trying to find and rescue young Robert—

Suddenly they emerged from the trees into a clearing. The sparse grass under the feet of their horses ended abruptly in a line at which another type of landscape started—a stony, forbidding landscape, though thick with stunted trees. A silver light coldly flooded all he looked upon; and something like a white sun was barely visible above the trees.

But it was not just this that had jolted him so suddenly from his self-examination. It was a voice, calling out to them.

"Stop!" cried the voice—and it belonged to Carolinus.

Chapter 21

What struck Jim immediately was that Carolinus looked as if he had been in a fight with a bear. His red robe was ragged and stained along the bottom edge. His face looked gaunt and weary, as if he had gone without sleep. But his voice was as strong as ever.

He was, however, still only a projection rather than a living three-dimensional actual Carolinus. Jim, Brian, and Dafydd had all automatically reined in their horses at his first word. Now, they stared at him, seemingly standing about half a foot off the ground, and perhaps ten feet in front of them. His eyes did not so much look at them as past them, as if he could not see them.

"Before you enter Lyonesse, you must hear a warning." His voice rang oddly—formal and oracular. "Note well that you are about to enter a black-and-silver Land, where none but those colors exist. Keep always alert that what is around you remains black-and-silver. Little by little, it may seem to fade toward the colors of an ordinary world. But before the black-and-silver is gone completely, be you gone yourselves! If you wait until you see no more black-and-silver, but all seems as if it were seen in honest sunlight, you have already been captured. You can never go home to stay. You will have to remain in Lyonesse forever. Now, I must—"

"Still!" shouted Jim, pointing his finger at the red-robed magician. It was a forlorn hope, almost a desperate reflex action, to keep Carolinus from disappearing again; as Jim had suddenly felt sure he would, once he stopped speaking. It produced an odd result.

The projection broke off at the last word spoken before Jim interrupted it; and suddenly Carolinus was starting again from the beginning, repeating the same words.

"Stop! Before you enter Lyonesse . . ."

The image of Carolinus continued, to the point where Jim had stopped it; and wound up suddenly in the magician's ordinary, testy tone and everyday speech pattern ". . . must go because I have only a moment to talk to you. But let me say one more thing. Lyonesse is a Land of Magick, old, old Magick. Do not trust what you see. A dwarf may be a giant, a hovel may be a castle, or a castle a hovel. A maiden in distress may be indeed a maiden in distress— but also might be a deadly foe. Where you see one knight, there may be twenty. I must leave now. Fare—"

There was a bright flash of red, even as Jim quickly repeated his earlier command; but this time it had no effect—Carolinus winked out like a suddenly snuffed candle.

Jim looked at Brian and Dafydd on their horses beside him, suddenly feeling guilty. He was the only one who had a real duty to cross this border, and it might be that he should go on alone. Just in time he checked himself from suggesting it, realizing that instead of welcoming the proposal, they would be offended by his making it.

He was learning, he thought grimly to himself. Perversely, that realization made him feel better.

"What think you, James," said Brian. "Is there any lesson we should take from this, before we go forward?"

"Well," said Jim, "it's clear that we should be careful." He paused to think for a moment, then went on: "It also seems that it would be dangerous to prolong our stay in this Lyonesse place; so we should try to move through it as fast as is possible."

His friends nodded solemnly; naturally, they would look to him for decision, where things magical were concerned. "In fact," he said, looking up at the sky, "it seems to me that the evening is coming upon us. If we proceed into Lyonesse, we'll soon have to make camp for the night—don't you think it might be better if we go back a little way, to stop overnight? Then we can enter Lyonesse with a full day to move through it."

They rode back beyond the dark forest to make their camp; but they found no water and so made a dry camp in a fold between two bare hillsides. They talked little, and in the morning Jim wondered if Brian and Dafydd had slept as badly as he.

As they mounted once more, Jim looked at his friends somberly. "I'll keep my eye out to protect us from anything like Carolinus mentioned, any deception of magic. But it'd be best if we all watched for the change in the color, as Carolinus said."

"Amen," said Brian; and Jim thought he heard Dafydd echo him, but in a much lower tone.

They lifted the reins and rode forward, Jim wincing internally as he did so. The other two had utter faith in his ability to make decisions in this area, and he now found it bothered him greatly. This was something new; a part of his new sensitivity to the way people around him reacted. He had not been made uncomfortable by their complete belief in him before.

Maybe, in this case, it was also that, so recently, Brian had demonstrated his ability to make a hard decision swiftly and surely—and stick with it. And Dafydd had, only a short distance from here, also faced a like hard decision; and been firm and immediate in rejecting what was offered to him.

It was not just that these two seemed decisive where he was not. Everyone in this medieval world seemed to show that ability. Their decisions might end up being wrong, but they were made without hesitation and were stuck to. These people did not wander around in their own heads as he seemed to do, worrying about finding the right answer.

Lost in his own thoughts, Jim came to himself to realize that they had again reached the spot where the projection of Carolinus had appeared; but nothing happened this time. They moved on into Lyonesse.

Silence surrounded them in this wood—no sound of birds singing, no leaves rustling, not even the soft breathing of a breeze among the branches and tree trunks. But he began to be aware of a sound, irritating to him in the stillness, like the buzzing of a particularly annoying insect. It began to resolve into a voice talking some distance off, insistently and even pompously.

He roused himself enough to make out what the voice was actually saying. It was Hob's voice.

"—And I said to him," the hobgoblin's voice was announcing, " 'Varlet,' I said to him, 'I am Hob-One de Malencontri, and you . . .' "

Jim tried to close his mind to the words, but now that he had tracked the sound to its lair, he found himself paying attention to it, whether he wanted to or not. Hob, of course, was boasting about his experiences at the Earl of Somerset's Castle last Christmas, and how he had lorded it over that Castle's

Hob, who only had for name the simple three-letter one by which all hob-goblins were called.

Happily, since Hill either could not talk, or talked by some strange mode that Jim could not perceive, there was only one voice for Jim to endure. It ought to be possible to shut it out by picking something that would keep his mind off it.

But then an inspiration occurred to him. The question of how Hob and, earlier, Rrrnlf, had talked back and forth with Hill, and how Hill could talk to them, was a puzzle that had to have a solution. So far, in this world of magic, he had found nothing so mysterious that it did not have some kind of a rational solution.

Was it possible that Hill was sending some kind of signals in a way other than with his voice, and both Rrrnlf and Hob were reading those signals without realizing they were doing anything unusual?

It was certainly a possibility, but no sooner had he thought of this than objections began to occur to him. Certainly Hob, if not Rrrnlf, would have realized by this time that Jim was not picking up the signals, and tell him about the different way Hill "talked."

But what if what Hill did sounded to them just like ordinary speech? Jim remembered hearing once that some people suspected that whales could communicate with each other over long distances, by making sounds in—what was it again?—the subsonic range?—the supersonic? In fact—Jim tried to remember—had not dolphins actually been found to "talk" up into the super-sonic range among themselves?

It was a real possibility, he decided, his spirits suddenly perking up over the chance of it being true. Now if there were just some way to check on it—

"M'Lord! M'Lord!"

It was Hob calling him directly, now. Jim lifted his reins to check Gorp and waited for first Dafydd, then the sumpter-horse, to draw level with him. Both Hob and Hill were completely out from under the cover on the horse's back, Hill sitting there staring at him.

"What is it, Hob?" Jim asked.

"M'Lord!" said Hob. "It's important! Hill has something he has to tell you!"

"Well, what's he saying—" Jim broke off suddenly as his thoughts of a moment before returned to him. He turned to speak to Dafydd. "Dafydd," he said, "leave the sumpter-horse with me, would you? Ride up and tell Brian that I want to stop to talk for a moment with Hill, so Brian doesn't get too far ahead of us and we lose him."

"Certainly, James," said Dafydd, untying the lead-rope of the sumpter-horse from his saddle and passing it to Jim. He rode forward to Brian. But Brian, able to hear clearly in the stillness what had been said, had already halted Blanchard and turned in his saddle. Dafydd joined him, and the two of them sat on their horses, watching and listening.

Jim turned in his saddle again to face the two Naturals.

They had halted in a setting that was suddenly, completely Lyonesse as Carolinus had described it. All at once, the land might have been forever moonlit. The light was as adequate as it might have been on a clouded day; but the shadows of the trees, the rocks—their own shadows—were impenetrably black, and where the light fell on rock or tree or ground, what it illuminated seemed silvery-white. Even the upper surfaces of the leaves, on the few trees that caught the light, were bright silver.

Ignoring all this, Jim turned to the two on the sumpter-horse.

"Hill," he said to the small man, "I want you to listen to me carefully and do what I ask. Hob, he can understand me all right, can't he, when I speak to him?"

"Oh, yes, m'Lord," said Hob. "*He* can understand you perfectly."

The emphasis on the word "he" had to be entirely unconscious on Hob's part. But it was still an uncomfortable thing for Jim to hear. He pushed the feeling from his mind.

"Now, Hill," he said again, finding it a little hard to keep his tone of authority in the face of that open, childlike stare, "what I want you to do is, first, to tell me what you have to tell me. Then stop, wait a little bit; and then when I signal you to talk, tell me again. I may have to ask you to tell it three or even four times. Possibly even more. Do you understand?"

"He doesn't understand," said Hob promptly. "He thinks you're very strange. But, since it's you, he doesn't mind. He'll do just as you say."

"Good. I want you to listen very closely and do exactly as I tell you," Jim went on, looking directly at Hill. "I'm going to ask you to repeat the words you say over and over again, while I try listening to them in different ways. You may not understand what I mean by that, but if you'll just stop talking when I lift my hand, and not start over again until I put it down, then stop again if I lift it, we'll be all right. Do you understand that?"

"He says he understands," said Hob.

"Thank you, Hob," said Jim. "But from now on, don't say anything, just let me listen and see if I can hear him talking for myself."

It was a matter of finding something he could visualize to focus the magical energy he could call on. He thought of the hearing of a bat—it seemed to him he remembered that bats could hear into the supersonic. He half-closed his eyes and imagined the auditory capability of the bat somehow added to his own hearing, his ears lifting into pointed bat-ears that could move and focus. . . .

"Go ahead, then, Hill," he said, "tell me what you have to tell me."

Hill stared at him—and nothing happened.

For a moment Jim was convinced Hill had either not understood him, or was simply not responding. Then he was sure Hill was doing his own form of talking, and he was still not hearing it.

Jim raised his hand and thought again. What had he been thinking of earlier? Oh, yes, dolphins and whales—both were possible candidates for supersonic hearing.

He looked at Hill and lowered his hand.

This time he thought he might have heard something—but then, it could well have been his own imagination; he had felt it rather than heard it. He was on the verge of giving up, when a plain old ordinary commonsense possibility plunked itself down in the forefront of his mind without even being asked.

What was wrong with him? He had completely forgotten he was in Lyonesse, where his magic might not be able to work. He thought for a moment, looking for a simple test; then he thought of his wedding ring, which did not fit him well and so was left behind at Malencontri. He tried to summon it to him.

Nothing happened. His magic was not available here.

So much for using it to give himself more-than-human hearing . . . wait a minute!

Dragons, he knew, could hear better than humans, and well into at least the subsonic range—he himself, as a dragon, had once been able to fly at night by picking up a sort of sonar-like image of the dark land below him, as he bellowed with his tremendous dragon voice.

—And his ability to change to his dragon body, or to parts of it, was not subject to the rules of ordinary magic. It was built into him, like the simple magic some Naturals had—something they could turn on, or off, but not otherwise control. He had before given his human body the hawk-like telescopic vision of his dragon-shape. Dragon-hearing should be just as available to him.

He made the change, and suddenly heard Hill in the middle of a sentence— Jim had forgotten to move his hand.

". . . 'ee should go that way, I keep telling 'ee!" Hill was saying with absolute, bell-like clarity. Hill's accent, Jim noticed, was not too far different from the accents of the local people in the Shire of Somerset.

"—I keep telling 'ee that!" Hill went on.

"I hear you, Hill!" said Jim. "But which way is 'that way'?"

Hill raised one of his strange long arms, completely covered by its even-longer sleeve. He was pointing with it.

"Off to our left is where 'ee should go."

"Why?" said Brian, quick to pick up what was going on. "Ask him why that way?"

"Why, Hill?" asked Jim.

" 'ee must!" said Hill stubbornly.

Jim looked where the arm pointed. It angled upward over the nearer tree-tops, pointing at something in the distance that might be a rocky pile, or the beginning of something farther off, like a mountain range on the horizon.

It was in the opposite direction from the round silver disk, enormous in size, that was shedding light over them.

"Can we trust him?" said Brian, frowning. "Carolinus said that this was a Land of magick and deception, and nothing could be trusted."

"Well, Hill, like us, came in here from outside," said Jim, turning back to look at the small man. To his surprise, tears were stealing down Hill's cheeks.

" 'ee must!" said Hill again.

"Can we trust him?" said Brian sharply again. Jim looked at Brian and Dafydd, sitting their horses only a few feet away now. Both had interpreted the pointing arm.

"I think so," said Jim, touched in spite of himself by the emotion behind Hill's words. "After all, he's only with us by chance, more than anything else; and he didn't know we were coming here."

He paused to think. "Besides," he said, as it occurred to him, "we don't know where we're going, anyway. So any direction's as good as another. We can keep a sharp lookout; and if it turns out to be dangerous, we can turn back. Also, then we'll know whether to trust Hill or not."

Conscious that Hill would have overheard the last words, and they might have hurt his feelings, Jim turned back to the small man.

"Actually, I believe I trust him now," he said.

Hill blinked, but there were no more tears.

"Do you know where we are?" Jim asked him.

"Nay," said Hill, shaking his head.

"You must say m'Lord when you speak to my Lord!" said Hob to him, sharply. "Always say m'Lord when you speak to him!"

"Quite right!" said Brian; and even Dafydd gave a slight nod in agreement. Hill said nothing.

"Let me hear you say m'Lord to him!" insisted Hob.

"Nay," said Hill, in Jim's head. Dafydd and Brian, who of course had not heard Hill, waited expectantly.

"Why won't you say it?" cried Hob.

" 'ee's not *my* Lord!" said Hill. The tears were beginning to start again.

It was ridiculous, Jim thought, but he found himself unreasonably moved by the sight of the small man's crying. It was like seeing a very young child cry because it was completely helpless to do anything else about a situation it was in. "What he calls me doesn't matter. Anyway, let's try the way he suggests for a while."

Brian looked shocked.

"In that case," he said stiffly, "I shall certainly continue to ride ahead. Keep me in sight at all times; and, if by chance you do lose sight of me, call me back at once. I must not go beyond voice-shout."

They started off again in the new direction, with Brian leading and Jim now riding at the back of the group, next to the sumpter-horse, trying to get Hill to talk to him some more.

Hill had evidently said all he had to say for the moment. In the end Jim gave up, let the sumpter-horse fall behind, and—since there was more space between the trees, here—rode ahead to be saddle-and-saddle with Dafydd as they went on over the stony ground, which was sparsely thatched with what should have been green. Ahead, the rising ramparts of dark stone now seemed much closer than they had before, as the great silver orb mounted in the sky, seeming to shrink in size as it did.

The time spent trying to get Hill to talk some more had not been completely lost, however, Jim decided. He was beginning to notice small things. For example, the " 'ee" that he heard from Hill did not stand indiscriminately for "you," "him," or "we." There were little differences of what would have been intonation—if Hill had been talking aloud—that made one " 'ee" into "thee," and, said in a couple of other different ways, could be either "ye," or "we."

The rise toward which they were headed, when glimpsed through the trees, was turning out not to be as distant as it had seemed. It had grown very much taller in the short time they had been riding toward it—although the tricky light of this black-and-silver land still made it difficult to say how far away it was.

They had moved into an area that seemed to be older forest. The trees were almost as large, if not as leafy as they were used to seeing back in their old, familiar forests on the surface of the earth under ordinary sunlight; interspersed with them were little glades or open spaces. After close to an hour, Brian unexpectedly halted, lifting his hand to signal them to do likewise

Jim, Dafydd, and the sumpter-horse—the last always alert for a chance to stop working—stopped immediately. Brian sat where he was on a motionless Blanchard, looking out through the trees before him into a clearing; after a moment he turned and walked Blanchard quietly back to them.

"There is a knight up ahead in that open space," he said in a low voice, when he came level with them.

"What makes you sure it's a knight?" Jim asked.

"It can hardly be anyone else," said Brian. "He has the belt, the sword, the spear upright in its socket, and he is in full, if somewhat old-fashioned, armor. Moreover, he sits his mount in knightly fashion; though his saddle is antique and a little strange. Its pommel and cantle are much less than a jouster would wish to have before and behind him at the moment of encounter."

"What's he doing there, did you notice?" asked Jim.

"He seems to be merely sitting his horse, deep in thought," said Brian. "Perhaps he is a traveler, pondering which way to take, even as we have been at times. Or perhaps he is trying to remember something he has forgotten to do, and may need to return home for."

"But there's only one of him?"

"That's right, James," said Brian. "He is alone. Except for his horse—which in this light I cannot be sure of. It appears black, but it may indeed be a dark brown, or some such. At any rate, it is a destrier, heavy and suitable for a man who is equipped for spear-running."

"Well, I think we ought to ahead and meet him," said Jim. "Don't you think the same thing, Brian? How about you, Dafydd?"

"I am no knight," said Dafydd, "and have no opinion."

"I think by all means we should go forward and speak to him," said Brian. "Such a chance is not to be missed. Perhaps he can put us more surely upon our path; or even give us some news that may raise your heart about your ward."

"You're right," said Jim.

Brian turned Blanchard about, and the three of them rode forward side by side. The sumpter-horse shrugged and followed, as its head-rope jerked at its halter, and all together they made their ways up and into the clearing.

Chapter 22

The knight was apparently so deep in thought that he did not look up and turn his head in their direction until they were well out into the clearing. Once he did, however, he immediately reined his horse about to face them.

The visor of his helm was up; and the face it revealed, possibly because of a few spots where the "sunlight" did not touch it—utterly black shadows about his eyes and on either side of his nose—gave him a grim, angry look.

Brian reined his horse to a stop, and the others stopped with him.

"Fair sir!" called Brian—there was still a good twenty feet of distance between them and the solitary knight—"We pray pardon for intruding upon your solitude this way. But perhaps you would be kind enough to set some travelers on their proper path?"

The fierce-looking face of the solitary knight broke into a large smile. He lifted his reins and trotted forward toward them.

"Certainly! Certainly!" he said, pulling up before them. "Be glad to. Damned lonely out here in all sorts of weather all the time. But have to do it, you know. The Ancestor's about, but you can never tell where he'll show up; so someone has to ride the woods, and since I'm head of the family, there's no choice to it. Give you any aid I can!"

"That is a great kindness in you, Sir," said Brian. "May I name to you the Baron Sir James Eckert de Bois de Malencontri. I am Sir Brian Neville-Smythe, of a cadet branch of the Nevilles. And this is our Companion, Master Bowman Dafydd ap Hywel."

"I am honored. You could not have come at a better moment. I was weary of riding about by myself. I am Sir Dinedan."

"Sir Dinedan?" Brian's voice cracked in a way Jim had never heard before, as he repeated the name. "This meeting is great honor to us, Sir Dinedan. You are most gentle to speak so freely and so friendly to us, who—though we both are knights—are not such as someone like yourself might have heard of."

"Why, that is true," said Sir Dinedan, "but I would hardly have thought it otherwise. You are clearly not Cornish knights, as I see by your armor and weapons. Also, never have I seen such a magnificent warhorse as the one you ride."

"I am once more honored," said Brian. "My steed's name is Blanchard of Tours, fair Sir. In a sense, you might say he was my father's gift to me on his deathbed, for it cost nearly all of my patrimony to buy him."

"I can well believe it," said Sir Dinedan. "But you said that you needed, perhaps, aid from me to set you on your proper way through these woods? I would be failing in my duty to my Ancestor if I did not assist two such courteous knights. Whither are you bound?"

"As for that," said Brian, "we do not know exactly. We search for the lost ward of Sir James, here, a mere babe who was stolen but recently—we believe, by some of the Faery ilk—and we seek to recover him."

Sir Dinedan gave a low whistle.

"That is no small task," he said. "It is not that the faeries do not abound, but finding them is something else again. You may have a long journey still before you. And there is little I can tell you, as far as the way you should take. If the Ancestor were here, or if you meet him on your way through these woods, he might be more help to you, being closer to such creatures than I am, since I am still alive. And perhaps if I ride along with you some small way, it will increase the chances of your meeting him, since I encounter him more than anyone else, being of the family."

"Indeed, that is very gentle of you!" said Brian. His voice quavered a little bit, and Jim looked at him in curiosity.

"In that case," Brian went on, "if we are to bear company, perhaps you would vouchsafe me the greatest possible favor a man could ask of someone like yourself. While I have had some small success in spear-runnings with other knights in the country from which I come, it is exceeding bold of me to ask. But it would forever be a golden memory for me, should I live, to remember that I had once encountered with a knight of King Arthur's Round Table. Would you consider breaking just a single spear with me?"

Sir Dinedan stared at him for a moment.

"I fear, Sir," he said at last, "you are confusing me with the Ancestor. It is true I am Sir Dinedan, but I am Sir Dinedan-of-now. It is the Ancestor who was of that great fellowship of the Table Round. But many generations have passed since then, and the name has remained in the family. I would that you not consider a spear-running with me to have value it does not."

"You are not the Sir Dinedan who rode with Sir Tristram against the thirty knights of Queen Morgan le Fay, to rescue Sir Lancelot du Lac from them?"

"I am not," said Sir Dinedan. "As I say, that was my Ancestor, and—by the by—that story has been much distorted by later generations, who have falsely given much of the praise of the encounter to Sir Tristram."

Brian opened his mouth, then closed it again.

"Yes," answered Sir Dinedan-of-now. "He, as you know, was also of the Table Round, and a valiant knight. Nevertheless, when word came that thirty knights lay in wait for Sir Lancelot, it was the Ancestor, instead of Sir Tristram, who immediately said that they two must assault and defeat those thirty knights, to save Lancelot. It was Sir Tristram who demurred, saying that adventuring against thirty other knights at once was too much; and that his cousin Sir Lancelot had gotten him into fights like that before, and he had determined never to be drawn into one again."

It seemed to Jim that this was coming out very patly, as if it had been told many times. But he said nothing as Sir Dinedan continued.

"Whereupon the Ancestor shamed him, by saying that if he would fight but one knight, the Ancestor would fight the other twenty-nine. Whereupon, Sir Tristram agreed, they went and battled the thirty, and indeed Sir Tristram, gaining courage, killed ten of the knights himself, after all. But it was my Ancestor that killed twenty, thus saving Sir Lancelot. I tell you this that you may not be misled by the tales others tell, who have it the wrong way around."

"Er-hem!" said Brian, clearing his throat with an embarrassed air; and making Jim quite certain that Brian was one who had heard the story the other way around. In fact, thought Jim, if he remembered anything about Malory's *Morte Darthur*, it *had* been the other way around, and it was the present Sir Dinedan who was giving a distorted version. For one thing, if Jim remembered correctly, it was Sir Dinedan who was Lancelot's cousin, not Sir Tristram.

However, that seemed to be somewhat beside the point. Sir Dinedan was already agreeing to break a lance with Brian, if a spear-running with a mere descendant of the original Sir Dinedan would please him; and Brian was eagerly taking him up on it. Jim thought about whether he ought to object to the project, on the grounds of Brian's recent wound; but he could think of no way to do so that was not certain to seriously offend his friend.

"I fear me the only spear I have with me is at my saddle," said Brian, "and it is sharpened, of course, as is usual for a knight in a strange land."

"Why, what else could we ride with but sharpened spears?" said Sir Dinedan, his shadow-darkened eyebrows rising in surprise. "Is it that you have broken spears with people, when the points were not sharp?"

"Oh, in sport, in play, you understand," said Brian airily, but to Jim's ear with another touch of embarrassment. "No, no, sharp they should be by all means. Do you have a choice as to the end of the clearing from which you would begin to ride—"

This commenced a small discussion as to the particulars of the meeting; but these were soon settled. Jim was drafted into the job of giving the signal. He sat Gorp halfway between them, raised his arm, and then dropped it again. The two knights hurtled together as Jim hastily backed Gorp away from their meeting-point.

The crash of their meeting sounded enormously loud in the silence of the black-and-silver wood; and the results were almost as spectacular. Sir Dinedan's spear glanced off Brian's shield, cunningly tilted at the last moment to produce exactly that effect, while Brian's spear hit Sir Dinedan's shield dead center and bore down not only the knight, but the horse he was riding.

The horse pulled himself from under the legs of the fallen knight and got to his feet, then shook himself vigorously. Brian had reined up, ridden back, and was staring at Sir Dinedan; who, however, remained motionless upon the ground.

"God have mercy!" cried Brian, leaping down. "Have I killed the good knight?" He knelt beside Sir Dinedan and lifted his visor. Sir Dinedan's eyes were tight shut.

"Sir Dinedan—?" said Brian.

"I am not quite dead," said Sir Dinedan, faintly. "Perhaps I may even live. A cup of wine from the flask at my saddle-bow . . ."

Brian leaped to his feet and caught the reins of Sir Dinedan's horse, soothing it with his voice as it started to react defensively; and plucked the flask from where it hung at the pommel of the saddle. He brought it back, pulled its stopper out, and gently lifted Sir Dinedan's head. He tilted the flask to the knight's lips, and the other took several swallows before Brian took the flask away

"More," said Sir Dinedan, opening one eye. Brian gave him more. "Aah, that revives me."

He opened the other eye.

"It may be I shall live after all. Nonetheless, Sir Brian, may I give you honor and joy of your victory over even such a feeble knight as myself."

"Why do you speak of yourself as feeble?" said Brian. "You are a lusty knight."

"Ah, but if it were only so—a trifle more wine, if you please—I give you thanks." Sir Dinedan opened his other eye. "But, it is not so. There has been a terrible weakness in our family handed down through the generations; so that, without warning, at times we become feeble all over; and it happened that just before we met, one such weakness struck me."

"Why did you not tell me this before?" said Brian, tenderly helping the other knight to his feet.

"What?" said Sir Dinedan, frowning down at Brian—he was a good three inches taller, and much wider of shoulder. "When it is my duty as head of my family to ride about the woods daily, looking for rencounters such as we have just had? I, who carry the blood of the original Sir Dinedan in my veins, who was ready to fight thirty knights single-handed, if Sir Tristram had not changed his mind and gone along to aid him?"

"Of course!" said Brian, contritely. "A gentleman need not mention such. Forgive me, I pray you."

"I freely do so," said Sir Dinedan, remounting his horse; then reaching down to take the flask from Brian's hands and tilt it once more to his lips, before rehanging it on his saddle. "Besides, it is only a weakness that comes and goes, beneath notice. I never complain of it."

"As a knight should not," said Brian, admiringly

Brian also remounted, and they all rode on, with Sir Dinedan and Brian in the lead, Sir Dinedan talking about his castle, which was full of relatives.

"   Actually, it is a relief to get out during the day   " he was saying. Jim was barely listening. Curiously, at the moment, for no reason he could think of, he was missing his ability to make magic. It was a feeling like that of something not being there, or perhaps more like the feeling which might cling to a person who knew very well he or she had forgotten, and left behind, something that might be needed at any moment. A sort of emotional void.

Trying to take his mind off it, he became aware of a rustling somewhere among the trees not too far away It was off to the right and far enough ahead of them so the woods hid whatever was causing it.

A moment later, however, there suddenly burst out from the same direction a sound like a hundred tied-up dogs yelping to get loose; and a few seconds after that, they entered a clearing just in time to see leaving it a creature like an oversized and elongated leopard, with a head like a boa constrictor and flames pouring from its nostrils, plus a long tufted tail like a lion's.

"The Questing Beast!" exclaimed Brian.

"Ah, yes," said Sir Dinedan, waving to it. He called after it. "I hope I see you well, QB!"

The Questing Beast turned its head to look at him, raised a paw briefly in a hasty wave, and disappeared into the trees, continuing to make what Jim now correctly identified as the sound of thirty couple of hounds questing. He hastily lifted Gorp's reins and rode up level with the other two knights.

"What is it questing for?" Brian was asking Dinedan.

"King Pellinore," replied the other. "The Original, you know—just as QB's the Original Questing Beast."

"But I thought that it was King Pellinore who was on a quest after the Beast?" Brian said.

"Well, they're both looking for each other, if you know what I mean," said Sir Dinedan. "Like the Ancestor. They keep moving around, but they don't run into each other often, except by accident. Great friends, really, you know."

"I didn't know that," said Brian.

"Oh, yes," said Sir Dinedan. "They used to hunt together when QB had a den right near Pellinore's castle, before a landslide covered the den and he moved elsewhere. Never very good at hunting, either of them, even then. But they both missed their little get-togethers, and so you see the result."

"Ah," said Brian thoughtfully.

"Sir Dinedan," said Jim, "where exactly are we in Lyonesse now?"

"Well, if things haven't changed around on us, as they do sometimes," said Sir Dinedan, "we are still in the Wood of Rencounters, and we should be approaching your next adventure very shortly."

"Next adventure?" echoed Brian, staring.

"Oh, yes," answered Sir Dinedan. "They're all over the place, you know. You can't avoid them."

"What—" Brian broke off. "Where do you think we'll find this next one, then?"

He stared about them, loosening his sword in its sheath.

"It should be anywhere just past this next patch of trees," said Sir Dinedan. "At least, that's the sort of place you find them lurking."

They passed through the trees; and came out in another open glade. All of them halted their horses.

To their left the silver sun had departed from the zenith and moved toward the horizon; it seemed to be growing larger as it did so, and was flooding the area before them with brilliant white light. This light illuminated not only the glade, but the upright face of a sheer rock cliff, rearing some fifty or sixty feet before them, with further rock looming higher beyond it, and higher rock even behind that.

It was a little hard to tell with this strange illumination, but the rock looked like granite; and it was unbroken except for the circular entrance of a cave or tunnel where the cliff met the forest floor, straight before them. An entrance which looked wide enough for all four horses to enter abreast.

The light also picked out what looked like some runes carved in the cliff face above the highest point of the hole. In the white light, the runes were black wounds in the rock. As they looked, however, the runes shifted and changed shape, until, to the eyes of Jim at least—and neither Brian nor Dafydd could read—they took on the appearance of words.

"What says it?" asked Brian, staring at them.

Jim read it off for him.

WHO ENTERS, DEPARTS
WHO DEPARTS, RETURNS

"Farewell," said Sir Dinedan, reining his horse around and starting back into the woods. Jim was the only one that paid any attention to his departure.

"Now, perhaps," said Brian, with satisfaction, "we close upon our quarry."

But their horses had only covered half the distance to the hole before they were interrupted by a woman's voice crying out.

"Help!" it cried. "Oh, help! Help me!"

All together, they reined in their horses and looked to their left; as a woman, in a white dress with a veil hiding her face, ran into sight from between the trees there. She stopped at the sight of them, staggered for a moment, and then stood still, her veil swelling in and out as she panted behind it, obviously trying to catch her breath.

They turned their horses and rode toward her She was relatively slim and about average height. Black hair showed beneath her headdress, but that was all. The rest of her face and body were hidden by the veil and gown.

"What troubles you, my Lady?" asked Brian courteously "Are you pursued?"

He cast a glance at the trees behind her; but just then she got her first words out.

"No!" she gasped. "Of your favor, fair Sirs, aid me—in this parlous moment! They are about—to kill my brother—and my father!"

"Where do the villains have them, my Lady?" said Brian, standing up in his stirrups and trying to see between the trees behind her.

"A short distance only—" she answered. Her gown heaved with her struggling breath. There was something familiar about her voice, Jim thought, but he could not put his finger on it. It was not the voice of a girl or a very young woman. "These devils—surrounded us. They have only clubs; but they are many. My father and brother are unarmed, except for their daggers. I pray you, help them. Help them, for God's sake!"

"That will we do, and straitly!" said Brian. "Otherwise, may I never draw sword again! Give me your hand."

She extended it, and he drew her up one-handed, without leaning sideways in his saddle or with any other indication of effort, onto Blanchard's back behind his saddle.

He had made the lift with no seeming effort at all, Jim noticed; and the woman appeared to take it as the most natural thing in the world. Jim was always forgetting how strong Brian was, in spite of being slim and several inches shorter than Jim. In fact, he tended to forget how strong everyone was in this time—he had seen a serf at Malencontri, the top of whose head came barely to Jim's shoulder, easily pick up and walk off with a bundle of firewood logs Jim could barely lift.

He remembered how after coming here, he had foolishly thought that his larger body and a lifetime of activity in a number of sports must have made him equal to or stronger than most of the people he would meet in the fourteenth century. That illusion had been swiftly corrected.

But he had no time for thoughts on that topic now. Brian had already touched his spurs to Blanchard's flanks; and, with the distressed maiden—as Jim found himself inescapably labeling her, in spite of himself—galloped off into the woods.

The rest followed as fast as they could, except for the sumpter-horse, which, no longer tethered to Dafydd's saddle, slowed, unnoticed, behind them, and then halted behind a bush that effectively hid it from view.

It could not have been more than thirty yards before the rest broke into another, smaller clearing, completely surrounded by trees. Brian reined Blanchard to a halt in the center of the space, and the maiden slid down from the horse's back.

Facing her, sure enough, were one older man and one younger, both wearing cotes-hardie over shirt and hose, with soft, dagged hoods lying about their shoulders and girdles worn just above their hips in decorative imitation of a knight's sword belt. The girdle of the older man had been tooled and inlaid— possibly with gold, although Jim could not tell that in this light—some of which had fallen out. The younger's girdle was merely painted. These were indoor clothes, and both men looked embarrassed and uncomfortable in them, outdoors here, rather than frightened.

They were indeed wearing daggers, but neither man had drawn his—a most unusual failure to act under attack. Jim stared at the woman. There was still something familiar about her—at that moment she pulled the knife at her own belt, as the men reached for theirs; and at the sight of her weapon, Jim's memory clicked—just as their assailants came out of the woods on all sides.

These most clearly were armed with nothing but clubs. Heavy clubs, however. But then, these weapons perfectly suited them, since they were giants, nine and ten feet tall, wearing kilts that looked like untanned skins.

Jim spurred Gorp to the woman, reached down, and snatched the veil from her face. The well-remembered features of Agatha Falon, Robert's aunt, looked up at him—ugly now with a wild triumph. In the same instant, she dissolved into nothingness, and the two men with her.

But the giants remained, silent but advancing—at least twenty of them—and clearly they meant business. Their great figures were coming from every direction. Brian's lance was already out of its socket and down into position. Jim imitated him, turning Gorp about to face in the opposite direction. He checked himself when he saw that Dafydd had already taken up a position so that the three of them could watch the complete circle of trees. Jim heard Dafydd's bow snap, and saw a giant fall silently; then another dropped his club to clutch with both hands at a broad-headed arrow driven through his right kneecap.

The giants, who had been advancing more or less at a walk, suddenly came on in a rush.

Without warning, there burst on all their ears the sound of thirty couple of hounds questing. The giants turned, snatching up the two now brought down by Dafydd's arrows and carrying these off with them. They vanished in all directions into the trees; and a second later the Questing Beast entered the clearing. Its long tongue was lolling out of its mouth, and it was smiling as much as a beast with a serpent's head could, as it trotted up to their small group.

It looked at Jim and began to bark with the sound of a single hound. It continued the barking; and it became obvious to Jim that it was trying to tell him something.

"Hob," Jim said, looking around for the little Natural, "—where's the sumpter-horse?"

Before anyone could answer, that beast came out from behind the bush, rather nonchalantly. Hob looked at them from between the horse's ears. "Yes, m'Lord?"

"Hob," Jim said, "do you know what he's saying?"

"Oh, yes, m'Lord," answered Hob. His voice changed, and his next words came out in a steady rush, as if they had been a memorized lesson. "He's saying that he and the Ancestors, those who were rightfully members of King Arthur's Round Table and loyal to him in that last battle, were the first-comers and own this land. All creatures like these must give way to them—and they do, or else the very trees reach down and strangle them as they pass. Seeing we were friends with one who belonged to the ancient Families, he came to aid us."

With another friendly bark, QB disappeared among the trees and they heard his full voice, a thirty couple of hounds questing, disappearing in the distance.

Chapter **23**

A**h,**" said Brian, with satisfaction,
"now we can get on into that hole!"

That hole, once they actually rode into it, turned out to be more than Jim,
at least, had expected. For one thing, the tunnel beyond it continued wide
enough for the three of them to ride abreast—the sumpter-horse trailing
grumpily behind on a lead—although Dafydd, out of a sensitivity to rank and
courtesy, lagged half a horse-length behind the two knights.

For another, the tunnel had a flat floor that seemed to slant downward as
far as they could see; though the walls and ceiling showed the continuous
curve of what must have originally been a circular cut through the rock.

The rock appeared to be a dark granite—and Jim noticed that colors were
once more visible down here—but light came from it—not from its surface,
but as if its source were buried inside the stone itself. This light allowed them
to see as much as thirty or forty feet, as they left the brighter circle that was
the entrance behind them.

"I see little strange about this, James," said Brian, conversationally. He
turned to Dafydd. "Do you, Dafydd?"

"I do not, Sir Brian," said Dafydd. "Yet I am not easy in my bones about where this goes. I have a feeling we would do well to keep our weapons ready."

"Indeed," said Brian, "that goes without saying in any unknown place. I have had it said to me when riding with others into the marketplace of an unfamiliar town. I mind me once, however, that the warning stood us in good stead. There were only four of us, though all knights, only a few miles short of Winchester—"

He pulled Blanchard to a sudden halt, and Jim and Dafydd both reflexively checked their horses also.

As if they had passed through some invisible door, they were no longer in a simple tunnel, but in a cave, the extent of which exceeded the strength of the light.

Stone fingers seemed to rise before them, a forest of stalagmites reaching upward from the cave floor, and stalactites growing down out of the gloom hiding the cavetop overhead—the cave was noisy with the dripping of water from the tips of the stalactites. What light there was came from the same buried illumination that had shown their way so far. Through this stone jungle, still slanting downward, their tunnel floor had become a road that went on as straight as if the Romans had been building here, too. It was as wide as the tunnel itself had been.

"A hellish, but convenient, light," remarked Brian.

"There's a glow from everything," Jim said. "As if under their surfaces the rocks were phosphorescent."

Brian and even Dafydd looked at him with respect. Occasionally, at moments like this, they were used to hearing Jim come up with long words that no one could have understood. Magick, without a doubt.

"A help in this hap, however," said Brian—more cheerfully, now that Jim had taken steps to counter the hellishness of their surroundings. They rode on.

Farther on the cave seemed to widen even more, into an enormous space whose walls could not be seen. Their road, shrinking to a mere trail, wound away into a wilderness of rock fingers until it was lost from sight among them; and still they descended.

The strange illumination seemed brighter—or perhaps their eyes had adapted to it. The quiet of the air here was accentuated by the dripping sound, that was all around them. Jim remembered a little mnemonic that a tour guide in the western United States had told his group, so that they could remember which name belonged to which kind of rock spire

Stalactites have to stick tight,
But stalagmites, might grow if they had more water.

Jim wondered if either of his companions had ever been in a cave like this, but since they gave no sign of anything being out of the usual, he did not ask.

By the light in the stone, he and the others went forward along the winding trail; and within moments, they had lost all sense of direction and had only the trail to guide them.

"M'Lord?" said Hob's voice, lowered and very small-seeming behind him—and yet at the same time, it echoed and reechoed among the stone spears.

"What is it, Hob?" answered Jim, without turning his head.

"There are—things. Around us."

"Things?" Jim glanced around, but saw nothing.

"Don't look for them, m'Lord," said Hob. "If you do, they hide. Just look straight ahead and watch for them out of the corners of your eyes."

Jim tried this; but for a moment—a long moment—he saw nothing—heard nothing but the clopping of hooves on the stone beneath them and the dripping. Then his eyes, focused straight ahead, picked up a flicker of movement off to his right; and then, a second later, another to his left.

As he watched in this unobtrusive way, he began to make out dark figures, essentially man-like—smaller versions of the giants Agatha had led them to confront back in Lyonesse. They moved upright but in a shambling, almost ape-like manner; they were covered with a very dark-colored fur, even to their faces; and they seemed to be carrying no weapons. But there were more than a few of them, and they were moving along with Jim and his party.

It seemed to Jim that they kept coming a little bit closer all the time.

Brian had heard Hob's warning, too. He did not touch his spear, but he loosened his sword in its sheath again and spoke out of the corner of his mouth to Jim.

"The hobgoblin was right," he murmured. "These are a small host; and they mean us no good. If we could but come to a place where we could put our backs to something, we would be in better case to meet their attack."

"Hob," said Jim, still without turning his head, "ask Hill if he knows what they are. Or has he said something about them?"

"I asked him, m'Lord," said Hob. "He says nothing, no word at all. It's as if he doesn't hear me."

Jim risked turning and looking at Hill. The small man's expressionless face was as uninformative as always, and his gaze looked not at Jim, but past him and into the forest of stone ahead, as if he rode alone and with his mind elsewhere.

"Hill, pay attention to me!" Jim said. "I've got something to ask you!"

There was no response from the small man. Jim spoke again; but Hill said nothing.

But, Jim realized, there had been a change about Hill after all. Although his face was exactly the same, now his mouth was closed; and there was a seriousness, almost a grimness, about him, that was new. He could be said to have the expression of a soldier going into battle; or, maybe, a man going to his own execution. In either case he seemed unapproachable.

"They come closer," said Brian.

His hands had crossed each other, the left still holding his reins but very close to the hilt of his dagger, and the right close to the hilt of his sword on his left side.

"I suggest sword and poignard," he said, still in that low voice but in an almost conversational tone. "In this case, James, our shields will do us little good, and our blades much more."

He raised his voice just a trifle.

"Dafydd," he said, without looking back to the archer, "I would suggest the same for you. The blade of that long knife you carry on your right leg, rather than your arrows, deadly though they may be. There are too many here for a few killed to stop them before the rest can rush us altogether."

"I have made ready so," said the voice of Dafydd in an equally low tone behind them. "I am close behind you; and no doubt it were best we three stand as next together as possible."

Jim felt something light land on his shoulder.

"Pray pardon, m'Lord," whispered Hob, perched there, "but I want to be with you."

"That's all right, Hob," said Jim under his breath.

But now Jim felt Gorp nudged from behind; and the sumpter-horse pushed its way between Gorp and Blanchard, taking the lead. On it, and without any visible control of the animal, Hill rode through and past them, sitting almost on the neck of the animal and taking the lead. His eyes were still looking straight forward, and he seemed not to see them, or the creatures about. He rode some little way out in front, until the sumpter-horse, again without any apparent direction, slowed down to its previous pace; so that they all went forward, but now with Hill a couple of horse-lengths in front, leading.

Hill's move seemed to affect the creatures circling them. Their movements slowed, and they ceased to come nearer. Also, their numbers seemed to have thinned somewhat.

"I had a suspicion the fellow knew something about all this," muttered Brian to Jim. "Mayhap he may now carry us safely through."

"Maybe," said Jim.

For the fur-clad creatures began to move faster in their circling, and to move in again toward them. They were now very close, some of them dodging out to stand for a second clearly in sight between two of the glowing stone columns, mouths open and teeth bared. Brian made the mark of the Cross on his breast.

"That is the one trouble with this adventuring in strange places, James," he said, again in a conversational tone. "How is a man to find a priest to shrive him, in such a place as this? *In manus tuus, Domine.*"

The creatures now began to thump with their fists on the vertical stone formations. It was a soft sound, but many times multiplied, so that it felt almost like a muffled drum beating inside Jim's head. He took it as a signal that they were just about to begin their rush, looped his own reins about the pommel of his saddle, and reached quite openly for the hilts of his sword and poignard.

It was a moment in which he was quite sure that there was no way out, that an attack would come at any minute. But, oddly, he found that instead of feeling fearful, regretful, or any other emotion he might have expected—there was only a sort of empty feeling inside him. He rode on, listening to the drumming.

Then, unexpectedly, something lanced through the soft heavy sound of the drumming—a sharp, almost musical note, a sound like a steel pick striking rock. It chimed like the note of a glass bell over the drumming—and the drumming stopped instantly. The chime repeated, and continued, as steady as a metronome.

Jim stared about him. The furry figures had frozen in place. For a long moment they stood unmoving; then, like dark lights going out, they began to vanish among the stony pillars of the cave. In less than a minute there was not a one to be seen.

"In God's name," said Brian, "it sounds as regular as a church bell. What is it?"

Jim had no answer. Brian rode forward until he was level with Hill and almost shouted at the small man.

"What is that?" he demanded.

Hill rode on, apparently unmoving and unresponding. On Jim's shoulder Hob called forward to Brian, before Jim himself could speak.

"Sir Brian!" Hob said. "Hill answered!"

"What did he say then?" asked Brian, looking back.

" *'It is my friends,'* " called Hob.

"I knew it!" said Brian, checking Blanchard, so that he stood for a moment until Jim caught up with him. "He is no stranger here! Now we need doubt no longer."

"Yes," said Jim, grimly. "And now maybe things will start to make sense."

"It is well past time," said Brian. He looked closely at Jim.

"I remember now," he went on. His face was perfectly humorless. "It comes to my mind," he said, "that you named that lady with the brother and father who vanished a while back. I was looking elsewhere; but you knew her. Is she somehow a part of this?"

"I didn't think so," said Jim, "but you're right. It was Agatha Falon, Robert's aunt."

"But she was wearing a veil," said Brian. "What was it led you suspect it was her?"

"I'd seen her hold a knife in her hand, before," Jim said. "You remember, I told you of the time, at the Earl's Christmas party—Angie found her in our room trying to smother Robert. She pulled a knife on Angie. Luckily, I came in just then and took it away from her."

"Ah, yes," Brian said. "I recall you telling me of it. Would that she had a husband, for that should call for a meeting between you and he!"

"Not only has she no husband," Jim said, "but she came in the train of young Prince Edward, having lately been favored by his Majesty the King. It was she who insisted on coming, though the Prince didn't want her. She had asked the King to let her go—and he let her, of course."

"Well, if not her husband, her Champion, then," said Brian, brushing the matter aside. "So no more was made of the matter. I was remiss not to speak to you about it. It was not properly done. Surely she could have found someone to meet you on her behalf. What if Angela had been killed?"

"It was not a simple, straightforward matter," said Jim. "Remember, she's been one of the King's favorites, and is again, it seems. Any uproar over such a happening could do nothing but harm to us."

"Nonetheless . . ." said Brian, a truculent set to his jaw

Down, down, and down they went, the chime still keeping them company. Their way changed once more, seeming to widen because the forest of stalactites and stalagmites dwindled into nothingness. The light was again coming from stone walls, off to their sides, and the ceiling was visible; although this section was clearly both higher and wider than the first tunnel had been.

The regularity of the chiming sound and the hoofbeats began to make a soporific rhythm in the back of Jim's mind. No one spoke. Dafydd was not a great talker under any conditions, and Brian was often silent when not in the grip of some strong emotion.

Jim's thoughts hopped from subject to subject. All during this trip, there had been no evidence that they were going in the right direction to find Robert. Still, it had all felt somehow *right* to him. If it was true, as Carolinus had hinted, that a magician could *feel* when magic was being used against him—maybe it was that feeling leading him now.

But how could that be true when he no longer had the use of his magic, here in this underground Kingdom?

Something else bothered him. Back there in Lyonesse, in a place he himself could not have predicted he would ever be, he had been ambushed by someone who should not have had any way to know he was there—much less have a way to get there for an attack, and then flee as she had.

That was bad enough. But when he thought of it, there was the fact that he had come to seek young Robert, whose enemy was the very Agatha Falon—his aunt—who wanted the Falon properties and who had just tried to stop Jim and his friends. Jim had little evidence that Robert had been taken here. But maybe Agatha's attack could be taken as coincidence.

Somewhere he had once read that there was no such thing as coincidence. If so, it would argue that Robert was indeed somewhere up ahead of them. But it also could mean that Agatha had been involved in the kidnapping; and it was hard to think how that could be possible.

Coincidence? Unlikely. Ever since he and Angie had come to this fourteenth-century world, they had been marked as enemies by the Dark Powers; those malignant forces who—or which, perhaps—Carolinus said were trying to alter the balance between Chance and History, in either direction.

But how could the kidnapping of young Robert affect such Powers? It seemed to make no sense.

Suddenly, too, he remembered the warning given by Carolinus' projection, about not letting himself be deceived by appearances in Lyonesse—how could he even be sure that that *had* in fact been Agatha?

There was too much here to figure out without further information.

He switched his mind off to the more immediate question of where this tunnel might lead them and what they might find at its end. So far, nothing that had happened gave him a clue to their destination, except that it was undoubtedly underground. They had been going down steadily—

"I like them," said the voice of Hob dreamily in his ear. The hobgoblin was still sitting on his shoulder; and, light as the little Natural was, Jim had completely forgotten he was there. But now Hob's voice pulled Jim from his thoughts, and he realized that the bell-like sound had ceased some time since But the clopping of their horses' hooves seemed to have picked up something like an echo—a regular drum-like beating that seemed almost within his ears, rather than outside them.

It seemed to come from everywhere around them, and no place in particular—Jim's laggard mind suddenly registered Hob's words. . . .

"Them?" he said. "Which 'them' are you talking about, Hob?"

"The Gnarlies. Behind us." said Hob.

"Behind us?"

Jim looked around, and saw behind him, marching ten abreast, rank on rank of manlike beings only slightly smaller than Hill, and all with the same expressionless faces. They came steadily along behind Jim and his party, their feet bare, slapping down on the stone floor in perfect time, and making the soft, drum-like sound Jim had heard. They moved all together and were all dressed alike.

Like Hill, they wore what looked to be leather kilts and shirts. Each one carried, thrust through his belt on his right side, a hammer with a metal head and a short wooden handle; balancing it on the other side was a metal-headed pick, pointed at both ends. Behind their backs, sticking up the way an unstrung bow might be carried by an archer, each bore a metal rod no thicker than Jim's little finger.

These baffled Jim for a moment, until it occurred to him that, here underground, these might be a mining variety of Natural; if so, the rods might be drilling rods, lengths of metal that could be hammered into a crack in a rock face, to force it to crack further, so that the rock itself could be broken more easily than straight pick-work could manage.

Like Hill, each had his long sleeves closed at the ends, well past the ends of the arms inside them.

"Who are they?" Jim asked Hob. "Why are they following us?"

"They're friends of Hill's," Hob said.

Jim felt a sudden spurt of hope and quickly pushed it back and firmly stoppered it up again.

"You like Hill now, don't you?" he asked Hob.

Hob did not answer immediately, apparently thinking it over

"Yes," he said at last. "But he mustn't think he can have what belongs to me. Malencontri and m'Lady and you, m'Lord, are mine!"

Jim tried to turn his head to get a look at the hobgoblin's face, but he was too close. Hob had never shown a jealous streak like this, before.

But he recognized a faint, but familiar, note in the little creature's voice, now It seemed to Jim like a note he had heard in the voices of his Malencontri servants when they were speaking to him, a proprietary note, as if they owned him, rather than the other way around.

"I don't think he particularly wants Malencontri and those of us who live there," said Jim.

"He wants you—part of you, anyway," said Hob. "But you're *my* Lord, not his."

"Of course," said Jim. "And I've no intention of being his Lord."

"You hear that, Hill?" said Hob, looking forward at the back of the small man.

Hill, however, did not answer.

A suspicion that had been building in the back of Jim's mind for some time, half-noticed, suddenly crystallized. He lifted his reins and urged Gorp forward with his heels; but the warhorse was strangely unwilling to draw level with Hill on the sumpter-horse. Jim finally gave up, Gorp's head only level with the withers of the sumpter-horse.

"Hill," he said to the back of Hill's head, "what are those metal rods used for? Are they used for driving through stone walls? And if they are, what kind of noise would they make?"

Hill still did not speak. But without turning his head to look, he held out one of his sleeve-enclosed arms to the side; and, although he gave no other signal that Jim could see, one of the marching little men broke ranks, ran forward, and passed up the rod he had been carrying.

Hill held the rod quite easily at one end with a hand still enclosed in his sleeve, and pointed the other end at the stone wall to the right of their passage. There was no sound at all, but suddenly there was a circular hole about five feet across and ten feet deep. It seemed to have opened into a parallel passage, in which could be seen more of the creatures Hob had called Gnarlies, moving about.

These stopped, staring at Hill. Their arms fell to their sides and their faces went blank. Hill paid them no attention, but rode on a few more yards and once more pointed the rod at the stone wall beside him.

Once more the stone opened up. But this time Jim heard the *boomp* he had become familiar with in Malencontri. The passage revealed at the far end this time was visible as if seen through a grimy, but transparent, circular window. And the Gnarlies Jim saw moving beyond it this time paid no attention to Hill and kept moving as if proceeding on their everyday errands.

It was certainly a kind of window, in the second case with some thin layer of stone left that could be seen through, somehow; probably to find out what was beyond. He must have all the walls tapped where there had been boomps heard, when he got home.

Clearly he, Brian, and Dafydd had found their way to the right place.

He looked balefully at Hill's back. *Luck,* indeed!

Hill had opened his grip on the rod and let it fall, as if no longer interested in it—and the Natural that had given it to him, running forward, had just made a desperate diving catch before it had hit the stone floor.

"Hill, what—damn you, Gorp!" said Jim, forcing the warhorse forward until the two of them were all but level with Hill. "Isn't it a mining tool, then? What's the rod for if not for mining?"

"Fighting," answered Hill unexpectedly, still without turning his head to look at Jim.

"Fighting? Who would you fight?"

"Goblins," said Hill. He turned his head then and looked—not at Jim, but at Gorp. Gorp stopped in his tracks; and Jim sat there, unable to make him move until Brian caught up with him.

"A curious breeze above us there," said Brian unexpectedly. "Hark how it sings."

Jim had not previously noticed any breeze, but Brian was right. One was indeed blowing, seemingly from above them. And looking about, he saw that they had just now emerged into what seemed an ever-widening cavern, with walls lit more strongly by the light in the stone—or whatever it was—but its farther distance, beyond a hundred yards or so, still lost in darkness.

Lost in the darkness above them also was any ceiling to this larger cave. The stone-light climbed the walls about them high enough to throw a little gleam on what seemed to be the end of more stalactites hanging down from the ceiling—hanging down, and in a number of cases, pierced by holes.

The breeze blowing from somewhere behind them whistled through these holes, sounding notes of different pitch. The breeze itself varied, as he could feel on the back of his neck, resulting in something almost resembling music—music in which the sound of the feet on the stone floor behind them, steadily beating, was like a tympani accompaniment.

But, Jim asked himself, was he hearing this with his human ears, or through the enlarged range of hearing which enabled him to hear Hill? He turned to Brian.

"Brian," he asked, "can you hear Hill when he talks?"

"Never heard him say a word," answered Brian.

"He can, but I had to find a special way of hearing before I could hear him."

"I remember," said Brian. He looked closely at Jim. "Is something amiss, James? You speak oddly."

"I think," said Jim, "that even though I don't have any magic down here, I may still be able to feel when other magic is around me, even if I can't tell what it is, or do anything about it."

"That is some help, surely, however," said Brian. "It may be we'll need no more."

"Well, yes. It might turn out to be an advantage," said Jim. "If no one else realizes that I'm aware of whatever magic's here, maybe I can take advantage of that in some way to help us."

"May the Saints aid you to do so," said Brian. "Meanwhile, I've had enough of riding behind that small fellow, whatever he is. Let us pass him and take the lead ourselves."

With that, Brian rode ahead, and Jim felt obligated to go with him. Their horses came level with Hill and his mount; but then, neither Blanchard nor Gorp moved ahead.

"What ails the beasts!" said Brian, angrily, urging Blanchard forward both with reins and spurs.

Hill, meanwhile, had not even bothered to glance at them.

Before Jim could answer, Hill spoke; a single word that came out sharply and commandingly, in a tone that was the last thing Jim would have expected from Hill.

"He said 'Stop!' " Jim informed Brian and Dafydd.

But in fact they had already stopped—their horses having done the stopping for them. Hill dismounted.

"Blanchard, damn you!" said Brian angrily, but under his breath. Blanchard put back his ears, but did not move.

"We'd better get down, I think," said Jim, softly.

"If you say so," said Brian, equally softly, but through his teeth. "But it were my rede—James, I do not understand this!"

"Neither do I," said Jim, as they all dismounted. "But, look at the floor."

Before them began a sort of path across the stone floor marked out by glittering jewels of about two inches' diameter, inset every six inches or so. Two lines of them led forward, laying out a trail whose far end could not be seen—whether because of distance or a mist, it was impossible to say. Hill evidently intended to walk it, for he was already starting down between the two lines.

"I think he wants us to go with him," Hob said timidly into Jim's ear, but loudly enough to be heard by the two other men. Jim looked at Brian and Dafydd.

"We might as well," said Jim. They both nodded.

Jim turned, and saw that the cave just behind them was solidly packed by the small miners who had been following them; and more were flooding in to spread right and left from the tunnel mouth, pressing into the mass already there. Brian and Dafydd had also seen this.

" 'Fore God," said Brian, "I think we have no choice."

They turned to walk forward, behind Hill, with the horses coming along on their own. The flood of small figures followed them closely.

Ahead, the murkiness that had obscured the farther reaches of the cavern seemed to roll back, but more slowly than their advance; so that now it was only about fifteen yards in front of them, but retreating steadily. Above, the wind had increased. The discordant music in Jim's head was louder, but oddly counterpointed by the sound of the naked feet of those who followed on the stone floor.

"I think there's someone who doesn't like Hill up ahead," said Hob in Jim's ear. His voice had become timid and uncertain. "M'Lord, would you like to tell Hill we're on his side?"

"What is his side, Hob?"

"I don't know," confessed Hob. "Maybe if you asked him . . ."

It was not the most unlikely suggestion. There was certainly no harm in trying.

"Hill," said Jim.

Hill turned his head briefly; and his eyes met Jim's. As usual, there was no expression in them, but he had plainly heard and understood what Jim and Hob had been saying. His own response came clearly to Jim.

" 'Ee'll see'm soon enough." There was a slight pause before the next few words. " 'Ee's my Uncle."

"Your uncle?" echoed Jim. "But why—"

He broke off, because Hill had looked away again and was obviously through talking. He walked on, and Jim, with Brian and Dafydd, walked after him—with the horses nodding and following, and the little miners crowding close behind.

But now, without warning and without sound, the darkness before them began to pull back faster. It did not have to roll far. In a moment they could see the farther end of the cave. Before it was a platform, with a chair like a throne on it, and a bulky figure in the chair, robed in flashing light.

Chapter 24

The cave came to an end at a wall that reared above them like a windowless, many-storied building. However, that wall was undercut at a height roughly comparable to two stories above the ground, the sheer vertical drop abruptly angling sharply inward. So that in effect the upper part projected outward like a massive awning above a tiny plaza.

In the large space underneath, at the very center, there was a raised stone platform, on which a throne literally glittered, as did the robe of its occupant. A ring of the same glittering gems that had outlined the path, marked an open space about and before the platform.

The back of the throne rose in an arched curve above the head of that occupant; and halfway down it sprouted ends that curved forward, flattened, and became ornately carved armrests, differently shaped at their forward ends, one like a pick, one like a hammer. The entire throne appeared to be of one piece, part of the living stone of the wall behind, but such was the effect of the bright jewels around it and the subdued light of the cave, that it seemed to float at head-height of those standing before it.

Jim looked more closely By heaven, it *was* floating!

He forced his gaze from the throne to the one sitting in it. There, clad in a floor-length, glittering robe, was a Natural just like Hill, but half a head taller and proportionately bigger.

As he looked more closely, Jim saw that the face of the enthroned individual, while very like Hill's in its heavy-boned, primitive appearance, was unpleasantly different in expression. Its eyes also stared at Jim and his friends, but with nothing of the innocence Jim had thought he had seen in Hill and those behind him. Then, abruptly, even that changed. The stare focused on Hill; and the Natural's face became almost human with a smile that did ugly things to the formerly emotionless face.

"Well, Nevvy—" Jim heard him begin.

"Well, Uncle!" Hill interrupted sharply. "Here I be again!"

Jim looked quickly; and Hill's face had also changed. It, too, had taken on personality such as Hill had not shown before in Jim's experience of him. His was a young face still, but now the vacantly open mouth was closed, the lower jaw set. He, too, looked more human now—but in his case, it was for the better.

"Why, so I see, Nevvy, as I was about to tell 'ee. 'Ee dug thyself out, did 'ee? I never looked to see 'ee back here for another hundred year."

" 'Twas help I had," said Hill, "from a friend."

"A friend? Oh, thee has friends up-surface now, do 'ee? What friend of 'ee's could dig 'ee faster from under a mountain than 'eeself?"

" 'Ee was called a Sea Devil," retorted Hill. "Ye never saw the like. 'Ee was as tall as eight o' ourn, piled head to foot; and 'ee could crush 'ye in one hand like a piece o' sandstone, so 'ee could."

Uncle's grin suddenly broadened, although nothing else about him changed—giving him a mad look.

"No living creetur can crush the Gnarly King, the King o' th' Hill, of Overhill, Underhill and all the other Underearth! 'Ee should know that, being a King's-son, Nevvy!"

"Thee be no True King, Uncle!" cried Hill.

"I be True King!" roared his uncle, half-rising from his chair. But he checked, and sank back onto the Throne. ". . . Or else thee just be stoopid. Thee was always stoopid. But I think, now thee's lying to me, as well. If thee's not, why bring here these Up-Earth Stoopids and beasts wi' thee, if not to back up thy story?"

Hill flung out one of his covered arms to point at Jim.

"Thee stole away his cheild!" he said. " 'Ee knows t'was thee did it."

"And if I did, what's that to me or thee, Nevvy?"

" 'Ee's my Luck!" cried Hill.

"Luck?" For a moment the King looked disturbed. But then he rocked with silent laughter. "Now I know thee's not only a liar but stoopid, Nevvy. A Stoopid from up-surface to be a Luck for a Gnarly?"

"My Luck beed the Sea Devil, who dug me out this fast," answered Hill. "Ask 'eeself, how could I be here so soon, otherhow? But the Sea Devil couldn't come to Overhill with me. So 'ee passed his Luck to thisun; and thisun's no simple Stoopid, neither. 'Ee's a Mage, 'ee is, full with magick. 'Ee was coming here for 'is cheild, anyhow!"

"Wants t'see it, does 'ee?" said the King. " 'Ee's magick don't be any good here. Here, it's I got the Robe and the Throne. So—"

He waved his hand toward a corner of the space in which his throne of flashing silver was centered; and suddenly, a few feet to the side, Robert Falon appeared, lying on a block of stone, his legs and arms waving. He was crying harder than Jim had ever seen him cry—but utterly without a sound. The fact that his crying was going unheard registered clearly in Jim's mind—and a moment later, he walked with considerable force into what felt like a wall of stone. With the impact came realization: the King had set up a ward about Robert.

The sudden understanding was like a door slammed in his face, just as he had tried to go through it.

"Look at 'ee standing there!" the King's voice rang behind him. "So stoopid 'ee thought I'd just let 'ee go take ee's cheild! 'Ay! Stoopid! Yon cheild's not 'ee's no more! I'll be given 'ee to a Stoopid Lady!"

The King laughed, like two blocks of stone grinding against each other.

"Look at 'ee!" he chortled, turning to Hill. "Fair mazed 'ee is! No wonder, neither. Five o' ourn I sent to steal the cheild; and 'ee all came back shaking after trying to dig out of rock into 'ee's cave—not so far from Stoopids 'eeselves—and there smelling Stoopids all around, crazy to kill poor Gnarlies. 'Twas 'un tried to steal the baybee from open surface in broad day's light and the cheild's watch-Stoopid sleeping under Sun beside the wee 'un, but came back 'feered of a wolf! 'Twas then I had to go meself!"

Jim, staring at Robert, had hardly heard any of this long speech. But abruptly, what the King had said just before that reechoed in his head.

"You said you'd give Robert to a Stoopid Lady!" he said to the King. "What Lady? A Lady named Agatha Falon?" His voice came out hard.

The King said nothing; but Jim now found himself being pushed backward by some invisible force, away from Robert. The King kept his attention on Hill, ignoring Jim.

Jim turned. He walked unsteadily back to stand beside Brian. This Gnarly

King, he found himself thinking, was someone he could kill with an easy conscience.

"Were you struck by some magick, James?" Brian's voice whispered in his ear. He put an arm around Jim, who was literally unsteady on his feet.

Jim shook his head, as much to clear it as to answer Brian's question. With an effort, he put his fury from him, and found steadiness. Magic had nothing to do with his sudden weakness, but to explain emotional shock to Brian was impractical.

"No, Brian," he said, and his own voice sounded strange to him, unreasonably hollow. "I'm all right. What's going on?"—For Hill's voice and the King's were clashing again.

"They are now in fierce discussion," said Brian, in a voice that sounded more normal. "He who calls himself the Gnarly King is taunting young Hill. I had no great love for the little fellow, but—by Our Lady! I would aid him in this moment, if I knew how."

"You, too?" said Jim. "How long have you been hearing their talk?"

"Why, since they started to speak out, a moment past," answered Brian, releasing him. "I knew you could hear these creatures speak—magick, of course—but to me they were dumb as stones. Now, however, it appears these two, at least, can utter some words if they will. Enough, at least, to make plain that the King of these people, there, is about to send Hill back beneath some mountain, and wishes to see him beg for mercy. Yet Hill has been standing up to him, almost as well as a man might. Only hark, James. You can hear them yourself."

"But how could you—" Jim began, then interrupted himself. "They're speaking in the normal human range now. Wait a minute—no, they're not. I wonder . . . Brian, listen to me for a moment—"

Jim edged forward, moving inside the ring of gems that outlined the space on the floor. The King had turned to face Hill, and Hill was concentrating only on the monarch. Jim spoke to Brian.

"*Gladiator Hill, amor Fortunae.*"

"Indeed, James, I am entirely of your opinion. But why did you walk away like that to say so?"

Jim stepped back toward him out of the ring and repeated the Latin words.

"What?" said Brian.

"Sorry," said Jim, in his own form of English, which for some unknown reason fourteenth-century individuals seemed to find perfectly understandable. "Frog in my throat. I said that Hill was a fighter and Fortune loves him."

"That is what you also said, a moment gone," replied Brian. "Good fortune is never to be despised, of course, in any bicker. I agree. Still, they do seem to insist on a lot of talk before they get to blows, down here. Almost makes one doubt their willingness to do so. Never do to act like that in dispute with an Englishman."

There was nothing Jim could think of to say to that.

"Besides," Brian went on, "how else should they speak? True, they have a common, country way of talking, but it is clear enough."

And indeed, it was.

"—I say it again," Hill was almost shouting in a tenor voice. The faces of both of them were now showing emotions Jim would never have thought possible to them.

"Killed thy father?" retorted the King. "Never I did! The old pooker just keeled over."

"That be'en't true!"

"Na, na, watch thy words!" said the King.

"Well, don't thee call my father a pooker!" cried the Prince. "If any Gnarly here's a pooker, it's thee!"

"Oh, thee's be now like a fine little Stoopid Knight with manners, be'en't 'ee? Besides, 'ee was a pooker. I was 'ee's next youngest brother, and I should know!"

"Stop that! 'Ee shouldn't never talk that way of anyone who's gone Overhill-Underhill—and 'ee thy full-blood brother!"

"Thee be'en't here when it happened, remember," retorted the King. "It were me, not thee, saw 'im fall. 'Ee just beed a weak old pooker and 'ee died."

"I be 'is closer kin. I be 'is son!" cried the Prince. "I'll scatter 'ee for saying that!"

The King laughed.

" 'Ee and 'oo to help 'ee?" he said. "Be'en't no other kin left to 'elp 'ee now. Them as stands behind 'ee at this moment won't lift a pick or rod to help 'ee—even if it would do good against my King's Power of Magick. What makes thee think thee could even touch me?"

"I've my Luck!" said Hill.

The King sneered.

"A Stoopid's no Luck to you!"

"Don't thee ever say that!" cried Hill. " 'Ee's Lucky. 'Ee couldn't be luckier. Thee knows that! What of all the baybees stole down the centuries? 'Twas because they were lucky to have. And this'n's a Magickian. That makes him twice as Lucky!"

"Magickian!" snorted the King. "I've a prime Magickian 'ere already—and look at 'ee!"

As suddenly as Robert had appeared, Carolinus appeared on the other side of the dais. Carolinus in a cage, holding to the front bars as if they were all that kept him on his feet. His face was ravaged with exhaustion, but he opened his mouth and his cracked voice rang out, not in Jim's head but plainly in his ears.

"Depart!" he cried. "Jim, DEPART!"

And Jim did.

With Carolinus' voice still sounding in his ears, he found himself in a large auditorium filled with men and women, many in red magician robes—more so-dressed than he had ever seen together before. On the stage on which Jim had appeared, a woman was standing, addressing the audience.

She was a woman he had seen once before, one of the only three AAA+ Magicians there were in this world; and she had been the referee—or whatever magicians called it—at the time of Carolinus' duel with a B-class magician named Son Won Phon, over the latter's accusation that Jim had been using Oriental Magic without having been properly instructed by an expert in that area.

The woman was of indeterminate age, by appearance perhaps in her thirties or forties; tall, but thin and somewhat cadaverous-looking. Her face was bony and long, and her expression stern. When Jim had seen her before, she had been wearing a dark green robe and a sort of skullcap of the same color; now she wore the magician's red. Her clothes were clean, but were obviously well-worn. Jim's mind scrambled to remember how to pronounce her name.

Whatever she had been saying to the audience, it had been interrupted by Jim's appearance. She, like everybody in the seats, now turned to look at him. For a moment there was a dead silence, and then murmurs swept through the audience . . . "Dragon Knight . . .", ". . . No, no more than a class C+, I assure you!" "Tremendous extra Drawing Accounts. They say . . . (mumble, mumble) . . . Carolinus, but . . ."

"How did you get here, Jim?" demanded the tall woman. At the sound of her voice, those from the audience ceased.

"I think Carolinus sent me," said Jim. "—In a way. Or maybe he just took advantage of something that was carved over the entrance, something about *WHO ENTERS DEPARTS, WHO DEPARTS RETURNS.* '"

"Hah!" she said, as fiercely as Jim had ever heard Brian say it. "That's our Carolinus—taking advantage of their own Natural, Gnarly Magick!"

There was a sudden storm of questions shouted at Jim from the audience. The woman turned to face them, held up her hand, and all voices except hers fell silent.

"Now, Jim," she said, turning back to him and speaking only slightly less severely than she had just looked at the audience, "how was it you were there where Carolinus could take advantage of this particular Gnarly command?"

"Well, you see, Mage Kinety—" he began.

"KinetetE," she scowled.

"I'm sorry." Jim tried to follow her pronunciation of her own name with that final emphatic E. "Kinetet . . . yah?" Jim's attempt to duplicate the sound was a total failure.

"No," she said. "Kin-eh-tet-E. Accent on the final E. Never mind. Pronounce it any way you want—but answer my question."

"Well," said Jim. He suddenly felt six years old again, facing a towering first-grade teacher—and, in fact, KinetetE was a good three inches taller than he was. In just a few sentences he outlined the events that had followed the kidnapping of young Robert. KinetetE interrupted him when he came to the part about Hill.

"What was he?" she snapped.

"A Gnarly—a Gnarly prince, I guess, but we didn't know that at first." He outlined the rest of their trip up to the confrontation with Hill's uncle. "Anyway," he concluded, "just about then, the King made Carolinus appear. Carolinus commanded 'DEPART'—and here I am."

Jim stopped and tried to catch his breath. The whole story had come out almost in one sentence.

"Hah!" said KinetetE again, thoughtfully this time, but still somewhat fiercely. "But you say you did see Carolinus. How was he?".

"The King had him in a cage, and he looked in bad shape. He could barely stand up."

Something like a moan came from the audience, with an undernote that was very like a growl of rage.

"Were you aware," snapped KinetetE, "that Carolinus had gone to whoever was King down there with special permission from our worldwide Collegiate of Magickians and full Ambassadorial Credentials, to look into a threat to unbalance the Kingdoms?"

"No, I wasn't," said Jim. "I saw and talked to him a short time before our journey—but even then he was a projection, rather than with us in person. He appeared once more, just before we went into Lyonesse; and he was a projection then, too—I think a message he deliberately left for us if we showed up; to be triggered into sight and sound by the fact we were there. But he only warned us then that Lyonesse was a land of magic, and dangerous for us."

"Well, now we know," said KinetetE. "The Gnarly King apparently thinks he can do what he wants with a AAA+ Mage. We'll have to teach him differently!" The audience snarled its approval—very unmagician-like in sound.

"But Hill's uncle has the only magic that's allowed in that Kingdom, isn't that so?" said Jim.

"He has it, but doesn't own it!" said KinetetE sharply. "He simply controls it as long as he rightfully wears that Robe bejeweled with Great Silver—do you know what that is?"

When Jim shook his head, she explained. "Great Silver forms a tiny part of ordinary tin, that only Gnarlies can recognize. Crushed by the Gnarly King's magic, as diamonds are made from the like of charcoal by the miles-deep weight of the Earth, it becomes like a jewel—the rarest jewel there is. It's from those jewels on his Robe and his Throne, that his magick springs. But he has to own these rightfully or they can be taken away. Then, someone else becomes King of the Gnarlies and has it."

She paused, her dark eyes focusing past Jim at nothing in particular for a moment. Then they returned to him.

"Yes," she said, almost to herself. "We must think matters out. You do not know why Carolinus sent you to us here?"

"He must have arranged it that way beforehand, against the time I might need to be Departed," said Jim.

"I thought so," said KinetetE. She turned her head and spoke to the audience. "Barron, I'm going to have to ask you to come up here."

There was a moment in which nothing happened, and then a small, fussy-looking man in his fifties, rotund, with a button of a nose, a small unimpressive mouth, and pale blue eyes that blinked frequently, appeared. He was wearing a red robe and a tall pointed red hat, neither of which seemed to fit him very well. He looked exactly like the sort of person who ought to be wearing a pair of metal-rimmed spectacles. But spectacles, of course, were not available in this time and place—and in any case, a magician would not need to wear them: he could make his eyesight as good or as bad as he wanted at any time, magically.

"If I must," he said, in an annoyed tenor voice.

"It'll be your mind and mine, plus whatever we can gain from our young Apprentice, here," said KinetetE. "If the Gnarly King can defy us like this and so mistreat one of our most valuable members, then this is something that threatens us all. I can't understand how the King could fail to realize that."

"Unless," said Jim, "it's because this new King, who seems to have killed the rightful ruler—Hill's father—to take the Throne, has something big in mind and thinks he's invulnerable now, for some reason."

"Speak when you're spoken to, boy!" barked the man who had come to share the stage with KinetetE. He was considerably smaller than either Jim or KinetetE.

"I tell you," said Jim, stubbornly continuing to talk, "there's got to be some kind of pattern to it all; and I think that's a part of it!"

Chapter 25

"**W**ell," said Barron, "here's pertness! Speak when you're spoken to, apprentice. Mage KinetetE and I will unravel this matter!"

It was not the other man's tone of voice or his assumption that Jim was incapable of helping that did it—it was his perfect pronunciation of KinetetE's name. Barron, Jim remembered now, was the name of the third AAA+ magician in this world; but despite that, Jim found himself growing angry—and when he got angry he also got stubborn. He had run into this kind of person in his own twentieth-century world, and he knew from experience that if he let someone like Barron get away with shutting him up, then he would never get anything said. The only way with this individual was to meet him head-on.

"No," he said. "None of you seem to be paying any attention to the fact that I said Carolinus' message to us just before we went into Lyonesse was a projection. And best odds are he sent that message from inside the Gnarly Kingdom."

"Where his magick would not work, you mean?" said KinetetE.

"And since magic doesn't work there," Jim continued, "he could only have done it with the permission of the Gnarly King. The King wanted me lured there, and wanted me not to take my friend Aargh—the English wolf—along; I suspect Gnarlies have an unusual fear of wolves. So he let Carolinus send his projection to me, and Carolinus managed to give me some hidden information."

"Not too bad reasoning for an Apprentice, don't you think, Barron?" KinetetE said.

"Lucky guess, I'd call it," said Barron. He hesitated, added grudgingly, "I suppose he has a few wits, this lad."

"So do I suppose," said KinetetE. "And I think we'll listen to him for the moment."

Her last words came in a tone of voice that would not have encouraged Jim to continue a discussion with her. Barron evidently felt the same way.

KinetetE turned back to Jim.

"Is there anything else you want to mention to us, now?"

"Just one thing that might tie in," he said. "I don't understand how it could happen, but while we were crossing Lyonesse, we were led into an ambush by a veiled woman." He explained about recognizing Agatha, and her disappearance.

"Agatha," Jim said, "stands to inherit the Falon lands and possessions, if her nephew dies. I was given Robert as a ward by the English King, and my wife and I thought we knew enough about Agatha to keep Robert safe from her—"

"We know all about this!" interrupted Barron.

"All right," said Jim. "But if it was Agatha—Carolinus warned me that Lyonesse was full of tricky magic, so it might not have been her—she'd have to be working with some sort of magical power, herself, to have gotten there."

"Hmmm," said KinetetE.

"Anyway," said Jim, "before Agatha and the two men with her vanished, I noticed that they were wearing Court clothes. And Carolinus had said something to me about the King—I mean, the English King—being in some sort of danger. So I think someone ought to go check this out at the Court."

This time both KinetetE and Barron were silent after he had finished speaking. Finally, Barron spoke.

"Probably has nothing to do with Carolinus' predicament at all!" he said.

"Clearly the woman could gain from taking the child," said KinetetE. "But how capturing Carolinus would involve the English Court—it may be Jim, here, sees a connection where you and I, Barron, don't."

Barron snorted.

"You're really ready to believe this Agatha woman might have something to do with Carolinus' being held by the Gnarly King?" he said.

"I do," answered KinetetE. "And I'll remind you, Barron, that I am unmatched in connective magicks. Just as Carolinus is in intuitiveness—and Carolinus trusts this boy. Remember, the woman is connected to the boy; the boy is connected to the Gnarly King; the King is connected to Carolinus; Carolinus is connected to Jim, here; and Jim is connected to the English Court."

"I am?" said Jim, but apparently unheard.

"Oh. Well, in that case," said Barron, "I suppose I'll have to go back to the Court myself, then." He made a face. "No help for it. None of our Collegiate is known there as I am; and above all, no one else from our Collegiate is as respected there as I am—"

Muttering in the crowd.

"Except perhaps Carolinus himself, of course," Barron went on, a little hastily. "But in any case, I know my way around the Court better than anyone else. I know the people there. You—"

His eyes focused on Jim.

"Yes, Mage?" answered Jim politely, feeling the time for manners had come.

"I suppose you'll have to go along with me to find this Agatha and the two men she tried to pass off as a brother and a father."

"Me?" said Jim. "But I can't! I have to go back to rescue Robert and Carolinus—"

"Not now," said KinetetE.

"We'll leave, then," said Barron. "—that is, if the Collegiate approves that manner of handling things. Do you all?"

He turned to face the audience below the stage.

Jim and KinetetE both looked with him and Jim was astonished to see every robe in the house turn a glowing magician's red.

"Very well, very well. If I must. Come along, Tim—or Jim, or whatever your name is—"

"Just a minute," said Jim.

Barron stared at him in honest astonishment. Jim turned quickly to KinetetE.

"I need to be able to go back to the Gnarly King's Throne Room," he said. "And as quickly as possible, because it looks as if a fight is developing there. Both Robert and Carolinus need help."

"I have never—" began Barron; but this time it was KinetetE who interrupted him.

"Don't worry about that, Jim," she said. "I'll make sure you don't miss anything. You can rest easy."

"Thank you," said Jim.

He turned back to see Barron glaring at him, and just in time to see Barron change the glare to a somewhat sickly smile. Jim looked again at KinetetE and saw her smiling at the other AAA+ magician, with a smile of her own that would have stopped a tiger in his tracks.

"I think it's probably for the best, Barron," said KinetetE. "I'm sure we can all count on you to make the most of young Jim here, by paying attention to what he says and thinks."

"Oh, that. Yes—of course," muttered Barron. "Are you ready—er, Jim?"

"I'm ready now, Mage," said Jim.

With the same suddenness with which Jim was used to being taken places by Carolinus, he now found himself standing with Barron inside a stone-walled room, the small, square window of which evidently gave on an inner court. All that could be seen through it, from Jim's position at least, was a small patch of blue sky above a somewhat distant wall of stone.

Probably that was the side of another building, Jim thought. From out of sight below rose up shouts and cheers, as if some kind of athletic contest were going on.

The room itself was obviously a bedroom, for there were only a couple of low, unpadded, semi-backed chairs, a table, and a curtained bed, with its curtains undrawn. On the table sat several wine bottles and a couple of tumbler-like glasses, one almost empty and one half-full of wine. The table was within arm's reach of the bed. Barron was looking annoyed.

He strode to the bed and grabbed the bare shoulder of the figure on the closest side of it, all that was not completely hidden under the covers. He shook it vigorously.

"Wake up!" he snapped. When neither shaking nor voice were answered he raised his voice and shook even harder.

"Edgar, you will wake up—now!"

The face belonging to the shoulders was half-buried in the pillow. But one closed eye had been showing, above half a mustache and the corner of a mouth.

Now the eye flew open. It stared upward at Barron. With a spasmodic jerk the man belonging to the eye and mustache sat bolt upright in bed, both eyes now wide open despite lank brownish-black hair falling into them. He pushed himself back against the headrest as tightly as he could, as if trying to get as far as possible from Barron.

"Mage!" he said in a thick voice. "Mage—thought you had left the Court!"

"I did. I'm back," said Barron. "This room used to be your sitting room. Why is it a bedroom?"

"Well, I—I—well, you see, it was like this—"

"Never mind!" said Barron. "There are two doors here—" Jim looked. There were indeed two doors in facing walls of the almost square room. "—Which one of them leads to your sitting room?"

The man called Edgar pointed past Barron and Jim at the door more behind them than in front of them.

"We will see you there in three minutes. You will be fully dressed, awake, and ready to talk!" said Barron.

"Yes, Mage—" said Edgar, half-falling out of bed and revealing himself completely naked. Just beyond him the crown of a blond head was barely revealed above the covers, now that he was no longer hiding it with his own form.

"Come, Jim," said Barron.

He turned about and marched toward the door Edgar had indicated. Jim went with him, into a room furnished with two plain wooden chairs and two with full backs and padding. Barron took one of the padded chairs and waved Jim into the other. They sat down.

This room also had a window, through which a burst of cheering could be heard. Jim tried to imagine what was being done or played there. A courtyard like that was not really built for any version of team game. Possibly tennis.

"Mage," he said, "what's his name? Whoever it was you just woke up in the bedroom there?"

"Edgar," said Barron, almost absentmindedly, "Edgar de Wiggin. He's taking his time in there."

"We just sat down, Mage," said Jim. "It can't have been three minutes yet."

"Maybe not." Barron had crossed his legs, and he drummed the fingers of his right hand on his knee. "Still, a slippery fellow like that. Have to keep a tight rein on him. Not that he isn't useful—oh, here he is!"

Edgar de Wiggin was just now coming through the door from the bedroom.

"You are a disgusting sight," said Barron coldly, looking at him. "Lace up your codpiece."

"Oh, pray forgive me, Mage." Attending to that particularly male piece of apparel, Edgar came up to them, hesitated, and then sat down in one of the unpadded chairs.

"It gladdens my heart to see you, Mage," he said. Under the lank hair, his spade-shaped face was managing to smile broadly while preserving a sort of background look of suspicion and insecurity. The kind of appearance, Jim thought, that you might not like to find on someone you had trusted to handle a large sum of money for you.

"Don't waste my time, Edgar," said Barron. "Do you know the Lady Agatha Falon?"

"Why, we aren't close," said Edgar, holding on to his smile. "But then, she spends so much of her time with His Majesty and the other people of importance here at Court. I am a Gentleman of the King's Chamber, of course, but she is kept far too busy by those far above my station. I would not presume—"

"Never mind your presumption," said Barron. "We want to know about her. Is she here all the time?"

"Oh, she hardly ever leaves the Court," said Edgar, "even to go into London to someplace like the Spanish Ambassador's ball, or an important dinner. I can get a message to her, if you like."

"I do not like," said Barron. "What I would like is information, as I said. Whom does she have about her? I do not mean servants, I mean lesser gentlemen who serve her in small ways?"

"Why, there are many who would seek her favor," said Edgar. The smile had finally vanished, but the appearance of closeness and secrecy was still in his face. "You don't mean those of rank like the Earl of Cumberland, for example?"

"No, no," said Barron. "I said *lesser* gentlemen, did I not? Besides, I thought you told us it was his Majesty she was interested in."

"Oh, it is, Mage," said Edgar. "But she is on very good terms with people like Cumberland and Gloucester and the Despensers. But there are many of lesser rank who hope to gain from her favor, since she is so welcome to his Majesty."

"Jim," commanded Barron, "describe those two men to him."

"Certainly, Mage," said Jim. "If you think it's wise."

"Wise? Wise?" snapped Barron.

"I'm afraid I don't know much about this gentleman," said Jim.

"What of it?" said Barron. "He's perfectly harmless—to us. As I told you, he's Edgar de Wiggin—actually a bastard son left behind by a member of a Spanish Embassy. He is tolerated here at Court as a private communication channel between the English Throne and the Spanish. He speaks Spanish and does a little spying on Spanish visitors to Court, for the King. His position as a member of the King's Wardrobe is in name only. That's all he is—a penniless petty Baron, actually."

Jim felt slightly nettled. He was, himself, among the pettiest of Barons; but it was not a good idea to show irritation just now.

"I'd like to find two men," he said to Edgar. "One is in his twenties, with lighter-colored hair and a rather silky, youthful sort of goatee, and a little mustache. He wears fashionable clothes, stands almost six feet tall, and has a ferret-like face with over-large, protruding front teeth. He does not look much like a warrior. The other is at least twenty years older, about five feet six inches tall, and slightly stooped in the shoulders. He has greying hair and a little mustache. Neither one had any particular scars or marks on their faces, or signs of disease like smallpox."

"Sir," said Edgar, "may I ask what they were wearing?"

Jim had forgotten that here in the fourteenth century, if you were in a situation where your best suit of clothes was required, you lived in them day after day, with only an occasional stab at brushing or cleaning by some servant; until the day came when they were too worn, stained, or ragged to appear in. Then you did your best to obtain a newer garment, giving away or selling the older one—and proceeded to live in the new one for as long as it would last. The clothes he had seen the two wearing in Lyonesse were probably the only clothes they had been seen in lately.

"I can't tell you the colors," Jim said, remembering for the first time that he had only seen those men in Lyonesse, where all was black-and-silver. "The younger wears a cote-hardie, and the older a mantle that covered much of his clothing."

Edgar stared at Jim, and then slowly shook his head. "There are several gentlemen of the height and age you describe who could each be wearing such clothing as you mention," he said.

"Well, then, we're going to have to go look at them," said Jim, a little more sharply than he had planned. It was true KinetetE had promised to get him back to the Throne Room of the Gnarly King quickly, but he had a sinking feeling that things here were threatening to become too complicated to handle in short order.

"Exactly," said Barron, getting to his feet. "You go with him, Jim. Edgar, you take him to see anyone who could possibly fit that description. If at any time you want me, Jim, call me. I'm sure you know how to do that. Carolinus must have taught you that, at least."

Jim had actually taught it to himself. But he held his tongue again; and, in fact, he did not have time to say anything because Barron had already disappeared.

"If you will come along with me then, Sir," said Edgar de Wiggin.

Jim followed him out into a narrow, musty, stone hallway. Edgar continued to lead the way.

"I'm afraid that Mage Barron forgot to name you to me, Sir," said Edgar as they went.

"That's right, he didn't," said Jim. "I'm Sir James Eckert, Baron de Bois de Malencontri in the Shire of Somerset."

"I am honored to have your acquaintance, Sir James," said Edgar.

"And I yours, Sir Edgar," said Jim, automatically

The other looked embarrassed.

"I pray you will not be offended to learn—to discover this, Sir James," he said. "But I have never been knighted."

"You haven't?" said Jim, genuinely astonished. So far, in this century, he had never encountered anyone of gentle rank, male, and of fighting age, who was not a knight—unless he was clearly on his way to eventual knighthood or in Holy Orders.

"I am afraid not, Sir James," said Edgar, as they started down a long flight of steep stairs built into a tall stone wall. "The King knights people here at Court—occasionally. It is a great mark of favor. Since knighthood conferred by the King is of such high value, it is generally felt that it would be offensive to his Majesty for anyone else—even though they might have the rank and right of knighting worthy individuals—to dub anyone knight at Court. Consequently, knighthood has never come my way."

He fell silent; and, since Jim could think of nothing to say to this, they went on. They did not speak, in fact, until they had reached the ground level and gone out to their right through a doorway with an arched top. Beyond this, they were in something that might have been the very courtyard down on which Edgar's bedroom had looked.

"Ah, tennis!" said Jim, pleased that his guess had been correct.

"Pray forgive me, Sir James," said Edgar, "but it is merely rakets. One of the two men you mentioned, the young one, may be standing over there watching along the right side of the court. Do you see him?"

Jim looked and saw a tall young man, but his hair was pale and he in no way resembled either of those Jim remembered seeing just before the giants with clubs moved in on them.

"No," said Jim. "That's not the man."

"Pray forgive me, Sir. We will search farther."

So they did. Moving about through dingy hallways and scantly populated courtyards, Edgar turned up three more possible candidates for the role of the younger man, and two for the role of the older man; but Jim shook his head at all of them.

"Pray forgiveness for asking, Sir James," said Edgar, "but are you completely sure that one of those we have looked at could not be one of those you saw? It is easily possible that even a good pair of eyes may make a mistake over something seen in a quick glance."

"I'm sure," said Jim. "We'll go on looking."

"Very well, Sir James. This way, if you please."

This time Edgar led him up a staircase, stepping off it at the first level above ground. He conducted Jim down a long, rather narrow stone passage, that was also, Jim found, very dusty, as if it was not normally used. Jim sneezed twice and Edgar made sympathetic noises.

"Just the dust," said Jim.

"I am relieved to hear it," said Edgar. He had lagged a little bit behind Jim. "It is not too much farther to the next person I would show you. But the corridor is somewhat narrow here, so perhaps you should walk ahead of me—"

The corridor was indeed narrowing, and Jim stepped out ahead. What warned him, even as he did so, he was never quite sure, but he suddenly started to turn around. In the same moment, he was struck a heavy blow high on the right side of his back. He staggered slightly and finished his turn to see Edgar standing, legs apart and staring in what could be either shock or fear. The sheath at his belt that held the knife he, like everyone else, carried— for purposes of eating and any other need that might arise—was empty.

It did not take the sight of an empty sheath to give Jim a full understanding of what had happened. He was already beginning to feel the effects of shock, though there was no pain. There was a definite feeling of something on or in his back.

He had apparently turned just in time, so that while the knife had gone in and was still there, it had struck and gone in at an angle, not as it had been aimed. He could feel his strength going, and a film was starting to obscure his vision. He lifted a heavy hand and thought, at least, that he had it pointed in Edgar's direction.

"*Still!*" he managed to say.

Chapter **26**

Edgar did not even have time to change his expression. He was suddenly halted, frozen, awkwardly balanced in the act of turning to run, a frightened look on his long face.

Leaning against the wall to keep from falling, Jim tried to reach for the knife still in his back, to pull it out. But it was in a difficult position, high on his back and apparently either in deeply, or somehow caught inside his body, chain-mail shirt, or clothes, so that it would not come out easily. He could barely get the fingertips of one hand on it. There was no hope of getting a grip firm enough to pull it out.

There was nothing in magic that he could think of at the moment that could help him, but simply focusing his attention on what he was doing might help. He went through the same process of trying to visualize as he did in creating magic, but in this moment it was a major effort to think.

He imagined himself with the mistiness that was threatening his eyesight pushed back so that it formed a globe within which he stood, and within that globe he could think clearly. There was still no pain, although he seemed to feel something unnatural inside him where no such thing should be. It felt like a weight pulling backward and downward—in fact, it felt like more of a weight than it possibly could be.

He would have to make use of Edgar.

"Edgar," he said out loud, turning his back once more on the man, "your body from the waist up is free. The rest of you stays *still*. You will take hold of the handle of your knife and pull it out of me. You will do that and nothing else. Now, stretch one arm out as far as you can."

He looked over his shoulder. It was almost eerie. Edgar's arm slowly extended, as if it had a life of its own. Jim lost sight of its hand behind his shoulder.

"Now," he said. "With your hand out like that, tell me as soon as your fingers touch the hilt of your knife—you can speak now, too," he added.

He felt the weight in his back increase.

"Are you touching the knife now?" he asked.

"Yes," gasped Edgar. "Mage, I did not know you were a Magickian. I should have known by Mage Barron bringing you to me. Believe me, Mage, if I had known—"

"Never mind that!" said Jim. "Have you got a grip on the hilt?"

"Yes, Mage."

"Then pull the damn thing out, now! Easy . . ."

"Yes, Mage—yes, I understand. I'll get it out just as neatly . . ." Edgar ran out of words.

"PULL, goddamn you!" said Jim.

He felt himself tugged backward, and braced himself to stay on his feet. The pull stopped suddenly, and he almost overbalanced forward. However, he caught himself in time, and immediately visualized the blood vessels in the wound closing up. He turned, to see Edgar still standing, completely paralyzed by Jim's magic order, except for his one arm, with the bloody-bladed knife in his hand.

"Throw the knife from you!" said Jim.

Edgar obeyed, clumsily, and the knife clattered through the dust twenty feet down the hall.

"*Unfreeze!*" said Jim.

Nothing happened; and after a moment Jim realized his mistake in using the wrong command. But on second thought, he decided to leave the other as he was for the moment.

Ignoring the motionless Edgar, Jim began to concentrate on visualizing the wound in him as healing—torn tissues knitting together, the previously sealed blood vessels linking up, infectious material vanishing—just as he had envisioned the healing of Brian's wound up in Cumberland. He felt a brief stab of pain, then nothing for a long moment; then a steady ache began to spread out over the whole area of his back. He reached back to feel at the area, and touched wetness. Blood. He concentrated on making that vanish as well, and felt to see if the area was now dry. It was. He turned his back once more on Edgar.

"Is there any blood showing?"

"No, Mage."

Jim turned back to face him.

"All right," he said—though things were actually very far from being all right. The ache in his back, the mist that hovered on the edges of his vision and the fogginess in his head that made thinking difficult, were threatening to overwhelm him. He felt very unsteady on his legs. "Do you know of an empty room somewhere close with a bed, where I can recline, or lie down?"

"Yes, Mage," said Edgar timidly. "But—"

"But what?"

"But we'd have to go back down the stairs and into another part of the building. This wing is empty; it has not been used for some years."

"That's why you brought me here to knife me," said Jim. "So nobody would find my body in a hurry!"

"Yes, Mage." Edgar's voice almost squeaked on the words.

"In this room you know of," said Jim, "is there anything that you know well enough to tell me exactly what it looks like? A chair, the bed itself, something in the room, a tapestry on the wall—"

"Well," said Edgar slowly, "there is one chair with a broken back—one of the plain wood chairs. Just one side of the back is broken away from the seat. The other's all right."

"What color and size is it?" said Jim. "Compared to the chairs that were in your rooms?"

"It was just like the ones in my rooms. The same color, too, Mage."

"All right." Jim summoned up a mental image of one of the unpadded chairs in Edgar's room, imagined one with its back broken on one side, and reached out for the nearest room that had such a chair. The view in his visualization seemed to open out to show a bedroom that had just a table and one other unpadded chair, plus the bed.

Magically he moved himself and Edgar to it. He found the bed only a couple of steps away, and staggered those two steps. As he started to crawl onto the bed, he recalled the likelihood that it would contain vermin such as fleas and lice, and he laid down a ward to seal them within the bed's fabrics themselves.

Lying half on his side, he propped himself against the headboard, with the help of a pillow. The pillow did not help the pain in his back; but the happiness of getting his weight off his legs and being able to cease the effort to stand upright, was tremendous.

Jim sighed with relief, and then took a deep breath to fill his lungs again. He sneezed explosively.

For the first time, he realized that the room was thick with dust and that the pillow he had put up behind him had also been dusty, so that now he was surrounded by a dust cloud.

"Edgar, would there be anyone at all in either of your rooms right now?" he asked.

"No, Mage," said Edgar; and added more cautiously "—I don't think so."

"There better not be," said Jim grimly. Edgar's bedroom, with its bed and all its pillows and blankets—nice and clean, relatively speaking—came sharp to his mind's eye. Magically he switched them to that, moving himself and his anti-bug ward directly into Edgar's bed. He propped himself up against the headboard with a pillow behind him.

He sighed again. This time there was no sneeze, and the relief was even greater. It seemed to him that the pain in his back had begun to lessen slightly.

He was suddenly aware of Edgar standing unnaturally still near the bed, his arm still outstretched but sagging. Jim's head was definitely clearing, and he thought now that he had really gone about this business of handling the knifing in a very clumsy fashion. But all that was necessary now was to put a ward around himself and the bed, with another around the inside walls of the room, so that Edgar couldn't get out, and then they could both relax.

He set up the two wards, specifying that he and Edgar would be able to talk back and forth through them; and then looked at Edgar almost with a touch of compassion.

"*Unstill,*" he said. Edgar slumped suddenly, almost collapsing. "Sit down in a chair."

Edgar made a short step to a chair and dropped into it, where he sat huddled up and catching his breath. Jim watched him, thinking what Brian's opinion, for example, would be of someone like Edgar being considered for knighthood.

Now that he was secure, Jim himself began to feel a serious exhaustion. It suddenly struck him that he hadn't slept or eaten for quite a long time. Back in the cave of the Gnarly King, he, Dafydd, and Brian, at least, had probably been too keyed up to think of food and sleep.

He opened his mouth to tell Edgar to call a servant and order food, or go himself to get some. Then he realized that he'd have to figure out what to do about the wards he had set up to protect himself, and to keep Edgar inside. Resolutely he put sleep and food from him while he thought about it.

The important thing was, he was now safe—with the wards about him there was nothing anybody could do to him—in fact, all the forces that this castle might be able to call upon would be unable to reach him. And the more he thought about it, the more sure he was that Edgar would almost surely obey orders—for the present, at least.

"Edgar," he said.

"Yes, Mage?"

"I'm going to rest. And you're going to go out and get me something to eat and drink. You will not tell anyone that I am here, and you will bring no one back with you. I will be listening and watching you magically, and I can strike from a distance. Tell no one—you hear? Tell *no one* I'm here."

"Oh, Mage," said Edgar, clasping his hands prayerfully, "I won't. You can trust me."

"I better be able to," growled Jim, thinking that he'd been using similar threatening words a lot lately. He lifted the ward from the door as Edgar left, and put it back, reminding it that only Edgar could enter, when he returned.

As the door closed, Jim's eyes drooped. He could not fall asleep, of course, he told himself, with all of this discomfort caused by the wound. He closed his eyes however, and tried to ignore it, as a good medieval knight should; and was understandably furious, accordingly, when—it seemed only a second or two later—he had to open them again because Edgar was standing beside the bed, calling him.

"What? What is it?" he snapped. "What went wrong?"

"Nothing, Mage," said Edgar, timorously. "The food and drink you wished—"

Edgar waved at the little table at the bedside. On it was a glass, a pitcher of wine, some chunks of cold meat, and dark bread on a wooden platter. Jim was still sitting up in the bed.

"Ah—I see," he grumphed. "All right. How long were you gone?"

"An hour. No more, Mage," said Edgar.

Jim grunted; and lost himself in the food and drink—the red wine was surprisingly good. After a while all the food was gone, and half the wine. He leaned back against the headboard, feeling better. The pain in his back was still there, but seemed easier to ignore now.

It made him think, however. Brian had never said a word about how his wounds still hurt him after Jim—or, once before, Carolinus—had mended them with magic. But then, that was part of this century's attitude toward pain: you couldn't do anything about it, so you put it out of your mind. It was like being caught in a rain with no place to shelter—since you couldn't get out of the rain, you just let it rain on you. That was the way life was.

So he told himself. The pain, however, did not grow any less. He turned his attention back to Edgar.

"Why did you try to kill me?" he asked.

"It was all a sad mistake, Mage," said Edgar, swiftly. "I thought you were a Devil that Mage Barron had set to watch me; and a man in my position at Court can't go around with a Devil following him all the time. I thought you would just disappear when I put my knife into you. That's what Devils do, don't they?"

"They do not," said Jim.

The fact was, he had no idea whether they did or not; but this hardly mattered, since it was obvious Edgar was lying to him. If Edgar had really believed him to be a Devil, the last thing he would have dared was to use a knife. Edgar clearly hoped to be thought simpleminded, rather than dangerous.

"So," said Jim, "you thought I'd disappear? That's why you carefully took me up to a deserted section of the castle, here, to use your knife?"

"Well," said Edgar, "you see, I didn't want anyone to see me doing it. You've no idea how difficult it is for me at Court here. I only manage to stay on and stay alive, and get my stipend as a Gentleman of the King's Wardrobe, because I can pick up little bits of harmless gossip and pass them on to those who may gain some small, harmless advantage from knowing them. To do that, you have to go carefully—that is, you must be alone with whoever you are speaking with; and having a Devil with me—"

"Let's forget about any Devil being involved in this," said Jim. "Just get one thing clear: I'm going to be with you until we get to the bottom of this. Now, pretty obviously, you're not a practiced assassin."

"Oh no! I'm not at all, Mage," said Edgar. "I knew someone like yourself would see that right away. I couldn't be that sort of person. I just couldn't live with myself if I was."

"Then what made you try it?" said Jim. "And let's not have any more of your imaginative answers. Something large had to be at stake for you—and don't tell me it was just a matter of keeping your place here at Court."

"I promise you, Mage—"

"Promise me, hell!" Jim checked a sudden, unusual flare of furious anger, remembering Robert and the others back in the Gnarly cave. "There's a young child and several good men with their lives at stake because of this; and I'm through listening to your made-up answers! You're afraid of someone—well, be more afraid of me! What is going on to cause all this? Is it something to do with the two men that I'm looking for? Is it Agatha Falon, herself?"

"Neither, Mage, I swear it—"

"Think before you speak!" said Jim. He lifted a forefinger slowly until it pointed at Edgar. "Do you know what I can do to you?"

Edgar's face went a papery white. Jim had no idea what he could do, but right at the moment he was willing to do it, and the Magickian's Law of using Magick only in self-defense be damned.

Edgar burst into tears and fell on his knees, his hands clasped before him, staring up at Jim on the bed.

"I dare not, Mage!" he said. "I never wanted anything to do with them; but how can I refuse when a Lord of the Realm tells me to play the spy? He could crush me with a wave of his hand!"

"Who could crush you?"

"Mage, I can't tell you!"

"Who were you supposed to be spying upon?"

"All of them!" said Edgar. "But in especial the Earl of Oxford and Sir John Chandos!"

A bell rang in Jim's mind. The last time he had heard the name of the Earl of Oxford mentioned, it had been in relation to the raid on the Earl of Cumberland's land.

"The Lord you are so afraid of, then," said Jim at a venture, "is my Lord of Cumberland! Don't deny it!"

Edgar wrung his hands. He had stopped crying to talk, but now he started again. Jim looked at him with disgust, not unmixed with a tinge of shame at having pushed him to act so.

"I will be killed!" Edgar was sobbing. "Not only will I lose everything— what little I have—but they will kill me. Kill me most cruelly and hideously— perhaps as the father of our present King, God rest his soul, was killed, so no mark would be left on him!"

"I'll protect you," said Jim pompously. Once more he was talking at a venture. He had no idea whether Barron, KinetetE, or any other magician would back up any promises he made. But he had to get answers out of this man.

"So, at Cumberland's order, you spied on Sir John Chandos, the Earl of Oxford, and others. It was about their stopping a raid that might be made on my Lord Earl's estates, wasn't it?"

"What can I do? What can I do?" said Edgar, more to himself than to Jim. "You know everything, Mage! Why do you even trouble to question me?"

"I have my reasons," said Jim. "Now tell me, what's the connection between the men I was looking for and the Lady Agatha, and the rest of this business of the raid?"

"I dare not tell you," said Edgar He had stopped crying, and his face was pale but calm. "Do what you will to me, Mage, she and they can do worse. The woman is a witch!"

"As a magician, I know she is not a witch," said Jim.

"Oh, but she is, Mage!" said Edgar, looking up suddenly. "I saw her once myself, at a distance down a corridor, turning into a room. But when I came up to that room afterward, opened the door, and stepped in—intending to say that I had come to the wrong room by mistake—there was no one in it."

He stared at Jim.

"And there were no secret passages or doorways out of that room," he added. "Believe me, Mage, I know it well."

Jim doubted that.

"Magicians do not explain themselves," he said. "But I repeat, she is not a witch. Now, how did you come to see her down the corridor, and why did you enter the room yourself, with an excuse on your lips?"

"I just happened to be in the corridor and see her," said Edgar.

"You have only answered half of what I asked you," said Jim. "Your reason for entering the room?"

"I thought if she was visiting someone my Lord might like to know about, then I'd find out who it was. If it was somebody unimportant, I would simply put it out of mind, make my excuses, and leave."

"You're so afraid of her because she's a witch," said Jim, "but you walked right in, intending just to make your excuses and go out again?" He snapped the rest of his words at Edgar suddenly. "Were you set to spy on her, too?"

Edgar slumped on the floor. "I am lost," he said, as much to himself as Jim.

"Tell me the truth," said Jim, "and I'll protect you. How well-known is this story about Lady Agatha being a witch?"

"Oh, it is generally known," said Edgar, apathetically. "She has never pretended to be so. But it is talked of by all at Court. It is said the high Lords and those around her—except, possibly, the King himself—know of it, but admit it only among themselves. She vanishes from Court at times. She was gone secretly all the Twelve Nights of Christmas. It was given out she was visiting the Earl of Somerset with Prince Edward, but instead she had traffic and intercourse with various trolls and other demons—"

"Nonsense!" said Jim. "I was at the Earl's myself last Christmas and saw her there. She did no such thing!"

"She did not?" Edgar stared.

"She did not!" snapped Jim. "Answer my question!"

"She, too," said Edgar miserably. "I am set to watch her, too. But Mage, there are other matters, not so easily explained. She is not in truth well-favored in face or body, but the King dotes on her. If she is indeed not a witch—"

"That's enough of that!" interrupted Jim. "If I hear the word 'witch' from you one more time—"

"You will not! You will not, I promise, Mage!" cried Edgar.

"Good. Now tell me how you know the King dotes on her," said Jim.

"Why, the whole Court knows, Mage. She has the high favor of a suite of rooms in the main tower, all but next to his Majesty's quarters; and it is in that part of the tower where the King's Advisors are lodged in suites of their own. When she is about the Court, but not with the King, it is usually with one of those Lords who advise the King."

"How close are her rooms to Cumberland's?"

Edgar's eyes widened a little bit, for just a moment, but that was all.

"Next to Cumberland," he said, "of course, Mage."

"Why 'of course'?" growled Jim. His back felt a lot better, but it still hurt.

"Why, Cumberland was the patron who introduced her at Court. No one can be introduced at Court except by a patron already here—except someone like me—" Edgar attempted a knowing smile, but it appeared on his face as rather more of a sad expression than anything else. "—I was born here."

"How did Cumberland get to know her?" he asked.

"The story is she met him at a party in one of his castles, and showed him how his Steward there was stealing from him in the accounts the Steward kept."

"Hmmm," said Jim. "Cumberland must have brought her here, not knowing what a handful she could be. Next to Cumberland, then, is she?"

"And Cumberland's rooms are next to the Royal space, Mage," he said. "But you must understand, she is the *King's* friend."

"Then she is seen more with Cumberland, than with others?"

"Yes!" said Edgar. "My Lord the Earl of Cumberland is his Majesty's Chief Advisor. It is only natural she is seen most with him, among all the great Lords."

For the first time Jim felt his spirits lift—even though he could not pin down exactly what gave him that feeling. He had been throwing questions at Edgar almost at random, just as they occurred to him. Sometimes that meant the back of his head was working and now, perhaps, that unconscious part of him had a scent of what he was after

"Perhaps then you could tell me—" he was beginning, when a sheet of greyish-white paper—the kind they used at Malencontri—came slip-sliding, wafting down toward his lap from the ceiling.

"Close your eyes," snapped Jim at Edgar and, when the other had done so, gave the *still* command again.

Chapter 27

Jim caught the piece of paper just before it went past him on its way to the floor. Happily, his reflexes had always been fast; and this, coupled with the years of volleyball, had taught him, like any old hand in that sport, to receive any incoming object close to the ground rather than up in the air. His fingers closed on the paper and held it. He looked at it.

It was blank. He stared at it for a second; then, understanding breaking through, he turned it over. On the other side was a note in Angie's handwriting. It was in ordinary twentieth-century script, rather than the fourteenth-century script she had taught herself to write since they had been at Malencontri, so that she could use her knowledge of Latin to answer any rare missive that managed to make its way to them.

It was a good thing she had. Jim, to this day, could not make sense of the flourishes which scribes here used. Conversely, of course, the best of those clerks would have been badly puzzled by twentieth-century handwriting; so this note Angie had sent would probably have been safe, even if it had fallen into the wrong hands.

But it had come by magic—and that was a strange thing, for Angie had no magic. Certainly she had possessed none since Carolinus learned that she had managed, more or less by sheer willpower, to turn herself into a dragon. Carolinus, appearing almost immediately, had reversed the change, and then put a ward on her to keep her from discovering any more such things. He had said that Jim was already more than a man his age should have to deal with—two of them doing the sorts of things Jim found to do would be too much.

Greedily, Jim began to read the note. It was headed by block capital letters:

EMERGENCY

My love,
Carolinus gave me the ability to write you in an emergency, like this. He had promised me, when you went on that trip to the Holy Land, that he would find some way for me to get a message to you if I really needed to; and later he gave me a small supply of this magic paper—I guess I only have to write on it, and when I tell it to, it will go and find you. Forgive me for not telling you about it, but I didn't know when or how I might need to get in touch with you, so I kept it to myself.

A man named Sir William Wilson, with a troop of King's soldiers, showed up, with another letter from Prince Edward, asking once more for your help against Agatha Falon. He really sounds desperate, and must have sent this second letter before hearing the results of his first one.

His second letter says that things have gotten much worse; and at any moment now he might be disowned by the King, or charged with High Treason, or some disastrous thing like that. I don't understand it—King's men seem like odd people to carry a letter like that from the Prince, when Agatha is his father's current favorite. Has it occurred to you how strangely coincidental it is, that both Robert and the Prince are in danger now—and both have Agatha as their major enemy? But I can't see how she could have taken Robert, unless she has some sort of alliance with some magical being—I wouldn't put it past her, either!

Anyway, I'd like to know where you are and what you're doing. Are you all right? I always want to know that; but Carolinus made such a point of my using this only in a great emergency, that I haven't written you like this before now to find out how things are.

I won't worry if you don't answer this; because I know you're all right and it just isn't practical for you to send me messages as often as I'd like to have them. But I miss you and I love you more than anyone else in the world. More than little Robert, even, much as I've come to love him in the little time we've had him.

Do take care of yourself. I lied. I do worry. I worry all the time; but I can't help it and there's nothing that can be done about it; so don't pay any attention to it. But message me when you can. All the love in all the world.

Angie

Jim reached out into thin air, saying "Handkerchief" quietly and visualizing one. His fingers closed on it, a little above the surface of the bed, and he blew his nose, and cleared his throat. He was glad Edgar could not see any of this. He carefully folded the letter and tucked it away; then wadded up the handkerchief and was about to tell it simply to vanish, when he had a better idea.

"Disintegrate!" he told it firmly.

The handkerchief hesitated a moment, winked out, winked in again, but finally disappeared in a small white flash of light.

Relieved that the present era of magic could understand at least that one modern word, Jim turned his attention back to Edgar.

"*Unstill!*" he told Edgar, in a more kindly voice. Edgar opened his eyes but said nothing.

"Now, back to business," said Jim. "You did say Agatha Falon's quarters were next to those of the Earl of Cumberland?"

"Why—yes," said Edgar.

"I see," said Jim. "Now, on another subject. How are matters between Agatha and Prince Edward?"

"Much as you might expect, Mage," said Edgar. "They are well with each other, although of course since she is interested with his father the King, they have little occasion for direct conversation. But they are certainly cordial."

At the Earl of Somerset's Christmas Party, Jim remembered, it had been obvious to all that that relationship had been anything but cordial. No one had said anything about it—at least aloud and in his hearing. But it had been no secret then, and it could hardly be a secret here at Court, which was undoubtedly worse than your ordinary small village as far as internal gossip went.

"If you continue to lie to me," said Jim, slowly and in his deepest voice, "you will begin to grow smaller and more like a worm than a human being; you will continue getting smaller and smaller until you are very small, on the floor, and fully a worm. Then I shall step on you."

"Mage!" Edgar started to cry again.

"Stop that!" said Jim. It was a thing about this era that he could not accustom himself to. No one should have to abase himself or herself in such a fashion, and he always felt shamed when such went on about him. He took a deep breath to calm himself down and went on in a more ordinary voice. "Just keep in mind what I said, and answer me truthfully. How are things with Agatha and the Prince?"

"They have no love for each other. That is true," said Edgar with great sincerity.

"Closer to the truth, anyway," said Jim. "All right, from now on you will answer me truthfully, or else. Next question: are there any secret passages between Agatha Falon's rooms and the Earl of Cumberland's?"

"Mage, I swear by God I have no knowledge of secret passages here or anywhere! There is always talk of them, but I know nothing with certainty. Nothing!"

"Yet you told me that you went into a room Agatha'd entered, and found no one there; and that you knew the room was empty because you searched for secret passages."

"I lied about that, too, Mage," said Edgar unhappily. "I really do not know about secret passages. There is some talk of a passage between the Earl of Cumberland's and the King's suites; and more talk, of course, of secret passages from the King's suites to other areas of the Castle—and even to without the walls, so that he may come and go secretly. But I have no true knowledge."

"Then we'd better find out right now," said Jim. "Take me to Cumberland's quarters, to the place where they come up against, or close to, the King's area."

"But, Mage," said Edgar, "I cannot take you openly through the Castle and to that part where are the rooms of the King, as you are. You carry sword and poignard at your belt, and are wearing a mail shirt—to say nothing of the fact that your face is not known about Court." He paused, and seemed to swallow before continuing.

"—Before, I took care to take you only in areas little-frequented and far from the King—places where a stranger would not look too unusual. But if you—armed and unknown—come close to him, we should both be challenged and thrown into chains, without question, immediately!"

"Were those also places you knew would not be frequented by the men I was seeking?" Jim asked.

Edgar cringed, and nodded rather shakily.

"Well, it makes no difference for the moment," said Jim. "I'll make both of us invisible and inaudible."

In his mind's eye he envisioned the room they were in, with Edgar and himself still in it, but the room appearing absolutely empty. Once he had thought it impossible to make himself—or anything else—invisible, but had found a way to accomplish a similar effect in another way. But with experience, he could now do it more simply.

"But, Mage—by your favor—we aren't invisible," said Edgar in a small voice. "I can see you clearly; and I can see parts of myself."

"That's right," said Jim. "I can see you, and you can see me, and we can see ourselves. But nobody else can see us. You have to take care that anyone else we meet doesn't walk into you, thinking there's nothing there. We don't want people to know we're there."

"No, Mage," said Edgar. "Of course not."

"Well, lead me to the Earl of Cumberland's suite, then."

Edgar led him back down to the courtyard where another game was in progress, although with fewer spectators. From there they took a different doorway and a long passage; another stairway; more corridors . . . and, eventually, a wider, cleaner set of stairs than any they had yet climbed.

Atop these, they entered a wide corridor. A long walk, but it had taken Jim's mind off the ache in his back.

In this corridor servants were coming and going, with full or empty trays, or, occasionally, articles of clothing.

"Can they hear us?" Edgar whispered in Jim's ear.

Jim shook his head.

"They can't hear us either," he said in his ordinary voice. "Now show me where the Earl of Cumberland's quarters end and the King's begin."

Edgar stared at him.

"Well?" demanded Jim.

"Mage, I—I don't know where it is," he said. "In fact, I don't know exactly where the Earl of Cumberland's quarters are."

"Hell's bells!"

"In fact, Mage," said Edgar miserably, "I'm not even sure which doors might open on the quarters of any Lord here. You see, someone of little importance like me . . . I—I've never been here before. This is my first time."

Jim stared at him. Edgar shrank back.

"If you could give me a couple of weeks," he said hastily, "possibly I could ferret it out and give you the information—"

"Hell's bells!" said Jim again, realized he was repeating himself, and moved them both back to Edgar's room so fast that Edgar wobbled a little on his feet and gasped uncertainly. Jim looked around the room.

"Get me a bowl of clean water," he ordered. "No, wait, you'd take too long."

He searched his memory for a moment, trying to remember where at Malencontri or anyplace else he'd seen the kind of bowl he wanted. One came to mind—a bowl in Carolinus' cottage. The idea of taking any of Carolinus' belongings made him feel uncomfortable. But then, he reminded himself, Carolinus was locked in a cage and might never get out unless Jim did something about it. He visualized the bowl he had in mind—one of a sea-green ceramic material with a high scalloped rim and small fish set inside it. It appeared on the table before him.

"Get me some water," he said to Edgar. "*Clean* water!"

Edgar hurried into the next room, and came back with a leather pitcher. He offered it to Jim.

"Thanks," said Jim shortly. He poured from the pitcher into the bowl, but immediately saw that the water was full of small floating bits of something— possibly leather, but possibly something worse.

Jim picked up the bowl and, with Brian's best sort of casual gesture, tossed its contents on the floor. He set the bowl back down on the table.

"Go back to Carolinus' cottage," he told the bowl. "Rinse yourself thoroughly in the pool of the Fountain of Tinkling Water. Then come back to me, filled with clean water."

The bowl vanished and was back almost immediately, filled to the brim with water so clean it shamed the room around it.

"Now, we're getting someplace," said Jim. He pulled up a chair, sat down at the table, and focused on the surface of the water. He was no longer in the Gnarly Kingdom, and his magic ought to enable him to look in on the cave of the King and everyone there.

It was scrying, of course, as he had seen it done by Abu al-Qusayr, when Jim, with Brian, was hunting for Geronde's father. The Eastern magician had used a bowl of water rather than the crystal globe which Carolinus and most northern European magicians used. Jim concentrated, and the scene in the cave formed before his eyes, everyone in it apparently motionless.

Hill still stood facing the King, who was leaning out from his throne— obviously they were still in argument. Jim puzzled a moment over why nobody seemed to be moving; then he dismissed the problem—he had suspected, from stories he had heard, that sometimes time was different between Kingdoms.

He looked for Hob and did not see him, until he peered more carefully at the sumpter-horse, dozing on its feet, and saw Hob's little face barely peeking out from under the weather-cover

Now the question became whether his magic could reach into the King's cave. The best way to find out was to try what had come to his mind. There was every reason it shouldn't work, since it could be thought of as trying to make magic in a Kingdom where foreign magic was not allowed. But then, Carolinus had somehow sent his projection, and that implied his Master-in-Magic had some way of taking at least some of his magic to the Gnarly Kingdom.

Foreign magic might not work on anything physical in another Kingdom, but maybe it could on something that was pure energy.

"A puff of smoke, six cubic inches," Jim commanded—and such a puff appeared, hovering in the air before him.

"Now," he told it, "everything physical about you will cease to be. Only the energy in you will remain."

The small cloud of smoke bobbed in the air for a second or two, uncertainly. Then it disappeared.

"And now," he told the space where he had last seen it, pointing at the apparently motionless little face peeking out from under the cover of the sumpter-horse, "go to him!" Hastily he prepared magic to make Hob as invisible as he and Edgar were.

For a long moment nothing seemed to happen. Then Hob's face suddenly seemed to speed up, changing in expression to startlement. A second later, Hob himself, wearing a grin, appeared before Jim; and the thin air beneath him suddenly became a puff of smoke. He launched himself to Jim's nearest shoulder, throwing both his arms around Jim's neck as he arrived.

"M'Lord! I *knew* you sent that smoke! I knew you did. I rode it right back to you!" he said, hugging Jim's neck fiercely with both arms.

"Guk!" said Jim.

"Oh, I'm sorry, m'Lord!" said Hob, loosening his grip. "Did I seize you too stoutly? I'm so glad to see you! How did you get here? What is this place? Who's he—"

Hob pointed at Edgar.

"Name's Edgar," said Jim, on his first lungful of air. "—Wait a minute."

He had just remembered the bowl which he had used to scry the Gnarly cave. Carolinus might raise a fuss if it was lost or stolen—though it was obviously an old bowl and unimportant. At the same time, Jim might need it again. Not only the bowl, but its sparkling-clear Tinkling Water.

"You—" he pointed at it, "stay with me, but be inaudible and invisible; and none of your water is to fall out. That's a magical command."

The bowl disappeared. "Now," said Jim, turning back to Hob, "what were you asking me?"

"With your pardon, m'Lord," answered Hob, a little timidly, "I just asked who *he* was. But you told me. He is an Edgar."

"Oh," said Jim. "I meant his name was Edgar. Look—I'll explain things later.

We're in the King's Castle near London. It's a very big place; but if we find a fireplace, can you go into it, and ride up and down chimneys until you find some secret passages in the wall?"

"Of course, m'Lord," said Hob. "Your Lordship knows that!"

"Well, that's what I want you to do. I'll take you to as close as we were able to get before—remember now, we're all invisible and we can talk, but nobody can hear us talk." They were suddenly back again in the corridor busy with servants.

"Invisible, really, m'Lord?"

"Yes, really; and you can loosen up on my neck again."

"Very sorry, m'Lord."

"Now," Jim went on. "Somewhere along here there're the rooms of the Earl of Cumberland. They end at a wall, on the other side of which we'll find all the rooms of the King. I'm sure there has to be a secret passage through that wall. Do you think you can find it?"

"Oh, yes, m'Lord," said Hob. "If I just have a place to start—like a fireplace?"

"Well . . ." Jim turned around and, as luck would have it, not too far away, a servant was carrying a tray to a door. It was a tray that required both hands, so that he had to rather balance it in mid-air with one hand, while scratching on the door. He waited—and in that moment of waiting, Jim reached him, with Hob on his shoulder, and Edgar close behind.

The servant opened the door and shouldered his way in, reaching back with an elbow to try to pull the door closed behind him. It gave a slight swing inward; but Jim caught it with invisible fingertips, and he, Hob, and Edgar slipped through.

"Close that door!" snarled a voice.

Jim had heard that voice before—in France. He had been trying to stop a potentially bloody battle between the English and French armies; and, with the help of the French Dragons, as well as both Prince Edward and Carolinus, had succeeded—though the encounter had managed to be bloody enough. But in the aftermath of the affair, Jim had earned the enmity of an Earl.

The speaker was a large burly man with a round, greying head of hair and a short-cropped greying beard on a square, heavy-boned face—his body bulky in red velvet cote-hardie and hose and his face set in a scowl that made the beard jut forward belligerently: Robert de Clifford, the Earl of Cumberland—the same man who had refused to allow Jim and Brian to take the body of their friend, Giles, to the sea for the burial he had wanted.

Clearly, Jim thought, nothing had changed with the Earl, in any way

The servant they had followed carefully put his platter down on a table in front of the Earl. Jim and his party continued across the room, to pass invisibly through a half-open door that might lead them to the connecting wall with the King's quarters. Jim was deep in thought as he went.

Agatha Falon did not like Angie, or him, at all—it would not be going too far to say that she hated both of them with a vicious hatred—simply because they had thwarted her plans to inherit the vast Falon estates by controlling or murdering her baby nephew, Robert.

It was bad enough to be up against Agatha alone, now that she was apparently reinstated as the King's favorite. It was much worse if she were also working, somehow, with one of the King's chief Advisors—perhaps the most important of them—and him already disposed to be an enemy to Jim.

But Jim still could not understand how Agatha could have persuaded the Gnarly King to steal Robert for her, or how she could have gotten to Lyonesse to try to ambush Jim and his party.

While Jim pondered this, he and his party had passed through two rooms and still not come up against a wall with no door in it—a lack indicating a dividing wall between suites of rooms. But as they headed for the next door, it opened before them.

Through it appeared the King himself, walking heavily right at them—not seeing them at all, of course—and, Jim supposed, heading toward a meeting with the Earl of Cumberland.

Chapter 28

There was no doubt he was the King. Edward Plantagenet, under God King of England, Duke of Aquitaine, Duke of Brittany, Duke of Carabella, Prince of Tours, Prince of the Two Sicilies—and too many other places for Jim to remember right at the moment—had been a tall, soldierly Royal-appearing figure in his early manhood.

Now, the years had shrunk him and padded his lower figure with fat. He wore no crown; but, though his mustache and beard were untidy and stained with wine—as was his mulberry-colored gown—the golden belt around his waist, although naked of sword or poignard, proclaimed him no common man. He advanced, if unsteadily, still with the authority of someone who owned the ground he walked on—which, legally, of course he did. And all the other ground in the Kingdom, too.

Moving quietly, Edgar, and Jim with Hob on his shoulder, got out of the Royal way and watched him go in the direction from which they had just come. Then they went through the door by which his Highness had come and found themselves at last in a room with no further visible exit.

It did, however, have a fireplace, with the remains of a few logs burning in it, and a large curtained bed with two bedside tables and a couple of padded chairs. Tapestries hung on the walls, and the curtains of the bed were of heavy material—a dark blue velvet. At the moment, these had been pulled back to show a rumpled, unmade bed with at least six enormous pillows and any number of sheets and blankets.

"Oh, look, m'Lord!" said Hob, pointing at the fireplace.

"I see it," said Jim. The logs in it were burned down to charred stubs, and only a tiny wisp of smoke came up from their faintly glowing ends. "Don't you need more of a fire than that, to make smoke?"

"Just fine, m'Lord!" cried Hob cheerfully—and launched himself from Jim's shoulder into the fireplace, on a dive that caused him to plane in just above the flames.

"Wait!" called Jim. Hob had already disappeared up the chimney, but now he reappeared, upside-down, his face peering at Jim inquiringly, just below the upper edge of the fireplace opening.

"Yes, m'Lord?"

"What are you going to do if you run into the Hob who belongs to this place?" asked Jim.

"Oh, I'll say 'Greetings!' " said Hob. "And he'll say 'Greetings—' "

"He won't be able to see you," Jim pointed out. "Let me change the magic so that other Hobs can see you.—There! But what if he isn't all that friendly to you?"

"Oh, m'Lord," said Hob, "all Hobs are friendly to each other. We're never like, like . . . well, like some of you big people."

"Well," said Jim, "you remember, you gave the Hob at the Earl's Castle rather rough treatment when you first went there, according to what you told me."

"I did?" Hob's face was a mirror of upside-down astonishment.

"Certainly," said Jim. "You ordered him about and called him 'Sirrah!' "

"I did?" said Hob again.

"That's right," said Jim.

Hob's face abruptly stopped looking astonished.

"Oh, that was different, m'Lord. You see, you'd just given me that magnificent name I wasn't able to keep—you remember? Can I say it?"

Jim nodded.

"Hob-One-de-Malencontri," said Hob, a couple of tears rolling up his forehead.

"Well," said Jim, touched with remembered guilt, "Carolinus told me I wasn't allowed to give names to a Hob. But maybe we can get it back for you someday."

"D'you think so, m'Lord?"

"We'll see," said Jim. "Anyway, be prepared, because this Hob will be the King's Hob, and he just may think he's got higher rank than you. Now, are you sure you can find the secret passage in this wall—if there is one?"

"Certainly, m'Lord," said Hob. "You see, I'll make the smoke feel over everything. And if there's a crack someplace, or some sort of a little hole, the smoke will work its way into it even if it has to go out into a room and back in again to do that. It may take me a little while, though."

"That's all right," said Jim, struck by a sudden thought. "You go ahead. Edgar will stay here and wait for you, so he can come for me when you've found it."

Hob disappeared, then almost immediately popped back into sight again.

"I don't suppose you could make me invisible every time I come out of a fireplace, m'Lord?"

"No," said Jim, thinking of what might happen at Malencontri if he did.

"Oh, well," said Hob, and disappeared again.

"Where are you going, Mage?" asked Edgar, sounding alarmed.

"Just back to where Cumberland was sitting," said Jim. "Don't worry now. If anyone comes in, they can't see you. Just make it a point to keep out of their way, so that they don't bump into you."

"I will, Mage. You can trust me," said Edgar.

Fairly sure that he could trust Edgar, for that at least, Jim went back through the various rooms to the door of the room where Cumberland had been seated. The door was ajar, but not enough that Jim could see the Earl. He slipped quietly through the opening, shouldering it slightly to do so, and stepped into the room, counting on his invisibility to make this a safe move.

Cumberland was standing now, almost but not quite in front of the fire. Seated in the best chair was the King, looking less than majestic now that he was not on his feet.

"—Where the Devil did you say she had gone?" demanded the King.

"Riding, your Highness," said Cumberland.

"Riding! What does she want with that? Lately, anytime I want her, she's 'riding,' " the King muttered, more to himself than to Cumberland. He looked up at the Earl. "Robert, give me to drink."

Cumberland moved to the table that was actually within arm's reach of the King, poured from a bottle—rather than a pitcher—into a large painted-glass goblet; and, with only an abrupt small bow, handed the goblet to the King; who took it absentmindedly, but drank rather thirstily from it.

"Damn women," said the King. "They've always got things to do. I don't ask much of her time. I believe I leave her free to do what she wants for most of it. But it would put the Saints to wonder the way there are always things coming up to interfere when I want to see her."

He looked sharply at Cumberland.

"In the name of all that's Holy, Robert! I give you permission to sit! Stop hovering there like a bull about to be let out among the cows."

"Thank you, your Highness," said Cumberland stiffly, sitting down on the other padded chair.

"Where was I?" went on the King. "Oh, yes, hair-dressing, fitting a new robe, any number of things . . . Robert, is she still paying visits to that whatever-he-is down in the dungeons?"

"I believe she goes down from time to time, Highness," said Cumberland. "There was a time in which he seemed to have escaped. Broke his chains somehow—they should have held a bear—broke his chains, and dug his way out of the pit he was in, or, at least, dug so far down that the man we sent in came back saying he had been blocked by a fall of earth. But three days later the creature was back again. We put heavier irons on him, and blocked up the hole; and yes, Lady Agatha has been down at least once since, I think."

"Why does she do these things?" demanded the King.

"I do not know, Highness," said Cumberland. "Perhaps—you know how women are, with small things—children, birds, and the like. They keep them to play with them. Perhaps she was trying to see if this strange, odd-made man could be trained like a lap-dog."

"If he's trainable, I want him for a Fool at my Court," said the King. "But someone of her rank, mucking around in those dungeons—I wish she wouldn't!"

"You could speak to her about it, Highness," said Cumberland.

"Why don't you speak to her, first," said the King. "I don't know how it is, but when I try to talk to her about things like that, somehow the conversation never goes the right way. Speak to her sharply, Cumberland. Tell her it ill-befits someone who is in close contact with the King, going down below the Castle like that and coming back possibly covered with filth."

"Whatever is your Royal desire, of course," said Cumberland.

"You are a good servant, Robert," said the King. "I appreciate your taking care of these little things as well as the larger ones."

"Thank you, your Highness," said Cumberland.

"Yes," said the King, "it is comforting to know I can entrust you with certain matters—oh, Robert, you have let my wine-cup become empty."

The Earl got up, refilled the wine-cup, and sat down again. "I am happy to have your approval, Highness," he said heavily. "If I may pray for your attention to the matter, perhaps this might be a good time to talk some more about the raid on my properties in the North."

"Not that, Robert, not that!" said the King, pettishly. "We've talked about that already. Do what you want. Take care of it yourself. I shouldn't have to hold your hand in everything you do. It's your property, after all."

"It is not the property that concerns me, Highness. If that were all, I would never disturb you with the matter. But you remember, I pointed out that the raid was intended to protest the Royal taxes, which makes it a matter of concern to the Throne—to your Highness and all England."

The King sighed. He closed his eyes wearily; and for a second Jim, watching, saw a small, grim smile touch the corners of Cumberland's lips.

"Very well," said the King, opening his eyes. "Which tax is it they were protesting?"

"All of them. That is what makes for the seriousness of the lawless action, Highness," said Cumberland. "It is the tax on inheritance they protest, the tax on sales and transfers of property—and a mort of others. I have mentioned to you before this that there is a treasonous element in this Kingdom, intent on making cause to disturb the peace of your Realm. You may remember I mentioned the names of the Earl of Oxford and Sir John Chandos."

"Not Chandos, Heart of God!" said the King, angrily. "Chandos is a man and warrior after my own heart. Also, he is far too useful to think of replacing in any of his many duties. I wonder sometimes at how he manages to do as much as he does. Also, was it not Chandos who put down this troop of raiders that would have damaged your estates?"

"Chandos has long experience in clevernesses of various kind," said Cumberland. "You remember, it was remarked that among the raiders was one Somerset knight, Sir Brian Neville-Smythe; and with Chandos' party there was his close friend, the Dragon Knight. It is not beyond imagining that perhaps each was present, but on separate sides, to control those they were with so that Chandos would have the easy and almost bloodless dealing with the raiders that he did. You remember, I told you how I suspected there had been some evidence of magick during the encounter."

"Damn it! Now you sound just like Lady Falon!" said the King. "If there was magick—well, the Dragon Knight is a Mage, is he not? Perhaps there was some reason for him to make use of his art. What matters it? Your property was not bothered, after all. The protest—if it was indeed a protest—failed. Why need we bother ourselves further?"

"Because we still have people about Court, like Oxford, Chandos, and others," said Cumberland, "who are too clever to openly oppose your Highness, but contrive to raise opposition to you in other ways like this I speak of."

"Yes, yes, Agatha is always on me about that point," said the King. "I can understand that she dislikes this mage—this Dragon Knight, I mean—and it is very possible she does not like Chandos. But both have been useful in the past and may be useful in the future. I have seen no real proof they pose any danger to my Kingdom and me."

Jim smiled a little grimly himself. It was obvious to him—and must be to Cumberland—that the King was at the old ruler's game of divide and conquer. He wanted as many of those around him as possible at each others' throats, so that not enough of them could combine to make a serious try at his.

But Cumberland was going on to answer smoothly, wearing down his royal half-brother.

"Lady Falon works constantly for your Highness' good in all ways, here at Court and even outside it, and at such places as the Earl of Somerset's Christmas Party—when she did her best to keep your Royal son from overindulging in drink and foolishness. Indeed, almost she has tried to be like a mother to him, but he will have none of it. Yet she does not stop trying."

"Well, well"—the King drank from his cup—"that may be true. She is a few years too young to be much of a mother to him. But certainly she shows me all proper signs of affection. However, Cumberland, we must not forget that she is still a woman, poor thing, and cannot be thought to understand things as you and I do."

"But I wish," he added wistfully, "she would come back from this eternal riding of hers and stay put. In any case, as far as this other matter is concerned, I have said repeatedly it is yours to deal with. I wash my hands of the matter. Deal with it as you wish—simply don't lose me the services of valuable people like Chandos, and even Oxford, for that matter. Oxford is not indeed one of our lesser English nobles."

"It shall be as you wish, Highness," said Cumberland. "But it might be wise to keep in mind that while the Lady Falon is, as you say, a mere woman, with all the strangenesses of her sex—which I freely confess I do not understand, being a practical man who has had little time for women—still, the sex has been said, like cats, to have understandings that they may not be able to prove, but which nonetheless are right. It may be that while I am still hunting the proofs your Highness needs, the Lady Falon's instincts have already identified those who would work you ill. It may be that the scenting of such attitudes in people is simply a strange sense they are born with."

"It may be," said the King, gloomily. "She gets her way with me often enough. I am always finding I have agreed to somewhat I had no intention of agreeing to—"

Whatever the King said next was lost to Jim's ears completely, in a shriek that seemed no more than a few inches from his right ear.

"M'Lord! I have found it. Come quickly!" cried the excited voice of Hob, now back on his shoulder. "I've found them—not one passage, but two! Come quickly, while I still have them both open!"

Jim blessed the moment in which he had made all three of them, himself, Hob, and Edgar, inaudible as well as invisible.

"Quiet down!" he said to Hob, and turned his attention back to the King and Cumberland. But whatever had been said during the few seconds of Hob's interruption was gone for good.

"—Spanish wine," the King was saying to Cumberland. "Don't tell me we are out of it already. Is there a new shipment due?"

"I do not know, Highness," Cumberland was saying. "Inquiries can be made—"

"All right, Hob," said Jim, turning away into the next room. "Show me these passages."

When Jim arrived in the last room, he found part of the brickwork around the fireplace had apparently slipped backward into the wall and moved sideways to leave an opening. Edgar was standing by it almost proudly, as if on guard. Hob leaped from Jim's shoulder into the darkness of the opening.

"Well done!" said Jim, stepping into the opening. "I didn't expect you to get done anywhere nearly this quickly."

"Actually, I didn't do it, m'Lord," said Hob. "It was the smoke that did it."

"Oh, I see," said Jim. "In that case, you both should be congratulated. Edgar, you stay here. I'm going to look into this."

"This way, m'Lord," murmured Hob. "You turn to the right just within, here."

Jim ducked under the low, dank entrance, turned to the right, and found himself in a narrow, dusty corridor between two stone walls, a passage so narrow he could not extend an arm to full length. It went on for three steps, past an unexpected flight of stairs leading down, that was dimly lit by a thick candle on the wall; then the corridor turned sharply again, to face a wall of darkness. Jim stopped.

"Just a moment," said Hob. There was an ominous clanking noise, and light flooded in to reveal a much larger room than he had yet seen here. Its furniture was sparklingly clean—clean floors, clean ceiling, and a bright window with glass in it, as well as a carpet in the middle of the floor. No one was there; but if anything had ever tried to look like a chamber belonging to a medieval King, this was it.

"That does it then, Hob," said Jim, peering into the room without entering it. "There's no doubt now the King's got a way through to Cumberland; and seeing this, I'm almost ready to bet there's something like it—maybe just a plain door—between the last room of Cumberland's, at the far end of his quarters, and the rooms of Agatha Falon. This tells us a lot."

"If m'Lord wants to go down the stairs inside the wall," said Hob mysteriously, "he may learn even more."

"Down the stairs?" said Jim. "There was some talk of the King having passageways to the outside of this palace."

"It doesn't lead to the outside—or maybe it does," said Hob. There was something very close to a mischievous tone in his voice. A pleased, mischievous tone, as if he was about to give Jim an unexpected present. "Why doesn't m'Lord go down and see?"

"Have you been down already?" asked Jim.

"Yes, m'Lord," said Hob. "But please, you go down and look for yourself."

Jim hesitated. He could make Hob tell him, of course, but plainly what he would find at the bottom of the stairs was supposed to be an agreeable discovery; and Hob was clearly proud of himself for finding it.

"This won't take long?"

"Oh, no, m'Lord."

"All right."

Jim turned back into the passage and stopped. "How do we close this entrance here, again?" he asked.

"Oh, that's easy," said Hob. "Do you see the chain?"

Jim looked at where the hobgoblin was pointing. There was indeed a chain, visible now in the light from the entrance.

"Are the stairs lighted, all the way?"

"Yes, m'Lord. Candles all the way down."

Well, that was all right then. Still, it wouldn't do to find himself suddenly lightless down there. Be prepared. He pointed his index finger down the stairs when he got to them.

"You're an eight-cell flashlight," he told it. "—turned on!" he added hastily.

A bright beam of light lanced down the steps from his fingertip. He had just about given up anyway on any attempts to save his magic. Saving simply was not possible. Shining his finger down the steps ahead of him, he saw that the dust on them had been disturbed by someone walking this way not too long before.

His own light was much more powerful than the occasional candle on the wall, but he still had to be careful. The steps were steep, with nothing like a handrail to grasp as he went down; and the further steps outreached the light thrown by his finger

"Is it very far down?" he asked Hob.

"It's not as far as from the ground floor of your tower at Malencontri up to your room and m'Lady's," answered Hob. "Maybe a little more than half as far."

This was still a considerable distance. Jim continued to descend carefully, leaning a little bit backward so that if his feet did slip, he might be able to throw himself back on the stairs and stop himself with his heels after sliding only a short distance.

After what seemed like a very long time, the stairs ended at a blank wall, beside which hung another chain. Jim pulled on it, and the wall opened almost noiselessly to reveal another narrow, dusty corridor. A distinctly unpleasant smell flooded into his nostrils—something between sewage and a refrigerator full of food that had gone rotten because power was off. The short hallway led to three more stone steps down onto an earthen floor, and there he faced a closed door.

"Wait, m'Lord," said Hob. "Let me look first."

Jim looked to see Hob hovering in mid-air on a level with Jim's head, riding a waft of smoke that had apparently come from nowhere.

"I'll be right back!" said Hob. The front of the waft of smoke before him reached out, slipped through the crack between the edge of the door and the frame in which it was set. As Jim watched, the rest of the smoke—and somehow Hob as well—slipped through after it.

Jim was never quite sure whether Hob somehow thinned down to the point where he could go through such a narrow crack, or whether the crack momentarily widened—one moment Hob had been approaching it, then he was gone.

Jim spent a moment playing the magic light of his finger on his surroundings and feeling somewhat ridiculous. And then Hob was suddenly back, still riding the smoke.

"It's all right, m'Lord," he said. "But if you could come through the door without opening it, it'd be better, because it squeaks when it's opened."

Another small use of his magical energy. But necessary. Jim spent a moment in thought, and then stood directly before the closed door. He looked at the door before him and visualized it, still standing upright, directly behind him. Abruptly, he could see into the room ahead of him.

Chapter 29

After the King's remarks, and the smell, Jim was not surprised to find himself in the dungeons. Although the moat would have been his second guess—it was usually an even bet which would have the worst odor.

These were upper-class as dungeons went—not so much in comfort and decor, as in facilities. Those nearest him were stone-floored, stone-walled dungeons, facing each other across the passageway and apparently quite dry, and cleaned since they were last occupied. Toward the far end, he could see some of the earth-walled pits that were more ordinary dungeons.

Beyond, some forty feet from him, was the doorless entrance to a larger chamber. He could see what was obviously a rack, and parts of other instruments were also visible—undoubtedly other machines useful for encouraging people to talk.

Cressets hung along the walkway before him, the light from their burning wood illuminating—and heating—the corridor and the dungeons. The place seemed to be empty except for Agatha Falon, who was in the passage looking down into the last stone-walled pit, talking to someone in it.

Suddenly wary, Jim turned off his magic fingerlight and walked softly down the line, with Hob riding the smoke beside him, until he came close enough to look down into the pit that was getting the benefit of her attention.

Agatha's sharp voice ordinarily had good carrying quality. Here, strangely muffled by the echoes of this dungeon space, it had been familiar, but not understandable, at a distance. Now that Jim, safe in his invisibility, was closer, her words came clearly to his ears.

"—Oh, no, he doesn't!" she was saying. "He'll give me that boy when I'm ready for him! Only then, if everything works out well at this end, will I see about getting him what he wants—as far as perhaps a third of the tin-mining area in Cornwall. But at most a third! That mining is valuable to England, which means it will be valuable to me. Now, stop whining and take that message back to him!"

Metal clinked on metal; and Jim, moving a little farther forward, saw what had been hidden by the depth of the dungeon. The figure was grimy; but the dirt and filth could not hide the fact that it was a Gnarly Man—but a Gnarly Man lacking his pick, hammer, and rod. He was chained to a post driven deep into the bottom of the pit, by links that looked heavy and strong enough to hold an elephant.

Whoever it was, he was indeed whining—with a strange sort of voice that echoed in Jim's ear, as if he was hearing it twice. Abruptly he realized that Agatha could plainly hear what the creature was saying, and so could Jim's own human ears. Probably the Gnarly King had used his magic to ensure that his messenger—as this clearly was—could be understood by Agatha. But Jim, having earlier expanded his hearing to dragon-range, was hearing both ranges.

Now that he was close, the grimy prisoner's words also came clearly.

". . . But 'ee'll slay me! 'Tis the second time 'ee sent me back t'im!"

"What's that to do with me, sirrah?" snapped Agatha. She was making no effort to keep her voice down; not only this part of the dungeons, but the torture-room beyond, must presently be unoccupied. It was hardly likely she would speak so openly where she might be overheard. "Can you break those heavier chains they've put on you?"

"Oh, them," said the Gnarly, glancing down at the links. The tied-at-the-end sleeves on his abnormally long arms dangled over the chain. "Ay, them's easy enow. But 'ee'll slay me—'tis bad luck having a messenger bring 'ee bad news, without you slays 'im!"

"Well, you belong to him, not to me," said Agatha. "You have my answer; and your task is to take it back to your King. So take it! If he tries to keep that boy when I require him—our deal will be done, and he will get nothing. What do I want with a Mage? But once I am ready here, all is possible. I shall decide then how much tin-mine land your King may get. He can agree to those terms, or have nothing! I must get back to my rooms, now."

She turned and began to walk toward Jim. Startled, he turned, hurriedly, himself, to hastily return the door to its frame, and himself to the other side of it. He started climbing the stairs, Hob riding the smoke up beside him.

"She has to come back this way, doesn't she?" Jim panted at the hobgoblin.

"Yes, m'Lord." said Hob.

Jim climbed faster. He was becoming short of breath, but Agatha could hardly be mounting the stairs any more quickly than he was. Thanks to the tower stairs at Malencontri his legs had plenty of spring in them. If his wind would just last him until the top of the steps at least. . . .

"How'll Agatha get back to her own quarters? The King's with Cumberland. She'll have to go past them," he panted.

"I don't know, m'Lord," Hob answered. "Maybe she could go through a door to the hall. Then she can go down the hall to the outside door of her own rooms. Would you like to ride the smoke the rest of the way up?"

"Oh," said Jim breathlessly, feeling foolish. Things were getting to a fair pass when he was out-thought by a hobgoblin. "Never mind. I'm almost there now." Indeed he was. The end of the stairs was in sight, and his thoughts were racing.

Maybe the situation was beginning to take shape, finally. Agatha Falon was acting as if she really had a chance to become not merely the King's favorite, but his wife and Queen. The very idea was ridiculous: she was no more than minor nobility. The Court had been said, for a year now, to be gleefully awaiting her downfall and certain disgrace—if not banishment or even execution. Surprisingly, so far, she had obstinately escaped any such thing.

It seemed impossible that the King could marry someone like her. True, his first Queen was dead; but there were other massive obstacles—obstacles of Church and State. Theoretically a King should only marry someone of Royal blood. Further, the marriage—his taking of a new Queen—should be an action benefiting not only him, but his country, such as cementing an alliance with another national power that would prove a help in time of need.

But still—could it be possible she had some plan in mind that actually might give her a chance to win the King?

It was all but inconceivable, but she had talked to the Gnarly messenger as if she was confident of it.

However, that evidence alone was no help to Jim. Whether her plan had any real hope of success was beside the point, just now; Jim had to deal with the current situation, which was that she was already in a position of influence with the King, and in some sort of alliance with the Gnarly King, who had young Robert Falon.

Her ambition had to be overreaching itself. There were no two ways about that. But whatever she was doing was much more complicated than he could have guessed.

And where did the Earl of Cumberland come into all this? Jim could well believe what Chandos had said about the Earl's plots against the young Prince, but he could see no way that the affair of young Robert Falon affected that. Still, Carolinus had said that the King and Prince must be protected; this must be what he had referred to.

It was lucky he had at least this much of a head start on Agatha. It struck him suddenly that there was one thing he should do immediately: Edgar was a spy, not only by profession, but by nature. If he, while tagging along with Jim, heard anything at all important, he would immediately begin to think of ways to turn it to his own advantage. It would be like adding the Town Crier to their company.

"Come on, Hob," he said.

Hob followed him as he hurried back along the stone passage and out into Cumberland's quarters. Edgar was still there, waiting.

"Edgar," Jim said, "I'm going to send you back to your own room. I'm also going to put a ward around it, so you can't get out and no one can get in. Don't worry. I'll be along to set you free in a little while."

Edgar's face paled, taking on a rather pasty look, so that his little mustache and Van Dyke beard looked like cheap bits of makeup attached to his face.

"It'll be all right, I say!" said Jim impatiently, clamping his teeth on the words. Without waiting to hear any protest, Jim visualized the man back in his own two small rooms, with the ward surrounding both and the invisibility spell gone. Edgar disappeared.

"Have I got to leave, too, m'Lord?" Hob said in a small voice next to his ear.

"No, not you, Hob. You stay with me," answered Jim. "Now, nobody can hear or see us, but don't say anything to me unless you think it's really necessary—and don't bother me for a minute."

"Yes, m'Lord."

Jim was wondering just how far behind him Agatha was, while reflecting that he had inadvertently saved some magic, after all, by climbing up from the dungeons. Certainly, he must still have some lead over her.

He headed toward the first room of Cumberland's suite—the room where Cumberland and the King had been talking. He hoped they still were; it would be interesting to see what Agatha would do on discovering she had to pass by them to get out. Of course, she might take another route, but . . .

Hob abandoned his waft of smoke, hopping onto Jim's shoulder, as Jim tracked back through the intervening rooms. Cumberland, he found, had by this time pushed the King into something perilously close to argument.

"—I tell you, Robert," the King was saying testily, "things are all very well as they are. Chandos is the last man I'd suspect of anything treasonable; and if others want to dabble in it, let them dabble. They'll lose their heads in due time. But when they are capable men, doing as they ought, and there's no one I can think of who could replace them, leave them as they are, for God's sake!"

"Oh, my Liege," said Cumberland. "On my honor, there are a number of men of family and title who could take their place and do their duties as well, if not much better."

"Maybe so, maybe so," said the King. "But I'm used to the men I have. The way things are now, my governing works. Why must we always go around looking under bedsheets and behind curtains and trying to find reason to get rid of men who are giving me no trouble? I believe you when you say there are many who grumble and groan under my taxes. But, if you will remember, a number of those taxes were at your suggestion. You also, at the time, agreed to the men charged with gathering the monies—some of those you suspect of high treason now. No, no, I shall need a great deal more reason before taking some of the actions you suggest."

There was finally some sound of Royal wrath in the King's voice, but otherwise nothing new and interesting to be learned here at the moment, Jim thought. It was simply more of the same debate between King and Earl. He looked back into the room he had just left and was almost run into by Agatha.

Hastily, Jim ducked out of her path. Still invisible, he and Hob moved back into a corner of the room.

Agatha was walking quickly, like someone who knew her way well. But the sound of the King's voice checked her before she reached the half-open door. She stopped dead, then moved forward in short, quick, silent steps until she could see through the opening without being seen herself.

Jim, trusting to his invisibility, moved quietly up behind her, to see what she was seeing. Her position gave her a full view of Cumberland; and, if Cumberland looked in the right direction, he would see her. But the King could not be seen at all from this angle and, therefore, could not see her.

Meanwhile, both she and Jim could hear him talking. The subject had changed to horses, and, temporarily at least, Cumberland seemed to have given up trying to hold his monarch on the subject of lords with treasonable intentions.

"—sending me a stallion from Tours, which I have bought," the King was saying. "If the beast is half as good as those Frenchmen promised, I should have a warhorse beyond price."

Cumberland did not make the obvious answer, that the King was well beyond the age of needing a warhorse and his only use for one would be to look at it and preen himself on possessing it.

"I know a young man," said Cumberland, "of the Lockyear family, who are known to have an excellent eye for horses. Perhaps I could send him to look at the horse?"

"Never heard of them," said the King. "In any case, I have already made up my mind about this horse. They tell me that at the gallop he will leave any other destrier behind. . . ."

Jim's mind was doing some galloping of its own. Somehow, the King would have to be maneuvered out of this room, if Agatha was to escape to the hall unseen. He waited with interest to see how she would manage it.

He moved from behind her to a position at her right, from which he could see into the room at an angle that showed him the King. His Majesty was sagging a little in his chair, as if the wine was getting to him. Not surprising if it did, thought Jim, considering his age and probable physical condition.

As he watched, the King looked down at the floor and his eyes closed, momentarily, as if he might be about to slip into a doze. Cumberland's gaze lifted. He exchanged looks through the partly open door with Agatha, then nodded slightly and looked again at the King, who was opening his eyes once more.

"In any case," said Cumberland, "let us drink to this new horse of yours, your Highness. A noble steed like that deserves a toast." He filled up their glasses, lifted his to the King, and poured its contents down his throat, almost ostentatiously emptying the container.

The King took up his wine more slowly. "A toast—" he said, but his voice had thickened—not a great deal, but enough to be noticeable if you were listening for it. He also emptied his glass, but he took somewhat longer than Cumberland had; and when he put it down, hand and glass together dropped heavily onto the table beside his chair. The empty glass goblet toppled over.

He took a deep breath.

"Robert," he said heavily, "since Agatha has chosen to ride and you will have things to do, I think I shall rest me a little while—*'lay me down to bleed a while, and rise to fight again . . .'* eh, Robert?"

Cumberland smiled that grim smile again and reached down with one arm, literally hoisting the older man to his feet—and revealing considerable strength. He had not even bent his body to do so; and the King was heavy from years of rich living and idleness.

"Your arm, Robert..." Edward said again, the thickness in his voice now blurring his words almost beyond understanding.

Cumberland offered his arm, and the King passed his own through its angle. Leaning heavily on the taller, middle-aged Earl, and with uncertain steps, the older man first let himself be led, then stopped and pulled back, on seeing the direction they were going.

"I thought, Majesty," said the Earl, in answer to an uncertain mumble from the King, "since a bed of mine was closer... for a short nap..."

"You're a good lad, Robert. Let us go...." The two of them disappeared from view.

"Bah!" said Agatha to the thin air. She strode into the room, took the Earl's goblet, filled it with wine, and, sitting in the chair the King had abandoned, took some hearty swallows.

"Well?" she said, when Cumberland reappeared and sat down. "How did his Highness take it when you told him I was riding?"

"He did not take it happily, my Lady," said the Earl. "But he accepted it. Still, I would suggest the excuse is wearing thin."

"And why do you call it an excuse, my Lord?"

"Yesterday, you were riding," said Cumberland. "But today you were down visiting that manling in the dungeons, were you not?"

"And what gives you the right to say that?" said Agatha. "Do you have spies following me now?"

"Of course," growled the Earl. He poured a small amount of wine into the goblet the King had emptied and sipped at it, then set it down again. "Do you not have your spies on me? Does not everybody have their spies on everybody else here at Court? Do not take me for a child, my Lady."

"I would take it amiss, my Lord," said Agatha slowly, "if you were to insist to his Majesty I have done anything but ride, this day."

The Earl laughed shortly, and drank a little more.

"Your wits are astray, I think, Lady Falon. You have one claim on the King. I have several. This I have told you before: Those who last long around the Throne do not do it on a single moment of favor. It is a game I know well. You will find that out if you count me as one you can play with."

"I think not in my case, Sir."

"Time will tell, Lady Falon."

"What do you want from me, then?"

"Some of whatever you get. You surely did not expect it otherwise? There are only two powers here. One is the King. The other is those of us who advise him. And of those, I am the strongest."

"And you are the King's half-brother, after all," said Agatha. "It could be that has bred in you, somewhat, and given you an illusion of greater strength than indeed you have. I may be a weak enemy, my Lord, but I warrant you I can be a valuable friend."

"This is not a public market, my Lady. I am neither to be frightened nor bought. I repeat, there are those of us who advise his Majesty—too many for you to think of having your own way with all, even if you were powerful enough to do so. Like the King himself, you will have to live with us, as we live with each other. His Majesty is not a fool, you know. He will not have forgotten the hard death of his father, strangely and secretly, after he had been forced to resign the throne. He will make sure nothing like that happens to him; and the best way he may do so is to keep the powers of those about him in balance."

"And what then is supposed to be the sum of this lesson you rede me, my most wise and experienced Lord?" said Agatha.

"Simply that he has a use for me in keeping that balance," said the Earl. "Not so you. I may control him utterly one day. You never will. For now you have my assistance as long as I earn by it in the long run. There may come a time when I will demand of you what your aim and plans are. When that time comes I would counsel you against telling me less than the full truth, Lady Agatha."

"I thank you most graciously for your kind advice, my Lord Earl," said Agatha, standing up. "Now, I must return to my own rooms."

The Earl bowed from the chair where he sat and she turned, heading toward the door that opened to the hallway outside. Time to go, Jim told himself. He paused only to work the magic that would remove the ward on Edgar's room.

"KinetetE?" he said; aloud, but safely, since neither the Earl nor Agatha could hear him.

Abruptly he was back with that one of the three most potent magicians in this world.

Chapter 30

He was back on the stage of the auditorium, but this time it was empty, except for KinetetE and Barron, who had turned to look at him.

"So you found what you were after?" said KinetetE.

"Not exactly," said Jim. "Cumberland's trying to control the King. So's Agatha. I think she and Cumberland are working together—they talked like partners that don't like each other, at all. Agatha's also ready to trade the Gnarly King a third of England's tin mines for little Robert; though how she can do that when she doesn't own one of them—but I suppose you already knew all this."

"Of course we did!" snapped Barron.

"Not about Agatha and the tin mines," said KinetetE.

"Anyway," Jim went on, "it's time I got back to Robert, Carolinus, and the rest in the Gnarly cave. Can you send me there now? Or should I try to use my own magic to get there?"

"I'll send you," said KinetetE. "I assume you want the hobgoblin, there on your shoulder, to go back with you?"

"Well—" Jim began.

"Oh, yes," said Hob, quickly. "I must be at my Lord's side if peril threatens."

"Very good," said KinetetE. "But first I want to know more about Agatha and the tin mines. How did you find that out?"

"I heard her talking to the Gnarly King's messenger," Jim said. "He's chained up in a dungeon directly below the King's quarters at Court; and he seemed to have just carried a proposal to her from the Gnarly King. I heard her turning down his latest offer."

Then, to the best of his memory, he repeated the conversation he had overheard between Agatha and the Earl.

"Interesting," said KinetetE.

"I thought so, too," said Jim. "But it doesn't explain how she managed to get to Lyonesse the way she did at just the right time to try and have us killed by those giants. Also, Edgar couldn't help me find the two men who'd been with her in Lyonesse."

"They're probably unimportant," said KinetetE.

"Maybe," said Jim, "but I wanted to ask them why she did it. It was a lot of trouble just to kill me if it was only out of sheer spite. I know she doesn't like Angie and me, or anyone who likes us."

"No," said KinetetE dryly.

"Do you think it was the Gnarly King who moved her magically into Lyonesse?"

"Impossible," said KinetetE. "The King of a Land of Naturals could only move you out of his Kingdom back to wherever you came from. Any competent magickian could move you to him. True, once she was in his Kingdom, the Gnarly King could have moved her to the opening of that tunnel you used to enter his Kingdom from Lyonesse. But that still leaves the question of how she got there in the first place and afterward got herself and those two courtiers back to Court, where you just saw her. Unless she had help from somewhere else—"

Very unusually for her, KinetetE broke off in the middle of her sentence, and frowned.

"Edgar," Jim ventured, "did say there was a rumor at Court that Agatha was a witch. He very much believed it, himself."

"Hah!" said KinetetE. "She's about as much of a witch as you are. Merlin alone would know what you are—unless Carolinus knows. But if so, he's not even telling me."

"Anyway, I thought there was nothing to it," Jim said, deliberately ignoring her last words. "But, if then—"

"Oh, there's a grain of truth to it," said KinetetE. "You remember what came out at the Earl's Christmas Party, about some of her early years when she lived with that very old and powerful Troll. Not that the Troll—"

"Mnrogar," said Jim.

"What?"

"The name of the Troll."

"His name has nothing to do with it. I'm saying he couldn't have taught her any magick, anyway. She doesn't know any magick—I wish you'd learn to pronounce the word properly!"

"I've called it 'magic' all my life," said Jim, his stubbornness getting the better of him.

"Ah?" said KinetetE. "There were some people who knew magick where you came from?"

"Magic."

"Magick!"

" 'Magic' is what I've always called it; and 'magic' is what I'm going to go on calling it!"

"Well," said KinetetE, "I suppose I can't blame you for your faulty foreign upbringing. Anyway, we'll go into that another time."

There was a moment of silence in which they stared hostilely at each other.

"In any case," went on KinetetE, "the point I was trying to make was that, like all Naturals, what simple magick the Troll had would be innate. He wouldn't know why it worked—like your Hob riding the smoke."

"I know that," said Jim, still stiff.

"Good. But what you probably don't know is that it wouldn't be unusual for a child, especially a little girl, with only a troll for company and cut off from normal human society and emotions, to look elsewhere for a place to belong. As it happens, I know she did seek out and experiment with Witchery. But when she found out that a mastery of the Lore requires a life-long, nun-like devotion, she dropped it. Never cut out for it, actually. But she might have picked up enough to continue some study on her own. Enough to know of the Gnarlies and how to get to the Gnarly Kingdom."

"But then," Jim said, "what could she offer the King of the Gnarlies that he'd want, for helping her?"

"Power," said Barron, speaking up for the first time, words tumbling out of him, "and riches—in this case, Great Silver, riches and power both in one. No ruler ever gets enough of either. Cumberland owns many of the mines, but only at the King of England's pleasure. But as everyone at Court knows, Agatha is well with the King there. Moving those mines into the hands of a ruler of a Natural Kingdom would upset History. So, the Dark Powers and politics come into it—"

"If you don't mind, Charles?" said KinetetE sharply. "I think I'm dealing with this matter?"

"Oh, very well," said Barron, looking sulkily off at the far-stretching left wall of the empty auditorium.

"And if a Mage can send people to the Gnarly Kingdom," said Jim, taking advantage of the moment to ask a question he had been holding, "why didn't Carolinus just import us, or anyone else he needed to help him, instead of leaving Brian, Daffyd, and me to make our own way by land to there?"

"Because once there," answered KinetetE, "he could no longer access his Magickal energy, unless allowed by the King."

"You're right, I'd forgotten that."

"Competent Magickians," said KinetetE icily, "do not forget. Now, if you and Charles don't mind, I was on the subject of Agatha Falon."

"Oh, yes," said Jim. "I'm sorry. Go ahead."

"I had intended to, with or without your permission. What I was about to say concerning Agatha and Witchery was this. It wouldn't be unusual for a little girl with a childhood like hers, and especially her years with the Troll, to end up feeling more at home with his like, seeing all other people as different—and enemies."

Jim was getting a little tired of the subject of Agatha. He thought of Robert—and Carolinus, Brian, and Dafydd—down with the Gnarly King. But mainly of Robert in Gnarly hands, so small and alone.

"Anyway," he said, "what's all this got to do with Robert being stolen by the Gnarlies? From what I overheard between Agatha and the messenger, Agatha is willing to pay a great price for him. But what's Robert got to do with Agatha, the mines, and the Gnarly King?"

"Even down there in deepest Somerset," said Barron—Jim had been watching him out of the corner of his eye as he talked to KinetetE, and clearly the third of only three Triple-A-class magicians in this world had been itching to get back into the conversation. "You must have heard how, after the Christmas holiday gathering at your Earl's, Agatha went to a nunnery in Devon. It was said she went only for a retreat of a few months, but actually it was because she was pregnant, and she could have her child quietly there. If she did so, and it died, she might have a replacement, though why—"

"Charles!" Jim had never heard quite that note of command in KenetetE's voice before. Barron stopped what he had been about to say, shutting up with the reflex of an oyster attacked by a starfish.

"Very well," he said, "if I'm not needed . . ."

He vanished.

"In a snit, of course," said KinetetE, looking at the space where he had been. "But he'll get over it."

"Why would she want a replacement?" asked Jim, suddenly very interested in Agatha again.

"I don't know," said KinetetE. "The by-blow of someone of rank is usually either conveniently left behind or disposed of. That's part of the puzzle, but it's not as important that you know, since Gnarly possession of the English mines would upset History—and that indicates the Dark Powers being behind all this. Your Master-in-Magick went to the Gnarly King as an Ambassador from the Collegiate of Magickians."

"Yes," Jim said, "you told me."

"And of course," KinetetE said, "the King treated him well at first, let him move about and use a little magick. But then the King, against all diplomatic custom between Kingdoms, made him a prisoner."

"What will the Collegiate do? If they decide to do it?"

"Apprentices aren't supposed—" KinetetE broke off. "There doesn't seem to be anything we can do to free Carolinus. It'll be up to you, as well as getting back your Robert. Don't come back without both of them."

"Of course I wouldn't—but he sent those projections to me. He must have been able to keep some of his magic!"

"Anything could be, with Carolinus. Or he could have foreseen what would happen, even Robert being taken. But if he managed to hold on to any of his magick, it's not enough to free himself. It's in the power of any ruler of a Kingdom to make sure no outsider can access his magickal energy. Surely you know that."

"Yes—yes, you're right, of course," he said hastily, to get KinetetE off the subject of his memory. "I should get down to the Gnarly King's cave as soon as possible. You said you could send me back before anything happened. When you send me back now, isn't there any way at all you can arrange for me to hold on to my magic?"

"No," she said. She lifted a hand as though to dismiss him, then hesitated. "I could, of course, send you back with a ward that includes some of the *Here* around you. While the ward holds, you could strike out of it with your own magick. But if you do that even once, or if the Gnarly King guesses you're warded, he can wipe the ward out as easily as you breathe on a snowflake to melt it. Then your *Here* will be gone and your Magickal power with it."

"But he might not guess I had a ward until I use my magic—and then it might be too late for him."

"It would not be too late," said KinetetE. "The instant you use your magick, the Great Silver on his Robe and Throne will turn bright red. The King will wipe out the ward and all foreign Magick in the same moment you use it. Probably you as well. Your Magick would be canceled out before it could take effect. Carolinus had you swallow a copy of the *Encyclopaedie Necromantick*, didn't he?"

"Yes," said Jim, remembering how Carolinus had shrunk that immense volume down to a pill, and how nonetheless he had felt like he had ingested a whale after getting it down.

"Consult it again. RELATIVE POWERS: Footnote 5, page 7—*LAWS AND RULES* '. . . *Resident Magick uttered in the same instant as non-Resident Magick shall have priority over any and all non-Resident utterances.*' "

"Ah . . . yes," said Jim. "But you say you can still send me back in a ward with part of the *Here* around me?"

"I said I would. But will you remember that footnote in *LAWS AND RULES?*"

"Carolinus must have trusted my memory for such, enough to hope I could rescue him as well as Robert."

KinetetE looked at him for a long, penetrating moment.

"Maybe Carolinus knows what he's doing with you," she said at last. "What will you do, then, once you're there?"

"I won't know until I'm there," answered Jim.

KinetetE shrugged.

"RETURN!" she said.

—And he was back in the great cave of the Gnarly King.

No one, apparently, had noticed his return, or reacted to his absence; and the memory of the way the scene in the scrying bowl had appeared frozen, came back to him—possibly some anomaly of time had worked in his favor, so that only seconds had passed here . . . or maybe it was something KinetetE had done. Certainly Hill and the Gnarly King seemed still involved in the same argument they had been carrying on when Carolinus had sent him away.

A feeling like a slight increase in air pressure reassured him that the ward was about him.

Everyone else was intent on the argument between Hill and the Gnarly King; and for a small, odd moment, he knew he was perfectly visible but felt strangely invisible.

In that moment, he had time to get a better look at the cave. There was a band of darkness staining the first four or so feet of the stone walls above the cave floor—now mostly hidden by the bodies of the mass of Gnarlies, who had packed all the space behind Brian, Dafydd, and the horses.

There must, Jim thought, *be at least a couple of thousand ordinary Gnarlies present. Gatherings like this must not be unusual.* The dark band might have been made by greasy clothing, rubbing up against the clean, brown granite. Still, he had never expected their expedition to attract a crowd like this. Hill was the cause, of course.

None of that crowd moved, even slightly. They stood as if carved, illuminated by the light from the cavern walls. Yet, above that light, the roof of the cave itself was lost in a sooty darkness that seemed to reject any light that reached it. A darkness suggestive of endless spiderwebs and massive bats—but no movement, no sound, came to suggest that anything lived there above, bats or otherwise.

The coin-sized squares of the silvery jewel-like metal glittered like cut gems in the stony light, marking the path they had followed and ending in the ring he had noted before, a circle on the floor that included the dais with its throne, a circle perhaps twenty feet in diameter. Upon the dais in that circle the throne and the cloak of the Gnarly King were covered by the metal bits. Their constant, changing glitter—almost on the verge of color changes—seemed to become more agitated as the voices of Hill and the King clashed with each other, rising in volume.

"—a cheild, yes. But never no growed Stoopid beed a Luck!" the Gnarly King was roaring.

Hill and his uncle were clearly still in the same argument they had been engaged with when he left. Both had lost the apparently normal—to Gnarlies—open-mouthed stare. The King seemed to be feeling uneasy, Jim thought, over Hill's repeated mention of "Luck," in spite of what he said.

It was just possible, Jim thought, that "Luck," as the Gnarlies thought of it, was something to be taken more seriously than what the same word might mean to humans.

It puzzled him how he could bring any kind of luck to Hill. Hill clearly had no doubt; and the King looked almost as convinced. Jim felt a sudden spurt of anger. If he only understood what their concept of Luck was, there might be something he could do to help the situation.

"No Luck to a Gnarly?" Hill was almost crowing. " 'Ee thinks that, does 'ee? Then step into the Ring with me—or does 'ee wish to simply give me the Robe and the Throne and step down? I'll be light on 'ee if 'ee does."

"Ye be light on *me!*" The King surged up to a standing position from his Throne, and began shrugging out of his heavy Robe. The metal plaques, which covered the outside of it, put on a sudden sparkling display, like miniature fireworks, that for a moment outshone the light from the walls as he tossed the garment aside, to fall clashing on the dais. He stepped forward and down into the ring.

Exposed now to the waist, he showed a chest and body like one thick barrel, with very little difference in size between the chest and stomach. Otherwise he looked very human.

But it was in the arms he and Hill—for Hill had now also torn off his shirt—showed their Gnarly inhumanness.

The tops of their arms were so close to their necks that they could almost be thought of as having no shoulders at all. But a great hump of muscle ran over the upper end of each arm, giving the impression of power to move each with great strength in unusual directions.

Their upper arms were ape-like and almost double the length of the lower arms, wrapped in heavy, rope-like muscle, under tight, greyish skin.

Also, the lower arms were almost lost behind the huge hands that had been hidden in their long sleeves—hands so massive and long that one of them could have clasped clear around the waist of its owner's body. The palms, unfolded now, were as wide as canoe-paddles, the fingers three times the length of those of a large human. They splayed out from the oversize palms so that their grasping abilities were all too plain.

The King raised his hands like a wrestler ready to grapple and stepped forward, kicking aside Hill's shirt, which lay where Hill had dropped it. Hill already had his own hands up in the same wrestler's position—but it was very plain to see that his were hardly more than three-quarters the size of the King's, and that the King's body in general was taller and heavier than Hill's by the same proportions. They circled slowly, facing each other.

The Gnarlies packing the cave were still silent; but they had moved backward, either compressing their ranks or crowding those in the rear out into the corridor, because they had now left an open space a good three to five yards from the circle, in which there were left only the Gnarly King, Hill, and Jim, with Brian, Dafydd, and the horses. For the first time Jim noticed that Hob was somehow back on the sumpter-horse, peering out from under its pack-cover.

Jim looked beyond the King, to the dimmer areas beside the throne's dais. Perhaps now, with everyone watching the two opponents, was his chance to use his magic to save Carolinus and Robert. Robert, he saw, was sleeping. Carolinus, clinging to the bars of his cage, was watching.

"Hah!" said the voice of Brian in Jim's ear. "The little fellow has forced the fight. Well done, Hill!" The last three words were half-shouted at Hill, who paid no attention to them.

"It looks more like suicide to me," said Jim, looking back at the fight.

"Why, James!" said Brian, turning on him in surprise, "what has the sin of self-murder to do with such as this?"

Their voices attracted the attention of the King.

"Move ye back!" he snarled at them; and Jim realized the space inside the ring had to be cleared for the fight. He backed automatically; the horses, with the sumpter-horse moving first, were already moving as if they had independently heard and understood the King. Dafydd stepped back with Jim. Only Brian stood where he was.

"Brian—" Jim was beginning; but in that same instant, the Gnarly King, seeing him still there, made a sudden, slow but powerful, swipe at him with one enormous hand.

Brian's reaction was pure reflex. Moving much faster, he drew his sword; and its blade met the great hand in mid-swing, cutting square across its palm. There was a sound as if the steel blade had hit one of the stone walls. Brian looked startled, the Gnarly King looked puzzled and stopped to stare at his palm. There was a red line across it, but the skin—if whatever integument covered that massive hand was skin—was not even broken.

"Brian! Back up! Come back with us!" called Jim.

Brian, sword still ready for use, risked a glance over his shoulder in Jim's direction, saw him beckoning, and backed up.

"The damned creature attacked me!" he said to Jim.

"Put the weapon away," said Jim. "Please, Brian! The Gnarly King and Hill are going to have a personal combat. You were inside the circle."

"Circle?" said Brian. "Of course. I crave pardon," he added to the King, who had ceased to pay attention to him. Brian sighed.

"No manners, of course," he confided to Jim, and turned all his attention to the circular space where the two opponents were facing each other. "But I would wish them to meet with weapons, James!"

"It looks like they're going to fight without them."

"Not gentlemanly, of course," said Brian. "But then, they are hardly like Christians, poor creatures."

"I think those hands of theirs are going to be the weapons," said Jim. "The first time Rrrnlf brought Hill to me, he told me he'd found Hill digging his way out from under the same mountain that Rrrnlf was digging himself out of, and took Hill along because Rrrnlf could dig so much faster. I got the impression Rrrnlf had been digging through solid rock with just his hands, so maybe Gnarlies can, too."

While they had been talking, the King and Hill had been circling each other, without making contact—still like two human wrestlers warily looking for a favorable chance to get to grips.

"All the same," Jim continued, "I wish I could believe Hill had even a ghost of a chance of winning. The King must outweigh him two to one."

"The little one has pluck, though," answered Brian. "He may win, at that.

Pluck is everything. Every man must show himself to have it, to prove himself a man, win or lose. And even though these are not men, it goes not amiss for one to act as a man should."

Jim hardly heard the last words. His mind was racing, trying to think of something he could do to keep Hill from losing. Clearly, something more than pluck was needed here. Otherwise, he and those with him, including baby Robert, had no hope of coming out alive.

If Hill could only overcome his opponent, however, they might have a chance of surviving. Hill had spoken of Jim as his "Luck." Surely he would not destroy his Luck if he won. Or would he suddenly turn into the same sort of King as the present one was, when he owned the Robe and the Throne?

In any case, the odds for Jim and the rest had to be better if Hill could win.

But, watching the two circling closer and closer in the ring, he felt the slimness of this hope. More and more, as they neared, it became evident Hill could be no physical match for the King. The King was not that much taller— a matter of inches only—but beyond this, the match was like that of a man against a half-grown boy. Not only were the King's muscles more massive, but his movements looked more practiced and certain. Hill had to know that, too, Jim thought to himself; Brian had said it right—he had pluck.

Now, even as Jim watched, the two closed enough to exchange a couple of slow but strong, swinging blows with their open hands. Surprisingly, in contrast to the way the King had used his hand as if he would flip Brian aside with the back of it, the two now were striking out with fingers together and straight. They used them, thought Jim, much the way Brian used his broadsword: as if the hands themselves were weapons manipulated by the rest of the body. But there was that strange slowness to their blows, as if their hands were indeed so heavy they were an effort to move.

If this was true—if those hands were actually as hard and heavy as they seemed—then a blow from one of them could be devastating; though, on the other hand, possibly the King's and Hill's bodies were also made of the same heavy material and could absorb considerable punishment.

Nonetheless, Hill was clearly at a disadvantage. As Jim watched, a strike by Hill's right hand fell short of the Gnarly King's body, where shoulder, such as it was, met neck; and Hill himself ducked a crosswise swing at his head by the King, while both stood with their feet planted facing each other. The King had a considerable advantage in reach.

Jim fidgeted. With all this going on, the King had evidently so far not noticed his ward. Jim could still make use of his own magic at least. But common sense said that if he used it to help Hill, he should do so in such a way that Hill would never suspect he had been helped. It might make the contest null and void by Gnarly rules. The magic could be wasted, and the King still on the throne.

Then it came to him that nothing could be easier than helping unnoticed. All he had to do was make the King trip as he started one of his ponderous arm-swings, and leave it to Hill to take advantage of the opportunity. Jim focused on the bigger Gnarly as the other's arm went back. He visualized.

Nothing happened.

The King's hand and arm reached their furthest extent behind him and swung forward in another horizontal arc. Once again, Hill ducked the blow, but so slowly as to barely escape.

Hastily, Jim tried the magic again. Nothing. He tried several other variations. Nothing worked. In desperation he went back to his early days as a magician and made up a spell to the tune of *Yankee Doodle*. Absolutely nothing. Why?

"Accounting Office," he whispered. "Is there something wrong with my account?"

"I will transfer you to the Auditing Department, Jim Eckert," boomed out the invisible bass voice that Jim had always dealt with, on matters regarding his supply of magical energy.

"Shhhh—!" Jim was unable to stop himself from trying to quiet the resonant voice.

"Be reassured," boomed the voice, "our words are not audible outside the ward around you."

"I knew that!" snapped Jim at ordinary volume. He hadn't; but he was damned if he was going to be talked down to by something that always sounded like a machine.

"This is the Auditing Department," said the same—as far as Jim could tell— voice. "Your account is empty because you have used up your available credit."

Jim stared at the fight going on in the ring, seeing none of it. So this was as far as the magical energy he had had when he left Malencontri, had been able to take him. Remembering the Auditing Department was probably still there, he made an effort to speak calmly. He went on aloud. "Well, I guess that's it, then . . . Farewell."

"Chin up!" said the Auditing Department, sounding unexpectedly human. Silence followed within Jim's ward. In this situation where he finally might have made all the difference, he was not going to be able to do so; simply because he was, for the moment, no longer a magician.

He focused numbly, once more, on the fight.

Hill had been merely dodging blows. But the King's great hand-swipes were coming closer, if more slowly. As Jim watched, Hill moved toward the King and stood. This time several solid blows were exchanged, with the odd, clacking sound of one stone striking another. Hill reeled back from the last of these. There was no mark upon him, but he shook his head as if dazed and stumbled slightly, as he began to circle away from, rather than toward, the King. The King came after him like a hunter after a prey.

Jim raged at himself for his own helplessness. Here he might have made all the difference; and he could do nothing. Nothing.

As had happened before when he had run out of magic, he was probably still able to change himself into his dragon body—but what good could that do against beings who apparently had rock-hard bodies?—Wait a minute!

His ability to change into a dragon was *innate* magic, like a Natural's—independent of the Accounting Office. It had been owed him by this world of magic because of the very accident of his presence in this world. Might it be possible to use that same source of magic in another way?

Perhaps he could be *in* another body, just as he had been at the time of his arrival in this world, when he found he had involuntarily occupied the body of the dragon Gorbash, taking control of it away from its owner. If he could now take over Hill's body the same way, maybe he could win the fight for the smaller Gnarly.

Hill might turn tyrannical on them if he became King. But their chances were at least better with him than with the present Gnarly ruler.

The method of fighting he was watching favored the larger, heavier Gnarly, but made him slower than his opponent. If Jim took over Hill's body, maybe he could put to use some moves from his own twentieth century that the King would never know. Also, he was ready to bet he could move faster than Hill.

There was nothing to do but try.

He tried, trying to use the same feeling he had when he changed into his dragon body, but concentrating on Hill. Abruptly, his eyes were looking at the looming figure of the Gnarly King, only a couple of steps away. He had a brief glimpse of an enormous grey hand coming at him like the prow of an ocean liner at a small rowboat, that only just then discovered that, after all, it could not get out of the way as fast as it had imagined it could. . . .

Chapter 31

There was a terrible impact. Jim found himself flying through the air. He was perfectly conscious, but could not remember the blow. He landed and began frantically rolling over and over as fast as he could. After covering some little distance this way, he stopped. He lay where he was for a moment, expecting to find most of his bones broken. But apparently they were not.

He looked for the King and located him standing, staring blankly at Jim. Perhaps he was not used to opponents who rolled away once they were knocked down.

Jim had been operating on the early-learned reflex that once you were down you wanted to put distance between you and your opponent, before trying to get back to your feet. He had done just that. Now he would spring to his feet—

He got up; but it could hardly have been called a spring. In Hill's body, he, too, moved in slow motion. Hill's body was like a granite statue come to life, with all the joints and muscles operable, but with a great deal of inertia. He gained his feet just in time to see the King coming ponderously and unstoppably, if slowly, toward him.

Now, he thought, a little bitterly, would be the time to use his magic—if only he had some—the thought was suddenly interrupted by his realization that he and the King were now as close as cellmates; but the King hadn't seemed to notice yet that there was alien magic in his Kingdom. Jim thought it unlikely that the ward KinetetE had put around him before sending him back here had moved with him when he had taken over Hill's body; but could the King still be so mentally involved with this fight that he had ignored what was under his nose—

Of course not! Jim's mind pounced on the answer. The King was no longer seated on his Throne, and he had taken off the Robe to step into the ring against Hill as an ordinary Gnarly. He would be as blind to the ward as Hill, or any other of this tribe of Naturals at this moment.

But the King was now close to him. Jim struggled to move a body that felt as if made of lead. There was clearly no point in standing still and attempting to dazzle the Gnarly Monarch with boxing or wrestling techniques from the twentieth century. There was not even any hope of trying to use one of the two or three martial arts moves he thought he might remember having learned, years ago. Not with someone as powerful as the King.

Besides, he was too much of an amateur at any of them; and the King was far heavier, far longer-armed and stronger than Hill. Hill and his "Luck"! Jim could use some of that "Luck" himself, right now.

The King was still lumbering toward him.

There remained the dirty-trick department.

Jim crouched in plenty of time to avoid a swing from one of the King's massive hands as they came just within reach. He moved aside at his top slow-motion speed. The King came to a stop in preparation to turn and pursue him. For a moment, the larger Gnarly was standing still, and Jim took advantage of the first dirty trick he could remember.

He had only been third string on his high-school football team and had abandoned it for volleyball, at which he could and did shine. Now, he threw a football-style block at the King's lower legs.

Two things went wrong. In the first place, he was not able to throw his body as far as he had thought he could. In fact, the only reason he reached the King at all was because the other had turned and was again advancing toward him. And instead of hitting hard across the lower parts of both the King's legs, he merely dropped on the King's toes.

The King gave an agonized grunt, and limped aside, retreating for the first time. Jim's mind raced. He felt a mild plucking sort of sensation inside him— that would be Hill trying to take back control of his own body, as Gorbash the dragon had struggled for his—occasionally succeeding when Jim's mind was very much occupied. Jim ignored the feeling.

The football block hadn't worked. Well, there were other ways. This time, when the King got close, Jim spun—slowly—past him and gave him an elbow low in the kidneys—or where kidneys would have been in a human.

He got in a very solid blow, though he himself felt nothing. It had been so solid, in fact, that Jim pumped his arm a few times to see if his elbow was not broken. It was not. The King was turning toward him once again, looking as if he had not felt the blow, either.

He was, however, still limping slightly. Hill's body must have dropped more heavily on his toes than Jim had thought—or perhaps Gnarly toes were particularly sensitive.

However, making the King's toes sore would not win the fight. What was necessary, Jim told himself, was to somehow get the other off his feet; and do that often enough, and hit the King hard enough in the process, so that the other would have to admit he had lost.

Jim tried ducking aside from the massive hands and trailing a leg to trip the Gnarly King up. That didn't work. The Gnarly King's leg kept moving, and it was Jim's leg that nearly got pulled out from under him. He barely escaped that time.

He tried standing off and kicking at the king—and was reminded almost too late that the Gnarly legs were short and the Gnarly arms were long— they had much more reach than the legs did.

Beginning to run out of ideas, Jim paused for a moment to catch his breath. It was a mistake. The King's continual advances were slow, but relentless. Jim had gotten a little too used to being able to dodge out of the bigger Natural's way at the last minute.

He was still searching for something to do, when he saw the King starting one of his long arm-swings with his right arm. He ducked under it and almost directly into the King's left arm, which was thrusting out just a little behind the right arm.

Jim made a frantic, spasmodic attempt to leap to his left, but the thick, thrusting fingertips scored a direct hit on his chest. He found himself airborne once more, flying off at an angle to the King's right and past him—an angle that was the product of the vectors of two forces, one being the King's blow and the other, his own desperate leap. He went some little distance through the air and fell to the stone floor with an unbelievable impact.

I'm done for, Jim told himself.

But he wasn't. He had not broken every bone in his—Hill's—body this time either. In fact, he had not broken any at all. He was not even dented. The Gnarly body must be very resistant to damage. While scrambling slowly to his feet, he saw that this time he had landed to the right of and behind the King, who was now turning to face him.

For the first time, he noticed how the King turned. He did not simply pivot around on his toes as a human being might do, but needed several steps—moving the right foot partway around the turn, then the left foot to join it. Then another move with the right foot, and so on. Jim half-ran to stay behind the heavy figure, still trying to put mind and body back together.

He managed it; and after the King had made almost a full-circle turn without finding him, the Gnarly stopped and looked about uncertainly. Then he started turning once more, his arms a little bit out from his sides to balance his body as it swiveled.

Suddenly, from the mists of memory—triggered by the relative positions of the King and himself—Jim recalled an aikido throw that had once so struck him with its elegance, its magnificent simplicity and devastating effectiveness, he had told himself he would never forget it. Well, he had forgotten; but now memory served it up again. He plunged toward the king's back almost without needing to think.

He reached the King in two steps and put his left hand on the King's head, to push it forward and down. At the same time, he closed his right hand over and around the back of the King's right hand.

Instinctively, the King tried to straighten up, throwing the balance of his body backward—and as he did, Jim began pulling him back and around to his left. Jim was pulling the king into a turn; and, staying behind the King, keeping him off-balance, continued the turn. The King had no choice but to keep spinning slowly about, or fall. They began to turn together faster and faster, Jim congratulating himself—until it suddenly struck him he did not know what to do next. Memory had turned traitor on him.

Not only that, but the King's stumbling, massive body had acquired a circular momentum of its own; and Jim was beginning to be the one who was being towed around, like a stone on the end of a rope. If he did not let go in a moment, Jim thought desperately, he would be airborne.

Reluctantly, chagrined, he let go. But to his surprise as well as that of the caveful of Gnarlies—who gave a general, astonishingly audible moan at the sight—the King kept spinning, frantically struggling to keep his feet, until the effort failed him—his legs crossed and he crashed to the floor with a sound like a truckload of bricks being dumped on cement. His head bounced on the stone floor in a way that made Jim wince.

He lay still.

For a long moment, nothing happened. Jim stood, stunned by the unexpected victory.

Hill took advantage of the opportunity to take back his own body. Jim found himself back in his, watching Hill walk toward the fallen King. Hill prodded the King's body with a toe. It did not stir. He stepped back, turned to face the caveful of Gnarlies, and spread his arms wide to them.

And the Gnarlies whistled—a roar of continuing whistling that bounced off the cave walls and deafened Jim. A wave of them rushed forward to surround Hill and sweep him up to the Throne. Then the wave receded, leaving Hill behind, with the sparkling Royal Robe draped around his shoulders. Only when all the ordinary Gnarlies were back in their ranks did the whistling stop.

Slowly, Hill sat down on the Throne, and as he did so, Jim, even back in his own body, felt something like a powerful electric current that seemed to surge upward from deep in the planet toward the new King. Suddenly, all the little shapes of glinting metal on the Robe, and the Throne itself, glowed like molten gold.

"Ah, well," said Brian, "so the little fellow was the true heir to the kingdom, after all."

Jim turned his head to stare at the knight.

"How—" he said. "Why do you think his uncle didn't have as good a claim?"

"Come, James. No Pretender to a throne would receive these sorts of Greater Tributes. All these common fellows could whistle like that for the big one—probably did, in fear of their lives. But the shaking underfoot, that silver all turned to gold? Hah! It's all gone back to silver again now—you see? But it was gold there for an eye-wink, you saw that, too, yourself. The one we brought here was right about what happened to his father. It stands to reason."

Jim opened his mouth, and then closed it again. This place and these Naturals were part of the world Brian had been born into. Jim knew he would get nowhere trying to make Brian see his conclusion was more guess than fact. Jim's logic-dominated twentieth-century mind was probably more likely to be wrong than his friend's instincts and beliefs, anyway. Besides, Jim himself had wanted to believe Hill rather than his uncle.

Jim turned back to look at the Throne and saw Hill was looking at him. Indeed, Hill was glaring at him. Whatever the rules were around here—whether it was simply a matter of manners that only the Royal family was allowed to show emotion, or whether the ordinary Gnarlies were not or could not—hardly mattered. The important point was that Hill was definitely scowling down from his seat of Majesty.

"—Damn fine little fellow, actually!" Brian was saying cheerfully in Jim's ear. "Did you notice how he upended the bigger one? Well done indeed! Wish I could tell him so."

"You already have—" Jim was beginning incautiously, when a very King-like roar from the Throne interrupted him.

"Ye!" Hill was saying. "Luck! Come here to me!"

Jim had spent some time earlier in an effort to have an excuse ready, in case he was asked why he had mixed himself up in the contest between Hill and the former King. But he had been interrupted and never gotten back to it. Now, Hill was not leaving him much time to think of anything. He went, somewhat slowly, toward the dais, thinking rapidly, and stopped at its edge.

"Up here!" ordered Hill.

Jim stepped up on the dais and approached the new King. He stopped finally when he was right up against the resplendent Throne itself. His face and Hill's were only about a foot and a half apart.

"What did ye mean by interfering?" Hill demanded, in so low a voice that Jim could hardly hear him. Jim guessed that this was the Gnarly equivalent of a whisper that the rest would not hear. He lowered his own voice.

"Me?" he said.

"Yes! Ye!" muttered Hill. "Ye came and fought my fight. Ye threw my uncle down and scattered 'im—well, nigh-on scattered 'im. Don't think I didn't know 'twas thy doing!"

"But what difference does it make—" Jim was beginning, when Hill interrupted in a choking low-voiced outburst that was nevertheless crackling with fury.

"*I wanted to do it myself!*"

You couldn't, thought Jim, stopping himself just in time from saying it out loud.

"But you did!" he said instead. "Congratulations, your Highness! A famous victory!"

Hill stared. A look of perplexity came over his face, which for a moment almost faded back to the expressionless open-mouthed gape Jim had become so familiar with.

"I did not!" growled Hill. " 'Twas ye! I felt ye, holding me still and doing all thyself!"

"No, no," said Jim patiently. "Forgive me if I seem impolite, Highness, but I think you have things mixed up a little. You said yourself I was your Luck. That Luck just went to work for you. I had nothing to do with it. Did it really feel as if something was holding you prisoner?"

Hill hesitated. Jim sympathized with him. If Hill continued to insist that

Jim had taken charge of him, then he would be denying himself the credit for the victory. And it was a victory that had earned him the Robe and Throne.

At this point a human might have grumbled something noncommittal, or stammered, trying to find some way to agree with Jim. Being a Gnarly, however, Hill's face simply went open-mouthed blank, and stayed so while he thought out the situation. Jim waited patiently.

Gradually, Hill got a more Gnarly King-like expression on his face; but it was not an angry expression anymore. It was a look of rather innocent happiness.

"Well, so, thee was my Luck after all, then!" said Hill. "I was worried for naught!"

He almost beamed on Jim.

"Thee be indeed a good Luck!" he said. "Is there anything thee wants, now I be King? I can give thee whatever wish with my magick."

Jim looked down at Hill's robe.

"Well," he said, "I'd rather like to have a couple of these—" He reached out to finger the little faceted, flashing silvery jewel-like objects that covered the Robe.

"Thee would?" Hill's face had fallen a little. "Thee does not ask for somat small. It were centuries to gather th' Great Silver thee sees, and magick it to cover all this Robe."

"Is it that hard to find?" said Jim.

"Ay," said Hill. "Being a Stoopid, thee wouldn't know. But some silver lies close wi' tin in the Earth, and a rare part of that silver is Great Silver. 'Tis wedded to the tin. All our Gnarlies search for it in their mining, to find and bring it back. Once magicked by the King—by me—Great Silver holds that magick and turns into what you see here. But it has to be that rare fine special Silver, first; and 'tis hard to find. That is why my people work so close to the Stoopids that mine the tin, up where the World stops and the Air begins."

"Is that so?" said Jim. "Well, I'm very glad you told me that. It explains why your uncle's left you a Kingdom in very serious trouble."

"Trouble?" said Hill. His voice wobbled. "TROUBLE? What kind of trouble?"

"He's been negotiating with a Lady of the human Court."

"Go-shaying?" echoed Hill, staring. "A Gnarly 'go-shaying wi'a Stoopid Lady? 'Ee never had no shame! But why'd 'ee do such a thing as that?"

Jim left Hill with his own interpretation.

"Why, to get control of all the lands where human miners mine. . . ."

"But that's good. Maybe worth it, then," said Hill. "But a Stoopid female!"

"I suppose you could call her that," said Jim. "Only, she and the others like me really aren't stupid, you know."

"But for thousands of years, none o'ye never could see the Great Silver married in the tin ye mined," said Hill. "Stoopid miners mines it, but never knows it's no'but tin. If such's na stoopid, what is?"

"Well, the point is," said Jim. "to do this, your uncle made a number of bad mistakes. For one thing, he stole my ward."

"I can cure thee of warts," said Hill.

"Ward," said Jim, pointing at young Robert, who was still peacefully sleeping.

"That's what 'ee is?" said Hill seriously. "Well, in that case, thee can just have him back for being so good a Luck."

"But that's just the beginning of what your uncle tangled himself in," said Jim. "He also took the Mage Carolinus, and put him in a cage, there—" Jim turned and pointed. "Carolinus is one of the three most important magicians in the world, and hundreds—maybe thousands of the World's magicians are now against you."

"I've no fear of up-surface Magickians, down 'ere!"

"Of course not, Highness. But what if they got so angry they magically take all the Great Silver out of the tin in the ground? A light metal like tin must be up near the surface."

" 'Oo's to tell 'im?" said Hill, sounding every inch a King, and staring accusingly at Jim. "Thee?"

"Oh, no," said Jim. "That's not necessary. They'll probably just look into a scrying glass or dish of water, and command it show them where your magic is hid."

Hill stared at him.

" 'Crying glass?"

Jim nodded.

"And this 'ere . . . it'd tell them?"

"It would have to," said Jim solemnly.

Hill stared at him for another long moment.

"What a dirty, Stoopid trick!" he burst out. " 'Ees'd do that, would 'ees?"

"Unless they get my ward and Carolinus back; and this Lady that was negotiating with your uncle is stopped."

"Thee, 'eeself, Luck, can take the Magickian, too, back wi' 'ees!" said Hill. "But will the Stoopid Lady be stopped if my uncle beed kept here?"

"No," said Jim.

Tears began to brim in Hill's eyes.

"But maybe I can stop her. I'm a magician, too, you know."

" 'Ee can stop that Lady?"

"Maybe I can stop her—if I can call on you for help when I need it."

"Ay, dear Luck! Call anytime, from anywhere. I will that! I can help thee—now!"

"Fine," said Jim. "Then I'll take all my people and horses and you send us, now, back to the courtyard. Remember my Castle, where we left from with Rrrnlf?"

"Ay," said Hill. "I do that. T'was back up-Surface."

"Well, send us there. I'll be taking everyone else I mentioned, including the horses and the hobgoblin."

"Hobgoblin?" said Hill. "Oh, thee means the little creatur'. Is that what 'ee calls 'isself?"

"That's right," said Jim.

He turned. Robert still seemed to be asleep, so he went first to the cage, where Carolinus was hanging on the bars. Carolinus smiled a little as he got close.

"Does 'ee need me to help wi' the cage?" called Hill.

"No, no—!" said Jim, smug still inside his ward and pointing at the bars. Hill was about to be astonished. "Disappear!"

Nothing happened. Jim had forgotten again. He was still out of magic. He turned back uncomfortably to look at Hill, still on the Throne.

"Er, Highness . . ." he said.

Chapter 32

W hat is it, Luck?" asked Hill.

"Can you make this cage vanish?" Jim asked.

"I can," said Hill. "Now I've Robe and Throne."

Hill made no move, but Jim, out of the corner of an eye, saw the bars disappear. He turned back just in time to catch Carolinus as the old man fell forward, his eyes closed. Jim had handled unconscious or dead bodies before—they had usually been unbelievably heavy. But Carolinus seemed as light as a package of old, dry bones. Jim carried the red-robed figure toward the horses. Dafydd met him halfway and took his burden from him.

Jim went to the stone on which Robert rested; the child did not wake as Jim took him in his arms. He returned to Hill.

"One more thing, then," he said to the new Gnarly King. "How do I call you when I want you?"

"Just thee call. Call me 'Hill,' though. 'Tis the hill in the earth over us now that gives my fambly name. 'Ee must call me 'Highness' any other time, though."

"I will," said Jim. "Now you can send us—"

But he had no chance to finish speaking. They were already back at Malencontri.

The sun was blinding in the courtyard. A few servants passing through stopped, stared at the group, and stood frozen for a second before—first one or two, then in a mass—breaking out with a mixed chorus of the usual, formal welcoming scream/shout of alarm they had determined was the proper way to greet their Lord when he showed up in a magickal way.

"To me!" shouted Jim, blinking away sundazzle.

The visible servants and men-at-arms ran toward him; and others, also at a run, appeared from various outbuildings and the doors of the Great Hall. Among them was the blacksmith, still holding his hammer and with his face showing a strange mixture of annoyance at being interrupted at his work, and astonishment—not only at their appearance, but at the remarkable sight of his Lord, sworded and in armor, holding a child, and Dafydd carrying what looked like a sleeping Carolinus in his arms.

"Ho!" shouted Jim. "Bring my Lady at once! Prepare a room for the Mage! Fetch me John Steward! Four of you, fetch a litter to carry the Mage up to his room in the tower! Stable hands, here! Take the horses! Move, all of you!"

Startled, not a little alarmed—on general principles—at this unexpected happening, but also enraptured by the excitement of it all, the servants ran to obey his orders. Within moments, the horses had disappeared into the stables and a litter had been located. Carolinus was put on it, and they were all proceeding toward the front door of the Great Hall when John Steward came out—at as good a compromise between a run and a stately walk as he evidently felt his position would allow him.

Shoutings and the sound of servants swearing at each other for being slow echoed all around the courtyard.

"M'Lord!" panted John Steward, coming to a stop before Jim, and then trying to walk backward with dignity as they all proceeded to the door. "M'Lord, what is your will of me? What may I do?"

"Take charge of everything!" snapped Jim. "Where is my Lady?"

But at that moment, Angie appeared through the front door of the Hall with Robert's nurse behind her, the two of them running the last few steps to meet Jim and bringing all to a full stop. Angie hugged Jim, kissed him, kissed a now awake and gurgling Robert, snatched Robert out of Jim's arms and kissed him several more times. Robert laughed happily at this new game and punched Angie in the nose.

"Slow down," Jim said, "you'll wear him down to a nub."

Hastily, still holding Robert, Angie kissed Jim once more for possibly ignoring him.

"Shall I take him now, m'Lady?" asked the nurse, timidly.

"NO!" said Angie, turning sharply from her, and they finally got the parade moving. John Steward was already taking charge.

Jim gave her a very brief account of their activities as they walked down the length of the Great Hall. "I'll tell you the full story later."

"Fine. When you can. Eat something now. You litter-men, follow me. Jim— I'll be back as soon as I can. By the way, the priest you sent for came."

She disappeared in the direction of the tower stairs, while Jim remembered that he had indeed sent for a priest, to exorcise the *boomp* noises. Well, he would not be needed now.

Dafydd and Brian were seating themselves at the High Table. It already had pitchers of wine and water and an assortment of foods on it; and servants were arriving with more food every moment.

"Aumph!" said Brian, clearly trying to express his pleasure with his mouth full. He managed to swallow and speak clearly. "James, I believe I could eat half of what's on this table by myself. Then I could sleep for a week."

"I wish you hadn't said that," said Jim, who just happened to have his own mouth empty enough to answer at the moment. He turned to John Steward, who had just come back into the Great Hall.

"How long have I been gone?" he asked.

"Gone, m'Lord?" John Steward looked blank for a moment, then recovered himself. "Oh—this is the sixth day since you left in the hands of the giant," he said.

Jim nodded, his mouth already full once more. He was growing somewhat used to the fact that time did not seem to act normally when he was dealing with magic and Naturals, he reflected; but perhaps that explained a little of why they were all so hungry.

He had not realized how hungry he was until he started eating. And he had been reminded, too, that he yearned for sleep. He could not remember having any since—since—it was too much trouble to figure how long it had been. Of course, Jim reminded himself, he had slept after being stabbed by Edgar—if you could call that sleeping.

Dafydd said nothing. He kept eating.

Angie came back downstairs to find all of them slumbering at the table. Not a great deal of the food had been eaten before sleep overcame them. Only Hob, who had been on Jim's shoulder throughout, was bright-eyed, still perched there.

"I thought I ought to stay with him, m'Lady," he said to Angie, somewhat unsurely. "Was that the right thing to do?"

"Of course it was, Hob," she said. She turned her head and lifted her voice. "Servants here!"

Half a dozen servants, including May Heather and five men-at-arms, appeared almost immediately.

"Carry your Lord to the Solar," ordered Angie. "Take Sir Brian to *his* usual room—I don't care if it is dusty; clean it while he's sleeping, but be quiet while you do it—though he probably won't wake anyway. Find and clean another room for Master Hywel. May Heather, run ahead to Ellen Cinders to be sure that there are clean sheets and bedclothes on the beds."

Everybody obeyed.

Angie sat down at the table, poured herself half a cup of wine, looked at it with distaste, and pushed it away. She sighed heavily.

"Shall I tell you all about it, m'Lady?" Hob asked.

"Yes," said Angie. "You do that. Go ahead. I'll listen."

"Well," began Hob. "We got picked up by the giant and carried . . ."

"Where am I?" said Jim, waking up with the sun in his eyes.

"You're in your own bed in the Solar," answered Angie sleepily, from beside him. "It's four o'clock in the morning or something like that, and the sun's just up. Go back to sleep."

"Oh," said Jim. He closed his eyes, felt Angie nestling closer to him, and went back to sleep.

"What time is it?" he said, waking up again, and sitting up in bed.

Angie's face was all but buried in the pillow. She buried it a little deeper.

"Five A.M., maybe six," she said indistinctly. "Too early. Go back to sleep."

"I can't," said Jim. "There's too much to do."

But he was talking to an Angie who had returned to slumber.

Six in the morning, maybe, Jim thought. It had only been noon or something like that when they had arrived back here. A mere eighteen hours of sleep—or less. They had gone into the Great Hall and started to eat . . . and that was all he remembered.

If they had eaten for an hour—and it had probably been less—that meant he had been sleeping for only seventeen hours, or so. Well, even that was enough to explain why he was so wide-awake now. His mind was thronging with things that needed to be done. Quietly, he crept out of the bed and looked around for his clothes.

Since he was awake, he told himself, the chances were Brian and Dafydd were, too. In which case the most likely place to find them would be down in the Great Hall, eating what passed for breakfast. At the thought of lumps of cold meat and a choice of wine or small beer, his stomach rebelled. Angie usually had the Kitchen prepare something like eggs and bacon for them, but it was not the breakfast natives of this century were yet accustomed to. If he were to go down and eat with his friends, he would have to eat as they did. But maybe he could have something hot, first.

Coffee was not available, here; but they had tea, thanks to Carolinus. Jim made himself a cup—strong—and carried it with him down to the Great Hall. He passed no one on the stairs, and even the Serving Room was empty as he came through it.

Sure enough, Brian and Dafydd were at the table.

Food and drink were set out there, as expected; and the two were eating with the healthy appetites they usually showed. They all greeted each other, and Jim chose a chair beside Brian—in front of whom, for some reason, all the larger serving dishes were gathered. It seemed a strange assortment of foods—cold vegetables with vinegar, rather stale slabs of bread, small cakes, and chunks of roasted meats that had not even been cut up—different from what was usually on the table for breakfast.

"What is that you are drinking, James?" demanded Brian, peering into Jim's brass wine-cup.

"A magician's drink," said Jim.

"Sleeping on a pallet in all strange places," said Brian, "drinking all sorts of messes—forgive me, James, that I sometimes forget how hardly you Magickians must pay for your great powers; while even a simple country Knight like myself may avail himself freely of good wine and a bed."

Jim, who had just been saying to himself, *That's thinking on your feet, James,* found himself taken unawares.

"Oh, it's not all that hard, Brian." Somehow, he felt like a dirty dog. He sat down at the table, then almost immediately stood up again.

"Forgive me," he said. "I forgot to look in on Carolinus on the way down and see how he's doing."

"He does well," said Brian. "Both Dafydd and I visited him this morning. He was awake, but weak. He feels he may be himself in several days, with rest and food."

"Good!" said Jim. "But I think I'll just step up and see if he's still awake and have a word with him. I'll be right back."

When he opened the door to the room Carolinus was usually lodged in, he expected to see a servant on watch. But there was only Carolinus himself, propped up in bed, his eyes closed.

Jim went in, closed the door behind him, and approached the bed. Carolinus' eyes opened just as he got there.

"Hah!" His voice was weak and hoarse, but in it there was the same indomitable tone of challenge and defiance that Jim was used to hearing from Brian.

"I just wanted to speak to you for a moment," said Jim.

"Well, then?"

"I'm just about to sit down to breakfast with Brian and Dafydd—you do know you're back in Malencontri now, don't you?" asked Jim.

"I am neither blind nor deaf," said Carolinus. "Of course I know it. Go on."

"Well, how are you feeling?" asked Jim.

"Never better," said Carolinus, sharply, out of a face that looked as pale and sunken as that on a corpse. "Is that what you wanted to talk about?"

"Well, no," said Jim. "It's about what to do next with Brian. I've got to somehow get him cleared of any charges from his taking part in that attack on Cumberland's northern estates. Maybe I'll have to go to Court; Chandos could make it part of a deal with Cumberland, maybe."

"Never mind," said the elder magician. At Jim's stricken look, he relented and went on: "The Collegiate of Magickians does not meddle with the politics of the Court. But since this affair reached into a Natural Kingdom, we have precedence. Cumberland will not be in a position to deny this."

He closed his eyes, seeming almost to nod for a moment. But he spoke.

"KinetetE will see to it," he said.

Jim had been about to mention the fact of his being out of magic now; but Carolinus seemed on the verge of sleep, so he turned to the door and opened it softly.

". . . Silly nonsense," muttered Carolinus behind him. "Any trouble, tell KinetetE . . . silly . . . bureaucratic . . ."

The last words faded off into nothing. His eyes closed the last fraction of an inch and stayed closed. His head fell back against the headboard. He snored.

Jim went up another floor to the Solar, to get another hot cup of tea; he tried to be quiet, but Angie seemed to be on the edge of waking. He closed the door softly and headed for the stairs.

There was still no one in the Serving Room, and he wondered idly if they were all off watching a fight somewhere again. He went on to the High Table.

"Dafydd," he said, after he had taken the first edge off his hunger, "I don't know how to thank you enough. If it hadn't been for you getting us through the Drowned Land, so we could go on to Lyonesse, we'd never have gotten Robert and Carolinus back."

Like people of all ranks at this time, Dafydd and Brian were not only gargantuan eaters—compared to Jim—they were also very fast eaters. Both had apparently dealt with their own hunger by now and were sitting back, toying with their mazers and nibbling at an occasional sweet cake.

"Indeed, it could not have been a smaller thing," Dafydd answered. "For, look you, it was nothing but the chance of my having relations below the waves; apart from the matter that I would gladly adventure myself to rescue Carolinus at any time. You need not thank me for it, James."

"But I do," said Jim. "I needed to thank both of you. But what I thought I'd better say, Dafydd, is that Brian and I may have to go off to the Court in London. Because that is where the King is; and I may have to see about this business with Cumberland. Anyway, what I wanted was to tell you, I didn't need to impose on you any longer; I know Danielle has returned to your home, and if you want to get back to your family, you don't need to have any qualms about doing so, now."

The words had not come off his tongue sounding quite the way he had expected; and a cold, uneasy feeling grew in his chest as Dafydd did not answer immediately and Brian abruptly stopped nibbling on a sweet biscuit, and sat very still and expressionless.

"Why, my Lord," said Dafydd, quietly, with a perfectly calm face and casual voice—and Jim knew immediately he had said exactly the wrong thing. "—I honor your thoughtfulness in this, now. I'll return home at once, then."

"I," said Brian grimly, "feel we have the utmost need of Master ap Hywel in any further essay, James!"

"Oh, so do I!" said Jim, quickly. "In fact, I've been trying to think how we could possibly manage without him—and no way comes to mind. But still I thought I should offer—I had an impression that perhaps cares and duties at his home . . ."

"Ah," said Dafydd, "and might these cares and duties have been spoken of by some member of my family? The boys, perhaps? Or even Mistress ap Hywel, my best of wives?"

"I don't remember, exactly—I sort of picked up the impression generally, if you know what I mean."

"I do indeed, James. Look you, rest easy. I have no cares or duties that would hamper my accompanying you and Brian."

"Terrific! Excellent!" said Jim. "The fact is, I woke up this morning, remembering something I hadn't mentioned to either of you. A letter from the Prince Edward came for me while we were gone, asking my help—and yours— because he is afraid of that same Agatha Falon who laid the trap for us just outside the entrance to the Gnarly Kingdom. It was a Court matter, and I didn't want to mix you two into it unless you would really want—"

"But James!" said Brian, "you did say the letter asked for our help as well. Surely, we are in honor bound to help, then. I do not speak for Dafydd— that is," Brian went on rather hastily, "—anymore, I mean, than I would not speak for any other man. But Dafydd has already made his wishes known; and what is the Court that it should make any difference to us where a matter of honor is concerned?"

"Well," said Jim uncomfortably, remembering Brian had never admitted to being concerned over his stand on the Royal taxes.

He had been about to mention that they would also be concerned in freeing Brian from any danger of being hanged, drawn, and quartered on a charge of treason. But unless Brian admitted the danger, there was no way Jim could bring the subject up. He looked at Dafydd and found Dafydd looking at him. The bowman shrugged his shoulders slightly. Clearly they both knew and could say nothing. It did not matter.

"You're right, Brian," Jim said. "The only thing that's important is helping the Prince—a matter of honor."

"So do we all consider it, then!" said Brian. "Let us drink, therefore, to the further hunt."

They all drained their capacious mazers, following Brian's lead. Luckily, Jim's was less than a quarter full. He managed to stifle a coughing bout; and when they set the cups down again, they were back to being the same comfortable partnership they were used to.

"I'll just get a little food into me, here—" he said, shoveling some of what was closest to him into his mouth by way of showing his satisfaction with how things had just turned out. The other two watched him benignly for a while, then went to talk about hunting the three different kinds of deer—roebuck, fallow, and hart. Odd words like "brocket" and "staggard" bounced half-heard off his ears. They were clearly deep in a subject they had been discussing before.

"Well done, James," Brian interrupted the conversation for a moment to say. "It is one thing to go without food for several days or even longer when food is not available; but when the good viands are there before you, it is time to take advantage of them. Say no more, but eat!"

"I am," said Jim, and proceeded to make a much larger meal than he would have imagined he could. Necessarily this reduced him to silence. He was therefore free to think as he munched.

He had not had a chance to ask Carolinus about his magical account. But now that Carolinus had been rescued, he would soon be able to look into that. And Jim was sure that there was no one who would be willing to stand in the way of the wishes of the AAA+ magician—particularly since he, Jim, had been instrumental in rescuing his Master. So it was only a matter of a little time.

The discussion about deer was a pleasant background noise, and a glance told him that the two were no longer paying attention to him. His appetite was just about satisfied, and he discovered that he had been mindlessly popping comfits into his mouth simply because they were there. He pushed the plate from him.

Now feeling more full than he had thought, he sat back and tried to pick up the thread of the conversation, sprinkled though it was with obscure references.

He began to become aware of how quiet things were. Sound did not carry between floors, except by courtesy of the tall, echoing emptiness that was the inside of the tower. But on this, the main level of the Castle, there were always servants talking with or calling to each other, and the general bustling noise of necessary activity.

Now there was none of that. No one from the Serving Room had been out to refill the wine pitchers from which they had been refilling their mazers—in fact, Brian's was now empty. Usually the servants were interrupting him to check on such things more often than he could stand.

Dafydd and Brian were looking now toward the door beyond which the Serving Room lay. Jim looked, himself, and saw coming through its arched space a tall man in priest's garb.

"My Lord!" said the priest, as Jim's eyes came on him. He was walking toward Jim as he spoke, and he continued to come along at a steady, even pace toward the dais; and as he mounted it, Jim rose to his own feet to confront this stranger, and became conscious that the other was muttering something under his breath—muttering in Latin.

The priest had been looking downward as he approached; but as he got within a step of Jim, he stopped and lifted his head to show a long, grave, smooth-shaven face in early middle age—and said his final words.

"Benedicat te, Omnipotens Deus, Domine Jacobe Ekertis." He finished the sign of the Cross in the air.

It took Jim a couple of seconds to realize what had been done. He had been blessed, with the words: *"May the Omnipotent God bless you, Lord James Eckert."*

He had deliberately been blessed, which to a magician meant that for the next twenty-four hours, he could not make his magic.

Jim opened his mouth to explain how ridiculous it was to bless a magician who already had no magic left—and shut it again.

Armed men in chain mail, steel caps, swords, and all the other accoutrements of men-at-arms were pouring from the service entrance and from other doorways into the Hall—twenty or thirty of them at least—and converging on Jim, Brian, and Dafydd. Jim found himself driven back into three of them at once, his arms pinioned behind him, his wrists bound; and he was aware that his friends were also being overcome and bound in the same moment.

Chapter 33

"Well, well," said a voice behind Jim, as the last of his bonds were pulled tight. The voice was baritone, with an upper-class London accent. "It worked as it always does. Sooner or later, the rats come to the bait in the rat-trap."

The owner of the voice came around in front of Jim, moving through the crowd of men-at-arms, who got out of his way. He halted at the end of the table, where Jim, Brian, and Dafydd could all see him.

He was a little shorter than most of his men, but remarkably broad-shouldered and thin-waisted. He wore no armor or weapon at all, his shirt was open at the neck, and his hand held a mazer more than half-full of wine. There was a smile on his roughly triangular, suntanned face. A smile that at first glance seemed pleasant, but about which Jim had second thoughts almost immediately. The mouth that smiled was thin, and the smile was only at its corners. It was a narrow, hard face.

He sipped at his mazer and looked at them with something that might have been pleasure.

"I take you for a gentleman, sir," said Brian, very coldly and evenly. "But I do not know you."

"Sir Simon Lockyear, at your service. And I am here at the orders of our King, whom God preserve."

"I find you unpleasing," said Brian.

Sir Simon Lockyear laughed.

"Do you now?" he said. "And no doubt on that account you would wish to challenge me?"

"Exactly," said Brian. "If you would show the courtesy to have your men cut these bonds wherewith they have tied myself, the Lord James, and the archer, I would be most happy to meet you immediately, with sword or any other weapon you might choose."

Simon Lockyear laughed again.

"No, no," he said. "It would be enjoyable, no doubt. But I must not damage those I am sent to bring back. So, I fear you must stay bound, all of you. I hold Crown Warrants for arrest of you, Sir Brian, on a charge of treason for intent to engage in a rebellion against the peace of the Realm; and two other warrants: one for you, my Lord James, for harboring the said Sir Brian; and one for a Welsh archer—which I make little doubt is the third of you at this table—named Dafydd ap Hywel, also charged with assisting the traitor Sir Brian."

He paused, and produced a handkerchief whose scent Jim could catch clearly even across the four feet or so between them.

"But I must say," he wound up, "you are not over-nice about those you sit at table with, Sir Brian and my Lord James. An archer?"

Brian paid no attention to the last words.

"Duty is no knightly excuse, Sir Simon," he said.

"Perhaps not. Perhaps not. On the other hand, there is neither profit nor honor to be gained by playing at weapons with a traitor."

"Why, damn your soul!" exploded Brian. "I am no traitor, nor ever was! What is this nonsense?"

Sir Simon doffed his heavy leather gloves, revealing long sensitive fingers, and looked across the table at Brian.

"That you may argue before your appointed judges when you reach the Tower, Sir Brian," he said. "I am merely charged with bringing you in, and bring you in I shall."

He turned suddenly on a tall man-at-arms by his side.

"But why have you not brought Sir James' wife by now, Elias?" he snapped.

"We have a woman, Sir Simon. But we are not sure if she is the lady you want."

"God's Wounds! Dolts! Not able to tell a Lady from a servant wench! Look at the quality of her gown and whether it fits her! A tall woman, with dark hair. I'd know her in a wink! I spoke her once before this, on our first trip to this Castle. There will be no doubt when I see her. Bring her at once, I say! She will be all a-quiver, no doubt, to see her dear husband."

His voice had dropped on the last words to a conversational level again, and he sat down in one of the empty chairs. "I shall wait here."

He poured a little more wine into his mazer and addressed Jim, Brian, and Dafydd. "Seat yourselves, my prisoners. We will play that you are all three my guests."

Brian, Dafydd, and Jim were shoved into chairs. Elias spoke to four of the men-at-arms, who disappeared through the entrance to the Serving Room and the tower stairs beyond. The tall man-at-arms turned back to the table.

"Was there anything else you wished, Sir Simon?" he asked.

"Not for the moment," said Sir Simon. "Do you follow and make sure those men of yours are doing as they should. I'll have no time for capers with drink or smock-lifting."

Elias went out and Simon reached for one of the small cupcakes. He picked it up and nibbled it.

"Ah," he said, in a quiet, thoughtful voice, washing it down with wine, "my congratulations on your kitchen, Sir James. I would not despise such cooking in my own home."

"Who sent you here?" said Jim.

"Sent me?" Sir Simon ate another cupcake before answering. "I am at the orders of my Lord the Earl of Cumberland, so I suppose you could say it was he. Though the orders, in fact, reached me from the leading knight of his household, Sir Adam Turner. I have been searching for you for some small time now, and during the night I took your Castle and have been waiting for you to be in the right position—ah! Well and swiftly done, Elias!"

He swung around, pushing his chair away and standing up. His men had just brought in Angie. Her wrists had been bound before her with a strip of cloth rather than rawhide thongs. Her face was perfectly calm and composed; and she looked at Jim as if she would reassure *him*.

"Good day, my Lady," said Sir Simon. He advanced his right leg, and bowed over it in a courtly manner, but with that thin smile again at the corners of his lips. "I regret the necessity that forces us to meet thus. But my Lord, your husband, and the other two at this table, must be taken back to London, to face judgment for treason; and my spoken orders required me to bring you as well."

Angie looked slightly amused, but said nothing.

He turned again to his men. "Make ready to travel," he said. "The Lady will be allowed a maid and some clothes. We cannot take too great a care of them.

Prisoners are so apt to die on the way, and never arrive." He paused to smile at Jim.

"To be sure, this often saves time and trouble in the long run; but I have always thought it a pity, particularly when there is information to be got. Elias, send a man to see what there is in the stable here."

Elias went off, another of his men following him. Out of the corner of his eye, Jim saw one of the men-at-arms pick up a metal mazer standing at the far end of the table and slip it into a sack on his back. He suddenly realized all of them had such sacks—and they were bulging.

There was no more time to waste.

"Hob," he called to the fireplace. "Tell Carolinus!"

There was no answer.

"Calling a Devil to aid you from the fireplace, were you, Sir James?" Simon asked. "You should remember that the good Father, having blessed you, has taken away your magick. I entreat you and Sir Brian to sit quietly a little while longer, while my men make all ready for the trip back to London. It will not be long. Will my Lady sit?"

But Angie had already done so.

"That reminds me," said Sir Simon. "Have you a particular servant woman you would like to take with you, my Lady? I will have her fetched, and you can give her orders as to what to pack for your journey. I am a knight-bachelor in both senses, so I have no idea what a lady might require for such a journey. Who shall I send to fetch?"

"Send for Enna," said Angie coldly. "She will know what to pack."

"See to it," said Sir Brian, nodding at a man-at-arms, who immediately turned and left, through a side-passage doorway.

"There," said Sir Simon, "you see how smoothly things go when we are all agreed?"

He helped himself to more wine.

"Damme if I'd sit at table with you, if I had not been here before you," said Brian.

"I believe Sir Brian is not yet fully understanding of the situation. Perhaps we should put the shackles on them all now, to save time."

"Shackles!" Brian surged to his feet. Evidently he had been struggling with the thongs about his wrist and either broken them, or wetted them with his own blood to the point where the rawhide stretched. At any rate, his hands came around free in front of him, with cord still dangling from one torn wrist; and he went with hands alone for the throat of Sir Simon. It took five of the men-at-arms to stop him before he could reach the other knight.

"Lack-a-day!" said Sir Simon, shaking his head. He had not moved an inch.

"I am afraid the grief of being arrested has addled Sir Brian's wits. Shackle him first, and well; but then the rest must be also fitted with irons—even the Lady when we are a-horseback, and whoever is traveling with her as maid. We must not waste much more time here. There is still a full day before us. Move!"

The last word came out like the crack of a whip. Two men ran up the length of the Hall and out the double doors into the courtyard.

Jim realized that for himself, Angie, Dafydd, and Brian, there was no more time at all. Neither Hob nor Carolinus could help. He wondered what Sir Simon had done with his Malencontri men-at-arms—and the other servants. Not that a dozen men-at-arms could take on this troop. Even with some sent on errands, there were still almost thirty of them in the Great Hall, all weaponed and wearing the light armor of ordinary medieval foot-soldiers.

Jim was beginning to feel desperate. Usually, in a tight spot, his mind came up with some idea or solution to the situation. He had never missed his magic before the way he was missing it at this moment, in the Hall of his own Castle.

Like him, Brian and Dafydd were tied up and helpless. No one could offer even a hope of rescue—

Or—wait a minute!

There was still himself. A blessing took magic away only from humans; it did not affect the limited, in-born magic of Naturals.

Only yesterday, down in the Throne-cave of the Gnarly King, he had been able to use the power that let him change himself into a dragon, despite the fact that he no longer had the magic power controlled by the Accounting Office. It was more than possible, it seemed to him now, that that same power—akin to the in-born powers of such as Naturals—might still be available to him.

But, he was thinking when he ought to be acting. If he changed into his dragon form now, these bonds they had him tied with would snap like threads—he had lost whole suits of clothes in the early days when he had changed into a dragon, before he got control of the change process magically. But in any case, once free as a Dragon . . .

No—it was an attractive thought, but not practical. He might scare the liver and lights out of the men-at-arms, though less possibly out of the knight; but if that many armed men really set about him in this small Hall where he had no room to take to the air, they would be bound to win.

He wouldn't be able to rescue Angie and the rest immediately on changing. The best he could hope for would be to get away, and then come back with enough strength to handle them. What he needed was a plan that would take advantage of his becoming a dragon—after he had supposedly been stripped of his ability to make magic.

He could certainly recruit the young dragons from Cliffside to come back with him, once the men with their prisoners were out of the Castle and in the open where they were approachable from all sides. Something might be done under those conditions. The trouble was that the young dragons would go through the motions of attack, but not actually fight for him—and he dreaded to think of what the parental dragons would say, if they heard that he had deliberately taken their children into battle with georges—which even the strongest of adult dragons avoided nowadays.

He thought hard, but nothing else came to mind. Well, at least he could probably make his escape, follow them from the air, and maybe find some other help.

There were other possible sources of help—for instance, in Brian's rather tottery set of servants and few men-at-arms. Geronde had a solid group at Malvern Castle, and there were also Giles o' the Wold and his men, off in their forested lands. The problem would lie in finding them all and getting them here in time to be of any use—he himself could not afford to be gone long enough that Sir Simon and his party could get away.

Asking any of those people to take armed action against the King's men, would be unfair—and bloody. It would be better if he could find some way to scare the men-at-arms into abandoning their prisoners.

Sir Simon would be a separate problem. Jim had been in the fourteenth century long enough now to know that the other man—whatever his other defects of character—would not be one to panic or run from a fight.

But that was enough thinking for now. He turned to look at Angie, only a couple of feet from him, and moved his eyebrows up and down, slowly and deliberately, several times. She nodded slightly and he knew she understood. He looked back at the doorway, and judged its distance. Two long leaps, if his wings helped him to be air-borne a little on each one, should see him to the doorway. He was just about to make his dragon-change, when a roar stopped him.

It was a sound from many human throats at the same moment. On the instant, the two big doors of the entrance slammed inward; and from the courtyard outside and all the other entrances into the Hall, poured a mass of people.

He knew every one of them, but it took him a moment to realize they actually were what he was seeing. They were the Castle's servants, led by the full dozen of Malencontri's men-at-arms, now very dirty—they must have been taken prisoner and thrown into Malencontri's dungeons, which were simply pits in the earth, he thought dazedly—but all with their swords; and all the servants were armed with something capable of doing damage.

They could not have looked more savage if they had erupted out of the Stone Age. There was the Blacksmith, with a heavy hammer in each large fist and what was left of his teeth bared in his unshaven face. There was May Heather, carrying on her shoulder a clumsy battle-axe, her favorite weapon. She had first carried one against Jim himself, not knowing him in his dragon body; this one she carried with less difficulty, now that she was several years older.

All the rest had something. Mistress Plyseth was waving a long toasting-fork with two very nasty-looking tines on the end, that perhaps could slip right through links of chain mail into the body of its wearer.

For a split second, Jim stared at them. His heart had leaped with hope at the first sight; now it sank in horror. What they were doing was suicidal. This was a wilder thing than he had ever imagined, an impossible attempt. For all that there were twice as many of them as of Sir Simon's men-at-arms, they did not stand a chance of winning against properly armed and experienced soldiers, men used to fighting as a unit. Perhaps they had been carried away by all the stories and ballads about Jim's adventures and heroic deeds, to the point where they thought they could be heroes, too.

"STOP!" shouted Jim, striving to make his voice sound above the noise they were making. "Stop immediately! Stop this, now! Do you hear me? I SAID STOP!"

Their roar faded, like the tail-end of a long thunder-roll, and finally died. They came to a stop and ended up standing, glaring across perhaps five to ten feet of space at Sir Simon's men-at-arms, who glared back, not at all averse to chopping up this civilian crowd and knowing just how they would go about it.

In this interesting moment of silence, the two halves of the large front door of the Hall banged open once more, and in walked Secoh, the mere-dragon.

Secoh had been a Companion of Jim and the rest at the fight against the Dark Powers at the Loathly Tower. Since then he visited now and again, when not acting as a sort of combination storyteller-leader-and-idol of the younger dragons at Cliffside.

Now, he waddled down the aisle between the two long, lower tables of the room—walking being an awkward, if perfectly practicable, way of traveling for dragons. Sir Simon's troop stared at him in astonishment.

A dragon walking was something that they undoubtedly never imagined. An heraldic dragon rampant, possibly, on someone's shield, or a picture of a dragon dying at the point of St. George's sword; possibly even a dragon seen flying ominously overhead—but never a dragon stumping toward them like this.

They got out of his way. Mere-dragons were no more than three-quarters the size of normal dragons, such as those of Cliffside; but in the ceilinged Hall Secoh loomed large enough to make anyone cautious. The servants had already made way for him; and now the men-at-arms drew aside also, without a word, parting before him like the Red Sea before the Israelites.

"M'Lord!" called Secoh in his deep dragon-voice, halting before Jim at the High Table. With Jim seated on the dais and Secoh sitting on his haunches on the Hall floor below, their heads were more or less on a level. With dragonish single-mindedness, he ignored everybody else who was present. "Word just came to Cliffside you were back, so I came right away. M'Lord, can you tell me—have you seen a youngster from the Cliffside Caverns by the name of Garnacka, recently? He calls himself just Acka, mostly."

"Yes," said Jim. "He came up to me when I was flying a few days back. I told him to go back to Cliffside."

Secoh let out a huge puff of relief.

"Thank you, m'Lord!" he said. "I feel so much better. Was he a bother to you? I told them all very strictly they were never to bother you. But he's a very active young dragon, and Garaga—his mother—wanted me to find out if he'd bothered you. Of course, they all want to."

"He wasn't really a bother," said Jim.

There was something ridiculous about sitting here with his hands tied behind him, carrying on this conversation with Secoh. He was saying the first thing that came into his mind, while his wits scrambled for some way he could turn this unexpected development to his own benefit.

Right now, Secoh was not so much a potential help as an impediment. He was blocking the way Jim had planned to take out of the Hall in a couple of leaps. Clearly Secoh, who was so used to Jim's being in control of things here, could not imagine for a moment Jim might not be so now.

"No, not what you'd call a bother," said Jim. "In fact, in a way he was even useful."

"Useful?" There was something very like a tinge of jealousy in Secoh's voice, and his head came forward on his neck as he peered narrowly at Jim.

"Well, you know, as much as someone that young could be," said Jim. "You'd have been much more useful, for example, if it had been you there."

"Why didn't you call me?"

"I'm sorry," said Jim, "but it was just that he saw something on the ground and told me about it, and I needed to get back to the Castle right away. There wasn't time, and it wasn't worthwhile calling you just then."

"Oh," said Secoh. "Well . . . I quite understand, m'Lord. I understand. You know, if you ever want me, a word will bring me to you—though you may have to use your magick if you want me there immediately."

"I know that, Secoh. In this case it just happened that Acka was there, and mentioned seeing these people to me. But as I say, in any real need I'd have called you instead."

"Well, thank you, m'Lord," said Secoh, looking down modestly. "It's good of you to tell me that."

Jim was running out of small talk to keep Secoh in play, though his audience, both local and visiting, seemed to be fascinated. Happily, it appeared Secoh was ready to go on carrying the conversation himself, if necessary.

"While I'm here, m'Lord," he said, "would it be all right for me to see Carolinus? The word that reached us at Cliffside was that he had been through a very hard time because of being the prisoner of some gnomes—"

"Not gnomes," said Jim rapidly, seizing on the first opportunity to interrupt him. "Gnarlies—"

"Well, I just thought I'd look in for a moment and pass on the sympathy of the Cliffside dragons, as well as my own. We all love Carolinus. Besides, he's our own Mage, so to speak, living at the Tinkling Water real close here. I'd just say 'hello,' wouldn't wear him out or anything. He's just upstairs, isn't he? I could go out and fly up to the top of the Tower and walk down to him."

"No, no," said Jim. "No, he's not up there—and besides, now wouldn't be a good time anyway. I'll pass the word along—"

But it was too late. Sir Simon was already talking to some of his men-at-arms.

"You six," he said pointing, "up in the tower with you. Search it from top to bottom. Father"—he turned to the priest—"you go with them. If there's a Mage up there, I want him blessed immediately, even if he's unconscious. We don't want to take any chances with a Magickian of that rank."

The priest and the six men-at-arms, clearly glad to be given an excuse to leave the vicinity of this walking dragon, literally ran out.

"Hell's bells!" said Jim; and was just about to turn himself into a dragon in a desperate attempt to reach Carolinus before the men-at-arms and the priest did—even if he had to knock Secoh over in the process—when he felt his bonds drop away from his wrists. He saw from the change in Brian's face and Angie's that theirs had also gone. Dafydd had preserved an unchanged countenance, but Jim was pretty sure that his hands were now free.

"Sit still, James!" snapped a familiar, if feeble, voice; and Jim turned his gaze to see Carolinus, sagging rather than standing at the far end of the dais—

supported on one side by the Earl of Cumberland and on the other by another familiar figure, wearing black monastic robes with a large jeweled cross hanging from his neck and a sizable amethyst ring on a powerful finger.

"I must sit down," said Carolinus feebly, and the two big men helped him into one of the padded and backed chairs at the High Table. He sank into it with a sigh of relief. "Simon, bring that priest back here right away!"

Simon Lockyear stared at him blankly.

"You heard him, damn your liver and eyeballs!" roared Cumberland. "Get that priest back!"

"Yes, m'Lord," said Sir Simon, starting like someone coming out of a trance. "Forgive me, m'Lord, but I don't—I don't understand—"

"Nobody needs you to!" growled Cumberland. "Have I ever been in the habit of having my orders questioned, sirrah?"

"Of course not, m'Lord," said Sir Simon, quickly. "Hebert, you and your two fastest men, chase after them. Find the priest and bring him back as fast as you can drag him down here. Never mind if he gets bumped around a bit in the process!"

The big man with the pectoral cross cleared his throat in an ominous manner.

"On second thought," said Sir Simon rapidly, "treat him tenderly, don't let him hurt himself—but get him here as quick as possible! My Lord needs him!"

The three men broke away from the semicircle of men-at-arms about the dais and ran at top speed through the entrance to the Serving Room.

Everybody waited. The pause in affairs caused something like a relaxation of the tension in the Hall. The Royal men-at-arms had to keep their formation and stay ready for battle, and the Malencontri men-at-arms clearly felt a professional obligation to do the same; but no such constraint was on the Malencontri servants. Imperceptibly they began to edge forward; and the various items they were carrying as weapons began to drop into inoffensive positions, although still kept in their hands.

A low murmur of conversation was coming to life between the two groups. The Royal men-at-arms, with their backs to the dais, wanted to know what was going on there; and the Malencontri people—though ready still to stab, smash, or stick basting forks into them, were obligingly telling them.

Jim had dropped his idea of turning into a dragon right away. He could always do that; and Secoh was still in his path. Moreover, he had recognized the big man with the pectoral cross. He was Richard de Bisby, Bishop of Bath and Wells, whose acquaintance Jim and Angie had made at the Earl of Somerset's last Christmas Party. Richard de Bisby was clearly on Carolinus' side—which meant he would be on Jim's, most probably. And Richard de Bisby feared neither man, beast, nor Natural—to which catalog the good Bishop added Devils, Demons, and anything else Magickal or Supernatural—in his vocation as a Prince of the Church.

The good Bishop's was a martial spirit, which longed for earlier days, such as those of Bishop Odo; who, three centuries before, had fought in William's invasion of England and ended his life on a Crusade to the Holy Land.

Odo had found his holy occupation no barrier at all to his own zeal— though he had thoughtfully carried a mace as his weapon, so as to not be guilty of the shedding of human blood. That sort of fighting Bishop was unthinkable here and now in this fourteenth century; but in this world there were still Devils, Demons, Fiends, and such, and Richard de Bisby had hopes of running some to earth one day and dealing with them personally.

It was the Bishop who had made sure Jim and Angie had gotten the wardship of Robert Falon. He had done this by going to the Court at London and, effectively, telling the King repeatedly that any other disposal of Robert was unthinkable. The King, whose blood was just as Norman as that of the good Bishop, would at one time have been just as likely as the cleric to argue.

That would have been true, perhaps, twenty or thirty years before. But while de Bisby was in the prime of life—which in his case meant his middle forties—time had laid its heavy hand upon the crowned head; and the King wanted nothing so much as to be left in peace to follow his whims.

The King could not evade the Bishop, he could not out-shout him; the easiest thing was simply to give in. Besides, Sir James Eckert was a popular name, particularly after the fight at the Loathly Tower, which was still being sung in England.

At the present moment, however, the Bishop was paying no attention to Jim or Angie, but a good deal of it to Carolinus, who had fallen asleep in his chair. They were old friends—so Jim understood—and the Bishop had always been very solicitous of the very much older—no one knew how much—man.

But at this moment Sir Simon's men-at-arms returned through the Serving Room entrance, hurrying the priest in their midst.

Chapter 34

T he unfortunate priest, hurried along by the press of bodies around him, and with his sight restricted to what he could see between the men on either side and a little ahead of him, caught sight of Carolinus' red robe first.

He automatically went into the Latin of his blessing for another four steps, until he stumbled and fell, tripping on the edge of the dais; and pulled himself back on his feet to step up onto it—only to find himself less than six feet from the jeweled pectoral cross and the amethyst ring.

He stared, turned pale, hastily took several more steps forward, and went down on one knee before the Bishop, lifting his hands toward the Bishop's ringed hand.

De Bisby automatically extended that hand to be taken by the priest, though his eyes glared down at the man. The priest devoutly kissed the ring, relinquished the hand, and stood up.

"My Lord Bishop—" he began.

"Who are you?" snapped de Bisby. "Where are you from? Who is your Bishop?"

The priest became even more pale.

"The Bishop of London, my Lord," he said, looking down at the floor of the dais.

"Where then is his Episcopal letter sending you into my Diocese?"

The priest raised his eyes unhappily.

"My Lord," he began, "you see, my Lord—"

"You haven't got one?"

"Well, no, my Lord," said the priest.

De Bisby seemed to grow in height and swell visibly, the picture of outrage.

"Are you not aware, unhappy priest, that it is a principle in Canon law that *'A Bishop is Pope in his own Diocese'?*"

"Yes, my Lord," said the priest. He might not be able to quote chapter and verse—even if there were such—but the practical truth of that principle was one with which he was thoroughly familiar.

"You are consequently here without proper authority! You will return to London for a proper letter before you come again; and I lay this penance upon you: if you have a horse, you will not ride. If you have coin, you will not spend it. You will return to your Bishop's residence on foot and beg your food and shelter as you go. Do you hear me?"

"Yes, my Lord," said the priest, staring at the floor.

"Then what are you waiting for?"

The priest knelt again briefly, rose, turned, stepped down from the dais, and walked past Secoh—passing as far away from him as the nearest table would allow—and went slowly down the length of the Hall, out the door, and into the sunlight.

A movement by Angie caught Jim's eye. He turned his head and saw she was holding up her wrists to show that they, too, were unbound. Jim lifted his own to show her, and saw the expression on her face change. She was staring at his wrists. He looked at them, and was astonished to see them almost as bloody as Brian's had been. Now, when had he done that? He did not remember struggling against the bindings.

"You!" said Carolinus, in a sudden, remarkably strong voice. Jim jumped and turned his head. But Carolinus was pointing not at him but at Secoh. "Where did you come from? Cliffside?"

"Yes, Mage," said Secoh. "But if I might stay—"

"*Cliffside!*" said Carolinus, his finger still pointing at Secoh. Secoh disappeared.

"As for the rest of you—" began Carolinus, sweeping his eyes over the servants and men-at-arms. But they were all already on the run for the nearest exit they could find. In much less than two minutes there was not one to be seen in the Hall.

The Royal men-at-arms held their positions, but they were now looking somewhat pale themselves, particularly those who were enough at an angle with Carolinus' position on the dais to see that his finger could have been pointing at them as much as the servants. Where had the dragon gone when he disappeared like that, they were obviously thinking? Had the Mage sent him to Hell? And would they be sent there also, without even the chance to shrive themselves first?

"You and the knight—out into the courtyard!" Carolinus said.

Sir Simon Longyear and his men-at-arms also winked out. And KinetetE winked in, appearing on the dais beside the chair in which Carolinus was slumped.

Jim, his friends, the Earl, and the Bishop, with the two senior magicians, were alone in a Great Hall that seemed to Jim suddenly very large, very empty.

But that impression was abruptly shattered by KinetetE.

"Carolinus!" she snapped. "What are you doing here? You're supposed to be in bed. Why aren't you in bed?"

"None of your business!" said Carolinus, but the strength of his voice broke before he got through this last word, and he squeaked slightly on it.

"You can't bullyrag the whole Collegiate, telling them you were the one mistreated and you'll handle the whole matter yourself, whether they like it or not, and then kill yourself. That would be shameful behavior, even for a single-A Class Magickian!"

A faint snore from Carolinus' chair was all that answered her.

She looked at the Bishop, who looked back at her.

"Mage," said the Bishop.

"My Lord Bishop," said KinetetE.

They exchanged a pair of cool, mutually respectful but frosty, nods.

Another snore came from Carolinus in his chair. Without warning, Jim found himself alone with KinetetE and Carolinus in a room just big enough to hold the three of them, and which greatly resembled the inside of a very large, empty egg. Its walls were a flat but brilliant white and there were no windows or furniture, except for the chair in which Carolinus still slumped.

"All right, Carolinus," said KinetetE, "you can wake up now. I understood you perfectly."

Carolinus' eyes opened and he focused on KinetetE.

"Kin," he said weakly. "Give me strength!"

"You don't need strength," said KinetetE. "What you need is a bed. You'll just tear yourself down further if I help you now. Oh, all right, then, if you must have it!"

Jim, who had now been around magic for several years, had used it himself and thought he was ready to expect anything, almost jumped as color suddenly came into Carolinus' face; his eyes opened all the way, and he sat up in the chair, looking years younger.

"Once again, a Magickian's Blessing on you, KinetetE," he said. "It's only for a few minutes. You can have what's left back then. But I've got to talk to the boy, here. Jim!"

"Yes?" said Jim, staring at him.

"It's all up to you now!" said Carolinus. "Don't ask me why. I haven't the strength or the patience to put up with someone who knows nothing, essentially, about Magick and when I tell them a hard-won fact about the Art, that I have acquired with sweat and blood over many years, they take it as merely a debatable point and wish to argue with me about it!"

"I won't argue," said Jim. "Are you all right?"

"For the moment," said Carolinus. "Never mind me. What I want to tell you is that from now on, it's all up to you. You're in your own Castle, you're free, and while you can't use any Magick of your own, you can use some of mine—"

"Carolinus!" cried KinetetE. "This is the second time you promised—"

"I don't give a damn!" said Carolinus. "As I say, Jim, you can use as much of my Magick as you need. Just go ahead as if you had—as if it were your own Magick—only remember, it's a great deal more powerful than what you're used to. What you have to do is bind the Earl of Cumberland to backing away from his current course of action, before it does irreparable harm—and, of course, setting you and your friends free of any kind of arrest or trouble now."

Jim stared.

"I thought, from the fact you brought him along with you, you'd already gotten his agreement."

"I have!" said Carolinus. "But it's only a present promise. You must bind him for the future to one he dare not break! As I say, you have your Castle, you have your strength, you have your freedom, and you have Magick. It's up to you!"

"But how do I do that?" said Jim.

"Up to you!"

"I suppose," said Jim, only half joking, "I could turn him into a beetle, the way you do."

"I don't turn anyone into a beetle!" said Carolinus.

"But you're always threatening to turn people into beetles or creatures into beetles!" Jim stared at him. "Come to think of it, I saw you turn Rrrnlf, the Sea Devil, into one!"

"You thought I did. In fact, I merely made him believe, and all the rest of you believe, he had become one. Something entirely different."

"How did you do that?" Jim stared at him.

"I JUST TOLD YOU—" began Carolinus, but KinetetE cut in quickly.

"Jim, he just warned you about not taking his word for matters! Calm down, Carolinus. The boy just forgot. Jim—" she turned the full frost of her gaze on him, "—James Montgomery Eckert, watch what you say!"

Jim stared back. He could have sworn no one in this fourteenth-century world knew he had a middle name, let alone what it was.

"How did you—" he began to ask, but checked himself in time. "Sorry," he said.

"Yes, yes," said Carolinus. "Never mind that now. KinetetE, Jim and I have to get back to his Great Hall—back there at as close to the time we left as possible. Will you send us back?"

"I'll do that," said KinetetE. "I'll also take back the rest of that strength I gave you, Carolinus, so we'll leave you some of your own reserves to recover with before you burn them all up doing things you shouldn't. Also, I'm going back with you. Don't worry, I'll stay invisible. Nobody else will know I'm there."

"Wait a minute—" said Jim. "Leave him with strength a minute longer, Mage, please. Surely I can ask this one quick question—Carolinus, the last I knew of you you were upstairs. How did you know about Sir Simon and his men being here; and how did you gather up the Bishop and Cumberland to get them here in time?"

"Simon and his men came in during the night," Carolinus said. "That priest had come in earlier, pretending to be the one you had sent for to exorcise those noises in the walls. Your people were so relieved to see him that they allowed him free run of your Castle; and during the night he opened the postern to let the rest of Sir Simon's party in. They were able to take your people asleep, and then wait for you to come down. But I'm a AAA+ Magickian; and it's hard to sneak up on me."

"Not that you were in any shape to do anything," put in KinetetE, icily. "That's all, Jim! Back with all of us to the Hall!"

As suddenly as they had left, Jim and Carolinus were back on the dais in the Great Hall. As far as Jim could see, nobody had moved, nothing had been changed since the second in which they had left. He smiled reassuringly, confidently, at Angie, and she smiled back.

It was all right for the moment—but only for the moment. His mind had begun to go into emergency high gear. Under such circumstances, it sometimes galloped so fast he was not quite sure he was understanding his own thoughts. It was as if they flashed into being in his mind, and vanished again almost before he had the time to consider them. Nothing wrong with that, of course, as long as he did consider each one. When he thought of something really useful the process would stop.

His only worry in this case was, would it ever stop? Maybe there was no solution, and his mind would go on flashing uselessly, indefinitely. Maybe what Carolinus was asking him to do was impossible. Nonetheless, his mind went right on leaping ahead, from possibility to possibility, at dizzying speed, while he almost forgot the rest of the people on the dais.

So, he told himself, turning Cumberland into a beetle was not the answer. But then he had never really been serious about doing so—it might be immoral and was probably illegal, magically speaking.

It struck him now, however, that beetle-changing was in a way the kind of transformation that Carolinus was asking him to perform—but on another level. The more Jim considered Cumberland, the less he thought it likely that any ordinary promise made by the Earl would bind him in the future. He was more politician than knight and peer.

His mental galloping suddenly skidded to a stop.

Of course Cumberland was a politician. The fourteenth century had no lack of them, like any other era; the only difference between politicians here and those in the world where Jim had grown up, was that the medieval variety were all ready, if not eager, to promote their agendas with sword, lance, and hangman's rope (or headsman's axe, if their opponents were of high enough rank).

Jim had not immediately recognized the politicians here as such, simply because those like Cumberland aimed at a slightly different goal from those Jim had been familiar with. In the century of his birth, politicians had competed for the approval of the general public. Here the competition was for control of as large a share as possible of the Royal power and privilege—or as much as an individual could get the King to delegate to him.

The great peers had to be politicians. In fact, the total population of the Court consisted of either politicians or political hangers-on. Perhaps an exception could be made for someone like Sir John Chandos, who might more properly be called a statesman than a politician, since he was concerned with the relationship between England as a whole and all other national bodies.

And what was most important to a politician in any historical period? It was his reputation. Cumberland was, of course, the bastard half-brother of the

King, himself—effectively a "Royal" in his own right, in this rough age. But he was nonetheless vulnerable in his reputation.

Only—how to put handcuffs on that reputation so that he would not be able to break loose later? Jim was prohibited from doing harm to the Earl; but then, Carolinus had not actually turned Rrrnlf into a beetle, either. . . .

Jim did not know the outline of what he would do, yet; but there was an odd sort of certainty growing in him that what he wanted was there to be found. All he could do was to keep reaching for it. He turned to Cumberland, who had helped himself to a seat at the table, appropriated a mazer, poured some wine into it, and was now drinking.

"Welcome to my Hall," said Jim. "I hope my Lord finds my wine sufficiently drinkable?"

Cumberland only grunted.

"I would like to thank your Lordship for freeing us," said Jim. Cumberland darted a quick glance at Carolinus, who now seemed deeply asleep in his chair. Then the Earl turned back to Jim.

"I wasn't the one who set you loose," he said. "As I think you know very well, Sir Dragon Knight—or whatever your Hell-bound name is! As for being set free, don't say your prayers of thanks too soon. We'll see about that!"

"I am the Baron Sir James Eckert," said Jim. "Perhaps if your Lordship and I could talk about this matter—"

"If there's any talking to be done, I'll do it, sirrah!" said Cumberland.

The Bishop's calm but powerful voice floated into the midst of this conversation.

"My Lord seems to be having some small difficulty with his eyes, Sir James," it said, melodiously. "He does not appear to have remembered me, either; and such as I, who am a caring shepherd to my flock, are not used to being ignored—save by those with guilty minds and souls."

Cumberland's head snapped around. For a moment his eyes glittered at the Bishop; and then the glitter went out of them and he was immediately on his feet.

"Forgive me, my Lord Bishop," he said in a voice almost as smooth as the Bishop's. "I have been so concerned with many responsibilities that I have fallen into the habit of paying little attention to what is around me. But that is no excuse. Would you give me your blessing again, as you did at Court early last spring?"

"Of course, my son," said the Bishop. Cumberland had been on the way toward the other man even as he was talking, and as the Bishop answered, he stopped in front of him, dropped rather heavily to one knee, and reached for the hand with the ring that the Bishop extended.

He kissed the ring and started to rise; but the Bishop's hand had turned over, and his fist closed around Cumberland's fingers and the back of his hand, holding the Earl where he was.

"O Lord," said the Bishop in a strong voice, gazing at the rafters overhead, "grant Thy blessing to this sinner, however black his sins—" His voice rose to a fine round pulpit pitch that echoed through the Hall. "Thou Who hast forgiven all who truly repent, show him the way to cleanse his soul, being mindful of the heaven that awaits those who have walked righteously; and remembering also the fate of the knight who lifted his hand to summon devils; and how that knight was shortly after struck dead by a levin-flash; and who, when he was attempted to be laid to rest, could not rest. His hand, that would have summoned evil against the innocent, rose up, even out of his sealed coffin; and not all the strong men of the Kingdom, struggling together, were able to make it lie down!"

He released Cumberland, who got to his feet rapidly, his jaw set, his eyes glittering once more, but his face now as pale as those of Sir Simon's men-at-arms had been.

"My Lord Bishop," he said, in a voice that struggled to sound calm and reasonable, "the Gnarlies are not devils. They are but familiars, Naturals as some call them, of the same kind, but nowhere near as dangerous as the trolls—which any good man with a sword need not fear. But we seldom see them for they are of an Under-Earth persuasion, and only occasionally share our mine-workings with us—normally fleeing at the very sound of a Christian voice or movement. Nor did I summon them."

"Will you chop words with me, unhappy Lord?" said the Bishop. "I blessed you, as you asked. If that blessing woke you to some deep sin in your own soul, best you examine yourself and see your confessor. I am not he."

"That's right," said Jim, before Cumberland could say anything further. "It's me you should be chopping words with, my Lord."

Cumberland turned sharply upon him. "You! What have you got to say to me?"

"Even the greatest Lord does well not to ignore what he may learn from even an unimportant knight and Baron. I only ask that you listen."

Cumberland twitched slightly as if he would turn back to the Bishop, and then evidently thought better of it.

"Well, what is it?"

"You have been at Court all your life," said Jim, "and it has been well there with you. But none can tell when the warmest place on a bright and cloudless day may suddenly lose its warmth as a cloud covers the face of the sun and shadows begin to fall about him—"

"Warm spots? Shadows? What in the name of the Devil himself are you talking about?" roared the Earl.

Jim held up a placating hand.

It was his own fault. The Earl's lack of understanding was something he should have expected.

The Earl was not short of intelligence. He had not held his position at the right hand of the King, all these years, only by the uncertain tie of blood. He was alert and quick to use his mind profitably.

But it had been a mistake to start making mysterious allusions. That might have worked in Jim's own time, to make someone uneasy. But hinting at what one meant simply was not the way of the fourteenth century—at least in England. The Middle Ages had been a time of plain speaking—or at least the appearance of such—where a man had to be as good as his word, and his word plainly understandable.

Jim put mysterious allusions aside.

"If certain rumors started circulating about you, my Lord," he said now, "you might find that there was no longer any room for you at Court."

"No room for *me*?" Cumberland burst into laughter, quite hearty, natural laughter.

"Rumors of Witchery, my Lord," said Jim.

The Earl stopped laughing and sobered up, but his answer was almost good-natured. "Oh, that gabble about the Lady Agatha," he said. "I have answered that quite plainly, and in public. All nonsense, of course!"

"But you did sponsor her introduction to the Court," said Jim. "And I was thinking more of rumors about you having no choice about doing that, because you were involved in Witchery yourself."

The hint of a smile on Cumberland's face, which had appeared there with his own last words, was suddenly wiped away. He stared at Jim.

Chapter 35

For a long moment, the Earl just stared at Jim. Then he snorted.

"You fool! Such a rumor might harm lesser men. But me? The King's brother?"

"Even Kings have been weakened by rumors, my Lord. Particularly when such start being passed about by the common man and woman. Rumor, rhymes—and a sudden silence in the marketplace when you and those with you ride through. Perhaps even a stone, or a lump of dung, flying out at you, suddenly, from the hand of someone hidden in the crowd."

"So, these are the shadows you would alarm me with," said Cumberland, heavily. "Let me tell you I am not to be frightened by such. There are none of those things you mentioned that will ever happen to me."

"Perhaps my Lord should not be too sure," said Jim. "After all, they can *happen* to anyone. The danger is what they do to power and place. Those who are not with one of whom tales are told, will tend to withdraw, so as not to be stained with the same color; and you know, my Lord—as well as any man—that in high places those who are not with you tend to be against you.

So it is that by the time there is marketplace talk and disrespect, there is already talk that the subject of rumor is ready to be brought down."

"Ah?" said Cumberland, jutting his lower jaw out at Jim. "And who is going to start such rumors, throw such clods, and bring me down when I am weakened? You?"

"I am distressed your Lordship should think so," said Jim.

"You did not answer me," Cumberland growled.

"I meant," said Jim, "to say that, as a magician, even though a lesser one, I can see shadows of the future. I am only warning your Lordship against them."

"Hah! So then I am warned!"

"That being so, my Lord," said Jim, "it only remains for you to tell me where the warrants are being kept that accuse us of treason, so that I may magically destroy them. I need not doubt, I take it, that no new warrants will be issued; nor that I, nor Sir Brian Neville-Smythe, nor Dafydd ap Hywel will be bothered by any such things in the future."

The Earl chuckled.

"Hah!" he said, again. "Well, now, Sir Dragon Knight, I am not at all sure those warrants can be delivered up to you, or that you can be assured that there will be no more investigation of your loyalty in the future. For one thing, such matters are out of my hands. It will be up to the Justices that may have already been named to judge you once you get to the Court."

"You think so, do you?" said Jim. "I am afraid I disagree with you, my Lord. I want those warrants now, and also your word that we won't be troubled again."

"And I said," replied Cumberland, his voice rising, "that you weren't going to get the Goddamn warrants. As for your being what you call 'bothered' in the future—"

Reaching inside himself for the link to Carolinus' supply of magic, Jim caused the daylight striking in through the windows of the Hall to be blanked out, and all light within the Hall to be extinguished. He allowed the moment of total darkness to last for perhaps ten seconds, before he brought light back.

"You were too late, my Lord," he said. "The word has already gone out throughout England and through the Court itself, that perhaps you, yourself, are involved in Witchery, and have been for many years. You will hear the whispering in the Court as you walk by, and in the streets you will find silence—and yes, even possibly some things thrown. I doubt that the King will long wish to have someone close to him of whom that is said."

He looked closely at Cumberland. The business of the moment of darkness had been no more than that, of course. Everything else depended upon how much the Earl would believe. He had certainly been shaken by the sermon that had resulted when he asked the Bishop's blessing, and Jim was now betting everything on his hope that the Earl's imagination would do the rest.

But he was mistaken. The Earl's face was very pale indeed this time, but his jaw was still set like a bulldog's.

"In the land from which I've—I came to England," added Jim for good measure, "the art of managing a rumor is well understood."

"Ah?" said Cumberland—but with a growing uneasiness Jim thought that the tone of his voice signaled not a further acceptance of defeat, but a sudden arousal of hope. "Yes, I doubt not, it is a high Art, and no one in England would know it as you know it. But as for these warrants you ask about, Sir Simon is carrying them. You will have to have him in here—though I see no one you could send for him. Perhaps the archer could go."

"Indeed," said Dafydd, before Jim could express his anger at the contemptuous tone in which the last words had been spoken, "I will be glad to do so. I will bring whoever is necessary back in a moment, Sir James."

He turned and started up the aisle between the two long tables, toward the door, carrying his longbow and with his quiver over his shoulder, having produced both from under the table the moment his hands were unbound. They all watched him in silence.

A faint scraping noise was almost drowned out by Brian's shout of warning. Jim turned swiftly to find the Earl had snatched up Jim's eating-knife from the table. It was nothing of a weapon, compared to ordinary daggers and swords, but it was some five inches long, with one keen edge and a sharp point. With it, the Earl was lunging at Jim.

Jim grabbed up his mazer, the only thing within easy reach, and met the point of the eating-knife with the inside of the metal vessel. Wine splashed all over the Earl's houppelande; and the knife-point jarred against the inside of the now empty table utensil. With a surprisingly quick move, the Earl pulled his arm back, weaving the unbroken knife in his big fist expertly, feinting this way and that, to draw the mazer out of line with Jim's body, where it could no longer protect it.

"*What's the matter with you?*" said the voice of KinetetE, with sharp disgust in Jim's head. "*What was the use of Carolinus so putting himself at odds with the Collegiate's rules—rules he helped write himself—if you're not going to use the Magick he gave you? Don't you know how to set up a ward?*"

Disgusted at himself, Jim envisioned a ward—not around himself but around Cumberland—who now suddenly found himself blocked by an invisible wall on all sides. Just in time, too—a moment after the ward was up, there was a scratching noise on the far side of the Earl; and Jim saw Angie had just barely been stopped from driving the blade of her own eating-knife into the Earl's back. The ward had been created just in time. She had a look on her face that Jim had never seen before; and it did not fade quickly as she stood staring at the now-encased Earl.

Jim reached across the small space between them and put his hand gently on the forearm of her hand that held the knife. She looked sharply at him; and as their eyes met, the fierce look slowly faded from her face.

"I just warded him," said Jim quietly. "It's all right. I think I can handle this, now."

She looked at him for a long moment, then put the knife down on the table and sat down in a chair, herself.

"It's all right—" Angie was beginning, when a roar from Cumberland interrupted her.

"Simon!" His voice rang out with surprising volume. "Now! All of you!"

The twin doors from the courtyard swung open with a speed that could only result if the men outside had been waiting closely beyond them, expecting some signal. Dafydd, who had stopped on his way to the doors when the Earl had attacked Jim, turned and ran back, easily and as swiftly as a deer, bounded to the dais, stepped around behind the table and was suddenly sending arrows from his bent bow, with devastating effect at this short range, into the front of the onrushing men-at-arms.

Simon alone, sword in hand, came on untouched.

"He is mine!" shouted Brian; Jim heard a ripping sound behind him and Brian burst into his sight, carrying in both hands the heavy, bladed pole of an ancient halberd, pulled down from among the weapons on the wall behind the dais.

"And so I have been leaving him for you," said Daffyd calmly, his voice pitched only high enough to be heard over the clamor of the attacking men. These were being channeled into a column four abreast by the long tables on either side; and those still on their feet were beginning to hang back slightly as the front rank fell to Dafydd's arrows.

The archer, Jim saw, had nowhere near enough arrows to deal with the rest of Simon's men; and as he watched, Dafydd nudged the quiver out of sight around his hip, quietly laid his bow, still strung, on the table, and loosened in its sheath the long, slim knife he wore on his leg.

Brian leaped from the dais, the halberd balanced in his hands and held diagonally across his chest with the blade at head height. Sir Simon had stopped some ten or twelve feet from the dais and was waiting for him, sword held high.

Three years—even two years—ago, Jim would have read nothing in that high-held blade. A couple of melees in which his one concern was to survive, plus having been put through an extended course of practice bouts with the friendly, but rough, Brian, had opened his eyes to many truths about broadswords and other medieval weapons.

Jim had learned that he was—despite the heroic legends about him—never going to be any kind of a match for anyone who had trained in the use of edged weapons on foot and horseback since childhood. But he now had a rough idea of what certain positions probably indicated.

In this case, Sir Simon's sword, carried high, signaled a clear purpose. His sword was too light to directly parry the massive steel head of the halberd. Simon was counting on making as little contact with it as possible, ducking or dodging Brian's first swipe of the polearm, then going in point-first for the kill, once the weight and force of Brian's swing had left him unable to get the heavy blade back up in time to block or parry the sword.

Brian took a step forward, the curved edge of the halberd above his head and pointing forward. Simon watched him intently. The eyes of each man focused on the other with no expressions of enmity or fury on their faces. They watched only each other, with the steady gazes of chess players.

Brian swept the head of his weapon in a sweeping curve downward, toward the middle of Simon's body—a blow not possible to dodge except by moving the whole body. Simon smiled thinly; and stepped—not back, to where his movements would be blocked by the men pressing close behind him, but one step forward.

Clearly he was planning to leap the pole itself behind its axe-head, and then drive in with his sword blade before Brian had a chance to check the momentum of his heavy weapon and bring it back in a parry.

It was a gamble on his own ability—but not that much of one for a knight of this century, trained to leap into the saddle of his already running horse, wearing full armor—five hundred years before the cowboy of the American West was doing the same thing, but without armor.

However, in the same moment, Brian's swing curved up from its downward arc, to become one aimed at Simon's head. It was the counterpart of a rather uncommon sword stroke that Brian had shown Jim, and Jim had seen him use in serious fights. But what made it remarkable here was that, even with Brian's two-handed grip on the polearm, the axe-head should have been so heavy that its momentum in its original direction could not have been changed as a sword blade's might have been.

But Brian did it. Jim had forgotten once more how strong the people of this time were from lifetimes of exercise. The sharp edge of the axe-head leaped back up toward Simon's chest and throat. Simon tried to both lean and back away in the same movement. He was partly successful, in that the axe-blade missed his chest—but the sweep of the axe-head brought it against the side of his head as it continued upward.

He dropped, loose-limbed, to the Hall floor and lay there, utterly without motion.

"A pretty blow! By Saint Michael, a pretty blow! Well struck!" shouted the Earl from inside his ward. "So, what are the rest of you waiting for? Take him!"

With a growling roar, the untouched men-at-arms rolled forward toward Brian. There was no more time for thought.

Jim took a deep breath and became a dragon. He leaped at the oncoming men-at-arms.

Chapter 36

T he last straw," said KinetetE in
Jim's head, sounding perilously close to chuckling—if a soundless voice could
be said to convey a near-chuckle.

Jim had landed on the bare floor between the tables where the forefront of
the men-at-arms had stood. Sir Simon still lay there, off to one side. As for
the rest—he turned to stare at KinetetE—to his astonishment, she was dem-
onstrating that she could magically send into his mind what the men-at-arms
were currently thinking.

It was not telepathy as Jim had ever imagined it. Rather, it was a sort of
mass telempathy—a sending to him of what Simon's men-at-arms as a group
were thinking and feeling—as if he were getting a sort of instant, condensed
report of their thoughts and feelings as a group.

His turning into a dragon and attacking them had clearly overloaded their
capacity for new threats. They none of them lacked courage where ordinary
opponents were concerned. But now they were each on their way to get as
far from Jim as fast as they could, by going over benches, under tables—
whatever was necessary—until they could reach the front door of the Hall
and escape.

They had, Jim learned, all been aware that this particular bit of duty was bad luck from the start. Arresting a magickian was nothing a man ought be ordered to do. They had all thought so, and they had all been right—this proved it. For a little while they had been reassured by the sight of the Bishop at the High Table; but plainly not even someone as holy as he could control a knight who could also become a dragon. Sir Simon should have known it was going to be like this.

Simon was a good knight, as knight-officers went. There had been a lot of merry sport, and profit, taking his orders.

But he was gentry. He should have known that old Fumblehand was sending them into trouble . . . magickians appearing from nowhere, and even bringing old Fumblehand with them; dragons walking in and then being sent to Hell— then a devil of an archer picking them off while Sir Simon himself got his head bashed in. And now this!

A knight who knowingly led his men into something where they weren't going to stand a chance, deserved to die. Usually, they'd be trying now to bring his body out with them, so as to give it to his lady—whoever she was at present—for proper burial. It was what they were supposed to do. But to hell with that! If he had cared for them the way he should have, they'd be caring for him now. So let him end up in the dragon's belly, instead—let him lie where he was, the bastard!

All this came to Jim in a sudden single flash of understanding, which his mind could divide up into words at his leisure. But at the moment there was no leisure. The men-at arms would be out of the Hall in seconds.

The inspiration he needed had come to him. He had not been ready for this before—it was too magically expensive; Carolinus might expend that much of his own magic for his own purposes, but Jim could not simply borrow an amount it would take to produce a crowd of people, just for his.

But he did not have to use magic. Here was his crowd, ready-made for him.

"*Still!*" he shouted, forgetting entirely that he was using his dragon-voice, which was enough to stop them dead even if the magic command had failed.

"Thank you, Jim," said KinetetE, sourly, in his head once more.

"Sorry," said Jim in a lower voice, sweeping his gaze over the other people on the platform. "*Unstill*, everyone on the dais. Oh, Brian, forgive me—I forgot you were down on the floor, too. *Unstill*, Brian. Now, would you step back up to the High Table? Good, thanks."

Hastily, he changed back to his human form.

"All you men-at-arms," he said, "may *unstill* enough to turn around and face the High Table. Good. Now, all of you have now forgotten everything that's

happened after Sir Brian bested Sir Simon; and you'll keep forgetting everything that happens, as it happens, until I tell you to start remembering,
again. . . ."

Jim turned back to face the High Table. "And you, my Lord Earl," he said,
"you also will forget everything that has happened since Sir Brian's fight with
Sir Simon. You will continue to forget every new thing that happens, as it
happens—until I tell you otherwise. . . ."

A sudden sense of caution made him pause.

"My Lord Bishop—Excellency—" he said, turning to the cleric, "I need to
work some magic now, if you'll permit it. It won't hurt anyone."

"My son," said the Bishop, trying to sound sour, himself, but not succeeding
as well as KinetetE had, "unless my own memory has been tampered with,
you have already just worked some magic without my permission."

"But my Lord, this is really harmless, to anyone. It's something Mage Carolinus does without hurting anyone, only making them imagine something.
Mage KinetetE"—Jim turned to the empty space on the dais where he was
pretty sure she was standing—"will you help me explain to my Lord
Bishop?"

KinetetE appeared, looking anything but helpful. She and the Bishop both
glanced at Carolinus, who continued to slumber in his chair.

She looked back up at the same moment the Bishop did, and spoke to him.

"My Lord Bishop," she said, "you know me. And I have known Mage Carolinus many more years than you have. Ridiculous as it seems, he would
approve what his Apprentice is going to do. Carolinus must be allowed to
rest now. I will take the responsibility for Jim's Magick upon myself."

The Bishop looked at Jim doubtfully.

"Remember," KinetetE went on, "this young man is only a class C+ Magickian, while I, like Carolinus, am one of only three AAA+ Mages in this
world. Where Jim is a hillock in his knowledge of our Art, I am a mountain;
and I will be watching him as he works, to prevent his doing anything of the
sort you would not wish done."

"I see." The Bishop cleared his throat. "Would you consider then, Mage—
bearing in mind the superiority of your rank over his—consider simply ordering him to make no Magick at all?"

"I would not."

"I see. Well, in that case . . . Mage, I've heard of you, from Carolinus, actually." He turned to Jim.

"I cannot approve anything to which the Church would object, of course,"
he said; "but provisionally, you may proceed with your magick, my son. But

with the utmost care to do no damage to your soul or that of any other son of the Church presently in this Hall."

"I might improve one or more," Jim said. "I certainly won't damage any."

"Then, proceed."

"Thanks, my Lord."

Jim stepped around the dais, and up, to stand beside the Earl, who seemed now almost to be sleeping on his feet. Jim looked at the men-at-arms down below them in the Hall.

He studied them critically. They made a pretty fair small crowd, spread about like that. The two long tables spread them out and divided them up into three groups; which in fact was not too unlike a marketplace, where rows of vendors' stalls would be dividing the customers. . . .

He turned to look at the Earl. He was still standing behind the ward Jim had locked him in, and, from the vague gaze of his eyes, he was also obeying the magic command to forget. Jim removed the ward.

"Now, these next magical commands are for you, alone, my Lord Earl," he said. "You can sit down again."

Jim hesitated. He was aware of Angie, looking doubtful and concerned, and of Dafydd and Brian, watching him with curiosity, but no doubt whatsoever. The Bishop was looking at him with severity. KinetetE had made herself invisible again, but he could feel her eyes on him.

The truth was, he was not planning to do the exact equivalent of making one person—and everyone watching as well—believe that person had been turned into a beetle. What he had in mind was going to be harder than that.

Harder, because Carolinus, making people think someone had been turned into a beetle, had done so with a single, all-encompassing command. But Jim intended to work not only with the Earl, but with the men-at-arms, separately. His commands would have to be detailed and specific.

He would also have to be careful not to include the other people on the dais with him in his magic. He wanted only the Earl to experience what Jim had in mind for him; not any of the others—least of all the Bishop, who might start to think it all had some claim to reality; he had, like many in this century, been seen to get carried away by even a simple play performance, in the past.

KinetetE, of course, could not be kept from seeing and hearing everything Jim did; but there was nothing much he could do about that.

He moved over to stand behind the chair that Cumberland now sat in, and spoke to him in a low voice.

"I'm out of your sight," he said in a low voice. "But you can hear me. You can hear only me. And you can't see anything but the images in your mind, as I tell you about them. Now, you're riding—"

The Earl's left hand reached out a little above the top of the table at which he sat, to gather up invisible reins—

"—and you've got four or five retainers with you, also on horseback, behind you. You know who they are. The group of you are just coming into a marketplace, crowded because it's market day, with common people in every kind of clothing. You can hear the crowd now; you can smell the dust and the other smells of the marketplace. You intend to ride straight through, of course; because you are Cumberland, and they must get out of your way. They do, but grudgingly. . . ."

From here on, Jim intended, there would be little for the others in the Hall to hear. Standing behind the Earl, with his magic he would be looking out through the Earl's eyes, guiding the Earl's own imagination, with occasional manipulation of the men-at-arms before them.

Magic visualization was not for the lazy. To visualize a convincing—which meant a complete—image for someone else's eyes, you had to know what you wanted to visualize. If that was a castle, you had to know how a castle was made and laid out—even what it was made of. Either that, or you had to be able to summon up the image of a castle you had once seen.

If the castle you were envisioning were real to you, it would be real to the one you were causing to see it. Not otherwise. That meant imaginary scenes had to be made up out of bits and pieces of things you had experienced yourself.

The marketplace Jim was envisioning was based on a small town he had himself ridden through, in the Cheddar district of Somerset. With the men-at-arms placed in its image, garbed in the clothes that both Jim and the Earl often saw on common folk, it would do as an imaginary marketplace in just about any town in the southern part of England.

He looked now, through the Earl's eyes. The Earl knew well what it felt like to ride a horse, and immediately Jim felt as if he were himself bouncing along in the saddle of a trotting horse. He had a view of the Earl from the back, just behind his head, as they entered a marketplace. Before them were the men-at-arms, but the Earl's imagination saw them as typical country people, of the sort to be found in any marketplace in the country. . . .

C h a p t e r *37*

. . . $\overset{\text{\Large A}}{}$ muttering began in the marketplace crowd and grew to a clamor of angry voices. The Earl rode on, erect in his saddle, his face as unchanged as if he were crossing an empty plain on horseback. Those riding behind him lifted their reins and moved their horses closer to him.

The voices rose to a roar of combined shouting. The Earl went on, neither changing his expression nor increasing the easy motion of his horse. A few dozen more yards would see him past the market. . . .

Something that winked black against the glare of the sunlight overhead arced through the air. It hit his chest and stuck there for a second before falling away. It was a half-decayed fish about a foot long, and it left a dark stain on the burgundy-colored cote-hardie he was wearing.

He still showed no emotion, moving steadily toward the trees that closed thickly about the road just beyond. But the crowd had found a single word in common, finally, and they were now chanting at him in unison. . . .

"Witch! Witch! Witch!"

The voices drowned out the sound of galloping hoofbeats until a man on a lathered horse, dressed in livery of the Earl's colors and moving at such speed that he had to rein his animal back on its haunches to keep from riding directly into the peer, burst out of the woods.

Wordlessly, he offered the Earl a piece of brown parchment, folded and bound by a black ribbon. The Earl took it without a word, ripped off the ribbon, and unfolded the parchment.

My Lord,

The Lady Agatha Falon hath confessed under question, after having been taken up at the King's orders; and admitted to being a witch, herself. She does say that she was enticed into witchery by your Lordship and that you have been a witch more years than she has had life. But that your intent has been to drive our Sovran King into madness and death and desired her help in this, therefore induced her into the foul practise to which you both then belonged.

Some of the northern lords, and others, put small faith in her confession, saying it is most likely to have come out so because of the wishes of her questioners and the rigor of the questioning. They suggest you might wish to go north to your own shire and there find friends and force to face whatever army those at court who wish you ill may be able to raise.

Long life and good fortune to your Lordship; and my prayer that you may be safe and remember I was able, at hard risk to myself, to send you this word, herein.

in obedience,
Edgar de Wiggin

The market crowd had grown silent with curiosity, seeing the messenger arrive.

The Earl read without changing expression, folded the letter up again, and thrust it under his cote-hardie.

"We go north," he said over his shoulder to those now sitting their restless horses behind him.

He looked forward and put his horse in motion again. The others rode after him. In the sudden gloom of the treetops overarching the road, after the bright sunlight of the marketplace, they were momentarily blind—

—The greyish-white tent walls were open to let in light and air; and outside them could be seen a large clearing hemmed in by forest. A score of men moved about the clearing, mostly younger knights, squires, and men-at-arms. Some were looking in the direction of the tent, while holding the reins of horses. Others—the older ones—were watching the woods.

Inside the tent, a table had been set up, simple boards laid atop trestles; and, even here and now—such were fourteenth-century manners—covered with a tablecloth, white as any wedding gown, if somewhat wrinkled by the creases where it had been folded for carrying.

There was wine on the table, in silver pitchers and mazers.

Six people were seated about the table with the Earl, all richly dressed. It was a cool day up here, hard by the Scottish border, and a strong breeze was stealing whatever heat their bodies brought to the tent.

The Earl knew the faces of these men. He knew the way they talked.

Right now, he was merely listening, with the same sort of bulldog look he had worn after reading the letter.

One large man, in early middle-age and wearing a red-dyed fur cloak, spoke in a baritone voice that slipped up into the tenor register when excitement took him. As it had, for he had been trying to outshout the others, and was finally winding up.

"—And I can bring you a hundred knights, my Lord, along with their armsmen!" he said, with a high-pitched, triumphant note.

"Can you have them here, ready to fight, by tomorrow se'ennight?" The Earl's voice overrode the others around the table, as each tried to get control of the conversation.

There was a sudden silence in the tent. The six all stared at the Earl.

"Why—why no, my Lord," said the man in the red-dyed cloak. "I must rouse the countryside, speaking to all the gentlemen who are my near neighbors. They will all be eager to come in their strengths, once they hear from me. Say a month at the earliest, if all would go well."

"Yes," said the Earl, looking at them each in turn, savagely, "and did any of you others come prepared with the numbers you could bring in one week?"

The silence continued.

"My Lords," said the Earl, in a tone that verged on sneering, "you are all my good friends, come to help me in my trouble—and for which help both I and you know you will have cause to gain in the long run. But in anything of war, you are babes, with the milk still wet upon your mouths! Now, listen to me!"

"Gladly—gladly indeed will we listen to you, my Lord," said the other man, quickly, "who are so well-known as a great and successful Captain. But—"

"Then do so!" The Earl's voice rose to a volume that had been used before this on troops lined up facing the enemy. "I want numbers of the men you can have ready to fight in a week; because in a week we will be fighting!"

He stared at their suddenly stiff and paling faces.

"You none of you understand, do you?" he demanded. "So let me tell you there will be not one battle, but at least two—at the very least, two! Have none of you realized that Chandos will have known of that letter I received at least a day before it found me? Indeed, he may have taken the letter as soon as it was written, and then had his choice whether to keep it—which could do me no great harm—or send it on, to trap not only me, but the rest of you, in active talk of treason against the King."

The faces listening had forgotten how to pale years since—for one thing, they all had healthy coats of weather-beaten tan—but they had now acquired a remarkable rigidity.

"Only his honor—which, with his wits, must be credited him—would keep him from using it to condemn, rather than merely set a trap for me. But in any case, be sure he has known we were to meet for some time. He knows these woods, too, and he will have sent a force to take us. When we meet them, that will be our first battle. They may be less in numbers than we are, but they will be seasoned warriors, perhaps with mounted archers in company."

The Earl stopped talking. None of the others ventured to say anything. He smiled at them, his lips tight together.

"That understood, then," he said, "how many knights, squires—and, 'fore God, I'd rather have a squire who is knowledgeable in war to back me at any time, than a knight who is not—and so on down all degrees of armsmen. But how many can each of you gather in six days—so we may honestly reckon up our strength?"

There was a certain amount of hemming and hawing. Only one of them, a short, spare young man with a cap of curly brown hair and a long, livid scar above his right eyebrow, spoke up promptly.

"Eight knights and eleven squires, my Lord," he said, "by tomorrow if necessary. All of my own family. But beyond that, who knows how many or how swiftly found? I will raise and bring what I can, but my neighbors do not leap at my bidding, as those of my Lord of Athernockie—" he glanced across the table at the man in the red-dyed cloak—"seem to do. Of armsmen, perhaps as many as thirty, given time; but how much time I cannot say, for hope of heaven."

The cross-talk at the table began to quiet down as the Earl sat waiting. Finally, they arrived at a tentative figure of sixty to eighty knights and squires, plus a hundred or more men-at-arms and no more than twenty crossbowmen. Local archers would be hardly worth bringing, since those Chandos brought would have a vast advantage in range.

"Very well," said the Earl, finally. "As soon as I think we have gathered anything like the number needed, we move to meet Chandos. All of you should send to discover any talk of his men approaching."

"One more word, my Lord," said a square-faced older man sitting closest of them all to the Earl. "Beyond the knights, squires, and armsmen, do you want country people?"

He was referring, Jim realized, out of what was now developing into a blinding headache, to the local common people, who would come with any kind of weapon they could make or find—often simply a farm tool—in hopes of some excitement in their lives—if not plunder. Jim had not thought of this himself; the Earl's own experience was already feeding this illusion. . . .

". . . If they stay from underfoot when the fighting begins, I have no objection. It never does any harm to let the foe think you more numerous than you are. But now about supplies, extra riding and baggage beasts . . ."

"—My Lords, my Lords," the Earl interrupted them later, "it is useless to consider how you are going to fight the enemy until you know his strength, disposition upon the ground, the look of the ground itself, and how eager he is to fight—to say nothing of the way the weather is shaping, and many other things. Cease discussion of this now, and let us not confuse each other with half-thought-out plans. Now, have any of you given proper orders for meals here—and, if so, when are we to dine?"

—A platter of small cakes was just being set down in the center of the table by a thin man in green-and-red livery. He took away with him several platters and bowls that had been emptied.

"That brings me to mind," the Earl said, "—what will you tell these neighbors of yours about my reasons for being here in the north now? These gentlemanly neighbors you are hoping will join us?"

He held a cake in mid-air, again smiling his close-lipped, tigerish smile.

"Why, my Lord," said Athernockie, "we will tell them the glorious truth. That, sickened with the heavy blight of Crown taxes upon us, and corruption in the Court, you have finally reached the point where you must take a stand and strike out boldly—possibly for the Throne itself, if that is God's will."

"I counsel all of you that you say no such thing for your own safety," said the Earl. "By those words you announce yourself to all men as being of the intent to commit treason." He looked at them squarely.

"Rather," he went on, "tell them what is the true truth: that the word I have received recently is the last fardel I choose to bear. I feel myself foully insulted by the apparent belief at Court in the confession wrung from Agatha Falon under cruel questioning, which would indeed bring any man or woman to confess whatever her questioners wanted. Say that as a result, I have withdrawn to my shire—only to find that I am in danger of attack by some at Court, who seem to hope for personal gain by bringing me back a prisoner."

His smile broadened, making him look more like a tiger than ever.

"Such as the good Sir John Chandos, when he finally meets us," he said.

There was a prolonged moment of silence around the table.

"Indeed, my Lord Earl," said the brown-haired, younger man, "your words are far better than any we could make. Well do you deserve to be known as you are for your wits in matters such as these."

"I would not have lived these many years without them," said the Earl, dryly. "Remember, however, not the value of my wits, but the first of at least two battles—in no more than a week of time."

It was a field of open ground with only a few scattered, spiny gorse bushes. The opposing line began to walk its horses toward the Earl and his line—a walk that would become a trot, then a canter, and at last a gallop, just before the two forces met. The Earl, in his position in the middle, but slightly forward, of the line of his men, lifted his arm and waved, setting them all to moving. It was not hard to pick out the narrow, erect figure of Sir John Chandos, in armor of full plate; and the Earl recognized him. Both Earl and knight headed toward each other.

Chandos, however, in the middle of his line, was a little to the Earl's left, so that the peer had to lay his right rein to his horse's neck to move him to meet the other man when the lines finally clashed.

It was what was to be expected of the two leaders; and being the men they were, neither would do anything but seek out such an encounter. The horsemen on either side of the Earl tried to give him room to move over.

Chandos was agreeable, the Earl was agreeable, the close-by knights and squires were agreeable—the Earl's mount was not.

There had been time, here in the north, to send for one of his own warhorses—a stallion, an animal of quality only an Earl could buy; an instinctive fighter and trained. But it was not the one he was most used to and would have preferred.

Man and horse knew each other. But they had not spoken to each other in some time; and the horse—as excited by the prospect of battle as the armored men—had his own idea of how he wanted to charge at the enemy. Straight ahead.

"The Devil roast your guts and stones!" roared the Earl, driving his knees powerfully against the destrier's rib cage to cut off his breath, sawing the rein and jabbing the prickspur on his heel to give the stupid animal an idea of where he should go.

The horse belatedly recognized a familiar voice and familiar discomforts. He decided to go where his rider wanted; and stretched out at a full gallop. But the damage had already been done. The line of which the Earl had been a part was well ahead of him now. The two ranks of eager enemies were approaching each other at a combined speed of around twenty miles an hour.

They collided just before the Earl could catch up; and amid the screaming of horses, the shouts of men, and the clang of metal, broke up into small groups as individuals struggled with one another. Riding into the midst of this with lance still in hand, the Earl had only a glimpse of someone approaching from his left, and there was a crash that shut out all other sounds as he dropped into darkness.

He woke, it seemed, immediately. But plainly, time had passed. He was lying in the shade of a lone tree in an open area.

No fewer than six men-at-arms were standing around him and watching him; and he had been stripped of his weapons and armor. His head felt ready to break open.

He had no time to concern himself with that now. He let his eyes roam idly around the space beyond his watchers. If there was a horse of any reasonable power close enough for him to reach it in a short run, then it would only remain to somehow get past or disable those watching him. Once on horseback, his chances of getting free would be doubled.

But there were no horses within a reasonable distance; and his wandering gaze instead picked up the somewhat blurry image of Sir John Chandos walking toward him with another man-at-arms—very likely a messenger sent to tell Sir John that the prisoner had come to.

In a moment, the knight had reached him.

"How are you, my Lord?" asked Chandos. "You took a shrewd knock on the side of the head."

"A nothing," said the Earl. He made an effort to pull himself up into a sitting position with his back to the tree trunk; and a quick nod of Chandos' head brought the hands of men-at-arms to help him. "And you, Sir John?"

"By chance and God's grace," said Chandos, "I was untouched. Are you able to ride?"

"I cannot remember when I was not."

Chandos considered him for a moment.

"Still," he said, "we can wait an hour or so. Some small rest will do you no harm—and food. I will have some and wine sent you. You will ride without your armor, my Lord. It will be kept safely with your weapons, my word upon it. But then we must ride."

"Where to?" said the Earl, bluntly.

"To the Tower in London," said Chandos. "We will put no irons upon you, my Lord, but you will ride with picked men of mine about you at all times, and sleep equally guarded. You are charged with treason in attempting to use witchcraft against the King; and your trial will be held immediately upon your imprisonment there."

—The high-ceilinged chamber had appropriately small, windows high in the two long walls. What daylight came through in the late afternoon fell mainly on the small stage at one end. Overhead, the height of the ceiling seemed lost in the obscurity that also hid the lower part of the walls.

Seven men sat upon the stage, older men in rich robes. Two wore the chain of office of high City functionaries. The rest were Church authorities and Lords he knew. To one side of the stage was a small table, at which a somewhat younger man in monk-like dark robes was writing. The men on the stage sat in sturdy armchairs.

The Earl stood in the center of the open floor between two tall men-at-arms; and others, bearing halberds, were spaced around the walls of the room. The Earl spat contemptuously on the floor in the direction of the stage.

"That is just to show you gentlemen," he told them, "that the sight of you sitting here does not make my mouth go dry with fear."

"Silence!" said Lord Oxford. He sat in the middle of the panel; and his somewhat high, reedy voice had the dryness of an armorer's hacksaw biting through metal. "Your trial is over. You are brought here only to hear sentence read upon you."

"What sort of trial was that?" shouted the Earl. "Oxford, who named you and these others Justices? Who signed the warrant for my arrest? You have not even heard me answer whatever charges there may have been made against me!"

"Silence! Gag the prisoner if he speaks again! Robert de Clifford, Earl of Cumberland, I repeat you have been brought here only to hear sentence read out against you."

Oxford looked down at the monkish figure at the table.

"Read the sentence!" he said.

The man put a last flourish of his pen-point on the parchment before him and, laying down the feathery tool, pulled out some other sheets, one of which he tilted up in the dim light. He stood, to deliver it with greater authority.

What he read was in Latin; but the Earl, like Chandos—in this age when most of the knightly class could not read, write, or understand that Churchly language—combined some of the abilities of the scholar with his fighting skills.

"*My Lord,*" the Latin would have translated into English, "*This Court denies you any right of answer because you can no longer be regarded as a man, it having been proved against you by confession of one of your own kind that you are a Witch. As such you have traitorously attempted for your own gain and profit to disturb the wits of our Lord King, whom may God preserve. You have so done in defiance of Holy Church, which holds you therefore accursed. Wherefore, the Court awards that you be drawn for treason, hanged for indulging in foul practices, beheaded for misdeeds against the Church—"*

His upper lip twisted, the Earl spat again, at the very feet of the man announcing the verdict, who broke off, starting backward.

"Go on," directed the Earl of Oxford.

The clerk started reading once more.

"—and because your deeds have dishonoured the order of chivalry, the Court awards that when you are hung and drawn for treason, you shall be in a surcote quartered with your arms and that your name and those arms be destroyed forever!"

"Noooo!" howled the Earl suddenly like a madman, struggling now against the six armsmen who were trying to gag him and at the same time hold his large, powerful body back from its effort to reach the judges.

"My arms! My name! You cannot take those from me! You do not have that right—"

The gag finally choked him off. The armsmen half-carried, half-dragged him away.

Chapter 38

Jim stood staring at the Earl, appalled. The magic was done and over with; and if the Earl would just look now, he would see nothing but Malencontri's Hall, and the men-at-arms of Sir Simon, standing among the tables and looking both uncertain and unhappy.

But the Earl, himself, was looking at nothing. He sat hunched over in his chair with his face in his hands, making hoarse, choking sounds, which—after a lifetime of showing no weaknesses that others might take advantage of—were probably the best he could do in the way of sobbing.

Jim would never have believed that the illusions he had created could have such a powerful effect; and that the last words of the sentence handed down by the Judges could have produced such a change in a man who, only seconds before, had spat contemptuously at the Court condemning him. Not only at the Judges, but at the award to be drawn—which meant that after he had been strung up and choked to near-death by the noose, he would be cut down, still living, just long enough to be disemboweled, before being hanged again, permanently.

All that Cumberland had scorned. But the knowledge that his coat of arms, and therefore all heraldic record of him, should be destroyed forever, had destroyed him, too.

Jim could hardly believe it. All he had done was paraphrase the sentence passed upon Sir Hugh Despenser of this same period in the history of Jim's world.

But Sir Hugh had only been a King's favorite. Cumberland was of blood royal and a King's half-brother—with an enviable record as a knight and warrior in history. What he was and what he had done was all that mattered, as it would have been also to Brian or Chandos. With those few words, everything he had spent his life making had been swept away.

Jim caught sight of a movement on the dais. Angie had taken an instinctive step toward the Earl. But as he turned to look, he saw KinetetE step between them.

"No, Angie," KinetetE said.

"No?" echoed Angie.

"He wouldn't understand." KinetetE looked at her sympathetically. "If you were his mother, or his sister, perhaps . . . but any attempt at comfort from you, who are no connection to him—and worse, married to another man—he would not understand at all. Perhaps I should say he would completely misunderstand—would think you were making sport of his downfall. He does not know the feeling that moved you just now. It is so with most in this world."

"I don't believe it!" said Angie. "People are born with it. Empathy—"

"Is a child born with it, when it squeezes a living baby duck to death, or pokes out one of its eyes in sheer curiosity?" said KinetetE. "No, they learn it, by seeing their elders show it. Those in our world now are partway there. They will feel for close relatives and friends, for those they love—but never for the stranger. Look—"

She put a hand on Angie's arm and turned her so that she stared at Brian and Dafydd.

Jim, with Angie, looked at the others around the table. Not even the Bishop, let alone Dafydd or Brian, was watching the Earl with any signs of compassion. Their expressions were interested, but detached, as if the Earl was no more than a stag their dogs had been hunting, now torn and dying.

It abruptly occurred to Jim that everyone on the dais seemed to be aware of what he had just done inside the Earl's head. "How—?" he was beginning, when the voice of KinetetE interrupted him.

"I'm afraid," she said, "Carolinus has overridden me. You're his Apprentice, after all. Talk to him about it."

"But he's . . ."

Jim looked to see a fully awake Carolinus sitting upright in his chair. Not only fully awake, but looking remarkably rested.

"Ask me no questions, I'll tell you no lies," snapped the elder Mage, seeing Jim staring at him. "It's enough for you to know that I've decided those at this table are concerned in what you've been doing. I've assured my Lord Bishop no harm is going to come of it."

Perhaps not, thought Jim, glancing now at the Bishop, who was the one person whose reactions to what he had done, had concerned him. The Bishop was saying nothing, but his eyes were looking at Jim with no great friendliness.

"—But I do think," KinetetE was saying to Angie with an edge of severity in her voice, "it's probably time the one who put him into this state started to bring him out of it."

"Don't rush the boy, KinetetE," said Carolinus.

"No, there's no rush to it," said Jim, walking around so that he stood almost before the Earl. "My Lord Cumberland!"

The Earl paid no attention. He still sat with his face in his hands, making the painful, repetitive sounds that expressed his grief.

"My Lord!"

Still no response. Jim could as well have been trying to get the attention of someone ten miles distant on a mountain. He bent down, lowering his voice, speaking emotionlessly but emphatically into the Earl's right ear.

"My Lord," he said, in slow, distinct words, "everything you are remembering so strongly now has not yet happened—and still may not, if you behave rightly. All that took place was a dream of things that may be, but need not, if you do as you should."

The Earl did not move, and his choking went on. Jim waited; and finally, just before he was ready to give up, the Earl's hands slipped from his dry-eyed but pale face and he slowly looked up.

"No!" he said hoarsely, after staring at Jim for a long minute. "I know what I saw—what I heard! Let me be. It was no dream!"

"It was," said Jim. "I am a magician, as you know, and able to give you such dreams. It was only a dream—a warning dream, my Lord; but still one that need not come true if you heed its warning."

"It was not, I say!" the Earl's tones rose, but only to a shadow of the strength Jim had heard in them at earlier moments. "No dream was ever that real—"

He glared almost maniacally at Jim.

"And how could you—little more than a stripling, magickian or no—"

"By the round Earth itself!" Carolinus' voice broke in on a note Jim had never heard in it before. "To think I should live to see the day a mere Magickless man should have the effrontery to look a magickian in the eye and deny that he had the powers he claimed!"

"My son," contributed the Bishop dryly—but Jim thought he heard a small note of compassion in the words, after all—"your wits are astray. Our Lord made beasts, Naturals, and ordinary men, as well as Kings and men of great holiness. Is it so surprising then that he would also make some to be Magickians as well?"

Looking slowly around at both Carolinus and the Bishop, Cumberland nodded.

"Pray pardon, my Lord Bishop," he said; and he looked at Jim. "Pray pardon, Mage."

"I am not a Mage," said Jim. "But I am a magician. If you will let me aid you now, my Lord Earl, I can show you how you can gain by learning what your dream taught you."

"It taught me there is no escape from my enemies," said the Earl, emptily.

"No," said Jim. "It showed that if you try to destroy them, what you do will return to destroy you. You set up a false raid on your own property, so that you could push my Lord Oxford and others like him toward a point where they could be accused of high treason against the Crown."

Jim shook his head a little. "But your attack woke them to a need to stop you—and stopping you could be as simple as accusing you and the Lady Agatha of Witchery. An accusation of Witchery would be more to the taste of public gossip than the ordinary matter of a tax revolt. The dream just showed how it could bring you down."

"I am no witch," growled the Earl in a low voice.

"No," said Jim. "But you—and Lady Falon—saw a chance in what you were doing to pay off old scores against people like me, my wife, and my friends. To save yourself, you'll have to stop both efforts, yours and hers, before they go any further."

Jim tried to put a warning emphasis in his voice. "Your future might become impossible to stop, if it reaches the point where the Lady Agatha is actually questioned and forced to confess to Witchery. But if you stop her now—stop everything now—those you call your enemies will not be moved to drastic action. They will not push the King to sign a warrant of treason against her. Only in desperation would they take such a risk."

"Hah!" said the Earl, beginning to sound like his old self again. "That is true. As true as the matter that questioning could not fail to wring accusations from any but a few like myself."

"Of course," said Jim, "you'll also have to withdraw the warrants against Sir

Brian, Dafydd, and myself, as well as anyone else who was to be unfairly attacked or accused."

The Earl grunted, a displeased but not negative grunt. Jim let him sit a moment in silence.

"You would do well to consider yourself as having got off lightly in this matter," he said then, wincing a little at the pompous sound of his words; but unable to think of a better way of impressing the Earl with the necessary message.

He need not have winced. Here again the medieval reaction was different. The Earl heard not pompousness, but the now-established and vouched-for voice of authority.

"Very well," he growled. "But in six months Oxford and his friends will own the King—and the Kingdom."

"They'll do nothing of the kind," said Jim, hoping he was right.

"How can they?" he went on, "as long as you still have your strength and are known as the King's most loyal supporter? And as long as you don't push them over the edge by arranging for raids on your own estates and spreading the word that they're the ones doing it, or by persuading his Majesty to levy higher taxes. Taxes, from which most of the money—as they and the whole kingdom know—went mostly into your coffers."

The Earl ventured a low grunt which was almost a growl, but he did not raise his eyes to meet Jim's.

"You are a magickian and I crave your pardon for my words. You have sought to guide me away from a dangerous path," he said, "for which I am grateful. But you are no courtier. Oxford and his ilk will find a way to attack me and the Throne. I will count on it; and you had best do also."

"All I want to count on," said Jim, "is that you will leave me and my friends alone—and make sure that Agatha Falon does likewise."

"A magickian like you should be able to protect yourself—" the Earl broke off on a cough, conscious he could be heading into dangerous territory—"but I will bridle and harness her, and keep her to other roads. There is no problem to that."

"All right," said Jim. "Then you can start by giving me the letters of warrant for arrest made out for Sir Brian, Dafydd ap Hwyel, myself, and anyone else like my wife who may have been warranted."

"I do not know who may have those letters at the moment—"

"Sir Simon said he did."

"He may have said some such thing, but such is never so. A Crown knight charged with the duty of bringing in—" the Earl checked his next word just in time—"those warranted, never carry the actual letters for fear that they may be lost or taken. Now—"

"My son, my son," said the Bishop, "barely are you shown the error of your ways than you leave the path again. Of course the poor knight, rest his soul, has the warrants with him."

The Earl kept himself from glaring at the Bishop, but the effort was visible in his face.

"I think so, too," said Jim. "So, my Lord Earl, if you will step down to his body and bring them back to—"

"By High Heaven, itself!" shouted the Earl. "A King's son to run and fetch for you? You may do as you like with me. I am no man's servant but that of my elder brother who sits on the Throne; and he would not require such service from me!"

"I will go," said Dafydd, speaking and getting to his feet so quickly that he was a shade ahead of both Brian and the Bishop.

"My Lord Bishop," said Dafydd, "I have handled dead bodies before now."

"As have I," said Brian.

"Bowman and Sir Knight," said the Bishop, rising with dignified slowness, "I am a Prince of Holy Church; and it is only fit that my hands should be the ones to touch a man who has died without a chance to confess his sins. Consider also that in finding and taking the warrants from his body you would be raping the dead, which in itself is a sin; whereas I can do so without committing it."

"Stay!" shouted the Earl abruptly. "Dammit all! I cannot permit this—I will go!"

"My Lord," said the Bishop calmly, stepping down from the dais, "I have already gone."

He reached Simon as he finished saying this.

"*Requiescat in pace,*" he said, making the sign of the Cross above the unmoving figure, and stooping to rummage inside the clothing on Simon's upper body. "Ah, here they are."

He drew forth what looked like a package wrapped in thin yellow leather. It was bound by a black ribbon; and without moving back to the dais he untied the ribbon and took from its outer cover a thickness of folded sheets of parchment. Standing there, he unfolded them one by one and looked at them.

Simon groaned.

There was suddenly a remarkable stillness in the Hall. It was most brief with Jim, Angie, and the two Mages; and most deep and lasting in the cases of Simon's men-at-arms, who were now without exception wide-eyed and pale-faced.

"Don't be a pack of fools, you men!" snapped KinetetE. "Your knight never was dead, after all; just knocked senseless! He's no dead man brought back to life to order you about!"

The men-at-arms stared at her and turned to look at each other. They remained pale and silent.

"Why didn't you tell them so if you knew it before this, then?" said Angie. KinetetE glared at her.

"Whether I did or not, it was just as likely he was unconscious as dead," she said. "I am out of patience with men who are perfectly familiar with death and wounds, but still must go seeing a miracle or magick in every second thing that happens—"

"This is very interesting," the Bishop's voice interrupted her. He was now examining the last parchment sheets. "My Lord Earl, aside from the question of how this knight of yours planned to make arrest of the Earl of Oxford or he of Winchester—what is this most remarkable document for the detaining of the King, *signed by you as Regent for Prince Edward?*"

"Those damn scribes of mine!" cried the Earl. "Always playing at some foolery when there is a moment's pause in the work. If they forged my signature to it, I'll have the hide off them."

"If they are of the Church and merely lent you for scribe-work, you will do no such thing!" said the Bishop sternly. "Privilege of Clergy is one of our dearest jewels, and the Crown of the Church; and the Church alone will consider their sin and correct them, if need be!"

"They are common men trained by those I set to do so," said the Earl. "Certain matters they must write which are secret to the Throne; and I would not put men of the clergy at such work, where those who write for me might fall into the hands of those who fear not God and would try to wring information from them. I will take that parchment, and those where they have played at ordering the arrests of such as Oxford and Winchester—the rest can go to Sir James, here."

"Nay," said the Bishop, "I will hand them all over."

"My Lord Bishop," said the Earl, clearly making an effort to keep his voice down. "This is not a court where you sit as judge, and these matters have no concern with the Church—"

"Hah!" said the Bishop, his eye lighting up with the same fire he showed whenever mention was made of Bishop Odo, his by-gone exemplar. "The King is king by appointment of God; and it is the duty of all in Holy Church to defend him from all who might try to do him harm. My concern is what threat this forgery might mean to his Royal Highness!"

He strode to the dais and the Earl and pushed the parchment in his hand at him.

"Do you warrant to me that your name written there is a forgery and not in your own hand?"

"By the—" the Earl choked, and stopped, his face going red with anger, but apparently holding second thoughts about the oath almost on his tongue. It was difficult to find something to swear by that would express his feelings and still not be improper, roared out in the face of a Lord of the Church.

"I—" KinetetE began, and broke off in her turn, looking at Carolinus.

"You're quite right, KinetetE," said Carolinus cheerfully, "pass me the parchment, if you would be so kind, my Lord Bishop—"

The Bishop, who clearly did not want to leave his commanding position standing over the seated Earl, passed the parchment to Dafydd, who passed it to Jim, who passed it to Carolinus.

"Ah, just as I thought," said Carolinus looking at it. "There is no need to question his Lordship. I can tell magickally if there has been forgery at work ... thank you. Yes, just as I thought. This was done by no trained scribe. Only one of a people who live very far from here and write in a fashion entirely different could have written my Lord Earl's signature, here. Look for yourself at its oddities."

The parchment came back by the same route. Jim glanced at it as it passed through his hands, then took another look to make sure. The signature was— now at least—one that had been forged in a thoroughly familiar hand. His own.

Dafydd had his hand outstretched. Jim passed him the parchment and turned to stare hard at Carolinus, who smiled back.

"Indeed," said the Bishop, considering the parchment with a somewhat puzzled air, "it does look even more false than it seemed to me at first glance."

"Hah!" said the Earl, with satisfaction. "Give it back to me, then."

He all but snatched at the sheet, but his fingers closed on empty air.

"No," said Carolinus, smoothly, now holding the parchment. "I will hold it and make some inquiries. Meanwhile, I'll put it in a safe place."

The parchment vanished from his hand. Both the Earl and the Bishop looked disconcerted.

But there was no time for them to say anything, because just at that moment a hollow, high-pitched voice, like that of a ghost speaking through a megaphone, made itself heard from the closest of the Hall's three fireplaces.

"M'Lord?" It was the voice of Hob. He was obviously hiding well inside the fireplace chimney because there were strangers present.

The men-at-arms had turned into statues again. Nothing now was ever going to alter their complete certainty that Jim could call devils to his aid if he wanted to. Telling them that what they had heard was just his Castle hobgoblin would make no impression. They had heard it, and now they knew with every fiber of their bodies what the real truth was. Even if they saw Hob, he would obviously be only a devil in disguise.

"M'Lord, the Lady Geronde sent me with a message for him. Pray forgive me, m'Lord, for speaking, but it's more important than anything!"

"Who's *him?*" demanded Jim. "What's *it?*"

"I have to whisper it to you, m'Lord. Would your Lordship come over to the fireplace, so no one else can hear?"

Chapter 39

Grumbling to himself, Jim started toward the fireplace, and bumped into Carolinus, who was also on his feet.

"It's all right, Carolinus," he said, a little more sharply than he had intended. "I can find out what Hob's worked up about by myself."

"Then do so!" snapped Carolinus. "It happens I'm on my way to heal Sir Simon's wound."

Carolinus pushed past him; and Jim, with an effort, kept the lid on his temper. But that lid was getting harder to hold down all the time. He had been outraged, seeing Angie tied up at Simon's order; but he had kept his surface calmness. He had been patient with the Earl, tolerant of KinetetE, and polite to the Bishop—all of whom had shown a tendency to act with a certain arrogance of authority, in spite of the fact that they had all come without invitation into his Hall, his home.

Now it looked as if he would have to humor Hob, who had been absent when needed, just a short time ago.

He tramped over to the fireplace, with Simon's armsmen watching him and nodding to each other in fairly obvious agreement that this was just the sort of thing they had expected him to do with his Devil. Ignoring them, he stuck his head into the fireplace—now down to a mere warmness—and tried to look up its chimney.

"Here . . . m'Lord," a faint whisper came to him; and, turning, he saw—much farther up than he had expected—an upside-down, shadowy, Hob-like shape, both arms and legs spread out against the two walls making a corner of the chimney; and holding its position either by sheer pressure against the walls or some handholds and footholds it was too dark for Jim to see.

"Come on down!" said Jim, "and speak a little louder. I can barely hear you!"

"Yes, m'Lord," whispered Hob, creeping down perhaps half the distance between them. "It's just . . . Court's Hob . . . not stiff . . . or, you . . . nose . . . in air; and told me . . . so . . . Malvern—"

"Closer! Louder!" snapped Jim. "I can't make sense out of what you say when I don't hear four words out of every five. Just tell me what's so important."

"M'Lord, he'll hear me!"

"No he won't. Who's *he*, I say? Anyway, no one's going to hear you."

"Oh, that's all right, then," said Hob, in his normal voice. "I was afraid—anyway, if it's all right now."

He scrambled down the chimney's interior without apparently needing anything to hold to, and stopped just before he could be seen by those in the Hall.

"You see, m'Lord," he said, "the King's Hob, at that place called the Court, turned out to be a very good Hob. I took Malvern Hob to meet him; and we were still at the Court when Mage Carolinus came magickally with my lord Bishop to get the Earl of-of Zunder . . . the big man out there—"

"Cumberland," said Jim.

"Yes," said Hob, "m'Lord of Cumberland. Malvern and King's Hob were with me and we were still listening to him, just as Carolinus and m'Lord Bishop got there. M'Lord Cumberland was talking again to that Lady you don't like—"

"Agatha Falon?"

"That's her name—telling her how he had arranged to hire men to plunder his own lands; but Chandos had heard of it too quickly, and stopped them—as you know, m'Lord. Anyway, King's Hob and Malvern Hob ducked away up a chimney as soon as Carolinus and m'Lord Bishop showed up. I left too, before the Bishop could know we were there—Bishops have special ways of knowing things—and Malvern Hob and I rode the smoke straight back to Malvern. But then a thing happened. I'm very sorry, m'Lord!"

"Sorry?" said Jim. "For what?"

"Well, you know we Hobs can always be trusted not to tell people things.

But of course I do tell you; and I forgot that Malvern Hob might tell m'Lady
Geronde. She was his own people, you see."

"I see. Well, all right. What did he tell her?"

"About m'Lord Cum—the big man; and she was all excited. She said Sir
Brian had to be told, so he could get it before the big man left Malencontri!"

"Hob," said Jim. "That's enough of this hinting. Come all the way down,
speak up, call things by their proper name, and tell me plainly what you want
to tell me! If you're worried about anyone, I'll protect you. This is your
home—you don't have to hide and whisper!"

"Oh, if you say so, m'Lord! I'm not afraid!"

Hob made a sudden flying leap from inside the chimney to Jim's shoulder.
He pointed at Brian.

"M'Lady Geronde is afraid Sir Brian might let the Earl of . . . the Earl go
away without paying him. He's to be sure to get the money he earned!"

The Earl's bellow would have taken over all possible conversation at this
point if it had not been for the fact that Brian's all but drowned him out.

"Money?" Brian said. "Geronde? Hob, what are you talking about?"

"The Lady Geronde says the Earl should pay you the forty pounds he owes
you, before he goes; and you're to make sure he does."

The Earl's response, more an explosion than a bellow, did seize the floor,
this time.

"Forty pounds!"

"So, my Lord," said Brian, getting up from his chair and stepping over to
look down at the Earl in his, "Now I discover it. You owe me forty pounds
for taking part in the appearance of a raid—a raid on your own property, by
all that's strange! But you owe it all the same."

The Earl shot to his own feet and towered over Brian, which did not change
Brian's attitude in the least.

"Like all the bloody flames in Hell, I do!" roared the Earl. "I never saw you
before in my life until Carolinus brought me here!"

"I was told," said Brian, "that the second portion of the moneys would be
paid me by the highest in the land, promptly after the work was done. It has
been some time now, and the second portion has never come; further, there
is certainly none higher than you in the land, my Lord—barring his Majesty,
our King, whom God preserve—and it is hard to give faith to the idea that
his Majesty would arrange a raid on a possession of his favorite Earl to protest
his Majesty's own taxes!"

"Who told you of this payment?"

"A certain gentleman in the service of my Lord of Chester. I had broken spears with him at a tourney; and knew him for an honorable knight, as well as one who held the post and duties he claimed."

"His name?"

"That concerns you not, my Lord. Our concern at this moment is with the forty pounds you owe me."

"On the promise of a man unknown to me. Pah!" said the Earl. "He promised it. Collect from him—if you can find him!"

"You deny you are the one who owes me?" Brian did not have the most forgiving temper, himself; and Jim, who knew him well, knew he was very close in this moment to losing it. Brian's hands were at his side, but they had already become fists.

"Hob," Jim got out, hastily, "just told us he heard you admit to Lady Falon you'd hired Sir Brian's party, my Lord."

"And I am to be held to account on the word of a creature, not merely not Christian but not even a man?" The Earl came close to spitting on the dais.

"Go seek your fairy gold elsewhere and—"

"Enough talk!" Brian's fragile grip on his temper had snapped. "Since you deny all, my Lord Cumberland, I name you under Heaven as liar and cheat— to which I will add 'craven' if you are not knightly enough to challenge and meet me over my words; and I will so proclaim you to all gentlemen I shall meet from this day forth!"

"By God—" Cumberland's large right hand flashed to his waist, found no weapon there, and balled itself into a fist raised to strike down at Brian.

"No!" said KinetetE. "There will be no fighting, no bloodletting. Carolinus, will you—or must I?"

"I'll take care of it," said Carolinus. "Robert de Clifford, look at me."

The Earl deliberately looked away from him.

"*Robert de Clifford,*" said Carolinus, slowly, "*you will look at me whether you wish to or not.*"

Jim felt it. They all felt it. It would not be Devils from a fireplace that Simon's armsmen would remember best about this day—and what it actually was, would be the one thing they would find no way to describe to anyone who had not been here. In his several years in this fourteenth century, and in all his own making of magic or that he had merely observed, he had never known anything like that which was touching him—touching all of them— now.

Power filled the Hall, and held all things animate and inanimate within it. The Earl's eyes were staring into those of Carolinus.

"We Magickians," said Carolinus to him, in a calm, quiet voice, "have our own rules about hurting anything, Christian, human, or otherwise; and indeed the craft that nearly all of our Art learn to use is, except in unusual hands, incapable of hurting. But there are a few like myself and Mage KinetetE, here, who have reached a point in our studies where we realized there was more to be learned by such as us—but that by its very nature it would not be Magick that could be confined by a Rule not to use it for hurt."

He paused. He and the Earl looked at each other.

"Robert de Clifford Plantagenet," Carolinus went on, "I only tell you this. I do not threaten you. But from this moment on you will speak the truth when asked. Now, were you responsible for the group of raiders sent against your own property?"

Something like pressure from what now filled the Hall closed around each of them.

"Yes," said the Earl, hoarsely.

"And was it your decision that the men approached were to be offered money for doing so?"

"Yes."

"Then pay him. Now."

The Earl lifted his empty hands helplessly.

"I carry no forty pounds."

"But there are places where you keep moneys, places having forty pounds and more in them?"

"Yes."

"Think of one such place."

There was a moment in which nothing happened. Then Carolinus winked out of existence and almost immediately winked in again. The Earl was looking surprised, having become seated in his chair without having sat down. A fawn-colored leather bag was on his knees. He stared at it.

"Brian," said Carolinus, "your forty pounds are in that bag. My Lord will give it to you."

Brian stared at the bag for a moment, and then stepped forward to the seated Earl, who mutely handed him the bag. In the silence of the Hall the chinking of its contents as it was lifted could be clearly heard. Brian's face lit up. He carried the bag back to his own chair.

"Sir Simon," went on Carolinus, still in his calm, slow voice, but louder, "you have been awake for some time, since I healed you. Stop pretending, get to your feet and take your men-at-arms back to where you and they came from. Take your dead with you. My Lord Earl, order it so."

"Go, Simon," said the Earl.

Simon stood up. For a moment his eyes met with Brian's. Brian beamed on him, but Simon did not smile back. He turned and walked slowly toward the front door of the Hall; and his men picked up the bodies of their comrades and followed him out of it.

"My Lord Earl," said Carolinus, "return from whence you came."

The Earl winked out.

"My Lord Bishop," Carolinus' voice seemed if anything to be slowing down, though it still rang as loudly in the Hall. "We are all indebted to you; and in especial, me. But I must go elsewhere now. May I send you back by Magick to your own place, now?"

"Cannot I be of some help to you, yourself, Carolinus?" The Bishop looked worried. "Surely you need care—"

"I thank you. I do indeed require some attention; but I must find it elsewhere after parting from you. You will help me most if I may send you safely home."

"Then do so."

—And the Bishop was no longer with them.

"Now—" said Angie, starting toward Carolinus. But before she had taken a step, Carolinus suddenly changed. His eyes closed and he slumped in his chair; at the same time he seemed to fall in upon himself. It was as if everything about him shrank, becoming fragile and very, very old.

"I'll take care of him," said KinetetE, stepping in front of Angie and going to the chair in which he now more lay than sat.

"We have to get him upstairs, to bed—" Angie tried to get back between KinetetE and Carolinus, but it was too late. "Don't you understand? He's exhausted. We need—"

"Exhausted in more ways than you know," said KinetetE, weaving her hands in the air inches above Carolinus' motionless form. "And in need of more than you can give him here in the way of care. It's my fault. I let him talk me into this last burst of energy—*stand aside!*" she snapped at Angie. *"This is something I understand and none of the rest of you do! I take him now, without delay.* He always would try too much. With luck and grace, you may see him again—"

She and Carolinus disappeared.

Angie, Jim, Brian, and Dafydd looked at each other.

"God send we do," said Brian.

Chapter 40

"At last," said Angie, coming into the Solar and throwing herself into a chair, "the Celebration banquet's ready. Ninety percent of it cooked and the rest only needs warming before being served. It can go on the table anytime in the next four hours without harm."

"Mmmp," said Jim, busy drawing something on a piece of paper.

"I do wish, though, Brian and Geronde hadn't decided to go for a ride without telling me, and Dafydd decide to test out some new arrows in the wood. Anyway, as soon as they get back, we can start. The servants can hardly wait to eat with us in the Great Hall—what're you doing?"

"Oh, this?" said Jim, self-consciously. Brian in particular had signaled, hinted, and all but commanded that the rescue of Robert and Carolinus, to say nothing of their victory over Sir Simon and Cumberland, should be celebrated. Jim had not expected Angie to walk in on him, busy as she had been at getting the meal ready.

"Drawing circles," he said. He lifted the sheet of heavy, greyish paper. "I was trying to visualize something being outside of everything, and the circles were to help. See?"

"Why did you want to do that?"

"Don't you remember how Carolinus told the Earl that there was a whole other area of magic beyond ordinary magic, that only a few top magicians knew about—those few like him and KinetetE who'd reached the point in their magical studies where they were face-to-face with it—and how it was as likely to hurt as help?"

"Of course I remember. But you don't have to worry about anything like that yet, do you?"

"I don't know. Twice I've had enough magic energy in my account to take us back to our own world, and both times we didn't use it—and then it got spent on other things. How would you like to be able to escape to our own century, anytime, at the drop of a hat?"

Angie stared at him with sudden shock and concern.

"Don't look at me like that," he said. "Of course we'd take Robert's best interest into consideration before doing anything like that. But you know I've been worried about people starting to see through me—and that the Castle staff already—"

"I wish," said Angie, "I really wish you'd get this idea about the servants out of your head—and all these other ideas connected with it—"

"It's not something to be just forgotten. How would you like to lose all of our friends at once, and still be stuck here? This business with Robert and the Gnarly King was proof enough we can't survive here alone. And if the servants are beginning to see through me, how much longer can it be before our best friends as well are going to see the truth, even though they may not want to?"

"Jim, this is downright ridiculous! This whole wild idea you've got is built on something you think you've seen and heard in the Castle people. If you believe that, ask them how they feel about you; ask them—"

"And I told you—"

He was interrupted by the wild screech of a voice from the tower-top overhead.

"To arms! To arms! Five knights in full armor and half a hundred men on horseback in light armor, coming fast against us, along the west road—"

The rest of the words were drowned out by the sound of hammering on the long strip of iron that was Malencontri Castle's alarm signal.

"Robert!" cried Angie, whirling about. "He'll be frightened to death!"

"Wait, Angie!" shouted Jim. "I may need you with me to hear what I order—"

But Angie was already out of the room, headed toward the separate chamber they had walled off for Robert and his nurse. Cursing, Jim went after her.

He came into Robert's room to find Angie holding the baby against her shoulder, patting him gently on the back as if she would burp him, and saying, "There, there . . ."

"But m'Lady—" the nurse was protesting.

"Nonsense!" said Angie. "He's just being brave about it."

Robert, looking bright-eyed at Jim over Angie's shoulder, took his thumb out of his mouth and crowed.

"Angie," said Jim, "he's fine; and I need you with me when I give orders for the Castle's defense, so you'll know what to do with your responsibilities."

"There," said Angie, handing Robert back to the nurse, "I think he's all right now." She turned with a cheerful smile to Jim. "Now, what was it you wanted?"

"Come on," Jim said.

He turned around and led the way out. They went down the passage and up the stairs to the tower roof.

It was empty. The metal alarm strip still quivered and swung slightly.

"What is this?" demanded Jim. He started toward the battlements to see for himself, but was stopped by a voice behind him.

"M'Lord!"

It was the voice of Yves Mortain, who had been promoted to Master of the Castle's men-at-arms, when their original Master—Theoluf—had been elevated to the rank of Jim's squire—an unusual but not unknown promotion, for an able common man, lifted from the ranks, particularly among fighting men.

It had been Brian who had suggested Theoluf. Jim had not been in Malencontri long enough to get the younger son of one of his neighbors for his squire, the most usual course for a country knight. Nor was Jim really capable of training a young squire from the gentry. The boy would know more than he—and be little help. Theoluf had instantly proved many times more useful than any inexperienced teenager.

And Theoluf had suggested Yves to replace him. Yves, a narrow-bodied, black-haired man with a prowling walk, was not far from being a younger edition of Theoluf—a lean, hardbitten veteran—and had been instantly at home in his new role.

Now, as Jim and Angie turned, they saw Yves had come up the stairs behind them. He was all but carrying an armsman young enough to have no more than a fuzz of beard on his chin and a look of panic on his face. The youngster was stumbling forward on the tips of his toes, because Yves had hold of the short hairs at the back of his neck and was using them to lift him into the toe-point position.

"M'Lord, m'Lady," Yves called as he approached them. "Of your grace, this is my fault. I had this wool-wit on watch, under my eye. But I left him here alone for a moment. And I have just found him in your Solar, to which he, without orders, ran, after giving the alarm, to warn you directly. I found him awaiting your return there."

He broke off as they all came together. He stopped and turned his captive by the hair so that he faced out through one of the embrasures.

"Now, pudding-head!" he said in a deadly voice. "What do you see out there? Tell us!"

The man-at-arms stammered wordlessly for a second, then found his speech.

"Six—"

"WHAT?" Yves hauled up on the back hair, producing a squeak from the armsman.

"Four—I mean, four only, of knights in full armor. That's all, Master, m'Lord, m'Lady—only four have the swordbelts of knights. Two others in like armor but with common swordbelts—squires, belike."

"And of the rest?" Yves' hard voice demanded.

"Twenty in light armor, such as armsmen wear, swords and spears. Ten mounted bowmen."

There was an ugly silence, and then Yves lifted on the hairs again.

"But there are no other fighting men, Master!" wailed the victim.

Jim winced internally. However, he had by now come to understand the sense behind the practice of not criticizing, or failing to back up a subordinate, in front of that one's own subordinates.

"I asked you to tell me what you *saw!*" Yves was saying. "There are twenty bodies a-horseback out there unmentioned. What of them?"

"Servants and pages!" gasped the ex-watchman. "Servants and pages with the extra weapons and baggage of the knights and squires!"

Yves released him at last with a shove that sent the youth staggering with enough momentum that he almost dived headfirst out the embrasure through which he had been looking.

"Bah!" said Yves, his tone suddenly almost indifferent, "and what if overnight in the darkness, those twenty should find armor and weapons within their baggage; and on the morrow we find ourselves facing twice as many fighting men?"

He turned to Jim and Angie.

"As I said, I take all the fault for this on myself, my Lord, my Lady. Do with me as you will regarding it. Meanwhile, if you would cast your eye over the wall here, you will recognize who comes."

"Why," said Angie, "the arms on that first shield—aren't they those of Sir John Chandos?"

Jim looked; the arms on the shield of the foremost knight showed indeed a golden triangle, occupying the center of the taller knight's shield, with its broad end against the shield's top and its point downward. All the rest of the shield surface around that upside-down, golden axe-head was a bright, light-hued blue. *Azure, a pile or,* as the heralds of this world would identify it.

C h a p t e r *41*

They took Sir John up to the Solar where they could speak in privacy, Angie explaining on the way about the banquet, its reason for being, and how they could not start without Brian, Geronde, and Dafydd. The knights with Chandos, and certainly he himself, would of course sit at the High Table, too. But with a full hall, they could not invite in the squires and all those of lower rank, since the people of the Castle would be filling nearly all the space available.

"I would not expect you to," said Chandos as they climbed the tower stairs. "It is great courtesy in you to invite myself and my knights, when we have come upon you so unexpectedly. If we have happened on a privy occasion here in your home, I would not wish to intrude—"

He was not doing so at all, Jim and Angie told him.

"I am relieved to hear it!" said Chandos. "I am come too late with my word of warning, from what you tell me—but that is all to the good."

What word of warning, his hosts wanted to know.

"It is no great matter, in the light of what you have been telling me; but I am happy to have a chance to say it, in any case," said Chandos.

They had reached the Solar by this time and taken seats. Food and drink had already been placed ready for them by the servants of the Serving Room.

"As I said," remarked Chandos, after he had tasted some of the wine and nibbled on one of the finger foods called "hanged men"—although it took a stretch of the imagination to see anything human in their shapes—"I came intending to warn, only to find you far ahead of me. It is a pleasant excuse to visit, however—though I venture to think the Mage KinetetE could have made it unnecessary when she saw me at Court, three days ago."

"KinetetE at Court?" said Angie. "I didn't know she went there. So you know KinetetE?"

"I have met her once before, but briefly, and not at Court," said Chandos. "But this time she came to tell me the why of your disappearance with Sir Brian from the field in Cumberland, where we had that small touch of arms—as you may remember, James."

"Oh? Oh, yes," said Jim, suddenly uneasy. "What did she tell you?"

"Why, that magickal business of great import had suddenly required the presence of both of you elsewhere. I had imagined the reason had been some such matter, but it was well to know it—in especial from a Mage of such rank."

"Well, good!" said Jim, "I mean, I'm glad she did." Magical business of great import had been involved, of course—for the preservation of Brian's life.

"But you were going to warn us about something," said Angie.

"Yes," said Chandos, "but you now know what I would have told you. I wished to put you on guard against the Earl of Cumberland, to warn you he is your enemy; not on behalf of or because of, the Lady Agatha Falon, but because he has never forgiven you for defying him over the burial of your friend, Sir Giles de Mer, at the battlefield in France you know of."

"Sir Giles was of silkie blood," Jim said, "and had to be buried at sea. Because we went ahead and did that, he turned into a seal once he was back in the sea, and a Bishop's blessing has now returned him to man-shape. We had no choice."

"I should think he'd hate Prince Edward, instead. It was Edward that made him give up Giles," said Angie.

"He does. His hates are undying; and he never forgets anyone who opposes him. The Prince stands between him and England's crown—and it is a crown he covets."

Chandos got to his feet uncomfortably and walked to one of the nearby open windows in the round Solar wall.

"The worst of it is, I can do little more than warn you. You are one of

England's paladins since your bicker at the Loathly Tower—and not easily disposed of without clear reason. But he will bide his time; and he is now urging war with France, in conjunction with John of Navarre and against the former Count of Valois—he who was chosen for the throne of France by the French magnates, over our Royal Edward. You will be called to our liege's banner if such war starts, and must obey. Cumberland will command any expedition that goes to France; and the war could give his chance to have you slain."

"Jim!" said Angie.

"So I thought I would come to suggest that you and your friends make haste to join me, if war seems close upon us," said Chandos. "I, also, will be in the field; as one of the war-captains; and to some extent I could then protect you as a member of my personal force . . ."

He broke off, staring out the window.

Jim and Angie waited for him to go on, but he continued staring at whatever had caught his attention. Jim was about to speak up when Chandos found his voice.

"I find this somewhat hard to believe," he said. "But if you will pardon me, I would that you both looked out this window, or one close to it."

"The window?" said Jim. He and Angie both got to their feet.

"—You may remember," Chandos was continuing, "I looked out one of these windows on my last visit and saw . . . at any rate, at the risk of getting a name as a bearer of ill tidings, there is a matter that might concern you, taking place in your courtyard. No fire this time, but another fight is going on—though so close those watching are pressed I cannot say whether the fighters are servants or armsmen. Most curious. Such usually settle their disputes in some quiet or hidden place where their superiors will not discover them at it."

Jim and Angie both moved to a window next to the one out of which Sir John was looking.

"It's them again!" said Angie, "May Heather and Tom; and—oh, Jim, he's got her pinned down this time and he's really pounding her. He could hurt her badly! Why don't all those older ones watching stop it?"

"Excuse me, Sir John," said Jim, already on his way to the door. Angie was right behind him, with Chandos right behind her, as they made all possible safe speed down the stairs of the tower.

As they ran through the empty Hall, with its white tablecloths already laid and some mazers, pitchers, and platters already put out, Angie was doing her best to catch up with Jim. It was not that she could not run fast. Back in the modern world from which she and Jim had come, she had owned a very small silver cup for winning the women's hundred-yard dash in her senior year of high school. But it is difficult to show your best speed when you are holding up a very heavy, floor-length skirt with both hands, and your competition is free to swing his arms as he runs.

At least, she told herself, she was outrunning Chandos.

But then, glancing over her shoulder, she saw the knight keeping a polite position some three paces behind her. She stayed ahead of him, therefore, through the door to the courtyard, still half-open from Jim's passage; and it swung so nearly closed behind her that Chandos would have to open it again for himself.

Jim had stopped just outside the door; and he caught her arm as she started to pass him. They walked forward together. None of the crowd had taken notice of them yet. It was an unnaturally silent crowd, though on its edges some were skipping and hopping like excited children—but still as quietly as possible.

"What's going on here?" roared Jim suddenly when they were not more than a dozen feet away. Everyone froze, some of them in awkward positions. All heads turned to stare at Jim—who, Angie suddenly realized, was now wearing a red magician's robe such as Carolinus habitually wore.

"I thought it was illegal until you became a class-A magician," she hissed in his ear.

"It is," he muttered back. "But only magicians are supposed to know that."

But whether it was the robe or not, if he had turned into his dragon form he could not have produced a greater effect. He decided to strike while the iron was hot.

"Do you all want to be turned into beetles?" he roared in his best magician's voice. "—Turned into beetles and sealed up in amber until the Day of Judgment?"

The threat clearly carried conviction—perhaps too much. None of them had ever seen him like this; and any threat involving magic was only too believable to all of them.

They were white-faced and silent as they opened a lane for him and Angie—Sir John was now politely but interestedly waiting, just outside the Great Hall door. At the end of that lane, right in front of the Kitchen entrance, Tom the Kitchen boy stood wide-legged and unsteady over a figure lying still on the hard-trodden ground.

"Oh!" burst out Angie on a note that was a curious mixture of sympathy and anger, running ahead to the fallen figure. She knelt beside it; and it lifted a blood-streaked head that was barely recognizable as belonging to May Heather.

" 'Tis all right, m'Lady," she said, if in a somewhat thin voice, "I'm all right— just winded, like."

"As for that," said Angie, ominously, "we'll carry you up to a bed and clean you up and then decide how right you are."

"You lost!" said Tom suddenly and fiercely.

"Ay," said May. "Lost, I did." Her head flopped back onto the ground.

"You, you, you, and you . . ." said Angie, jabbing a finger toward one male servant after another. "Pick her up. Carefully! And carry her—carefully, I said—to the first empty guest room on the lowest level of the tower—"

"M'Lord!" May Heather managed to lift her head again as the four men prepared to pick her up. "Pray m'Lord, don't turn Tom into a beetle!"

"Don't care!" muttered Tom in a low voice.

Jim turned his eyes with what he hoped was an awful slowness on the boy, who paled, but still stared back at him unyieldingly. The crowd held its collective breath to hear Tom's doom pronounced; and Jim let them hold it for a long minute before speaking.

"Since it's May Heather you beat so badly that asks it," he said, "just this once I'll leave you as you are."

The crowd breathed again.

"But, oh m'Lady! A room in the tower for a Serving Room apprentice—all to herself?" cried the voice of Mary Becket, the Wardrobe-Mistress, from the crowd.

"So, there you are, Mistress!" said Angie. "Watching this disgraceful exhibition with everyone else when you ought to have been at your duties. You go along with the men carrying May; and make sure it's a clean room with clean linen and everything as it should be."

"But the bed'll be lousy after she's lain in it—"

"Go!"

"Yes, m'Lady."

There was the murmur of quiet-voiced conversation beginning at the back of the crowd and Jim thought he heard something suspiciously like a relieved chuckle. It struck him that this could be turning into yet another instance in which he threatened them, but let them off after all. They might be beginning to count on him to talk tough but never follow it up with action.

"As for the rest of you—" he raised his voice, and abruptly there was neither talking nor breathing going on about him. "The only reason I don't turn you all into beetles this moment," he went on, "is because I want you to keep doing your necessary duties around the Castle for me—at present. But you're all going to have bad dreams, tonight!"

He whirled about and stalked off, red robe billowing above his feet. This time the silence behind him stayed unbroken. Angie hurried to catch up with him. Sir John was still politely waiting just outside the door to the Hall, so she had time enough to whisper a question to him.

"How can you come up with a dream for each of them between now and dark? And won't it use up a huge amount of your magic?"

"None," said Jim, grinning privately down at her. "I don't have to come up with even one dream: and I don't have to use any magic."

"Stop that!" she said, in a low, sharp voice. "Tell me!"

"They believe they're going to have them, so they will have them. They'll each have some kind of nightmare; and in the morning each one'll try to out-horrify all the rest telling what he dreamed. So anyone who actually didn't dream will make one up—and come to believe he actually had it, eventually. In the end, they'll remember tonight for the rest of their lives."

They joined Chandos. As they turned back through the door, Jim glanced back. The crowd in the courtyard had already vanished, except for a few laggard figures now making their best speed toward wherever they were supposed to be.

"Everything settled, Sir James?" asked Chandos as they went down the still-empty Hall toward the High Table.

"I think so," said Jim.

"I must say," said Chandos, "your servants know their duties admirably. Hardly a word. Only one question from that woman about the room—and all over in a second."

"It's good of you to say so," said Jim. "Look, why don't the two of you go ahead with dinner. I'll be right back down; but I've got to get out of this robe; and for magic reasons I can't use magic the way I did when I put it on. I'll run up to the Solar, change, and be back in no time at all. You might as well start eating."

He turned and left, taking their agreement for granted. He had suddenly become fully conscious of what he had done when he put on the robe. The sooner he had it off, the better.

He went rapidly through the now-populated Serving Room, where no one met his eye; and on to the foot of the tower stairs. As he started up, the warmth of self-congratulation that had come from the lucky thought of punishing Malencontri's people with their own bad dreams began to fade in him.

There was no good reason to congratulate himself. He had been feeling his oats when he had no oats to feel. All he had really done with the crowd outside was pull another quick trick on them. If and when they should realize it, it would only confirm whatever suspicions they already had of him.

The climb up the stairs seemed a long one, and at the same time it went too fast. Very shortly he would be going back to face Angie and Chandos again. Angie already knew he was a fake, of course, even though she loyally insisted on denying it; and he would not be surprised if Chandos already did also—it would be like the knight to keep the information to himself against a possible future need, meanwhile smiling to himself over it.

Jim reached the Solar and went in. He shut the door behind him, pulled the red robe off over his head, and laid it out carefully on the bed. For a moment he simply stood still in the empty room, the now-cool breeze from the open windows exploring his forearms and most of his legs, left bare by his fourteenth-century underwear.

Then he took a deep breath and spoke out loud to the emptiness.

"Carolinus?"

He waited. There was no answer.

"KinetetE?"

No answer.

"KinetetE, Mage," he said after a long moment. "I just called you because you might hear and be able to pass a message to Carolinus, wherever he is. I just wanted to say it was just a momentary impulse to put on the red robe—I didn't think. It was just the first thing that came to mind as a way of getting control of these servants of mine. I'm sorry. It was the wrong thing to do in any case. Anyway, I've taken it off now, and I won't be putting it on again until I have the right to wear it; and if I did any real harm while I was wearing it—it's only me who's responsible, no one else."

He waited; but there was no sign or answer. He sighed, dressed in the same sort of clothes he had been wearing when he had used magic to assume the red robe; and left the Solar once more to go downstairs.

On the way, it suddenly occurred to him that if he should go back down without looking in on how May Heather had been taken care of, that would undoubtedly be the first thing Angie would ask him about.

He stepped off the stairs, accordingly, on the lowest floor of rooms in the Tower, and went looking for the one that should contain May. There was an emptiness inside him, as strongly as it had been there after he had put his lance through Brian in Cumberland, and then had to be the one to tell Brian he had done so.

Magician, medieval warrior, knight, Lord of a castle—now that he looked at these things closely, it seemed to him he had failed at being each one of them. It should not be possible for him to tangle up a brief visit to a sickbed; but there was a sense of foreboding in him that told him he would find some way of doing it.

He put the thought resolutely out of his mind, and went on until he came to a door that had swollen, or sagged on the pintles that held it up, so that it would not shut completely. Peering through the crack between door and frame, he was able to see May Heather lying on a bed. She was wearing a robe, too big for her, of blue that had faded almost to white. She was awake, simply lying there and staring at the ceiling. He pushed the door all the way open and walked in.

"Well, May——" he began.

"M'Lord!" May started to scramble out of the bed.

"No, no!" he said, waving her back down. "Stay there. I'm just looking in so I can tell Lady Angela how I found you. How are you feeling?"

"Very good, m'Lord. Very good indeed. I feel like a princess, m'Lord; here in this great bed, in this fine room. Never I thought to know what it was like to be in such."

"Just see you stay there until you're told you can leave," said Jim, gruffly.

"Oh, indeed I will. But I ought to be downstairs, helping, like, with dinner. I really am very good, m'Lord."

She did not look very good. Her face was swollen in three places and there were several cuts on it—though none of them was bleeding; and both face and arms had obviously been washed—possibly more of her than that. Her hair had even been brushed, or perhaps combed.

Jim tried not to feel for her—her combat wounds, her lowly position in life, her ridiculous sense of duty—and failed. He had learned the hard way that the last thing any of these people wanted was sympathy.

Sympathy, evidently, implied weakness in the one sympathized with, and could be taken as veiled contempt or mockery—just as KinetetE had warned Angie when she had been moved to comfort the Earl of Cumberland, after Jim's magic had thrown him into the most desperate of despairs.

But now Jim's feelings won. A powerful urge to try one last time to think as one of them—from Brian down to this Serving Room apprentice—took him over. He looked around for something to sit on, found one of the armless chairs with which these rooms were furnished, carried it over to the bed, and sat down with his face more on a level with the girl's.

"Tell me, May," he said, "why do you and Tom fight so much?"

"We don't do it no more nor other folk, m'Lord," she said. "Everybody fights."

"Well, then," said Jim, "why do you always have your fights out in the courtyard; and why do all the other servants and men-at-arms come to watch?"

"Don't know, m'Lord. Just happens we get to fighting, more than not, outside the Kitchen where I used to get the foods from Tom's hands to take to the Serving Room—before I got to be apprenticed to Mistress Plyseth."

She would never tell him any more than that, he realized by the tone of her voice. Jim remembered the two men-at-arms he had heard outside Brian's room after he had brought his friend back from Cumberland. Their low-voiced conversation had clearly seemed to be about betting on whether May or Tom would win. But of course May would tell him nothing about that, either.

"What about all those coming to watch?"

"They just comes, is all."

"It wouldn't be because they've got some special interest in your fight that isn't there in all these other fights?"

Her face for the first time showed unhappiness; and for the first time he saw how pale and exhausted she looked. His conscience jabbed at him for cross-examining her like this.

"Never mind," he said, getting up from the chair. "We can talk about that sometime later. Just forget I asked, for now, and get some sleep—"

"But I *want* to tell you!" she burst out without warning. "You and m'Lady, m'Lord . . . I want to tell you!"

Jim opened his mouth to say there was no need to, recognized that would be doing the opposite of what they both wanted—and sat down again on the rock-hard chair.

May looked away from him.

"You and M'Lady ought to know!" she said. She kept looking away as she went on. "Like twins we was. From differ families but same age, same size, same weight. I even looked like Tom; and Tom, he looked like me. Then, when we both were let in to work at the Castle here, it couldn't ha' been no better, both of us here."

She stopped, and stared directly at Jim for a second, with shiny eyes.

"Am I saying it so's you'll understand, m'Lord?"

"Perfectly," said Jim. She looked away from him again.

"But then," she went on, "after a few years I started growing." She glanced back at him. " 'Ee grew, too, but not like me—you know how it is with women?"

Jim nodded. She looked away again.

"When we'd had our fights, sometimes I'd win and sometimes he'd win. But it came then that he couldn't no more. I was bigger nor him, and stronger; and that was bad enough. But then all the others started to notice it. So I told him to bide his time and not pick fights with me; and I'd walk wide o' him. But no, 'ee had to keep trying to fight and win; and by that time it was too late. Everybody knew."

She either ran out of voice or simply stopped talking. After a little silence, Jim spoke gently.

"You mean the other servants began making fun of him about it?"

"Ay, they did that. But worse, they started betting 'ee never would make no man; and when 'ee'd offer to fight the one who said it, whoever it was would say t'wouldn't be fair to do that to a lad who couldn't even win over a maid. He'd hit out anyway to make them fight; but you know 'ee couldn't prove nothing against a full-growed man. But he kept trying. . . ."

She looked down at the sheet and plucked at it with her thumb and middle finger.

"So it went on," said Jim, after the new silence had lasted a small while.

"It just went on," she said, nodding. And looked straight at him again, finally. "We're going to be husband and wife, M'Lord. We settled that atween ourselves long ago. There couldn't be no goodwife for him but me, and no goodman for me who wasn't him."

"So today you let him win," said Jim, sympathetically.

She sat up abruptly, fiercely, in the bed.

"Never I did! I don't lie down for nobody! Nobody, m'Lord!"

He looked into her angry, swollen face.

"I see," he said. "I was wrong."

" 'Ee just got his strength at last or 'ee had to win, or something—but he won, fair and square!"

"I believe you, I believe you," said Jim. "Lie back now. It's you we're worried about at the moment, not Tom."

Slowly, she did.

" 'Ee won it fair," she repeated in a voice that was almost a whisper. "Don't matter about me. But now, 'ee's as much a man as any one of them. Any making a mock of 'im now'll have to fight him, or back down! And we'll be husband and wife come apple-harvest time this fall."

Jim looked at her and a strange feeling, a deep, powerful affection, rose in him. These two children . . . but children in a time when they were considered old enough to take on the responsibility of marriage . . . he got to his feet and fumbled in the little leather purse hanging from his belt.

"Here," he said, grabbing a coin and passing it to her. She took it automatically, staring at it. "For your wedding."

She still stared, eyes and mouth open. Finally, the words in her came out.

"*A whole gold leopard, m'Lord?*"

A sick feeling made itself known in his stomach. His instinct had been right. He had made a mess of this visit, after all.

Like everyone else, she would know what the coin she held was worth. It was the smaller of two coins called florins, both minted in this century for the first time in England. Its value was that of three shillings—and a shilling a day was what a knight with a servitor and his own weapons, armor, and horses was paid for going into battle. Almost certainly, she would never have seen the actual coin in her life before, let alone handled one. She held it now, gingerly in her fingers, as if afraid it would vanish if she squeezed it too hard.

"Wedding present," said Jim, suddenly hoarse. He backed out of the room. "Lie down now. That's an order. Get some sleep."

May obediently closed her eyes. Jim slipped out the door, leaving it ajar. His conscience was already at work upon him—damn fool thing to do. Now probably every servant in the place would come up with some excuse to be given a coin. It was far too much of a gift for any servant, let alone a Serving Room apprentice.

He had been reaching into his purse for a groat, about the same size but thinner and silver—worth fourpence only. Even that would have been an eye-popping gift to someone like May or Tom. It could well be the only leopard they had in the Castle right now; and Angie, if she heard—he checked the way his thoughts were running. He might feel like the idiot of two universes, but—it was done and that was that.

At least it would make May and Tom happy . . . instead of just being included in part of some tax payment.

He stopped. Had she really obeyed him and tried to get some sleep? If she was still awake she could be doing anything. She might try to swallow the coin to keep it safe; and it was far too big for that. She would certainly choke herself to death if she tried. He turned and went quietly back to the unlatched door. Maybe it would be better for everyone if he simply explained that the leopard had been a mistake, and found a groat for her after all—or four silver pence, if it turned out he really did not have a groat.

He peered through the narrow crack. May was lying on her left side, facing him, her right hand clutching something that must be the coin to her breast, and her eyes tightly closed. A pair of the tears that had refused to show themselves while he was there, were sliding down her cheeks. No, he could not tell her, now. It was impossible.

But her stillness was profound enough to make it seem as if sleep had claimed her after all. Jim opened the door a little farther to poke his head into the room to make sure she was really asleep—it creaked; and her eyes flew open.

He jerked his head back swiftly, leaving the door agap. Outside, he stood frozen, listening; and for a few seconds, there was no sound within.

"M'Lord!" her voice called from the room. "Pray m'Lord, can I ask one question?"

He stopped, breathed deeply, turned and went in.

"You might as well," he said. He came slowly into the room.

She was sitting bolt upright in the bed now, her elbow at her side, her lower arm outstretched and the hand belonging to it open. The leopard lay in the center of her palm, glinting in the sunlight from the room's small, single window.

"Pray, m'Lord," she said. "Take it back."

"Why?" he managed to say.

Two more tears chased the path left by the earlier one, down her swollen cheeks.

"I'm afeared 'tis bad luck for me to keep it. Th-thanking you anyway, m'Lord."

"Nonsense!" snapped Jim, suddenly determined that hell, high water, and the whole population of the fourteenth century on this world was not going to stop him from making a gift of that coin to May now. "How can it be anything like bad luck? I tell you, as a magician, it isn't bad luck!"

"Oh, m'Lord! Then you're not never going to leave us after all? You and m'Lady!"

"Of course we—" Jim broke off, suddenly floundering at the change of topic. "That is, we haven't any plans—"

"We has to know, m'Lord. Not just me and Tom. All the Castle people has to know!"

"But why?"

"Because it's you we loves, m'Lord, you and m'Lady. Never could any of us settle to another Lord and Lady, here at Malencontri. Everyone says so. It'd be the end of everything if you left. So you never will, will you, m'Lord?"

He stared at her. She blinked hard, for the tears were starting again.

"No!" he said gruffly, after a moment.

Angie would never leave young Robert behind here. That was certain. Taking him from his native world, where he would be rich and lead as good a life as possible, was somehow also unthinkable.

"No, we won't be leaving," he said. "What gave all of you that idea in the first place, anyhow?"

"All that me and Tom planned"—she was looking at him with desperate earnestness—"it was with you and m'Lady and wouldn't never be with no other Lord and Lady! It's the same with everyone else here at the Castle; and they've all been trying and trying to make things so you like it here; but you don't seem to pay them no mind. So all been sure you were going. Not no other Castle people in England has such—a Lord and Lady like the two o' you."

"Well . . ." said Jim.

"We's Castle people, m'Lord; and we has to think of our childer, too. Tom and me—why, ours might all live to grow up; and some might come to be anybody, if you and m'Lady stay. Please, m'Lord, take the leopard back; and then I'll be sure everything'll be all right!"

Jim's throat was tight.

"No," he said strongly, putting his hand around hers and closing her fingers on it. "You keep it. I give you my word we'll stay. But if anything unexpected should happen to us, you've got my word—the word of a knight and magician—you'll all be taken care of as if we were here for the rest of your lives. Now, are you through worrying?"

May stared at him for a long moment, then really burst into tears.

"Oh yes, m'Lord!" she managed to say, clutching the coin.

"Good!" he said; and all but ran out of the room toward the stairs and the Hall below.

Chapter 42

He went down feeling a strange division of his spirits. The greater part of them was filled with happiness and relief, like a lighter-than-air gas within him, so that he fairly floated down the long spiral of stone steps. But a very much lesser part was concerned with giving his "word." He had never thought he would take it so seriously, or find it so hard to do.

There was a special seriousness to that word, however, in this time; and now that he was beginning to take this era itself seriously . . . but the happiness in him overwhelmed the concern for the moment. He could hardly wait to tell Angie everything.

He had been so used to thinking of each of the Castle's people as individuals, he had forgotten they were also a community; a village bounded by stone walls in which he and Angie were the monarchs. Like any community they had their own group feelings and aims.

He had even been aware of their continuity in time. He had known there were servants' children being born within these walls, quietly, well out of his and Angie's hearing. There was even a secret nursery for the youngest—called the "baby-room", though, officially, the two of them pretended not to know of it.

The children's chances of survival—an improved diet, the availability of extra caretakers, and the like—were indeed better in the Castle. Also, servants and their children shone in a reflection of the light from the higher ranks they served. They were generally thought to be more capable and of improved stock. No wonder May had dreams for the progeny she hoped to have.

He passed rapidly through the Serving Room. Nobody met his eye this time, either, but this was because they were all very busy. He passed on into the Hall and reached the High Table, with Angie at the end closest to him.

"Look who's here!" she said, leaning back so that he could see further along the table. Just beyond her sat KinetetE, and beyond KinetetE, Carolinus— looking thin and somewhat fragile, but otherwise as good as ever.

Jim felt a sudden coldness inside him. KinetetE's eyes under her dark brows were fixed upon him.

"Ah . . . KinetetE. Mage." It was difficult to meet the unblinking eyes under those eyebrows. "I called you a little while ago—may I talk to you privily?" He could not let his servants, nor even Sir John, know that he had no right to the red robe.

"I know," said KinetetE. "And that's the last I want to hear of it. I take it you're going to join us at table, now? Take the chair on the other side of Carolinus; and don't let him get excited."

Sir John's three young knights, Jim noticed as he moved toward Carolinus, were seated at the table's far end. They were silent, eyes on the others there— not surprising, thought Jim. They were sitting at table with two of the world's three top magicians . . . it didn't seem to have affected their appetites, how- ever. He sat down and greeted Carolinus, bone-thin, but looking unusually genial.

"—I must say," Carolinus was saying, a few moments later, in answer to a query from Angie, "I look forward to getting back to my cottage. It, and the Tinkling Water—both the way I made them. Restful, with everything in its proper place."

"I can understand—" Angie began, but broke off as a servant came up to whisper in her ear. "Crave pardon, all my guests, but I must leave you for a few moments."

She got up and hurried toward the Serving Room.

But Jim only heard her with half his attention. Everything else had been knocked out by a memory, exploding into life in his mind. One thing of Carolinus' was not back in its proper place. Jim cleared his throat and looked at Carolinus uncomfortably.

"There's something I meant to tell you," Jim said. "I was at Court and needed a scrying glass; and I'd seen a magician in the Holy Land using a bowl of water for scrying. There wasn't any proper bowl available, so I borrowed one from your cottage—"

Carolinus' white eyebrows waggled up and down.

"A bowl of mine? You borrowed it? What bowl?"

"Oh, it was just a bowl that didn't seem to have any particular use. Just a bowl you happened to have lying there. I was sure you wouldn't mind—"

"*What bowl?*"

Carolinus' voice had risen. KinetetE was looking around.

"A sort of green crockery bowl, its top edge bent for a lip and four little orange fishes—"

"NOT MY LUNG CH'UAN BOWL, FROM THE SUNG DYNASTY? My nearly three-thousand-year-old celadon bowl? Where is it?"

Jim stared at him, aghast.

"Well, that's the thing," he said. "At the moment I don't remember, exactly—"

"DON'T REMEMBER?"

"You see with everything going on—Hob!" called Jim desperately. "If you're listening, do you know what happened to that bowl?"

"I'm sorry, m'Lord. Pray pardon, m'Lord." said Hob, immediately appearing in the mouth of the nearest fireplace and soaring across to land on the High Table in front of Carolinus.

"I thought the children would like it; and you left it behind—oh!"

He covered his mouth with one hand. Too late.

"Left it behind, did he?" Carolinus' voice was now bouncing off the rafters overhead, and all other conversation in the Hall had stopped.

"But here it is, m'Lord, Mage," said Hob, producing the bowl from behind his back with his other hand and thrusting it into the grasp of Carolinus. "It's not at all hurt—"

An ominous shadow fell across all of them. A tall shadow.

"Carolinus!" said KinetetE's steely voice. "You promised me you wouldn't lose your temper! Jim, I told you not to excite him!"

"It's all sooty," said Carolinus sulkily, but in much lower tones.

"I'll clean it. Give it to me, Mage—" gabbled Hob. He and Jim reached for it, simultaneously. Carolinus pulled it away from them.

"And maybe scratch it?" he said. "Besides, it's not necessary, now."

It wasn't. The bowl had become sparkling clean.

"Very well," said KinetetE. "That's all very well. No harm done. But it was a mistake for you to try to come to this occasion, Carolinus. Here we go."

They both blinked out and almost immediately blinked back in again.

"No we don't!" said Carolinus.

"Do you want to kill yourself?"

"I want to stay through this meal, with my beloved Apprentice, Jim, and his beloved wife Angie—and all my other beloved friends. And I'm going to."

"All right!" said KinetetE. "But one more bout of temper, and you could be done for. So you stay—on one condition. When we leave, you come home with me until I say you're fit to leave. Otherwise I wash my hands of you."

"I shall go to my own cottage."

"Then that's that."

"However," said Carolinus, "if it'll make you happy I could pay you a small visit first."

"And you'll be calm and collected here?"

"Certainly. I—"

"Your word on both things?"

"Oh, if you must—" Carolinus looked ready to chew nails; but, of course, as Jim knew from his own recent experience, it was not all that easy to give one's word.

"Very well. *My word on it!*"

Jim looked at him with admiration. He had seen Carolinus work a lot of magic; but never suspected he could speak in small type. KinetetE turned to Jim.

"You should have realized," she said, "that when you went back to the Gnarly Kingdom, where your magick could not work, your command to the bowl to be invisible and stay with you would be negated."

"I understand," Jim said, feeling humble. "But how did it get here?"

"The Hobgoblin, I think, can answer that," KinetetE said. She looked at Hob.

"Right after we went back to that place, just before Hill's fight started, I saw the bowl just appear behind us and start to fall to the ground," Hob said. "I caught it before it could break on the ground, and took it back on the horse." He looked downcast. "Did I do wrong, my Lord?"

"Not at all, Hob," Jim said. Hob smiled. Jim turned to Carolinus.

"I really am very sorry, Carolinus," he said. "If I'd had any idea the bowl was so . . ."

But Carolinus was paying no attention to him, He was fondling the bowl, running a finger lovingly over its contours.

Jim stood up.

"If by your grace, the table will excuse me for a few moments," he said, "I must go in search of my Lady."

He walked off. It was not the most graceful of exits from what had been an embarrassing scene. All of those at the High Table table, of course, had heard every word said by him, Hob, Carolinus, and KinetetE. But his little politeness just now had set him free. He was still bursting with what he had to tell Angie—privately, of course. He almost bumped into her, coming out of the Serving Room.

"It was the pudding—" she began, and broke off. "You're grinning like a Cheshire Cat. What is it?"

He looked past her at Mistress Plyseth—who had apparently abandoned her seat in the Hall's celebration to oversee her domain—and the other servants in the Serving Room.

"Not here," he said in a low voice. "Come on."

He led her through the Serving Room to the dead spot at the foot of the tower stairs where voices did not carry. "You're acting very strange," she said. "What was all that out there with Carolinus?"

"Tell you later. Nothing. By the way," said Jim, "I promised May Heather—gave my word on it, actually. Hard to do, but it's not as impossible as it seems, however; Carolinus just had to give his at the Table—"

"What *are* you talking about?"

"Too much to tell you. Too little time. Not here. Later. The point is, I gave my word to May Heather, if you and I ever had to leave Malencontri, she and all the Castle people would be taken care of here for the rest of their lives."

"How could you promise something like that?" She stared at him. "How could you ever make sure that would be?"

"I can plan for it, talk to Brian and Carolinus about ways to handle it. Maybe give Malencontri to Brian and Geronde; probably use some magic to make it happen. But that's not the important thing."

"What could be more important? You say you told May—when did you see her?"

"On my way back down. I thought you might want to know how she's doing."

"How—"

"She's fine. Tell you more later. The important thing is I decided to have a talk with her, and in the process she told me about the servants. I was wrong. They hadn't been seeing through me, after all. Angie—they love us, all of them do, May said. They couldn't have the life they wanted with any other Lord and Lady. Angie, they *love* me, she said! That's why they were acting the way they were."

He was beaming at her; and Jim could see she was having to fight hard to keep from beaming back; because when one of them was happy, the other had a hard time not being happy, too.

"I told you so," said Angie, game to the last.

He kissed her, anyway.